MADNESS HAS GONE VIRAL

The world is not the same since the Pandoravirus outbreak changed the essence of human nature. Those affected by the disease are consumed by adrenal rage. They erupt in violence with the slightest provocation. And now, infected scientist Emma Miller is forging them into an army of merciless killers marching across America.

Emma's twin sister, neuroscientist Isabel Miller, is desperate to avert the chaos that threatens to engulf civilization. But her team has its hands full staying one step ahead of the civil unrest that's ravaging the country. Noah Miller, the twins' brother, thought he had created a safe haven for his family in the mountains of Virginia—until the arrival of Emma and her infected followers proved the folly of his plans.

The Millers' conflict is just one of many sweeping the nation. A nation divided into factions. A nation on the precipice of all-out civil war . . .

Visit us at www.kensingtonbooks.com

Also by Eric L. Harry

PANDORA: OUTBREAK
ARC LIGHT
SOCIETY OF THE MIND
PROTECT AND DEFEND
INVASION

Pandora: Contagion

Eric L. Harry

REBEL BASE BOOKS
Kensington Publishing Corp.
www.kensingtonbooks.com

First Electronic Edition: January 2019
ISBN-13: 978-1-63573-015-9
ISBN-10: 1-63573-015-5

First Print Edition: January 2019
ISBN-13: 978-1-63573-018-0
ISBN-10: 1-63573-018-X
Printed in the United States of America

Author's Note

Mankind's complex systems are both highly efficient and dangerously brittle. An average aluminum can is bought from a store shelf, taken home, consumed, dropped into a recycling bin, collected, melted down, refashioned into a new can, refilled, returned to the store shelf, and purchased again... all in 60 days. Humanity's enormous gains in productivity, logistics, and technology have ushered in an era of plenty, of ease, and of wealth. But removing any of the essential underpinnings of modern human organization causes a cascading sequence of failures that ripple through the economy with ever compounding results. Remove all of those underpinnings, all at once, and you have mass starvation, social disorder, and population collapse. Some novels and films deal with ominous pre-apocalyptic build-ups; many more depict post-apocalyptic hellscapes. This book series attempts to describe, realistically, the time in between: the apocalypse itself.

"Turning and turning in the widening gyre
The falcon cannot hear the falconer;
Things fall apart; the centre cannot hold;
Mere anarchy is loosed upon the world..."
– W.B. Yeats
The Second Coming

Chapter 1

The sound of the zipper was Emma Miller's cue. She leaned over the trucker's lap and reached into her boot for the rusty screwdriver she had found on the side of the highway. "That's a good girl," said the man—fat, ugly, and missing a front tooth—who had given Emma a ride in exchange for a promise. She looked up and attempted a smile. He sensed something was amiss. She drove the rusty screwdriver through his neck up to its handle. It sank into the voids of his mouth and sinuses with surprising ease.

She extracted her crude weapon before his hands found the spurting wound. He gurgled more than screamed, bug-eyed in shock. She dried the screwdriver and her hand on his tattered cloth upholstery. The driver made animal sounds and thrashed from side to side. His gaze never left Emma, but his hands remained clutched on his neck.

Emma's stomach rumbled. It was time for lunch. When the trucker finally slumped onto the steering wheel inert, she searched the filthy cab. The only thing of value was the man's wallet. "Bert Walker," his driver's license read. Age forty-seven. From the lone photo, with its shopping-mall quality backdrop of lazy palm trees and thatched huts, she gleaned he was married to a similarly unattractive woman and had two overweight children. She took only the roughly one hundred dollars he had in cash.

Emma considered trying to drive his truck, but grinding through gears would raise too many questions. She was a petite, five-foot-four epidemiologist trying not to attract attention, spark calls to 9-1-1, or trigger a manhunt. She climbed down and headed back to the state highway from the secluded parking spot. Bert had made a mistake, she noted and committed to memory. He shouldn't have performed his side of the bargain before her turn came. Contracts are tricky, Emma thought. She needed to discuss them with her brother Noah, who was a lawyer.

After leaving the NIH lab hours earlier, Emma had abandoned her blue mask and gloves in the woods, but she still carried her hospital-provided white plastic bag and its toiletries by the loops of its drawstring. She knew she would have trouble passing for uninfected. Several times, the trucker had cast sidelong glances her way after replies that he found odd. And Emma also wasn't sure just how contagious she remained. If she left a trail of infected people along the way, someone might plot her route and zero in on her location. Plus, she would have at most two hours until first symptoms appeared in her wake. She had to stay ahead of any outbreak she caused and the violence that inevitably ensued.

On reaching the highway, she walked down its shoulder but didn't hold out her thumb. The traffic was heavy, but not bumper-to-bumper like on the Interstate out of D.C. Cars and trucks flew by without stopping. Did Emma appear strange and out-of-place? It wouldn't take much of an incongruity for someone to phone the police. Everyone would be paranoid now that the disease had broken out in Vermont.

A large, older car, windows rolled down, passed slowly. A woman and her three kids scrutinized Emma before pulling off onto the roadside ahead. When Emma reached them, the African-American woman asked, "Did your car break down, hon?" Emma dared only a nod, not a verbal reply. "Well, hop in, then," the woman said.

The kids were young. She needed to worry mainly about killing their mother.

Emma climbed into the front passenger seat, displacing a long-legged girl of about ten who could probably run fast. "Where you headed?" the girl's mother asked as they drove off.

"South," Emma dared to reply.

"I understand. Tryin' to get...away?" She glanced at her children through the rearview mirror, then at Emma, who thought better of trying to smile and nodded again.

Wind rushed through the open windows. They probably wouldn't catch the virus, diluted as the air was in the sedan. Maybe Emma could avoid the hassles and slight risk of killing them all. Four was a large number to do all at the same time. It highlighted her need for a better weapon to make these things go more smoothly.

"What's your name?" the woman asked.

"Dorothy," Emma lied in case she spared their lives. The assumed name had popped into her head out of nowhere, along with the image of a yellow brick road leading south. The origin of these mysterious thoughts, which hinted at some deeper mental processes pondering questions not yet even posed, was increasingly curious. Where did they come from, and to whom did they occur? Were they, as proposed at the NIH lab by her neuroscientist twin sister Isabel, the product of unconscious reasoning? And if so, to whom were those solutions given if not some mystical, conscious *self?*

"I'm Francine. And that's Wanda, Marcus, and Brandon."

The woman glanced over as if it were Emma's turn to say something. "My sister's ex-boyfriend is named Brandon," came the thought out of nowhere. To Emma's ear, it sounded like suitable small talk. A semblance of a conversation.

"Hear that, Brandon? I *tol'* you it was a good name."

"It's not *Marcus,*" said the youngest of the three children, glaring for reasons that eluded Emma at his older brother of that name, who sat next to him, arms crossed, smirking.

"Where ya from?" Francine asked.

"Connecticut," Emma said, not lying where she didn't have to. That would help minimize later slipups and give her greater flexibility in choosing the time and place of their end.

"That's close," Francine replied. "To Vermont, I mean. How long do you guess it'll take for the *P.* to get down to Connecticut?"

"Six days," Emma replied. When Francine shot her a look, Emma appended, "More or less. I would guess." At least she hadn't said, *per my calculations.*

"Whatta you do up there in Connecticut?"

"I'm…in between jobs," Emma replied, which was true. But something seemed off about the conversation. Emma would have to get Francine to pull over before aiming one jab at Francine's face, then taking down the girl, then grabbing whichever boy was closest. She would probably have to chase the last one, hopefully into the woods and not down the public roadway. Or maybe she should attempt to salvage the conversation by asking a question, but what? Emma wasn't interested in anything Francine had to say. "What, *uhm...* Where are you headed?" Emma asked. *That sounded good,* came the silent pat on the back from the enigmatic hidden voice.

Francine shot Emma another look. Something in what Emma had said, or how she had said it, sounded off. "To Atlanta," Francine replied. "I got a cousin there with a big house. Takin' us all in."

"You shouldn't go to a city," Emma commented, but shouldn't have. When Francine asked why not, Emma said, "When SED arrives, cities will turn quickly." Again, not a lie.

"He's all stocked up and everything," Francine said, but her brow was now furrowed and she gripped and re-gripped the steering wheel. Emma's hand edged closer to her boot. "It's gettin' kinda chilly," Francine said. "Let's close these windows up."

"No," Isabel said, too sharply. Too abruptly. "I mean, can we keep them cracked?"

"Sure." They all adjusted their respective windows, alternately raising them above a howl from rushing airflow and lowering them below a squeal until the noise was tolerable. Isabel was now somewhat less certain whether the pathogen she exhaled with every breath would build in the car to levels dangerous for the susceptible family. If they got sick, the authorities would do contact tracing, inquiring about anyone they had met in the last few hours. The strange white girl, Dorothy, would sit at the top of their suspect list. But the relevant quotation—*dead men tell no tales*—arose from somewhere deep in her mind.

"What's in that plastic bag?" Francine asked Emma.

They're toiletries I was given upon my release from the National Institutes of Health after being studied for a month in their Bethesda laboratory. That was a bad answer. "It's my toothbrush and stuff," Emma said instead. There. That was better. Francine seemed calmer and smiled at her.

But the woman kept stealing looks at Emma. "I'm sorry, but you just look so *familiar*." Francine must have seen the Homeland Security video explaining the effects of *Pandoravirus horribilis* by reference to its first American victim.

"I'm fairly common looking," Emma replied, trying to avoid having to begin the killing right here and right now.

"Oh, no. You're *very* pretty! Don't ever sell yourself short, Dorothy. A girl has to have confidence, I always say. And don't worry about losing your job. Ever'body's gettin' laid off these days."

Emma surveyed Francine, then looked over her shoulder at the children. No one seemed particularly suspicious of her. "Are any of you sick?" Emma asked Francine.

"We ain't been anywhere near Vermont!"

"No, I mean regular sick," Emma explained.

"Oh. No. We all got good health."

That militated in favor of not killing them. Their immune systems might successfully fight off a low-level exposure to *Pandoravirus*. Their odds of survival rose even higher when Marcus passed gas, Wanda berated and punched him, Brandon and Marcus shared a laugh, and Francine had everyone lower their windows before apologizing to Emma. The now doubly tainted miasma was quickly swept out by the gale.

When they reached the junction with the Interstate, which looked like a parking lot, Francine pulled over. "We gotta head west from here," she told Emma.

It was now or never. If they were infected, how far away could Emma get before the dots connected back to her and every cop and sheriff for a hundred miles was given her description? She would have to try to do Francine with one jab, probably in through the eye socket. But if Francine flinched, it may take multiple stabs during which the kids would probably throw open their doors and scatter. There was a crowded gas station and convenience store a hundred yards away. Killing them here was not a good plan. Emma would just have to hope they hadn't contracted the virus.

"Thank you," Emma said, climbing out.

"Good luck!" said Francine.

"Good luck to all of you," replied Emma.

"You see," Emma heard Francine say to her kids as she headed off, "she was nice."

Emma was thirsty and hungry, so she went to the convenience store, which was busy despite its nearly empty shelves. Emma got in line with a large bottle of sports drink—the only consumable liquid she could find—and a package of miniature donuts dusted with confectionary sugar. On the small TV beside the cash register, a news helicopter filmed a large, angry crowd at a Vermont blockade formed by army Humvees. The people were loud, their gestures animated. They were clearly uninfected, presumably protesting their quarantine.

"Those poor people," said the woman in line ahead of Emma, who nodded in reply. The woman kept eyeing her warily. Could she, too, possibly have recognized Emma from the DHS video? On impulse, Emma took a knit cap from a rack and put it on. She needed to avoid interacting with people she couldn't kill.

When the woman in front of Emma finished paying, she turned to Emma, made a face, reached up to Emma's hat, and broke the plastic tie that attached to it a dangling price tag.

Emma left the store and resumed her march down the highway, eating her donuts and passing car after car waiting to ascend the ramp onto the Interstate. The shelter of the overpass was occupied not by the old and weathered homeless, but by the new homeless: clean-cut families and couples whose cars had died, or run out of gas, or money to buy gas. One tall man about her age, skinny, unwashed, and unkempt, fell in alongside her and said he liked her cap.

"Thank you."

He then asked if she had any money.

"Yes," Emma replied.

"Can I have enough to put some gas in my van?"

"No," she answered.

He grabbed her arm to slow her up and exclaimed, "Hey!" When she looked down at his grasp, he released her. "Why so unfriendly?" he said. "A perty girl like you, I woulda thought you'd be lookin' for somebody to hook up with. Maybe we help each other out."

"A contract?" she asked.

He shrugged. "Yeah, I guess. You give me gas money, and I give you a ride."

The order was again wrong. Emma would be making the same mistake as Bert: paying her price of the bargain at the front end and relying on the counterparty to honor the trade they had made. But then again, he would probably expect sex from her at some point. And she could always kill him and take his van then. *Good plan*, came to her out of nowhere, just like the silent voices Isabel said Uninfecteds heard in their heads.

"Okay," she said. "Where's your van?"

Chapter 2

Prof. Isabel Miller had thought that the difficult part had been the long walk up the bridge under the weight of the equipment that she bore: body armor, pouches bulging with gear and with a lifetime supply of ammunition, and a small rucksack—her "combat load"—with its goggles, disposable masks, gloves, coveralls, and meals of beef teriyaki and meatloaf in packets called "MREs." Plus, she had a Kevlar helmet on her head and a loaded rifle strapped across her chest in "patrol carry." At least they'd left, back at their Black Hawk helicopter, their huge backpacks full of camping accoutrements, which Isabel was convinced she couldn't lift, much less carry any great distance.

But when their Pentagon entourage reached the state police and National Guard barricade at the apex of the span, Isabel realized that the hard part was only beginning. She winced at the pleas shouted across the quarantine line established at the border. "For the love of *God*," a middle-aged man from the Vermont side yelled, "let us *through!* We're *Americans!*" He held what looked like a Boston Red Sox cap in both hands, straining as he begged from a hundred yards away, the picture of abject supplication. No, that was wrong. There was also undisguised indignation mixed with the man's visible anguish and fear. "How can you *do* this? They're right *behind* us! *Please!* We made it this far! We're almost safe! Just let us *cross!*"

Isabel looked up at Marine Capt. Rick Townsend, who shook his head in response.

"They're almost *here!*" The panicking refugee peered over his shoulder toward the bend in the still empty Vermont highway and the earthen causeway behind him that led up onto the bridge.

Isabel's nine-person "detail" had been sent by the Pentagon to observe and report on which containment policies worked and which did not. It consisted of Rick, Isabel's new wartime significant other, Dr. Brandon Plante, her peacetime ex whom she had recruited to study the Infecteds' crowd violence, and six army soldiers led by a Sgt. Vasquez.

Blue Dodge Chargers of the New York State Police and green Army Humvees were arranged across the top of the bridge to block passage into New York by potentially infected Vermonters. Opposite their blockade, hundreds of refugees beseeched the cops and troops to let them cross the Richelieu River before thousands of approaching Infecteds arrived.

Amid the spinning blue lights stood stoic but tense machine gunners gripping long black guns leveled at the increasingly despondent civilians. The refugees' representative ignored warnings against venturing past a flimsy line of orange traffic barrels connected by fluttering yellow police tape, which defined the beginning of the "killing fields." Isabel kept asking Rick for definitions of military terms, but killing fields was self-explanatory.

The chorus of voices confronting them hurled a mix of pleas, with hands clasped in prayer, and insults, with fists shaken in air. And these weren't all harmless women, children, and the elderly, Isabel realized. Rick scanned the crowd through binoculars and pointed out to a National Guard lieutenant a hunting rifle here, a coughing fit there.

Isabel's stomach churned as her sense of dread built. Brandon kept repeating, "This is bad. This is bad." Although Isabel had seen videos out of Asia of Infected mob rampages, Brandon was the expert. He had modeled dozens of mindless, primal clashes: clawing, stomping, gouging annihilations by Infecteds; grazing sheets of wanton machine gun fire unleashed by terrified troops. "*Look,*" he said to Isabel, his eyes wide and his pointing frantic as he turned her away from the quarantine line. "They're setting up more fucking machine guns. At the base of the bridge! *Behind* us!" He was right. That was worrisome.

Isabel turned reflexively back to Rick, who had witnessed the violence firsthand while observing the disease's advance. He had survived, and Isabel felt confident he would do everything within his power to ensure that she did too. Rick was an Annapolis grad and a Marine infantry officer, and like soldiers, policemen, firemen, and EMTs, he would be in demand by the vulnerable and the weak. She was incredibly lucky even to have met him while on her mission to Siberia to retrieve her infected twin sister.

The shot of confidence on recalling that good fortune, however, eroded while watching Rick peer over the bridge's guardrail as if measuring the distance to and depth of the water beneath them. "Can you swim?" he asked almost in a whisper. Isabel couldn't swallow the lump that formed in her throat. Her helmet flopped forward and backward on her head as she replied that yes, she could. "Dump your webbing and body armor before jumping, but hang onto your M4. It'll fire for a while even after it gets wet." Isabel realized that he was referring to her gun. She looked down and memorized where all her buckles and zippers were. "And remember to swim west." Rick then gave some version of the same instructions to a wide-eyed Brandon and a calm, nodding Vasquez.

The presumably frigid Richelieu flowed north to the St. Lawrence River and, under the clear skies, was a beautiful brilliant blue. Lake Champlain to the south glistened as late afternoon sunlight struck white spray whipped off wavelets in the brisk wind. The dancing branches of trees along the river's banks were thick and verdant. The picturesque New England landscape contrasted sharply with the scene on the concrete bridge, with its rending prayers and lacerating curses filling the last minutes before several hundred innocent people's almost certain doom.

Isabel turned away and forced the images from her mind. Their helicopter from D.C. to Vermont had diverted at the last minute. "The Vermont LZ is too hot," Rick had explained. "LZ" stood for "landing zone," she surmised from the context. When they set down in New York, they met the lieutenant colonel commanding a national guard battalion tasked with blocking the infection's passage into Clinton County. "I'm less worried about people coming across bridges from Vermont," he had told Rick in a low voice that Isabel had managed to overhear, "than through the woods straight down from Montreal, which is only about thirty clicks north. I've got combat patrols out there probing for contact 'cause the Coast Guard can't maintain a continuous presence up and down the St. Lawrence."

From their elevated vantage, Isabel could see thick woods all around, and they frightened her. *Think about something else.* Brandon's attention darted hyperactively from the quarantine line, to the men behind them setting up guns, to the water below. He had abandoned the white lab coat he had worn at the NIH hospital in Maryland, ridiculous attire for a social psychologist who modeled crowd behavior on computers. But he now wore even more absurd-looking camouflage battle dress, like the action figure he most assuredly wasn't.

After Isabel's smirk, eye roll, and scoff on first seeing him fully outfitted, however, she too had been issued her own "kit." It consisted of a helmet, body armor, pouches for ammo, compass, a first aid kit complete with bulky "quick-clot bandages" and a worrying number of tourniquets, a big backpack and little rucksack, wraparound amber eyewear called "ballistic eye protection", the water-filled bladder and feeder hose of a "hydration system," integrated "intra- and inter-team" radio, GPS locator, boots, and her very own camo uniform. When fully "kitted out," she looked ridiculous, to herself, like she had been miscast for her role. Only Rick wore his equipment naturally, as if he belonged in it.

Back where their helicopter had landed and, she hoped, still waited, a National Guard sergeant had handed Isabel a heavy black rifle, which he called a carbine, and she had pretended to understand the difference. He had asked her to read off the serial number stamped into the metal, then made a check mark on his clipboard. "You break it, you buy it," he had said. Isabel couldn't tell if he was joking, but hadn't felt in the mood to laugh.

When out of earshot, she had confided to Rick, "I don't really know how to shoot this." He had led her to the heavily guarded perimeter of the battalion headquarters, which was draped in netting, presumably out of habit and not in fear of an Infected air attack. Rick had stood behind Isabel and wrapped big arms around her as she raised the carbine to her shoulder. For an all-too-brief moment, Isabel had felt warm. Safe. At ease and at home.

"You're gonna have to open your eyes."

"Sorry!"

He had "chambered" a "round"—i.e., loaded a bullet—and shown her how to hold the ugly black gun. Flick the "selector switch"—the little lever beside the trigger—straight up with her thumb. Check that it was on "Semi," never "Auto." Aim. Pull the trigger. Pull it harder. *Bam!* The M4 had kicked. The shot had splashed the dirt on the riverbank into the air.

With Rick's face close, she had stolen a kiss from the corner of his mouth, apparently annoying him as he was going over how to clear jams and reload, which Isabel thought unnecessary. He'd always been so sweet. She'd never seen him irritated, or nervous…until then. And then again now, there, on the bridge.

"This is your final warning!" boomed from a patrol car's loudspeaker. "Clear this bridge immediately or risk grievous bodily harm or death!"

Isabel had trouble filling her lungs deeply enough. And the acoustics under the heavy helmet made everything seem surreal. This wasn't *her* standing on a windy New England bridge in full army combat gear. Maybe this was what an out-of-body experience felt like.

She tried to focus on her job. The Uninfecteds confronting their blockade from the Vermont side had isolated themselves into dozens and dozens of invisible little bubbles. They feared infection from anyone not an accepted member of whatever group to which they belonged. "I advise you to exit this bridge immediately!" boomed the voice from amid the patrol cars' flashing lights. "Before it's too late!" The little bubbles of people shifted this way and that, but none of them burst. They were staying together to the end.

"Look," the battalion commander said, "here they come." The front edge of a huge, trudging throng rounded the bend of the Vermont highway leading to the bridge. "Are we absolutely sure they're infected?" Even at over half a mile, it was clear there was something off about their behavior, though it was hard to describe what it was.

Brandon borrowed Rick's binoculars. "I don't see any subgroups. No families, or couples, or people who look like coworkers, or fellow students, or buddies. Just a random, heterogeneous collection of individuals."

Isabel copied Rick and several soldiers by peering at the approaching mass through her rifle's magnified sight. She added, "And they don't seem to be taking any precaution against infection. No masks. No gloves. They aren't avoiding each other."

"Why are they all coming this way?" the lieutenant colonel asked in a tone of desperation, not curiosity. "Can't they see what's about to *happen?*"

When no one else bothered to answer, Isabel tried to explain. "They all started out with some individual objective—find food, flee the same violence and chaos as the Uninfecteds down there, follow through on some old evacuation plan, whatever. When they somehow ended up at the same place and time, and the density of the crowd rose above some threshold, their individuality got submerged into that crowd. They then marched down the road, presumably recoiling from the chaos behind them, and they'll keep going in that semi-trancelike state till they either thin out and the hypnotic effect of the crowd is broken, or they reach an obstacle and their instinct of struggle compels them to overcome it."

"Give me an example of an obstacle," the colonel requested.

"*Us,*" Isabel replied.

"And there's no way to reason with them? Or scare them off, at least?" The colonel was running out of alternatives other than the obvious one.

Brandon said, in a drained monotone, "No way. They're packed forty to fifty-plus per ten square meters. They're totally immersed in that crowd." He was transfixed by the sight through Rick's binoculars. Gunshots rang out from the rear ranks of the refugees. Several of the approaching

Infecteds fell. "*That* didn't set them off," Brandon said. "But they're charged. Any second now..."

"Please! They're almost here!" shouted the man now crushing his baseball cap in his clutches.

A skirmish line of uninfected men at the Vermont base of the bridge fired scattered shots, retreated, fired again, and felled more Infecteds as they funneled onto the narrow causeway, which compressed the crowd even further and more dangerously. The Infecteds didn't cower or seek cover. It was as if they were completely indifferent to the deaths of a few from their ranks given the thousands more among their number.

But without any warning, an unearthly roar rose in volume and in pitch from the previously silent Infected horde. Isabel had been waiting for some trigger, but still she was unprepared for the deafening, demonic outcry, which marked the onset of the huge crowd's terrifying lurch, *en masse*, straight toward the few uninfected civilians' guns.

"Good *God!*" blurted out an astonished Guardsman from behind sunglasses.

The sound was familiar to Isabel from classified Pentagon videos, but unprecedented in her personal experience. The hair-raising screech chilled her spine and started her limbs shaking even before the Infected mob first set upon the outnumbered Uninfecteds. The quiver soon spread to her torso, and she could no longer hold the rifle's scope steady enough. A thick knot rose to a boil in her stomach, and she kept finding herself out of breath.

Rick caught Isabel's eye. The Infected crowd's wail was the sound he had warned her to flee if she ever heard it. The uninfected skirmishers at the foot of the causeway were quickly overwhelmed by the clamorous melee a few hundred yards distant in what was now, for Rick, Brandon, and Isabel, a familiar sight of flailing, gouging, clawing mutilation. But the sickening bloodshed hit the National Guardsmen and cops like body blows. Jaws agape. Eyes wide. "Christ Almighty," came one state policewoman's quivering comment.

"Everybody lock and *load!*" It was Rick's voice even though Rick, like Isabel and Brandon, was only supposed to be an observer. There were dozens of mechanical *clacks* from all around.

"What are my rules of engagement?" the National Guard lieutenant colonel demanded.

Rick, a Marine Corps captain, was craning his neck to count, Isabel realized, the number of guns under the colonel's command. Not the rifles of the individual soldiers, or the shotguns and pistols of the agitated state policemen, but the machine guns. There were three huge black weapons atop the Humvees, and another four Isabel saw—smaller machine guns whose bipods rested atop hoods or whose foregrips lay across the windowsills of open Humvee doors. Long belts studded with brass bullets dangled, ready to feed the fearsome beasts.

"What are my rules of engagement?" repeated the colonel. With his brow furrowed, Rick now scanned not the Uninfecteds, who crouched, some permanently on their knees with gazes lifted skyward, but the much larger and denser crowd of howling Infecteds, which approached the Uninfecteds from behind. "Captain!" snapped the National Guard colonel. "My-rules-of-*engagement?*" he demanded.

"What are your *orders*, sir?" Rick replied testily even though he knew the answer.

"Hold this bridge. Let no one pass." They almost had to shout at each other over the mass roar of the Infecteds and the frequent piercing screams of their victims.

"And you were authorized to use deadly force?" Again, Rick's question was rhetorical. *Hurry* up*!* Isabel urged silently. *They're coming!*

"If necessary," the colonel answered.

"It's gonna be necessary, sir. When the Infecteds reach the foot of the raised span, they're gonna be canalized between the guardrails." Rick stared into the colonel's ashen face. "Pour...it...*on*, sir," he enunciated slowly and unequivocally.

The colonel seemed sickened. He shook his head as he stared at the few hundred helpless civilians who recoiled past the orange barrels from the frenzied attack behind them. Infecteds ten or twenty times their number were tackling and ripping to shreds the scattering Uninfecteds farther down the bridge. The National Guard commander shouted into the patrol car's microphone, "*Run!* It's your last chance! Jump into the water! *Now!*"

Some people easily made it over the low rails of the causeway, but many were tackled short of the cold water and others were followed straight into it. *Leave them alone!* Isabel raged before closing her eyes to shut out the sights and sounds of the maulings, which in the water mimicked the splashing, flailing imagery of a shark attack.

But she had to watch. It was her only job. The railings along the raised portion of the bridge gave people time for internal debate. Some sat atop them, feet dangling in empty air. Their choice was often made for them right before the outstretched grasp of berserk Infecteds swallowed them whole. But if the jumper was a child, or elderly, or infirm, and they hesitated, they ended up being pulled backwards and disappearing under the fast-forming killing mounds.

"I'm gonna be sick," she said, but no one heard her over the clamor.

Each jump, sometimes by people in pairs holding hands, sometimes with mothers or fathers holding or first pushing or tossing their children, was followed by a dozen or more splashes as Infecteds, locked in on their intended victims, knew no limits in their zeal to kill. The sounds of splashes, however, were quickly overwhelmed by the sports stadium-like crescendo of the two main crowds merging with unrestrained violence.

"They're on the bridge, colonel!" Rick shouted.

"Please! You're supposed to *help* us!" came the final plea of the uninfected man with a long forgotten baseball cap, who now crawled on his hands and knees seventy-five yards away.

"Sir! You've gotta give the order!" The lieutenant colonel, eyes twitching, stared back at Rick, but appeared not to see him. "*Now*, sir!"

The Guardsman took a deep breath before emerging from his daze. "All right! Listen up! We hold this bridge! We stand our ground! On my command, I'm going to order you to fire at will!" There was an inordinately long pause during which the next words seemed several times to stick in the civilian/soldier's throat. "On… On my…" He gulped. "On my command! Commence…*firing!*"

What should have been a fusillade of automatic weapons was only a sporadic few shots aimed by riflemen who could single out targets in the more distant Infected crowd through the panicked and scattering Uninfecteds in between.

"*Colonel!*" Rick shouted.

The National Guard officer proceeded from gunner to gunner, climbing atop Humvees or squeezing between patrol cars to put an arm around each man in turn, speaking urgently into his ear and slapping him on the back or the helmet. One-by-one, the machine guns began to rattle. The gunners grimaced from what must surely be moral agony. Some Uninfecteds crawled across the pavement toward the railings; others writhed; still others lay unmoving in expanding puddles. The man with the baseball cap lay splayed on the pavement in the unnatural position of the dead. As more guns fired with ever greater abandon, more Uninfecteds spun and twisted on their way to the pavement, which attested to the violence of their tragic end.

Isabel threw up, but no one noticed. She pressed index fingers against her throbbing ears. In that relative silence, and after one more retch, she looked up to see the now solid mass of Infecteds—arms pumping, hands rigid and talonlike, faces frozen in bare-toothed sneers, eyes wide and unblinking—on the dead run up the bridge straight toward them. Gone was any hesitation from the troops or the cops. All could now clearly see the approach of certain death. Machine gunners slewed their blazing heavy weapons across the first rank, then the second, then the third. Flame burst from a female police officer's shotgun. She pumped and fired, pumped and fired, again and again, before pausing to reload awkwardly and hurriedly while trembling, lower lip quivering. Highway patrolmen held pistols in two shaking hands and emptied magazine after magazine. And yet the mob of howling Infecteds continued to close.

Rick and the Army soldiers in their detail crouched behind the cars and Humvees and fired straight into the crowd. But it took Isabel seeing Brandon—slack-jawed and paralyzed by the shock of the unfolding massacre—to realize what she had to do. She leaned over the hood of a patrol car, wincing at the tumult that now scraped at her unprotected eardrums, and raised her rifle to her shoulder. Long gone were the poor Uninfecteds caught in the middle. All Isabel saw now were crazed Infecteds intent on disemboweling her.

Isabel flicked the selector switch up, not all the way forward, just as Rick had shown her, and generally aimed at the onrushing mob. But when she squeezed the trigger, nothing happened. The thing should be ready to shoot. She looked at the switch beside the trigger guard. It was set to Semi, not Safe or Auto. She pulled harder. *Bam!* She had no idea whether she had hit anyone, but couldn't imagine how she could've missed. *Bam!* This time, she saw a young woman near the front rank of Infecteds fall. *Bam!* A boy with a brick in his hand took two steps before collapsing. *Please forgive me!* she prayed silently—*Bam!*—sickened by what she was doing and trying to swallow the bile that rose again to scald her throat.

The few orange barrels that remained upright at the quarantine line were toppled in unison. *One hundred yards away! Bam!* Everyone around her fired their weapons, even Brandon. The air stank of steely smoke. *Bam!* A heavy rain of brass shell casings cascaded off the roofs of the Humvees. *Bam!* She crunched cartridges underfoot with every redirection of her aim. *Bam!* The roar of weapons, now continuous, drowned out all other noise and blended with a ringing sound in her ears like a rock concert.

Bam! Isabel fired now without thinking. *Bam!* Without feeling. *Bam!* Like an Infected. *Bam!* She aimed right at "center mass," as Rick had instructed. *Bam!* Right at the middle of their chests. And at eighty yards away, more often than not, she saw through her small scope that she hit her target. *Bam!* Not a human being. A bull's eye. *Bam!* A thing that had to be stopped. *Bam!* Not a girl whose every sprinted stride kicked at her long purple skirt—*Bam!*—until her jaw exploded in mist. Not a paunchy man with a full beard whose round granny glasses—*Bam!*—flew from his face as his momentum was halted by the bullet to his abdomen. Not a white-haired woman in a hockey jersey—*Bam!*—who staggered forward a few steps despite losing a quarter of her cranium. Or a little boy with a multicolored cast on his forearm—*Bam!*—whose left leg went all floppy at the femur before he collapsed. Tears finally flooded her vision. Now, she fired at a roiling, amorphous blur that was impossible to miss at fifty yards and closing.

Bam! Bam! Bam! Bam! Bam! Bam! Bam! Bam! Bam! Bam!

When her magazine was empty after thirty rounds were fired, the nearest Infecteds still on their feet were over a hundred yards beyond the imaginary line where the orange barrels lay on their sides. They were struggling to keep their footing on the slippery concrete, some waist-deep in the carnage of still writhing bodies.

Despite no order having been given, the fire quickly abated. The tolling of the bells in Isabel's deadened ears filled the unsettling silence that followed. She looked up at the machine gunner atop the Humvee next to her. Heat shimmered off his blazing hot barrel. The man behind it slumped so low she feared he was wounded. And he was, she realized, but not physically. She couldn't see his eyes behind his sunglasses, but his jaw drooped, loose with horror and, possibly, guilt.

Little by little, her hearing returned. The bridge was covered in the dead and dying. A mere few hundred Infecteds retreated down the causeway on the run, the spell of the vastly diminished crowd broken. The only sounds came from the few surviving Uninfecteds. There were groans, the whine of a child, a faint call for aid from somewhere, and some splashing in the river. "Jonathon!" a woman cried out hoarsely. "Jon, *he-e-elp!*" That set Isabel's tears off again, and this time they wouldn't stop. She tried to regain control, but couldn't, letting her empty rifle dangle from its straps as she doubled over, grabbed her knees, and sobbed. At least she wasn't alone. She fought shame but looked around and saw male soldiers, here and there, wiping the tears from their faces.

Do your fucking job! she cursed silently, willing herself to look up and survey the carnage on which she would have to report to the Pentagon. The vast majority of the wounded were Infecteds, but they made not a single sound. Not a moan, or a plea, or a wail. They would die without any of the emotional distress of the similarly bullet-riddled Uninfecteds, who would rage and sob all the way to the oblivion awaiting them.

"Cease fire!" came the unnecessary command from the exhausted-sounding National Guard colonel. "Safeties on!" Rick clicked the selector switches to Safe on both Isabel and Brandon's rifles. Infecteds stumbled off the Vermont highway into the woods on the far shore. Many were wounded, but none were helped by anyone else. A blanket of the dead and dying, in places several deep, covered almost every square foot of roadway. Bright ski jackets. Dull work shirts. Red lumberjack flannel. An elbow rose, but the wounded woman couldn't lift herself. Thousands of bodies that were quickly falling still.

The cool, fresh air caught several times as Isabel struggled to fill her fluttery lungs. The pretty foliage on the far bank still danced in the wind. Puffy white clouds skittered across the pale blue sky. A flock of small black birds practiced their choreography, taking no notice of the insignificant events on the bridge below. Beneath Isabel's feet were countless huge, blackened, and spent machine gun and smaller yellowish rifle cartridges, alongside comparatively tiny brass casings from pistols, smoking red plastic shotgun shells, and a half a dozen puddles of vomit.

Rick slipped on the casings as he returned to Isabel. "You okay?"

She didn't know how to reply. Was she? Okay? What did that even mean? "I... I..." She couldn't compose an answer until she swallowed the burning reflux. She then raised her empty rifle and managed to ask, "How do I reload this?"

Chapter 3

"Good-bye, old life," Noah Miller heard his fifteen-year-old daughter Chloe say as they pulled off the state highway onto the ridgeline-hugging road that led up to the Old Place. Her mother Natalie had spent their last evening at home fashioning Chloe's now shorn blond hair into a trendy look. Noah had then found his wife sitting at her vanity, staring into the mirror at her own short blond hair, brush in hand, sobbing.

After Isabel's dramatic heliborne departure from their front lawn, Noah and his family's trip down to the Shenandoah Valley from McLean had been unusual, but blessedly uneventful. On their way to the Interstate, they had passed a police officer, shotgun propped on his hip, talking to a man behind the shattered glass windows of a small community bank branch. Then two buildings that were still burning while a single fire truck sprayed water onto a third. Then a cluster of young people brazenly drinking alcohol in the parking lot by the smashed door of a liquor store.

The Interstate itself was a parking lot, and people weren't ceding an inch. Noah engaged in a honking war and practically had to force the front fender of his huge SUV into the solid lane of traffic. The angry driver who followed him soon forgave the affront and became their neighbor for the next several hours.

But the farther they got from D.C., the freer the traffic flowed and the more normal life seemed, although the roadsides were now apparently permanently dotted with encampments of refugees from somewhere up north. Noah spent his time torturing himself with visions of finding their mountain refuge picked clean by workers he had insanely trusted to finish the job and leave. As the silent nightmare in his mind evolved, he imagined catching the workers in the act of looting their things, and them killing his whole family.

Just before the last bend at the top of the ridge road, Noah slowed to a stop.

"What is it?" his wife asked from the passenger seat beside him.

"I just wanna check it out. Give me a sec." He exited the SUV with his rifle.

Noah carefully made his way up the road. He looked back to see thirteen-year-old Jacob protruding from the sunroof, rifle raised. Natalie made Chloe take off her headphones and pay attention, which earned his wife a devastating eye roll. Noah peered over a dirt embankment. The house was still. The workers' trucks were gone.

He parked, led them up to the house, and held his breath as he unlocked the front door. The place was in perfect order. All their supplies were right where they had left them.

"Awww," he heard Natalie say. Noah joined her at the dining room table. She held a bottle of red wine with a bow on it and handed the note to Noah. "I hope you enjoy your new home," the contractor had written. "Please keep us in your prayers."

"What a nice man," Natalie said before she got busy cooking dinner.

Noah chided himself for so quickly losing all faith in humanity. The kids unloaded the SUVs. Noah went to the barn. Their house was off the grid. While the sun was shining, the rooftop solar panels were still producing surplus power as indicated by the needle that danced on the positive side of the battery's meter. But after they finished unloading the SUV and darkness fell, the needle sank to the left hand, negative side. The windmill still turned, but they were using more power than they produced. That began Noah's obsessive checking of the batteries every hour. He walked the fence line, locked the front gate, and agitated the chickens that had been delivered right on schedule. He grabbed the red handle in the barn that electrified the fence and pulled it down with a mechanical *clunk* to the "On" notch. The needle jumped more firmly toward the negative side, but the batteries' charges remained solid. The propane-powered generators never had to kick in.

"Dad! Dinner!" Chloe called from the front porch.

When Noah saw the plentiful quantities of food on the table, he thought Natalie had overdone it. They needed to ration. But it was delicious, and while Natalie supervised Jacob's washing of dishes—by hand, their son was aghast to discover—Noah was pleased to see Chloe collecting every uneaten morsel of food and refrigerating it.

After one last look out into the quiet, cool night air—tranquil despite what Noah knew was happening in New England, Canada, Europe, and Asia—the family settled around the lone big-screen television. They could receive two nearby broadcast stations—one well, one with ghosting. Both had local takes on the pandemic. Protestations by sheriffs, mayors, and clinic administrators that they were fully prepared. Rumors and eyewitness accounts of strangers, many armed, collecting amid ramshackle shelters constructed out of tarps and tents alongside highways, and official warnings against confrontations with them.

When Noah switched to satellite and a brilliant digital picture filled the screen, there were cheers. "Oh, I love that movie. Stop!" Chloe said, but Noah ignored her and settled on CNBC, eliciting his daughter's groan. "I'm *si-i-ick* of the news."

"…including New York City, Chicago, Los Angeles, Denver, Atlanta, and Miami."

"It's spread all the way *there?*" Natalie asked in alarm.

But the story wasn't about the arrival of SED—Severe Encephalopathic Disease—but about the looting and panic that preceded it. There were no reported cases of *Pandoravirus horribilis* yet outside Vermont. "Stores have been receiving their last shipments of food and are being emptied by frenzied shoppers. The National Guard is setting up centers for the emergency distribution of food and water, but civil unrest is hampering authorities' efforts."

In Philadelphia, straight lines of police faced off against ragged masses of rioters many times their number. Arcing trails of tear gas flew into crowds and back at cops. Fires spread unchecked in the distance as the news helicopter's camera panned back.

Breaking news interrupted other breaking news. The anchorman introduced a woman calling from her home outside Burlington, Vermont. "Can you hear me?"

"Yes," the caller whispered. "I hear you."

"Please tell our viewers what you see."

"They're outside," her caller replied softly. "There are police cars under a streetlamp at the corner, and they're meeting with them there. Please send help. They're everywhere!"

The journalist at the anchor desk was slow on the uptake. "I'm sorry, but didn't you say the police were already there?"

"The police are *infected*. Everybody has turned! They're meeting. Getting ready for something. They've got guns!"

"Are you saying that everybody you're seeing on your street has turned?"

"Everybody who survived," the woman said. "Ambulances have been removing bodies from our neighbors' houses. When the EMTs came up to my door this afternoon, I looked through the peephole and their eyes were black! They're not even wearing those masks and other getup anymore. I'm the only one left! Please, please, *please* send help!"

The anchorman asked, "So people who have turned are going back to their old jobs? The police? The EMTs?"

The distraught woman on the phone ignored his question. "They're coming up to the houses! They're knocking on doors! Oh-my-God! Oh-my-God! Please send help, right now!" She gave her address, twice, then blurted out, "There's shooting!"

"The police are shooting?" the anchorman asked. "The Infecteds are shooting?"

"No!" The caller was hyperventilating. "Two doors up. The Crenshaws, I think. Somebody inside shot one of the cops. The cops are shooting back. At the Crenshaws!"

"For our viewers who just joined, we have a caller on the line who's trapped in a quarantined zone in Burlington, Vermont. She reports that Infecteds who have turned have gone back to their jobs as police and medical personnel and are now going house-to-house in her neighborhood."

"They broke into the Crenshaws' house! Oh, God! There's a whole bunch of them. Oh, Jesus, Mary, and Joseph! They're going to the house next door to me!"

"Maybe you…need to get to *safety?*"

"I don't have anywhere to go! Please help!" More quietly now, the woman said, "My neighbors, the McDonalds, are on the porch talking to the police. Nobody's wearing a mask or anything. And they just shook hands! With the *Infecteds!* The McDonalds must've caught it too! They're going back inside!"

The woman was whispering, so the anchorman repeated what she said for viewers. "So your neighbors have turned, and they shook hands with the infected police?"

"They're coming up to my door!" the woman said urgently. "Our Father, who art in Heaven, hallowed be Thy name."

The woman didn't respond to the next few questions, but you could still hear the quivering, whispered Lord's Prayer above the pounding on the door. "I'm in the closet." There was a loud crash, and a whimper, and,

"They're inside. They're inside my house!" Despite long periods of silence, the anchorman listened with his face a mask of concern, almost as if he and the viewers were hiding in the closet with the woman. All at once, the woman shouted, "No! Please! Get back! No! *No-o-o!*" There was rustling. A brief struggle. The phone must have been dropped. The woman's pleas disappeared into the distance.

A man's voice came clearly over the line. "Hello?"

The stunned anchorman took a moment before replying, "Hello? Who is this?"

"Burlington PD," came the monotone reply. "I'm hanging up now." The phone line went dead.

Noah looked from face to face. The kids were pale and stunned. Natalie returned his gaze, sick with worry. Noah muted the television and said, "Enough TV. Anybody wanna play cards?"

"*What?*" Chloe asked, incredulous at the ridiculous suggestion.

But Natalie agreed. She went to find the new deck Jacob had bought on a whim—the last item remaining in the checkout lane rack at a CVS in Reston, Virginia. Noah joined her in the kitchen. Natalie threw her arms around his neck. "Noah, is that going to happen here? Are we fooling ourselves? Thinking we can just watch Armageddon pass by on TV? Come out when the dust settles with our guns and our seeds and start our new lives as farmers?"

He kissed her forehead. "One day at a time, Nat. Be strong."

When she was composed, they returned to the kids. Chloe, holding her phone, said, "Gracie is in Idaho with her whole family: aunts, uncles, cousins, a whole bunch of them. Why don't we have cousins?"

Jake answered. "Because Mom's an only child, and our aunts are both spinsters."

Noah objected. "Aunt Emma and Aunt Isabel are only thirty-two! Where'd you even learn that word?"

"Well Aunt Emma is infected," Jake continued, "so *she* isn't getting married any time soon."

"I dunno," Chloe said without raising her eyes from her apps. "After everybody turns it's Aunt *Isabel* who's gonna have a hard time finding a guy."

"Not that she was much good in that department before," Natalie commented.

"Oh!" Chloe exclaimed, reading her phone. "Trey and his folks are on an island somewhere. He won't say where. Why didn't we go to an island? That makes more sense, doesn't it?"

That annoyed Noah, and Natalie quickly intervened. "Your father worked his butt off to keep us all safe, so let's not second-guess his choices."

Chloe, oblivious to her parents, said, "Huh! Lucy Fong and her family are in Roanoke. That's in Virginia, right? I seem to be locked in some weird social orbit with her." She froze mid-sentence. Her jaw hung open. Her humor was gone.

"What?" Natalie asked. "What is it?"

Chloe lowered her phone, then threw it onto the sofa cushion beside her as it were an object of disgust instead of the center of her universe. "There's a picture of Janie and Justin! At Justin's church, handing out blankets and shit!" Natalie sat beside her daughter and put her arm around her. "I *told* you he'd leave me if I cut my hair!"

"Honey, they probably go to the same church."

"Janie's Jewish," came her daughter's sullen reply.

"Chloe, it could be nothing. But even if they got back together…"

"He said he'd come find me!" Chloe exclaimed, lips quivering. "*Now* who am I gonna have to settle for? That retarded boy down at the convenience store on the highway?"

"Chloe!" Noah snapped. "You can't call someone retarded."

"*Yes*, she can," Natalie replied, "because he's not. He's a perfectly good-looking boy. An athlete, just like Justin."

"He's a *hunter!*" Chloe corrected.

"Okay, an outdoorsman. You could do a lot worse in times like this."

"What the *hell*, Natalie?" Noah objected. "Are we marrying off our fifteen-year-old daughter now?"

"I'm just saying life goes on."

"No!" Chloe said. "It doesn't." She sat upright, freeing herself of her mother's embrace. "Not if you get infected. Or if some horde of crazies tears all the skin off your bones, life doesn't go on. It stops right then."

"No horde's tearing anything off *my* bones," Jacob said in what Noah mistakenly thought was bravado. "My last shot goes right here." He pointed his index finger at the roof of his mouth.

"Jake!" his mother cried out.

"But he's right, isn't he?" Chloe asked.

Natalie appealed to Noah for help with a look. Noah could only turn away. They all knew it was true. You saved your last bullet to avoid an agonizing end.

Natalie plopped the deck of cards noisily on the coffee table. "Chloe, you shuffle."

"*What?*"

"Shuffle. We're playing cards."

Noah mumbled that he needed to check the fence. He grabbed his rifle and went out into the cold. *Should we have gone to an island?* he thought, tormenting himself. *Or the desert? Or the Rockies? What have I overlooked, or forgotten, or failed to imagine?* When his eyes had adjusted to the darkness and he heard nothing but the wind in the trees, he walked the short distance to the barn. The battery levels weren't appreciably lower than before sundown even with the fence electrified. He could hear the windmill whirring on the hilltop. The ridge road beyond the gate was dark and empty. There was an eruption of clucking from the hens' cages as he moved about. He exited the far side of the barn and stood a few feet from the electric fence. He thought it would hum or make some other noise, and he considered a quick tap of it to ensure that it was electrified, but decided against it. All was still in the downhill sloping woodlands and quiet from the state highway a mile beyond.

"Noah!" Natalie called from the porch. He composed himself in the darkness, trying to erase all traces of the fear and doubt from his face, and only then returned for the family games of hearts and then spades.

Chapter 4

NORTHERN VIRGINIA
Infection Date 40, 1200 GMT (8:00 a.m. Local)

The old VW microbus sputtered to a stop on the two-lane blacktop in the Virginia woods. The gas tank was bone dry. The day before, Emma and the van's owner had made it only a dozen or so miles before night fell and the lanky guy had said he was tired. He built a fire along the roadside and heated soup from a can. "You don't say much," had been one of his few attempts to engage Emma in conversation. The rest of the time, he had talked about himself. Apparently, he considered his pointless roaming about the country and semi-homelessness before SED's arrival to be achievements worthy of boasting. Lots of talk about living off the grid and not selling out to corporate, but it all sounded to Emma like an attempt to turn failure into an ideology.

"What do you do?" he'd asked in a rare break from self-involvement.

"I'm a professor of epidemiology at Johns Hopkins University."

The guy cocked his head, then laughed and launched into a retelling of his life's story in which he was really the CEO of Fortune 500 company on an incognito tour of the hinterlands. His snickering hinted that he was pleased with his self-amusement.

"I'm going to sleep," Emma announced, rising and brushing the dust from the back of her jeans.

"I'll *join* you."

She gave him one last chance by saying, "No."

"Oh, come on. You're not gonna hold out on me. Not now, when we don't know how much longer we've got." In his case, it was about three minutes. Maybe five, if you counted until brain death.

Emma got out of the van and began stashing in a backpack the few useful items the loser had managed to accumulate—some canned food and a can opener, bottled water, matches, a fleece, a poncho, a wool blanket—plus Emma's own toiletry bag from the NIH hospital and rusty screw driver from the roadside now caked with the dried blood of two lecherous men.

Outside, a pickup truck pulled to a stop, and a man and woman got out. There was a shotgun in a rack at the rear window of the truck's cab, from which peered a young girl and boy. Emma exited the van and closed the door.

"Hello!" the woman called out to her and waved. The man walked up to the van's driver's side window and looked inside. "You have car trouble or something?" asked the overweight woman, in her late twenties, with a smile on her smooth, puffy face. She wore a silver cross on a silver chain.

"Out of gas," Emma said. The man was searching the dark van through its grimy side windows. Emma felt her level of agitation rise, and dug her fingernails into her palms inside clenched fists.

"You need a ride?" the woman asked. "We're not goin' far, but you're welcome to come along."

Emma hoisted her backpack onto her shoulder.

"What about him?" the man asked, his thumb pointing over his shoulder at the microbus. "Is he asleep?"

"I'm done with him."

The woman tilted her head and made some kind of pinch-lipped face that Emma couldn't decipher. But she locked her arm in Emma's and towed her toward their mud-covered pickup.

The man held his hand out, inviting Emma to get into the back of the vehicle, not the cab. Emma threw her backpack into the flatbed, climbed up the large knobby tire, and settled onto the cold, corrugated metal bed. She waved at the two little faces in the cab's rear window, and the kids waved back.

It quickly grew cold on the drive, and Emma donned the fleece and settled lower into the bed to get out of the breeze. Eventually, she lay her head on the backpack and dozed off watching the canopy of trees slide by overhead and the cab's rear window fog from the kids' breath.

She woke when the pickup's brakes squealed, and she sat up. Alert. Agitated. They had stopped in a small rural town. There was a civil war cannon in the square. A couple of dozen men, young and old, fat and slender, black and white, stood in formation with all manner of shotguns and rifles on one or the other of their shoulders.

"This is where we'll have to say good-bye," the cheery young woman announced as she appeared beside Emma. Her husband eyed Emma warily from a distance. She climbed down, thanked the woman, and exchanged a last wave with the kids.

They could connect her to the body in the microbus. Rather than continue south at the town square, Emma turned east. She would walk in that direction until out of their sight.

"Left shoulder...*arms!*" The ragtag collection of would-be citizen soldiers reshouldered their non-military weapons in a half dozen different, inexpert ways. "Port...*arms!*" Most didn't know what to do and belatedly copied their neighbors.

A small crowd had gathered to watch the martial display. They were clearly a mix of mostly elderly locals, and mostly younger refugees. She looked down. Her jeans, dusty boots, lightweight gray wool sweater, and backpack fit in well with the latter. But none seemed to be unaccompanied females. All the women were in couples, or families, or some other groupings; never alone.

She caught the eye of a boy and looked away, but tracked his approach in her peripheral vision. Before he had the chance to speak, Emma said, "Not interested," and kept walking without so much as a glance in his direction.

"You're that scientist." Emma stopped. "On TV." Emma turned. They were alone, but still visible from the square. He was a teenager, with a mop of dark hair, bangs near his eyes, facial stubble, and a gleaming white grin. She tried turning up the corners of her lips, but his smile disappeared and she quickly aborted. It didn't feel right anyway. "That's you, right? On CNN? You're, like, some brain doctor who's been studying the Infecteds?"

He thinks I'm Isabel, came the mysterious voice in her head. *Let him.* Emma nodded, both to the boy and...to whom? To her *self?*

"Charles. Charles Rankin. But people call me Chaz."

"Dr. Isabel Miller. Just...Dr. Miller."

"Right! I *knew* it." He seemed to celebrate his subpar powers of recognition. In fact, both Miller twins had been on nationwide TV— Isabel on CNN to discuss Infecteds' brain damage; Emma on a Homeland Security video as an example of *Pandoravirus's* effects. Isabel was the before to Emma's after. Emma was lucky for the boy's mistake. The boy was lucky too.

"Me and this guy were supposed to ride together all the way to St. Louis, but he ran outta gas and didn't wanna leave his car. I'm trying to get home to Boulder. I'm a Freshman at George Mason, or was, I guess." He paused as if it was Emma's turn to say something.

"What's your major?"

"What? Oh, uhm, undeclared. Prob'ly business admin." He was acting strange...or she was. "So, you're on foot? Me too," he said. "So-o-o...?" Emma waited, but Chaz never completed his sentence. "I wouldn't think you'd just be out here like a regular person. I woulda thought you'd be in some bunker or secret base or something."

Chaz stopped talking, so Emma filled the void. "Nope." The less said, the fewer clues she might give him. Though he did seem pretty dense.

"You wanna hook up?" he asked. "I mean...! I don't mean..." Emma had no idea what he meant other than he wanted to have sex with her. "I mean do you wanna be traveling companions? Throw in together for however long? Road trip!"

"I'm heading south." Isabel turned to leave in that direction. *You should have said east,* the voice said. *Now he knows the truth.*

"Me too."

After several steps, Emma turned back to him. He looked half her age of thirty-two, but he was handsome and had a nice physique, unlike the flabby truck driver and the lanky, yellow-toothed van guy. "Come on," she said. He fell in alongside her, grinning.

There, the voice said. *A normal looking couple.*

Chapter 5

Rick pulled Isabel up onto the bed of a big army truck. Six hundred murmuring soldiers fell quiet. They were the first *regular* army to arrive, Rick had informed her, the full significance of which she didn't comprehend. But unlike the National Guardsmen at the bridge, these men's heads were shaved to their skulls and faces were streaked black and green.

A lieutenant colonel, fitter than the senior National Guard officer on the bridge, bellowed, "Listen up!" No one uttered a word. "Dr. Miller here is an expert on Infecteds. She's gonna tell us exactly how we're gonna *kick their asses!*" There was a booming chorus of something that sounded like "*Hoo*-ah!" *What does that even mean?* The masculine ritual, joined in lustily by the women, was viscerally stirring, but also vaguely primal and more than a little disturbing.

Isabel said they usually just took questions. Their commander barked, "Questions?"—more an order than an invitation. Isabel was shown how to use a bullhorn. The first boy to stand was barely audible. "Shout it out, soldier!" interrupted the colonel.

The boy gathered himself and drew a deep breath. "Ma'am, can-you-get-sick-from-having-sex-with-an-Infected—*ma'am?*"

The obviously close-knit and keyed-up battalion howled in laughter. The questioner was pushed off balance, dragged to the ground, and put into a head lock. The smiling colonel's heavily armed, overgrown children were primed. Isabel was entertained because she liked men, and was amused by boys being boys. Their female comrades-in-arms, with low buns that fit under helmets, displayed timeworn smiles more of bemusement.

When they quieted down, Isabel said, in a greatly amplified voice, "*Yes*, you almost certainly would." There were more hoots and hilarity as their tremendous pent-up nervous energy found an outlet.

But when the next man—a lieutenant—rose to his feet, sergeants quieted their men with kicks, punches, and profanity. "I hear that when Infecteds attack, ma'am, suppressing fire won't work. They won't go to ground, or take cover, or chicken out. They'll keep coming, even if it's suicide." The battalion was entirely still now. "I hear they'll rip you to shreds with their bare hands. No mercy. No limits. No exceptions."

There was not a snicker or a cough to be heard. Rouses Point Bridge hadn't come up once in the briefings they'd given since the massacre. Not by pre-agreement, but because the memory of it was clearly too raw and disconcerting. Isabel, however, could still smell and taste her memories from that day. Not rotting bodies. That would come later. No attempt would be made to clear the thousands of corpses leaking the world's most dangerous pathogen. What Isabel recalled instead was the odor of urine, feces, blood, and vomit, and the acrid stench of gunfire.

She raised the bullhorn. "Yes, that's all true." Six hundred frozen faces stared back. "I don't know if you've heard about Rouses Point Bridge at the New York-Vermont border." Rick had written a detailed report to the Pentagon, which had instantly been classified Top Secret. "Once the crowd attacked, there was no stopping it. They only calm down when they've dispersed to a lower crowd density. Until then, every single Infected in a packed, charged crowd gets roused to unspeakable violence. Once triggered, possibly by some insignificant incident, that mob has only one goal: to kill you and only you, with their hands, with sticks and stones, or with knives and guns. They will focus on killing *you* with a single-mindedness never seen before. The only way to put a definitive end to a mob attack is to… to kill, basically, every last Infected in that mob."

No mercy. No limits. No exceptions.

Isabel caught sight of a fist bump here and an exchange of hard stares there. These weren't pre-game rituals designed to psyche up teammates. They were solemn vows: *you do your job; I'll do mine.*

She cleared the lump in her throat with a perfunctory cough. "Infecteds alone or in small groups are obviously *also* potentially violent. A fair number will be so brain damaged they're wildly unpredictable and highly volatile, but they'll only last a few hours or days before they succumb to the elements or are killed. The rest—the higher functioning—will attack you if you threaten them, or have something they want, or stop them from doing what they want to do or going where they want to go, or corner them. They'll become agitated, get a huge rush of adrenaline, and react in extreme ways—homicidal, suicidal, insanely irrational. But not as horrifically as when they're in a trancelike state in a crowd. Plus, if they don't have any of those reasons to kill you, they'll possibly leave you alone. In fact, they may cooperate with or obey you, so long as that course is rational. But you can never trust them. You don't know what they're planning or when the scales will tip and they'll turn on you without any remorse or guilt or conscience."

Foreboding seemed to suppress further questions until, finally, the same soldier who asked the first question rose. "What if you use a condom, ma'am?" The laughter was all out of proportion to the stale humor. But Isabel found herself chuckling, as did Rick and the battalion commander. Brandon, however, gazed blankly into the darkness, not returning Isabel's questioning gaze. Since the bridge, he had withdrawn from Isabel, from the horrible new world, from life itself.

After a half dozen other routine questions, the colonel took the bullhorn. "Our mission is to interdict infiltration into this country by Infecteds fleeing Canada. Follow your general orders. Challenge anyone you meet in a courteous manner and with a soldierly bearing. The sign is 'Thorough.' The password is 'Squirrel.' They were supposedly chosen because they're difficult words for French speakers to pronounce. If they want to parley, they send only one representative forward. The following special orders apply. If you order someone to halt and they fail to obey, you fire three warning shots into the air. Not two, not four: *three*. If they still fail to stop, fire for effect. You need no further authorization."

The colonel let that sink in before booming, "Second battalion, *mount* up!"

The troops belted out one more thunderous, "*Hoo*-ah!" before rising.

Snarled commands from sergeants herded underlings into lines at the tailgates of dozens of large, canvas-covered trucks. Isabel assumed that, briefing over, their detail would return to their helicopter like after each earlier stop. But Rick dipped his fingers into a can that looked like shoe polish and swiped them across Isabel's cheek. She recoiled in surprise. "We're gonna observe their blocking operation." Rick tilted her chin upward as if to kiss her. She closed her eyes. He applied more grease paint. "JCS thinks it'll inform our future briefings."

Rick painted Brandon's face and then his own as the battalion split into its constituent companies, platoons, squads, and fire teams. Their detail joined an infantry platoon and climbed aboard a covered truck. Rick returned the salute of a Second Lieutenant Brad Stockman, who looked to be about twelve.

On the drive, Isabel and Brandon sat on one of the hard wooden benches lining the walls of flapping canvas. Rick and Stockman knelt between the rows of knees and upright rifles. Isabel eavesdropped on their discussion, oftentimes shouted over the engine growl and the unending grind of gears.

In addition to Stockman and his platoon sergeant, she learned, there were thirty men in their platoon organized into three squads, each with a machine gun. Isabel now appreciated machine guns as an important contributor to her continued tenure on Earth. To Stockman's platoon had been added a weapons section with a fourth machine gun and its two-man crew, and two two-person *Javelin teams*, whatever they were. Thirty-eight troops, plus their nine-person Pentagon detail: Rick, Army Sgt. Vasquez, his five men, all with rifles and two with underslung grenade launchers, and the two scientists, also carrying rifles, but as an afterthought. That made for a total of forty-seven armed souls crammed into four trucks.

Rick bent over Stockman's paper map lit by Vasquez's flashlight. Their objective was to clear some woods, which Stockman illustrated with a sweep of his hand before stabbing at the blocking positions they would establish along an east-west stream two miles from their "line of departure." There was thermal imagery of activity in those woods—maybe animal, maybe human—but no "friendlies," in military-speak.

They went over the planned line of advance, the wooded but flattish terrain, landmarks and milestones along their route, the identity of the platoons to their left and right, radio frequencies to which both Rick and Vasquez tuned, and available fire support and medevac and the call signs for each. Isabel's eyes sank closed. She intended to continue listening. But when she rested her head against the wooden railing behind her, the noise of the engine and of the road's surface under the tires harmonized inside her helmet. The warm press of Brandon and an unknown child-soldier at Isabel's sides kept her upright.

When the truck's brakes groaned, she woke with an unnoticed gasp. They all climbed down at the edge of a dark and frankly terrifying forest wearing their combat loads, not their heavy backpacks. The platoon spread out in an extended line and lay prone in the roadside weeds behind raised rifles. Spectral figures descended from other trucks in the distance to either side. The few commands she heard were hushed, not shouted. Six hundred soldiers, all moving in deathly silence. Lethal silence, more like it.

Rick returned from a short meeting to brief Vasquez. Isabel listened in. Two squads, twenty soldiers, commanded by the platoon sergeant, would cover a front a hundred meters wide. Stockman led the reserves—the third squad and the weapons section—which would follow fifteen meters behind the main line. Vasquez, his five men, and the "two docs," were to remain immediately behind Stockman.

"Where are you gonna be?" Isabel whispered to Rick in the gloom.

"With Stockman. Stick with Vasquez, and stay low…and *quiet*." He must have read something on her face even in the dim starlight. Something like, *What the hell am I* doing *here?* "Don't worry. You'll be all right. There are no reports they've organized and armed themselves yet."

Yet?

Her helmet rattled when she nodded. Rick joined Stockman. Brandon looked just as lost as she felt. Stockman gave some secret hand signal, which was relayed off into the darkness. The prone soldiers all rose in unison and stepped off into the woods. The cumulative effects of the advancing platoon amounted to a hushed rustle: the chafing of fabric, the crush of weeds underfoot, the snapping of bushes brushed past.

When Rick and Stockman disappeared into the inky night, Vasquez followed. It was their turn. Isabel gripped her rifle in both hands and tried to focus on her breathing.

It grew darker when they left the highway. Isabel couldn't see Rick's line in front of her. She could barely see Brandon and Vasquez to either side. Invisible low branches scraped unexpectedly across her helmet, so she held her rifle vertically before her as if in preparation for a bayonet fight. Many of the soldiers wore monocular or binocular night vision devices on their helmets. Isabel stumbled blindly, at constant risk of turning an ankle.

Thonk! She was momentarily rattled after head butting her rifle and the branch with which it had collided. Leaves fell under her collar and she frantically brushed them away. *"Shhh!"* hissed someone rudely. Isabel caught up with her line. The growing perspiration under her body armor felt like crawling ants or spiders from the fallen leaves.

The monotony of their march and the sensory deprivation of the darkness soon freed her mind to wander. They had left the bridge immediately after the slaughter two days earlier, picked at MREs on a short helicopter flight to a high school auditorium, and been blinded by the stage lights like ill prepared understudies. Absolutely everything about that first briefing had felt off. "How many of you remember Dr. Miller from the CNN special? Show of hands." The beaming small-town mayor demonstrated the requested response by raising his own hand, and over half the audience of police, firemen, EMTs, and local officials did the same. He was starstruck by Isabel's fifteen minutes of fame. But less than an hour earlier, she had killed a person. And another, and a third, and who knows how many after firing all thirty bullets in her magazine. She stood on that stage, dazed, as if ready to be judged. What she got were innocuous medical questions.

And then there had risen the spot-lit profile of a diminutive female paramedic, who had awkwardly announced, to no one in particular, that, "If the order ever comes down that we have to…to eliminate, I guess, the Infecteds, well, my religious principles won't allow that." No one said a word, and she sat. How much stranger could this get?

They then flew from stop to stop in upstate New York and alternated briefings of troops, cops, and relief workers with debriefings of first responders, special forces, and talkative refugees. The former evolved slightly with each survivor's tale they heard in the latter. "One woman," Isabel had informed Red Cross volunteers, "said she talked her way past a group of Infecteds who came to the door of her motel room. She put on her mask and shoved her way through with a roller bag, saying, 'I'm-leaving-I'm-leaving-I'm-leaving,' and they let her go. Maybe they just wanted her room, or her gone. Who knows? Not something I'd recommend, but the point is that while every Infected is dangerous, they're not all totally *crazy*."

That first night after the bridge, she had told Rick she really needed to talk about what had happened. "Yeah, you do," Rick had agreed. "But not now. After." Rick had tucked her in to her sleeping bag in the city park and left to attend a meeting with the soldiers they bedded down with that night. She had lain there, thinking, *But what if there* is *no after?* He came and checked on her, then went to patrol the perimeter. Later, she saw him monitoring reports from nearby units over a Humvee's radio. Maybe he had insomnia. Or a case of nerves. Or maybe it was his training. Regardless, when Rick wasn't beside her, Isabel couldn't sleep.

The breeze through her hair had tickled her face. Vasquez's men snored. And every so often, distant firecrackers crackled, which she knew weren't firecrackers at all. Or the next night when Rick's nocturnal wanderings were revealed to be a habit of his, she couldn't sleep because the tiled back hallway of the medical clinic felt rocklike against her aching muscles. Then came the moans of a patient turning, and the wails of her parents when given the bad news. It was too cold outside in the park, and too hot inside at the clinic. Her underwear was itchy. She could smell her own body, and cringed at the thought that Rick might too. She was overdue for her period, which would add to her list of discomforts. At least she couldn't be pregnant since she hadn't had sex in about ten years and three months… and that had been with Brandon. How ridiculous was that these days to go so long? Was she picky, or just a failure?

Sometimes—to be honest, most times—when she couldn't fall asleep it was because she hadn't had sex in ten years and three months. She tossed and turned and fluffed the jacket she used as a pillow, and tried several times to process what was happening, but each ended with her having to stifle the gasping, hiccupping sobs and sniffles that erupted by surprise to avoid being overheard by the others. She needed time alone, or with Rick, and soon—before everything came to an end.

"Hubbardton, Vermont," she had read on her iPad instead of sleeping. Capt. Ramirez, Rick's classmate, had installed a DoD app on her tablet, and she read abstracts of field reports filed first in Asia, and now in New England. "48 civilians/officials trapped 40-80 feet AGL in steel lattice of radio tower, which is only structure in area tall enough to ensure death from leaps. Radio contact with Fish and Wildlife warden in tower. Est. 200-300 Probables at base. Guy wires prevent close approach, but observed 9 fatal falls from tower in 50 min. due to illness, fighting, or possible suicide. Mass jump planned if no relief by tomorrow p.m. Nearing bingo fuel but have 500 rds. 50 cal. and 7 x 2.75 inch rockets. Request permission to expend ordnance on Probables at base. [PERMISSION DENIED]."

Tomorrow p.m. had come and gone with no further updates.

Eventually, Rick had returned and lain down next to her. Only then did Isabel sleep.

Dangerously distracted, Isabel snapped back to the present when Sgt. Vasquez raised his right fist. Everyone halted except Isabel, who took one extra *crunch*. "Sorry!" she whispered. Vasquez flattened his palm downward. Everyone lay on their bellies like in a game of Simon Says. Isabel swatted a bug off her nose, pressed down on the weeds that tickled her neck, and rolled from one side to the other to look around until Vasquez shushed her. She drew more disapproval when she slowly, but apparently still too noisily, raised her rifle to her shoulder.

Three measured shots rang out from the distance to their left. Time seemed to slow in the few moments of silence that followed. She heard nothing. Saw nothing. But she viscerally felt the silent ticks of the clock.

Machine guns burst. Rifles fired. Grenades exploded. The cacophony erupted first from their left, and then—shockingly, stupendously loudly, and jarringly—from straight ahead of where she lay. Her heart rate, breathing, darting eyes, and quaking muscles all synchronized to the muzzle flashes that lit tree trunks in nearly continuous strobes, stripping away the previous anonymity of the night. She grew lightheaded and dizzy as vertigo set in despite her whole body pressing firmly to the solid ground beneath her.

Something crashed through the bushes beside her. A huge, antlered buck sprinted and leapt past. She heard a jarring snort as his front hooves landed heavily not four feet from where she lay. Other deer followed. Multiple people shouted, *"Cease fire!"* from the woods ahead.

It rapidly fell quiet again. Vasquez raised everyone to their feet and they proceeded forward. *It was just deer!* Isabel passed a soldier, who raised a knife overhead and sank to his knee while plunging it with a wet, hollow sound into a jerking form on the ground. The mercy killer, wearing night vision goggles, rose from the kicking hooves of the dying animal like a mutant in a post-apocalyptic nightmare. Isabel couldn't help but think that he'd shown more mercy to the deer than he would if it had been her infected sister Emma lying there wounded.

"Halt!" they all heard Stockman shout from ahead, and their entire line of troops froze. "Who goes there?" They couldn't hear a reply. "Thorough!" Nothing. *"Thorough!"* Again, no reply. Maybe it was more deer.

Isabel jumped at the *pop-pop-pop!* Three gunshots in rapid succession.

One breath. Her heart pounded. Two breaths. She exhaled raggedly. Three...

The woods exploded with gunfire. She followed Vasquez and dropped to the ground, cringing and plugging her ears against the resumption of the horrible noise. This was many times worse than the earlier shooting, and it showed no signs of letting up quickly.

Rick slid to the ground beside her, shouting something. *"What?"* she replied. His face, half lit in the flashes, looked grim. He almost wrenched her shoulder out of joint as he pulled her to her feet and shoved her back toward the road. She couldn't see the branches, or the forest floor, and relied more than she should have on Rick's grip to maintain her footing, course, and speed. Rick kept looking back over his shoulder, holding his heavy rifle one-handed by its pistol grip.

Other soldiers overtook them. "Faster!" Rick ordered.

"What's happening?" she shouted, but doubted that he heard her. *Did we somehow lose a battle?* She ran blindly. Her lungs and her thighs began to burn. A misstep almost felled her, but Rick kept her upright.

Stockman caught up with them breathing heavily. He stopped, turned, crouched, and fired into the darkness behind him, then raced past. Rick let go of her arm, knelt, and fired on full-auto, traversing left to right. Isabel waited for him. He turned, saw her, and shouted, *"Goddammit, run!"* before loosing another burst.

Something traveling at high speed cut through the branch beside Isabel. She stooped lower. Another zipping sound sliced through the air overhead.

Someone was shooting at *them*. From the *darkness*. The *woods!* She turned and saw a lone muzzle flash toward which Rick directed a burst of fire before reloading. "Isabel! I said get the hell outta here!"

"You come too! *With* me! Let's go!" She held her hand back to him.

He didn't take it, but they resumed their run together. Finally, she could see the road on which the trucks waited. As they passed a prone soldier, rifle pointing into the woods from which they'd come, the man rolled onto his side and shouted, "Forty-six and forty-*seven!*"

Stockman stood fully upright to yell, "Last man's in! Fire at will! Fire at will!" The forest erupted in shooting. Stockman headed down what Isabel saw was an organized line of troops parallel to the highway, encouraging each of his men on passing. Muzzles blazed from the troops' nearly straight line, which extended into the distance to both sides.

Rick practically tackled Isabel, who grunted when landing wrong. She grabbed Rick's body armor and shouted, "Who is shooting at us?"

"I don't know!" came his reply. "Them!" He then began firing into the darkness, his right eye aiming through his night vision monocular. Isabel raised her weapon, but couldn't see anything to shoot at. There was only an occasional flash coming from the woods and *zip* cutting through the brush within earshot.

Brandon crawled over to her. "I lost you!" he yelled over the cacophony. He, too, was just a spectator and didn't even bother raising his rifle.

After what seemed like the better part of an hour, but was probably only a minute or two, Stockman shouted the cease fire order, which Rick and sergeants up and down the line repeated until the guns all fell silent. "Fire in the hole!" came the only warning they received. Rick pressed his face into the dirt and said, "Get the fuck down!" in the direction of Isabel and Brandon. Both copied the Marine. *What fire in* what *hole?* she wondered.

What came next sounded like a biblical prophecy come true—*thy walls shall shake at the noise of the horsemen, and of the wheels, and of the chariots...* Some shrieking demon exited its hellmouth to their left and disappeared at incredibly high speed to their right, trailing a roaring crescendo of jet exhaust that was more felt in the chest than heard. Isabel raised her head to see what that noise had been. Rick jammed her helmet back down to the ground, tweaking a muscle in her neck. "*Ow!* Jeeze."

The world burst to pieces. The air itself shattered. It wasn't the rippling series of explosions, or the brilliant flashes of a dozen stupendous blasts, or the pounding by invisible walls of heat and overpressure, or the thuds emanating from the earth beneath her. It was all of those things, all at once. A staccato series of annihilating high explosive *booms* that shook Isabel's nerves as much as her innards.

"My *God!*" Isabel wailed, heard by no one. Dirt fell all around. Treetops crashed in great clumps. A finer volcanic rain of bristles, twigs, and ash followed, as did the smoke, and the stench, and the thought—*Why am I here?* The woods ahead of them settled again into a calm and dark broken only by the crackle and flickering of a hundred small blazes.

But the *pop* of rifles and *burp* of machine guns slowly filled the lull. Someone even closer to the explosions than they were had survived. Somehow many still managed to approach. "What was *that?*" Isabel asked Rick in horror.

"F/A-18. A dozen 500-pound bombs. Detail up! Sgt. Vasquez, back to the primary LZ. There are more fast-movers inbound!"

"*More?*" Isabel could hear an approaching helicopter. *Our* helicopter, she prayed. She felt guilty leaving Stockman and his men in the woods, but glad for an escape from the hell into which they had so unexpectedly and shockingly descended. Rick took her rifle and hoisted her aboard their Black Hawk. She, Rick, Brandon, Vasquez, and his five men all clung to the deck as the helicopter lurched skyward. In the calm after the door slid closed, Isabel stared at her palsied, quivering hand.

Rick and the other soldiers began cleaning their weapons, munching on energy bars, and putting adhesive bandages on small cuts as if what had just happened was somehow within the realm of the normal. "What...?" Isabel began. Rick looked up from his rifle, which lay in pieces large and small on his poncho. "What was *that?*"

"That? Technically, I guess you'd call it a meeting engagement." She looked at him as if he were speaking some strange tongue founded on extreme understatement. He sat back on his heels, still trying to bridge the language barrier. "And we *won* it."

"*Won* it? It didn't...It didn't *feel* like we won *anything*. It felt like...like everything went *wrong*, and...and we were almost..."

Rick seemed baffled. "That was about as good as firefights go. No friendly casualties. Maneuvers were organized. The line held. The fire mission hit the enemy, not us. Their objective was to block passage through those woods, and by the time they finish their work in there tonight I'm pretty sure it's gonna be accomplished."

Work? People do this for a *living? Rick* does this for a living? *Of course they do.* Isabel sighed. "Well, if that's winning," she muttered in a quaking voice, "I'd hate to see what *losing* is like."

"Yeah." Rick reassembled his M4 with mechanical *snaps* and *clacks*. "You would."

Chapter 6

Noah had to wake Jake, and then Chloe. "It's too *early!*" Chloe whined before pulling the pillow over her head to block the light from the hallway.

"It's the crack of nine am. Your chickens are hungry."

"*My* chickens? They're the *family's* chickens."

"Get your ass outta bed!"

"All right, all right. Jeez."

Back upstairs in the kitchen, Natalie had muted the TV news. Noah picked up the remote control. "That makes Ottawa, Canada, and Montpelier, New Hampshire, the latest North American cities to join Montreal and Burlington in reporting widespread and uncontrolled outbreaks of *Pandoravirus.*" Noah filled the water bottle he would wear on his belt like a cyclist. "In France, the disease has been reported as far north as Valenciennes, sparking violent clashes at the Belgian border with…"

The TV fell silent. Natalie held the remote pointed at the flat-screen on the wall, but looked at Noah. He kissed her and said, "We spend way too much time watching TV, and not neàrly enough tending to this place."

Noah headed to the top of the stairs. "Jacob!" he shouted down toward the kids' bedrooms. "Chloe! Get up here *now!* Let's go!" He heard something muffled from someone downstairs, then trudging, heavy footfalls on the steps. The basement, where the kids slept, was what Noah had planned to be the safest place in the house. His kids arrived scowling and bleary-eyed, technically complying with all the rules—rising on command, gathering at the breakfast table, awake and not asleep—but with deniable looks of protest at the impositions upon their lives.

"Why don't you and Mom plant some seeds today?" Noah suggested to Chloe.

His daughter looked back and forth between her parents, then asked, "What? Is this, like, a *girl* thing? Are we supposed to darn socks and make festive decorations for the holidays, too?"

"Come on," Natalie intervened. "Let's see if we can make something grow."

Noah told Jacob he was going to chop firewood. "Me *man!*" Chloe said in a caveman voice and beat her chest. Jake spit his multivitamins onto the table in laughter. Natalie nixed the idea as too dangerous and put the waffles and syrup on the table.

"The United Kingdom eased travel restrictions within the nation, but the Channel tunnel remains closed indefinitely." Jake had unmuted the TV on reflex.

Natalie grabbed the remote from him and turned the TV off. Jake protested to Noah. "This is, like, historic and stuff. Or historical? Whichever. Shouldn't we...?"

Natalie shot Noah a look before turning back to the kitchen counter. Noah shrugged in reply to Jake. Chloe unsurprisingly found something at which to roll her eyes.

Noah went to the living room and returned with a book entitled *Agriculture for Dummies.* "You should try tomatoes first," he suggested.

Chloe snorted. "We're not gonna be able to grow actual *food*, ya know."

"*Sure* you can!" replied Noah. "Necessity is the mother of invention. We *need* to grow food, so that's what you're gonna *do.*"

But before he finished his not overly long exhortation, Chloe was already reading texts on her phone. "Hey! Justin said everything is normal back in McLean, except that almost everybody is gone." She grinned as she typed rapidly with both thumbs.

"Justin's family is still planning on staying put?" Natalie asked.

"They don't think it's gonna be that bad, I guess, but, I mean, the *news*. Do you think maybe they're gonna be able to *stop* it? The P.? Before it gets down here?"

Noah's entire family looked at him. He had been forewarned of the pandemic by his scientist sisters so that he could make preparations that would help them survive. That had, for a month, made him an expert on the approaching menace by comparison to a world in which news of it was thoroughly suppressed. But how the hell did he know if they could stop the spread of the disease?

"We *could* watch TV and keep track of how it's going," Jake floated.

"Later," Noah said. "We'll all watch tonight. After our *chores*. Now let's get going. Chloe feeds the chickens and then joins Mom in the grow labs to begin our spring planting."

"It's not spring," Chloe couldn't fail to note glumly.

"Jake, you and I will go check the fence line, then I'll show you how to oil the gearbox on the windmill."

"Don't let him near any turning gears," Natalie warned. Another chore that would fall only to Noah.

A couple of hours later, Noah allowed Jake to take a break from clearing brush that spoiled sightlines and carrying the firewood that Noah had chopped, and went to the only grow lab of the four repurposed shipping containers whose door was ajar. Natalie and Chloe stood inside, staring at a trough filled with the finest potting soil in front of a packet of seeds and *Agriculture for Dummies*, which lay open on the brightly lit work table.

Natalie said, "This book says we should have a starting mix. Do we have one?"

"A what?"

"A...*starting*...mix," she repeated slowly, as if he were an imbecile. Then, she read, "Peat moss, ver-mi-cu-lite, and per-lite. Do we have any of that?"

"No! Of course not."

"*Da-a-ad!*" Chloe chastised.

He was exasperated. After all he'd done, all he'd thought *to* do, to have his wife and daughter come to a grinding halt over the first little hiccup. "Look, I'm sure it's optional. I mean, farmers a thousand years ago didn't have all that stuff, and they managed."

"They were starving, toothless, and died at thirty," Natalie noted, "but I guess we could just stick the seeds in the dirt and see what happens. But we're *supposed* to put them in little cups or containers first. Do we have any of *those?*"

Noah said they had paper cups in the pantry. Natalie sent their teenage daughter, perturbed at the unending demands, to go get them.

"After lunch," Noah said, "I'm gonna take Jake down to the highway to post some no-trespassing signs. We'll be back before dinner. I'm carrying my radio in case there's any trouble."

"That's it?" Natalie said. She picked up the farming book as if she were presenting it as evidence of the impossible complexity of her task. "I'm in charge of growing the food? And if our *crops* fail and we starve, it's on *me?*"

"How hard can it be, really?" Natalie stared back at him. "I gotta go."

Noah and Jacob drove down the long ridgeline road. It was barely passable as it was. A few more rains and maybe he wouldn't have to blow it. At the bottom, they exited their SUV and Noah relocked the gate behind them, which was discouraging enough to keep away casual visitors. But if people were sufficiently hungry...

The two-lane state highway was the downhill border of their property. Noah slipped a hammer into its loop on his tool belt and snapped off the price tag that still dangled from it. His pockets were heavy with non-rusting aluminum roofing nails. He shouldered his half-empty backpack, which contained only the essentials: water, radio, and six extra magazines filled with twenty-seven rounds of 5.56mm ammunition. After doing a radio check to make sure Natalie could hear him—"*Yes*, Noah?" she replied, annoyed—he told Jake, "I'd take about three of those," pointing to the spray cans of aluminum paint. Jacob shook one with a loud rattle, and put the other two in his own, similarly filled backpack. Both slung ARs over their shoulders.

"The paint marks need to be vertical. Two inches wide and eight inches long. Three to six feet off the ground." They headed for the barbed wire fence. "Paint the trees so they're visible from the highway."

"Paint *all* the trees?"

The woods were thick. The clinging, scratching undergrowth would dissuade people more than the double-strand barbed wire. "One mark about every ten feet or so."

"What does posting those signs and painting trees even do?"

"Legally, it raises the penalties for trespassing and poaching." He opened one of the Amazon boxes he carried and pulled out a sign. "POSTED," it read, and, in smaller letters underneath, "Trespassers Will Be Shot."

"Will we really do that? Shoot trespassers?"

"We may have to, son. But the main point is to scare people away."

Noah draped a carpet remnant over the barbed wire, grabbed a rickety fencepost, climbed onto the lower strand, and slung his leg across the carpet without snagging his jeans. Jacob followed suit, also without injury. Noah had read about the carpet trick on a survivalist blog when researching which wire cutters to buy.

"Are we gonna do this all the way around the whole property?"

"Yep."

"Seriously, Dad?" The walking was difficult through the brush and along the rocky, uneven ground. Not very inviting. Noah dropped his load and nailed a sign onto a tree beside their property's gate. Jacob stood frozen in front of his first tree six feet from the sign Noah had posted. "For *real?*"

Noah headed down the highway. "Yep. Get going." Noah posted the second sign onto a tree with a single hammer blow about a hundred feet from the first. Thus, it continued, with Jacob shaking his rattling can, painting tree after tree with a *whoosh*, and quickly falling behind and ultimately out of sight.

About a half an hour later, Noah nailed the last sign in the box onto a tree at a point where their property turned sharply uphill—unclimbable without ropes. He carefully traversed the barbed-wire fence without the aid of the carpet and headed back toward the SUV along the easier, paved roadway.

"Dad!" Noah heard Jacob yell from over a rise in the highway ahead.

Noah dropped the empty sign box, unslung his rifle, and ran. His heart raced. Outlaws holding Jake at gunpoint! Cannibals, maybe, licking their salivating chops. A trudging horde of insensate Infecteds raising dust all the way to the horizon. By the time he crested the rise, he was sweating as much from adrenaline—from mentally preparing to kill—as from exertion. A pickup truck with dark police lights and a star emblazoned on the door was parked next to Jake, whose rifle was propped against a nearby tree on the far side of the barbed wire. A khaki-clad man in a white cowboy hat casually spoke to his son from a distance with one boot on the fence that separated them. He turned to look at Noah clutching his rifle at the ready, and his hand drifted toward his holstered sidearm.

Noah slung his rifle over his shoulder before heading down. The man's hand left its perch atop the pistol butt, but his thumb remained hooked onto his leather belt, studded with bullets, only a short distance from his weapon. "What can I do for you?" Noah called out as he neared.

"You the Millers? Sheriff Walcott. Pleased to meet you. Didn't think we'd had any of your people up here in decades, but I'd heard somebody was workin' on the place."

"We moved down here from D.C. McLean, actually." Noah thought they might seem less like carpetbaggers if they had at least come from the same state.

"Good idea. I hear the army is keepin' D.C. in order, but there's a whole shit-pot full of lootin' out in the 'burbs. We're gettin' a lot of folks from up that way with some scary tales. Some of 'em don't have too much, and people are worried they'll run outta food and supplies and there'll be trouble. The churches are takin' turns feedin' 'em…fer now."

"Well, not to worry about us. We're pretty self-sufficient up there."

"Good, good. And it looks like you can defend your own, too. Good." He removed his cowboy hat and rubbed his forehead, which was as red as his short hair from where his hat band pressed. "Say, Mr. Miller, we're takin' a head count of people we can call on if we run into any trouble down in the Valley. Can we pencil in you and your boy over there, if push comes to shove?"

Goddammit, Noah thought. That wasn't part of his survival plans. Jake crept closer to listen.

"Me and my deputies should keep a lid on things. But you never know. The BCI—the state Bureau of Criminal Investigations—said, basically, shoot any Infecteds on sight. Then the Deputy Superintendent of the State Police, which is *over* the BCI, said use discretion, but don't use deadly force unless lives are at risk. Well, lives *are* at risk if you get *infected.* And that was the *Deputy* Superintendent who sent out that e-mail. Why not the Superintendent *hisself?* So...shit. I dunno. I guess, since the instructions are contradictory, we gotta decide for ourselves."

"Have you seen any around here? Anyone infected?"

"No, no. Not yet, anyways. But it's only a matter of time, I figure. And I don't know if I'm supposed to shoot 'em or give 'em milk and cookies. So we're holdin' a town meetin' down at the fire hall to talk about next steps, and I need to know who I can count on as part of an auxiliary force in case we approve it." He looked at the posted signs along the tree line behind Jacob, who leaned against a teetering fencepost barely held upright by the barbed wire. "You're invited. Only landowners and permanent residents. Day after tomorrow, eight o'clock in the p.m. We might even have some definitive word outta Richmond by then."

"I expect I'll be there," Noah lied. He hadn't planned to have any engagement at all with the local community.

"And your boy?"

"Jacob is only thirteen."

"He's a tall 'un," said the Sheriff. "And he knows his way around an AR?"

"You can count on *me.* But I want my son to stay here at the house."

The Sheriff unbuttoned the breast pocket on which he wore a big star. "I'll put you down as one. Noah," he said and presumably wrote on the pad he extracted, "Miller." He tapped the brim of his hat in salute before departing.

After he was gone, Jacob asked, "Are we in trouble? Because of the signs?"

"What? No! He's just looking for volunteers in case, you know, things get bad."

"And you unvolunteered me?"

"Someone has to take care of the house. Of your mom and Chloe."

Jake nodded. That made sense to him. "But *you* joined up? Don't you think you should run that by Mom?"

"I can make decisions on my own," Noah lied again, but Jacob looked skeptical.

"You're gonna have to drop all your g's to fit in," Jake said. "Puttin', gettin', fixin', spittin'…" He added a rural twang to his condescending tone.

"You shouldn't make fun of these people, Jake. We live here now."

Noah helped Jacob mark the trees along the highway. In the time it took to finish, several cars passed, filled with lost-looking families and piled high with belongings. Each time, Noah stopped what he was doing, turned, and faced them with his rifle in hand. Jake mimicked his father. Each time, after initially slowing, the city folk accelerated away from the possibly homicidal, possibly inbred mountain folk. Noah winked at Jacob.

As they worked their way past the alternate gate onto their property, carefully disguised per Noah's specifications, he showed Jacob where it was. The double strands of barbed wire were attached to a vertical metal bar that was padlocked to a fencepost. From the highway, you would never notice it or the overgrown old road that wound its way a mile up the hill to their house. Noah had walked it once. It was rocky, but passable with the higher clearance of a jeep or SUV.

On the way back up to the house on the ridge road, Noah and Jacob stopped to inspect the detonator and the wires leading two hundred yards away to explosives, wrapped tightly in waterproof plastic, that were buried under the road. "Is this far enough away?" Jacob asked. Noah assured him, with false confidence, that it was. "Can I come when you set it off?"

Noah put a hand on his shoulder. "I want you to know how to blow this all by yourself, just in case." Jacob fell quiet. Noah pulled the detonator out of its weatherproof box hidden under some drying branches beside the road and explained how to connect the wires running to the explosives and the battery to its leads.

Back at the house, Noah said nothing about the demolition instructions he'd given their thirteen-year-old son. Instead, he told Farmer Natalie about meeting the Cowboy Sheriff, but of course he wouldn't be attending the town hall meeting.

To his surprise, Natalie said, without catching his eye, "You should go."

"Did I mention the part about the Sheriff forming a local militia?"

"Yes. I think that's a great idea."

"But I thought we wanted to get *away* from everyone!"

"*You* wanted to get away from everyone. *I* want to keep the kids safe. Being part of a community sounds a whole lot safer than being up here all on our own like the Swiss Family Robinson."

Noah didn't agree. And even more offensively, it was a spur-of-the-moment major change of plans over which he'd obsessed, nearly sleeplessly, for an entire month. Only isolation, he had concluded, would keep them safe from the virus and the violence that accompanied it.

After Noah agreed to go to the town meeting, he snapped that he was heading out to "do some patrollin'." Natalie smirked as she poked seeds into moist soil filling paper cups. Her mood seemed improved by doing something productive. *Maybe* productive.

Noah muttered to himself in mockery of his wife—"I think that's a *great* idea"—before hesitating at the small side gate. He was sure the fence wasn't electrified, but just in case he tapped the metal with his fingertips, wondering throughout whether that would help at all in preventing his electrocution. It was fine.

Once outside, he chambered a round and set off uphill for the cabin. The whole way, he listened to the faint rustle of the breeze punctuated by the scrapes of his boots' soles. He smelled nothing but the fresh air of the outdoors. He saw nothing move but a few birds in the trees. Crossing the last of the three ridges before the cabin, Noah got down on his belly and crawled.

He peered over a rock outcropping. The cabin looked still and undisturbed. He pulled out his binoculars. Nothing stirred. No smoke rose from the chimney. No lantern light shone from within. No laundry on lines or plastic bags of trash piling up. The chair blocking the front door was right where he'd left it. He didn't know why he had expected anything different. It would take a long time for anyone to find the secluded cabin unless they knew where to look for it.

He headed back downhill, which was a much easier walk. If regular armies with tanks and bombers couldn't stop the spread of *Pandoravirus*, what could some ragtag county militia do? But Natalie was right, of course, about the importance of good relations with their neighbors. And the Bishops at the store on the highway seemed like good...

Chloe called out, *"Dad!"* from a distance, shattering his reverie. "Come quick!"

Noah's' heart thumped like a bass drum. He unshouldered his rifle and sprinted toward the shipping-container-turned-garden. It must be that sheriff, back with a posse of twisted redneck deviants. Instead, he found Jacob, Chloe, and Natalie kneeling, watching a gray rabbit with a white tail nibble on grass. "Shh. Isn't he *cute?*" Chloe said.

Natalie eyed the rifle in her sweating and winded husband's hands. "Jeez, Noah. Don't shoot the li'l fella." Noah put his rifle down. His blood pressure threatened to rupture blood vessels like popcorn. He was out of breath, not from the run but from forgetting to breathe. He flicked a cold bead of sweat off his brow. There was no one to kill. Yet.

Chapter 7

The college boy got sick in the middle of the night a few hours after he and Emma had sex. "It's *you!*" he shouted, shivering inside his sleeping bag as Emma packed her gear in the light of the half moon. She needed to put distance between herself and the newly infected Freshman. "Where are you *going?*"

"Away from here."

"You're *leaving* me?" he shouted. Luckily, they were all alone in the woods.

"You'll probably die. But if you don't—if you turn—you'll be pretty noticeable from your behavior and your popped pupils, so you'll get caught and they'll start contact tracing in an attempt to find me." *It would be safer to kill him now,* came the silent voice with ever helpful practical advice.

"But wait! If I turn—if I *live*—I...I'll join you. We can, you know, partner up."

The boy was bigger and stronger than Emma, and could hurt her or worse in a fight. He'd also been a competent if too hurried a lover. She hoisted onto her shoulder the backpack she'd stolen the day before from the lanky guy, which contained all her belongings. But she paused to listen to Chaz, who was proposing some form of contract.

"Why do I need you?" she asked, cocking her head. *He could wear sunglasses,* suggested the voice, ever nimble in its planning.

"For...I dunno! We could have sex again, whenever you want."

"There are lots of men who'll have sex." She turned to leave.

"Wait! I could…I'll *fight* for you. I'll protect you." Emma looked back at him. There was that old problem again. If she stayed by his side, nursed him, helped keep him hydrated, maybe he would live. But what would ensure that he honored pledges like *I'll fight for you?* What enforcement mechanism would bind him to his side of that bargain?

She left him there. Chaz's shouts at her—part repeated plea, part angry curses and threats—receded into the dark forest behind her. "*You bi-i-itch!*"

The two-lane state highway was virtually empty at that early hour. The few times she saw headlights approach, she hid. She would appear out of place if seen walking alone down the dark road, and also vulnerable without a visible weapon. After a couple of hours, her fatigue could no longer be ignored. Emma climbed an embankment and found a flat piece of ground perched above the road and hidden by rocks, trees, and brush. She covered herself in her rough wool blanket and lay her head on her backpack. With no thoughts troubling her easy mind, she fell asleep in minutes.

She woke on hearing a siren. The sun was high. The red ambulance raced toward where she had left Chaz. It could be unrelated, or it could be that he crawled out of the woods to the edge of the road and was spotted there.

She emptied her bladder and opened a can of peas, which she ate cold, with a spoon, while drinking a lukewarm Red Bull. In the time that that took, the sirens of two county sheriffs and one highway patrol car raced past. It was definitely Chaz. They would be looking for her now. She should have resisted the urge to have sex with the boy. Or killed him.

Where can I get a map?

There! What was that? Her mind was racing from the caffeine. Where did that question about a map come from? And to whom was it posed? Emma was curious about the mysterious inner voice that arose periodically with questions, but also sometimes proposed solutions to problems. Was that what her sister Isabel referred to as a *self?* Maybe it was more than the myth or the delusion she had earlier concluded it to be. Maybe it was not just a metaphor or handy self-referencing methodology; it was something real. Or some*one*, from somewhere deep inside.

She sat still and waited. Listening. There was only silence. She ignored the cars and trucks that by that hour trafficked the highway until her full attention was drawn to a pickup truck approaching slowly from the direction she had come. Armed men on each side of the truck's bed searched the roadway, presumably looking for her.

You should have killed Chaz popped into her head out of nowhere. She hadn't been thinking about Chaz, or about anything else for that matter, but maybe the voice had been. The thought—not exactly a voice, or even words as specific as those she had used to express it—was correct. She should have killed the boy.

Emma resolved to listen for such voices in the future and give each observation due consideration. They seemed to have her best interests in mind. She packed and climbed farther up the hill through which the two-lane road had been cut. At the top of the rise, she saw a highway junction less than a mile to the south and plotted a course through the rough, wooded terrain toward it. She had no idea where the intersecting road led, but at least it was not the same highway that they were searching.

I need a map. There it was again! It was insistent, and it was right.

Chapter 8

Isabel's helicopter descended into Boston's urban skyline along the Charles River bearing Rick, Brandon, Vasquez, and his five soldiers, plus the three-person crew. The gunner opened his door and unlimbered his weapon. Cambridge and MIT slid by to their left. On their right was their destination: Massachusetts General Hospital.

After their 'victory' in the New York woods, a strange fatigue had settled over Isabel. She had slept on helicopter and truck rides with her head on Rick's shoulder, lap, or backpack, periodically jolted awake by bullets whizzing by in her dreams. Each short trip was interrupted by another briefing or debriefing. Each farther south than the one before it.

At the briefings, a numb Isabel had to rouse herself from emotional and physical exhaustion and try not to drone on as she repeated her now wearisome song and dance. "Telltale signs of pre-assault agitation include stiffness, clenched fists and jaws, visible muscle tensing or quivering, shallow or rapid breathing. Then, if unarmed, a lunge, usually for the eyes or throat." The best way for her to keep from yawning was to force herself to make eye contact, for the second or two she could stand it, with the dismayed or cringing audience in the front row. *Yes, I'm talking about your eyes and your throat.*

Some briefings were detailed. Civilian first responders in West Chazy, New York asked about personal protective equipment, isolation shelters, the recommended duration of quarantines, and basic care for people who contract SED. Other briefings were thinly disguised pep rallies. A platoon of National Guardsmen in a parking lot amid a much larger gathering of volunteer militiamen in Au Sable. The undisciplined shouts from the gallery at every mention of the use of force clearly amped up the young Guardsmen. Their gazes alternated between Brandon's monotone description of crowd violence, and chants of "U-S-A! U-S-A!" that Isabel could still hear as the helicopter's engines spun up.

Interspersed with the briefings was their continuing research. There was the selfless school bus driver in Plattsburgh who had picked up everyone he passed until full, then driven south through heavy traffic. When night fell, most passengers slept despite a few stifled but alarming coughs. After a potty break took longer than expected, the driver thought he might have heard a moan quickly hushed in urgent whispers. When the child who had moaned retched, there was an instant riot. People literally pounded on the driver with their fists until he pulled over and the bus emptied in seconds just outside Wilmington, New York, except for a mother and her sick child, alone and wide-eyed in fear in the back. The driver, somehow, had not been infected, but eleven hours later all contact with Wilmington had been lost. That was how quickly it happened.

It had been south of Lake Champlain, around midday, that the true scale of the strategic disaster came into focus. After a calm and uneventful briefing of local police in aptly named Lake Placid, they had aborted three successive landings in Lake George, Queensbury, and Glens Falls. When they touched down on the infield of the race track in Saratoga Springs, it wasn't for a briefing. They were instructed to remain aboard their helicopter as they refueled from giant rubber bladders. Hot food on foam plates from the race track's kitchen—bland baked chicken that you couldn't cut with the accompanying plastic knife but which Rick's black combat knife sliced into chewable pieces, waterlogged green beans, and what had to be instant mashed potatoes—was the best meal Isabel had eaten in her entire life. In between the roar of arriving or departing helicopters came the piercing, snapping sounds of fighting in the distance.

They had next landed in Schenectady, but the briefing was called off just after assembling an army reserve transportation company—truck drivers—who were ordered back to their vehicles on the double. All Isabel could see as they ascended into the sky were a dozen columns of gray and black smoke. There was clearly no stopping the *P*. They were just its victims' grief counselors, Isabel thought, helping soldiers deal with lives they were about to lose, or take, just like the hundreds of millions or billions worldwide, by now, who had already endured what they were about to face.

Albany had only been a short hop, but Isabel woke when Rick went to the cockpit. He braced on the pilots' seatbacks, his head between the helmeted and visored man and woman. He spoke loudly but, to Isabel, still inaudibly. Each time he pointed through the windshield, the deck pitched in a sudden change of direction.

Tink. The soldiers seated around Isabel suddenly stirred at the sharp sound, like a rock hitting a windshield. The helicopter heeled over onto its right side with a sickening downward tug of G forces, a popping of Isabel's ears, and a thundering application of throttle. *Tink.* Soldiers one-by-one took helmets off their heads and put them on the cabin's deck under their folding fabric seats.

Someone on the ground was shooting at them! Although Isabel's anatomy differed from the men's, she nonetheless cared about it, so she put her own helmet beneath her seat. When Rick rejoined her, he didn't object, though they heard no more strikes on their airframe. "What was *that?*" she had asked.

"We're diverting." He looked at her as if his answer was significant. "To Boston."

Jesus. They were losing. Fast.

The helicopter began a sweeping right turn toward Mass General. The roofs of most buildings were green from eco-friendly plantings, or black from solar panels tilted southward, or filled with the spinning fans of HVAC equipment. But on one was a huge white "H" painted on black asphalt—their destination.

The baseball diamonds and outfields in the riverside park across the street were ringed in hastily erected fencing like a giant, open-air holding pen. At its fringes were green tents with large red crosses on their roofs. The city streets were all blocked in a semicircular perimeter hugging the Charles River and enclosing the hospital and its massive but as yet empty outdoor prison.

Farther afield, cars jammed bridges as the city fled in what would certainly be total panic. They had gone from watching seemingly distant CNN reports of a pandemic in Asia to the virus showing up at their front doors days, weeks ahead of all predictions.

The helicopter's wheels bounced once on the hospital's roof. When Isabel dragged her heavy pack into the hurricane-force winds at the opening, she saw a bullet hole in the fuselage beside her. Stooped under the weight, she lumbered through the gale with the soldiers toward an open door, and their helicopter roared as it left them there.

Isabel stared back at their departing ride. "They're just clearing the helipad," Rick said. "They'll refuel and stand by." It was suddenly quiet save the natural breeze, which quickly cleared away the gasoline fumes. Isabel took a deep breath of fresh air. "Don't worry," Rick said. "We're gonna get outta here. I'll *get* you outta here. I promise."

She was putting an awful lot of trust in whatever Rick said. He *seemed* confident. Annapolis-grad Rick. Marine Captain Rick. Dairy farmer Rick from a red state who might possibly know the tricks and cheats that would keep the overeducated blue state girl alive when there was no more helicopter and no place left to flee. And although it was his job to protect Brandon and her, she couldn't help but think that he really did care... about her. He had made a promise, and guys like him, she felt sure, took those things seriously. Isabel nodded resolutely to herself. Her protector chuckled, white teeth gleaming, the corners of his green eyes crinkling, as he tightened her floppy helmet's chinstrap.

The hospital was a hive of activity. But the soldiers in Isabel's detail—in camo, helmets, kneepads, their torsos thick with body armor and pouches bulging with ammo—were the only armed people in sight. They drew dark, nervous looks from the doctors and nurses in cheerful blue and green scrubs. "Any word?" asked an authoritative-sounding man whose gray hair peeked from beneath a surgical cap. No hands were proffered in greeting.

"Nashua's fallen," Rick reported. "It's broken out in Lowell. They're isolating a whole neighborhood in Medford."

"Medford! That's close."

"Everything north of the Massachusetts-New Hampshire-Vermont border extended, east of the mountains in upstate New York, and west of Augusta and Brunswick in Maine, is in some phase of outbreak."

Silent doctors and nurses now filled the brightly lit corridor. "How long do we have?" asked the senior physician.

"If I had to guess?" Rick replied. "It's probably already here. Someone, somewhere is coughing. Looking for a place to lie down. Probably already crossed paths with a handful of other people. Maybe they caught him as he stumbled, or held a door open as she passed. They'll be throwing up in an hour or two. But we probably won't see any evidence of mass infection for another six to twelve hours or so. Then, it'll get obvious pretty quickly."

It turned out the gray-haired man had come there to greet them. "Dr. Lawrence Goldschmidt. Chief of Surgery."

"Captain Rick Townsend, U.S. Marine Corps."

"Dr. Isabel Miller. Neuroscience. UC Santa Barbara."

The Mass General surgeon said, "I saw you on CNN. Sorry about your sister."

"Dr. Brandon Plante. I teach social psychology at Indiana University."

Their greeter escorted them through the busy hospital to the elevators. "Looks like you've got all your staff on hand," Isabel noted.

But Goldschmidt replied, "We've lost quite a few, actually. Most of the people you see here have been cannibalized from other area hospitals that have already closed." When they crowded into the oversized elevator meant for rolling hospital beds, their host said, "We're making Mass General our last stand, I guess."

He looked at Rick for some confirmation of the military advisability of that course. The normally direct Rick couldn't return the man's gaze. Even he had his limits. Mass General, Isabel and Rick knew, didn't stand a chance. Pressing close to Rick's side, Isabel snagged his pinky finger with hers for the briefest moment. It was something, but not enough to reassure her that his promise, given to her only minutes earlier on the roof, still stood.

The elevator doors opened. "They're gathering for your talk. But I thought first I'd show you what we're planning." The floor looked like a warren of cellular membranes with each cot surrounded by plastic, floor-to-ceiling sheeting. The tiny pods lined all the corridors in every direction, leaving only one-lane gurneyways. They filled waiting rooms, whose chairs had been removed and sofas turned into beds. They split private and semi-private rooms into four, each with its own, separate isolation shelters.

"You're planning on," Isabel asked, "receiving *patients?* Isolating them?"

"We're a hospital, Dr. Miller. We're here to treat the sick as best we can."

"You don't have restraints," Rick noted. Goldschmidt and his small medical entourage of older doctors and nurses stared back at him. "You need to restrain patients in the late stages of the acute phase. It'll make them panic, but I wouldn't wait too long."

The surgeon issued orders to prepare restraints. "See how many of those plastic, handcuff ties Boston PD can get us."

"What about intake?" Isabel asked. "What's your protocol?"

"We triage them in tents in the parking lot. People with ordinary medical issues or casualties of fighting are either turned away after first aid, if their injuries are survivable, or sent to an ordinary ward. People suspected of having been exposed to SED go into these isolation units." Isabel and Rick exchanged a look. "What?" Goldschmidt inquired.

Isabel answered for them both, speaking in slow and measured tones to allow her audience the time to change their understanding of the way the world works. "Every...single...person who comes from outside your perimeter is a potential SED carrier. You crowd them all into an enclosed, ordinary ward, and they'll *all* get sick. And this plastic in here restricts airflow and keeps high concentrations of the aerosolized pathogen in place to be stirred up into suspension for inhalation with every vitals check." The entire effort was so obviously doomed to failure. Why were they even trying?

Rick suggested, "Bust out the windows," never taking his gaze off Isabel. "It's breezy this high up. The ventilation will help."

"Okay." Goldschmidt turned to a similarly gray, similarly grim woman. "We isolate everyone we admit, and break out all the windows on this floor. Have maintenance nail some two-by-fours up as railings."

"How long will you quarantine patients?" Isabel asked.

"Eight hours."

"Four is probably safe. Symptoms usually arrive in two. I'd turn the beds faster. You won't be able to sterilize this area. It's airborne. You're just going to have to mask up all your patients and hope for the best."

The surgeon said, "We've set aside the parking garages for morgues. The survivors go into the MOAD." He pronounced it "mo-add."

"The what?"

"It's *your* facility," Goldschmidt said to Isabel. "Federal. 'Mass Open-Air Detention.' Our job ends when we hand them over to the navy corpsmen across the street." He led them to an amphitheater filled with chattering doctors and nurses in lab coats and scrubs. Unlike the briefings to troops, Rick remained beside the door. A pretty nurse, younger than Isabel and much more recently bathed, asked him questions, pointing at different parts of his rifle, smiling, and saying things like, "Oh! Wow. *Really?*"

Vasquez and his men milled about the corridor outside. A hush descended as Isabel and Brandon took to the stage in full combat regalia. She was getting used to her arrival casting palls over rooms. "How much does all that *weigh?*" asked the grinning young nurse as she squeezed Rick's ammo pouches.

Into the stillness boomed, "All right!" from a newly arriving man in a dark windbreaker with a blue emblem on its breast, who strode down the center aisle toward the front. "Let's start getting this place organized! I'm the Massachusetts Emergency Management Agency incident commander! This is the FEMA incident commander!" His thumb introduced his clone, on whose own windbreaker "FEMA" was helpfully inscribed. "We've just completed our delineation of jurisdictional authority, which I'd like to review with you all!"

Dr. Goldschmidt was crimson with anger, presumably having passed the more pastel shades of annoyance without Isabel noticing. "Watch out," whispered a female doctor who'd been on their tour. The senior surgeon asked to speak to the two bureaucrats alone.

"I've never *been* to Wisconsin. Are there lots of guys there like *you?*" The nurse's giggle was inappropriate to the somber mood of the room. But the shouts of the surgeon and the incident commanders from the corridor became audible to all and elicited a bemused stir among the hospital's staff.

The shattering of a window one floor above startled everyone. Tinted shards and stringers of glass plummeted past their view.

Goldschmidt returned—calm, peach-colored, alone—and introduced Isabel and Brandon both as "Doctor," but appended "PhD" lest anyone mistake them for an MD. As more glass rained past their view, he informed the gathering of his executive decisions like the ventilation plan, restraining late-stage SED victims, and shortening of the quarantine. Like most egotists, he'd already forgotten the ideas weren't his. He then motioned toward his PhD guests.

"We usually," Isabel said, "go straight to questions."

Several hands shot up. Isabel pointed at a man in a white lab coat. "From the abstracts we've gotten, the acute phase of the disease results in severe nausea and unconsciousness. If we cuff them to their cots on their backs, they may aspirate bile."

Goldschmidt clearly expected her to answer. "Can you cuff them face *down* and over a bucket?"

A senior nurse said they'd need more buckets. "A *lot* more." They really were going to attempt to handle this unprecedented medical emergency. It was both heartening that people were still trying, and heartbreaking in how, she knew, it would end.

The questions continued. Each identified a potentially disastrous failure, which in total slowly revealed the true hopelessness of their efforts. Where to do the triage? Whether to separate friends and loved ones from the potentially infected, or to quarantine them all? What about treating potentially infected patients suffering from other maladies? Criteria for discharging the uninfected. Barrier breaches that would require quarantining hospital staff. The importance of self-reporting lapses and reporting lapses by co-workers. Could they wash linens or do they need to be burned after first use? How many body bags do they have in stock and when did they make the call to begin reusing them solely for transport to the morgue? What constitutes "full" in those underground parking garages? In the end, Isabel knew, they would all be overwhelmed, infected, and die on their jobs or in belated attempts to flee their failing systems. *Pandoravirus* was a force of nature, as if Infecteds were the preordained successors to the former undisputed masters of the Earth.

Brandon stared into empty space. She had no idea where his head was. When a question related vaguely to security was asked, Isabel interrupted the pretty, industrious nurse by inviting Rick to answer it. He suggested to the gathering of medical staff that they arm themselves, then broke free of the nurse's clutches and hosted an off-to-the-side lecture of the private security, police, and military personnel.

After the briefing, their entire nine-person detail reassembled in the sandbagged, first-floor lobby where most of the armed men and women were located. *Their* peeps. Rick said to the entire detail, "Our orders are to observe the arrival of the infection from inside the city to see what we can learn about best practices." Brandon loosed a cynical scoff. "So, we've got two choices. We can bunk here for the night, or we can requisition some ground transportation and head up to Medford to observe the outbreak from there before falling back into the city after dark."

"I vote we bed down here for the night," Isabel said.

"I agree," Brandon quickly concurred.

They took food from the cafeteria to cots in the still empty maze of plastic sheeting. Isabel made sure she put herself next to Rick. The cell connection was good. They all typed their reports to the Pentagon. Isabel wondered how long people would be there to read them. "Giving the hospital staff," she typed with a kernel of guilt, "explicit instructions seems to afford them a glimmer of hope and may account for their continued dedication to their work," *as hopeless as that is*. She kept adding to her rambling observations every time she found that Rick was still typing.

After the Rouses Point Bridge massacre, she had read the report Rick would post to the DoD database, which had subsequently been classified Top Secret. Isabel's own e-mails back to the National Security Council were free-form and never secret. Rick's were composed from some sort of rigid template. "Memorandum: For the Joint Chiefs of Staff. From: Capt. Rick Townsend, USMC. Subject: After Action Report." Location, forces deployed, terrain, description of engagement, and ending in lessons learned. Her own observations seemed insignificant by comparison, like about Infecteds' migratory impulses and the tendency of crowds, once formed, to wander like sufferers of dissociative fugue, or the odd penchant for individual Infecteds' cooperativeness. Under lessons learned from fighting in the woods, Rick had typed, "Continuous lines unsustainable. Recommend checkerboard redoubts with interlocking fields of fire, and sallying."

"What's a redoubt?" she had asked him.

"A strong defensive position."

"And a *sally?*"

"It's, um, an attack—outbound—by the garrison of a redoubt."

"Like...lowering the drawbridge and charging out on horseback?"

"Exactly. Now I really need to upload this before the Midnight in the Tank," the Joint Chiefs' nickname, she knew, for their nightly meeting at eleven fifty p.m.

"Please quit bothering me," Isabel had replied. "I have to finish my report too...about drawbridges and moats and catapults." That elicited the faintest hint of amusement.

At around ten p.m., the hospital lights were lowered. After waiting in vain in the darkness for several minutes for the thick plastic to part and Rick's tall figure to appear, Isabel ended up saying, "Good night?"

Both Rick and Brandon replied, in unison, "Night."

Isabel's stifled sigh became a personal best exercise in deep breathing. She kept drifting off to sleep, still sort of waiting for Rick even with Brandon so close.

The next thing she knew—possibly minutes, possibly hours later—the lights were raised and there was a commotion. Orders were barked from behind masks.

Isabel parted the plastic into Rick's cot. He was climbing into his body armor and webbing. There were sirens audible through the black openings where the windows had once been. Isabel peered into the corridor. A patient was being rolled into the ward on a narrow gurney like those used by ambulances. The little girl on it was sitting upright holding a fraying teddy bear, eyes wide and pupils green above her mask, not yet black, as they wheeled her past. She stared at Isabel, too young to be in terror, but full of concern, which visibly grew as Isabel raised her own mask to cover her nose and mouth.

Chapter 9

Following a long day of work at the compound and a refreshing evening shower, Noah found Natalie in the kitchen pointing at the TV. "A college student at George Mason got sick in the next county over." On the muted flat-screen mounted to the wall was a boy in a one-piece white suit and hood. Only his black eyes were visible over his mask as he was led, handcuffed, from a patrol car into what looked to be a jail. "They don't know how he caught it. He has amnesia or something and is confused, but he mentioned some woman he met on the road. A professor."

Noah was instantly on alert. He wanted to ask if she was five-four with short, light brown hair and exhibited a special interest in epidemiology. But that would certainly rouse Natalie's concerns about Emma, who he grew increasingly certain was headed their way.

Noah found Jacob in the tower, as he and Jake called it. A small set of spiral stairs led to an unfinished attic space that Noah had opened to the outside, thereby creating an architecturally discordant watchtower of sorts with good sight lines over the barn, past the fence, and down the hill toward the distant highway. Jake sat on a built-in bench seat, flying the drone on his iPad, with his rifle propped against the waist-high, crenellated wall. "Jake, could we talk?"

"Yeah, sure. It's almost outta juice. I'll fly it home on autopilot."

Noah sank to the cushions on the floor. "First off, son, how many times…"

"Yeah! I know." Jacob slid off his perch and sat on the floor so that no one beyond the fence could see him there. Or, more importantly, shoot him. That was the whole point of the drones—to do recon without exposing themselves to any danger.

On the iPad, a video procession of trees and rocky outcroppings gave way to the fence line, barn, and main house. Its buzzing motor sounded like an angry bee as it grew louder. Jacob craned his neck to peer through the vertical slits in the tower's walls like in a medieval battlement, whose design, in fact, Noah had copied.

"Keep your head *down*," Noah again reminded. "You can watch it on the iPad." When the camera pointed—motionless—at a random copse of trees beside the relatively flat and open landing pad they had cleared of branches, the rotors fell silent and the iPad went black.

"So, Jake, I'm headed down to that town meeting this evening. Every night before sunset I walk the perimeter to make sure the fence is intact and the little gate leading up to the cabin is locked."

"You want me to do it tonight?"

"Yes. Take your rifle with you and chamber a round, but keep the safety on and your ears open. If anything appears off or different, or if you feel uncomfortable in any way, don't go check it out. Get back to the house, tell your Mom, lock up, and wait."

The soon-to-be fourteen-year-old boy agreed while wearing his serious look.

"If something goes really wrong—if there's big trouble up here—don't try to defend the house. You, your sister, and your mother go down into the basement, head out through the tunnel, and hike up to the cabin. *Quietly.* If you're not here, I'll look for you there. Okay?" Jake bobbed his head. Noah concluded yet again that he needed to make it back to his family. They would be far less safe if anything happened to him.

* * * *

The parking lot at the firehouse was nearly full. Noah walked up to the commotion at the door, where a crowd was arguing with a deputy. "You really oughta rethink this," a spokesman for the group was saying. His accent was definitely not local. Everyone wore some form of mask—an old-fashioned cloth surgical mask, a respirator like the ones used by house painters, various forms and thicknesses of bandanas, even a ghoulish-looking army surplus gas mask. Noah extracted an N95 mask and Latex gloves from the rucksack he carried.

The deputy, arms crossed, ignored the crowd. "Who are you?" he challenged as Noah edged his way forward.

"Name's Miller."

"*Noah* Miller?" The deputy waved him through without even checking his pack.

"What the fuck is *that* about?" the group's angry spokesman objected.

"Like I said, residents and landowners only."

Inside, several dozen locals were packed into the empty central hall where the fire truck, banished to the outside, was normally parked. Several people—by their attire farmers or not far removed from farming—acknowledged his arrival. Noah scanned the crowd. No one appeared visibly ill. Most carried sidearms; a few had shotguns. Noah decided to make a quick run back out to get his pistol.

One of the people from the crowd at the door fell into step alongside him. "Hey." The man's red-white-and-blue bandanna over his nose and mouth puffed outward with his greeting. "Alexei Kozlov," he said, pronouncing his surname "Kos-*LOFF*." He gave Noah his business card. *Senior salesman, AAA Jacuzzi Tubs, Hoboken, New Jersey.* "Look, we may not be from 'round these here parts," he said, sounding like an old cowboy in a B-grade western, but with a faint Russian accent, "but we're good people. We wanna join up. Be useful members of society." *Like if anyone needs a Jacuzzi.*

"You're talking to the wrong guy." Noah opened the SUV door, strapped his pistol belt around his waist, locked the truck, and turned to see the man heading off, checking Noah over his shoulder.

Back inside, armed, Noah felt more at ease and received additional silent greetings.

"Okay folks," announced the cowboy-hat wearing Sheriff whom Noah and Jacob had met on the state highway two days earlier. A pair of men joined Walcott atop one of several shrink-wrapped pallets of supplies. Behind them hung a huge American flag. "Now you all know me, and the mayor, and the fire chief. We called this meetin' to talk about organizin' a… Well, I guess I'd call it a militia. Y'all know I only got three deputies, and two auxiliaries. That's six of us for a county that used to have a population of about five thousand. But as you can see from outside, that's now swole to near double with refugees from up North."

"What's this militia of yers gonna be *for?*" asked an older man in overalls whose unshaven facial hair was gray trending toward white.

"Well sir," Sheriff Walcott replied, scratching his forehead underneath his hatband, "I guess you'd call 'em our last resort, if things get outta control with the Infecteds."

"Let's call 'em what they are!" someone else shouted. "We cain't afford all that political correctness comin' outta Warshington. They're *zombies*, is what they are. And the Bible warned us they was comin'. Revelations!"

"Now Teddy," the mayor said, "I don't think the Bible specifically foretold any zombie uprisings."

"They're *evil*, is what they are! They're gonna try and kill us and ours, or turn us into one of them, and take our places and our stuff! What would you call that if not the devil's work?"

There was a murmur of concurrence, but it wasn't universal. More than half, Noah estimated, were silent and taking it all in, like him. But the other half was engaged and potentially confrontational. Sheriff Walcott was tamping the crowd noise down with his hands, trying to keep the floor.

"What about the Army?" another farmer-type asked. "They's been convoys passin' my place every coupla days."

"We don't know yet 'bout the Army," the Sheriff replied. "Apparently, they're still arguin' about what to do in whatever bunker they're holed up in."

"That's *more* bullshit!" said Teddy, the anti-PC guy, garnering unanimous support for that sentiment. "That's what we *have* an army for, ain't it? Why are *we* havin' to do *their* job?"

"Cuz Pres. Stoddard is a *pussy!*"

Noah was surprised. Not by what people were saying, but that they were speaking their minds so freely. No shrinking violets here deferring to authority.

"The National Guard has been federalized," Walcott noted sanely.

"That's 'cause the gov'nors said they was plannin' on usin' the Guard to fight the zombies. That's why that *pussy*—no offense—we got for a president *federalized* 'em!"

The meeting was spinning out of control, with a dozen angry, irrelevant arguments breaking out. Walcott, the mayor, and the fire chief tried to rein them in. Noah grew tired of it. "Give the Sheriff a chance to talk!" he shouted.

Maybe it was because his remark was out of the blue, or maybe it was because no one knew who the hell he was, or maybe it was just louder than everyone else, but the crowd turned his way and quieted.

"Thank you, Mr. Miller," Walcott said. "For those of you who don't know Noah Miller here, he moved down from northern Virginia and fixed up the Old Miller Place."

Everyone waited for Noah to say something. "So, what *is* this militia gonna be for, Sheriff?" he asked.

"Well sir," Walcott replied, tipping his hat back off his forehead, "to help me and my deputies keep us all safe."

That wasn't sufficient for Noah. "Help *how?* Do you mean collectively defend the town from a horde of rampaging…zombies, or whatever? Correct me, Sheriff, if I'm wrong, but don't most people live out in the hills, not in town? If we come down here to serve in this militia, we're gonna leave our homes and families undefended."

There was a stir of agreement shared in whispers and amplified by repetition.

"So, Mr. Miller," replied Walcott in a tone not nearly as welcoming as before, "you wanna go every-man-for-hisself? When that horde is outside *your* house, *you* wanna deal with 'em with no help from the rest of us?"

"I just want to hear specifics, Sheriff. A plan—a *good* plan—before I leave my family to fend for themselves. What would this militia do *exactly?*"

Walcott looked at the mayor and fire chief. The only sounds were the muffled arguments outside the firehouse door. "Well sir, I s'pose that if Infecteds are unfit to live in society—if they'll be walkin' around spreadin' the virus, or they might go crazy at the drop of a hat…" The sheriff clearly didn't want to say it.

The residents all deferred to Noah and waited. "So what you're implying is that we have to decide—to *vote*—on whether we're going to kill anybody who gets sick?"

"I didn't say just because you get sick…" Walcott began, but Noah interrupted.

"Well it follows that if everybody who survives infection is a threat either because they're violent or contagious, then that threat begins the moment they're infected. After that, they'll either die or turn and threaten to attack or infect the rest of us. There is no third possibility."

"Then what are *you* proposin'?" the mayor asked, seemingly eager to have someone else say what the county's elected officials would not.

"I'm not proposing anything. I'm the new guy here. But I've got things to do, and I wanted to cut to the chase." He turned to the crowd. "The only reason to raise a militia, it seems to me, would be to go to war with the Infecteds, not to wait in barracks down here for problems to materialize. To engage in a campaign of eradication of them. All of them, because they're all contagious, and how can we tell the peaceful ones, if there are any, from the violent ones?"

Sheriff Walcott did not disagree. But neither he nor the other county leaders seemed willing to publicly endorse mass murder, which was still technically illegal, not to mention immoral for these presumably church-going people.

"So," said Teddy, the stubbled Book of Revelations scholar, "what does *that* mean? Somebody gets sick and we *shoot* 'em? Like puttin' down a *hog?*"

"Yes," Noah said. The crowd stirred. "That would be the plan we vote on." There were murmurs of heated rejection. Noah made it even more difficult. "And that means that if someone in *your* family gets sick, this militia will come into your house and put a bullet in them. Your wife. Your kid. Your grandkid."

There was now open rebellion in the firehouse. "Whoa!" and "Ain't nobody..." and, "Just like to see 'em *try*," were snippets of remarks Noah overheard.

"It's us or them!" came a shout from the crowd, which hushed the gathering. A man in a tattered green John Deere cap and unbuttoned red flannel shirt over a faded gray T-shirt said, "I don't plan on lettin' *my* fam'ly *git* sick. And if that means I have to serve in a militia, then that's what I'm gonna do!"

In what Noah thought was a ridiculous to and fro, the crowd seemed to tilt back toward that viewpoint. Everyone awaited Noah's rebuttal.

There was something about an argument, any argument, that had always roused competitiveness in Noah. He saw flaws in reasoning, unaddressed impracticalities in a proposal, or facts assumed without proof, and in pointing those defects out, he ended up picking a side without due regard for his true views. He lowered his mask to help connect with the impromptu jury. "Once anyone is infected, it's practically a hundred percent chance that everyone around that person will get sick too. So the plan we should vote on would be to kill everyone in a household once any one of them gets sick."

The harshness of that mission for Walcott's militia had its intended effect. A chill settled on the room as the men and a few women contemplated killing everyone—strangers, or friends and neighbors—unfortunate enough to have any among them get sick.

Noah's red-flanneled debate opponent, however, responded. "Or we can all agree that, if we get sick, we'll take care of the problem our *own* selves."

"Suicide?" Noah asked. The green John Deere hat bobbed resolutely. "Okay. Let's add that. An up-or-down, yes-or-no vote agreeing to kill ourselves and everyone we've been in contact with if any one of us gets sick. Problem is, do you really expect that the people who vote no on that plan tonight will follow through on it if they lose that vote? Or even the people who voted *yes*, when the time comes and they're standing over their sick kid's bed with a shotgun?"

Not without a solution, the pro to Noah's con said, "I guess that's where the militia comes in."

"Okay. Good point. Let's vote on *that* plan." Without any debate, Noah's repeated mention of voting had made that exercise in democracy a condition to adoption of any militia plan. "I move that we vote on a plan, A, to agree to kill ourselves and our entire family if any one of us catches *Pandoravirus*, and B, failing that, to consent to the summary execution of our entire household by the Sheriff and his militia. All in favor?"

There were shouts of, "Hold on there!" and "Wait just a doggone minute!" Noah's legal skills at framing the question had clearly prevailed.

"Lemme guess," came from the man in the John Deere hat. "You a lawyer?"

"Is there anything wrong with my *logic?*"

"I ain't killin' *nobody*," came a new voice, "unless it's self-defense. It ain't Christian."

Sheriff Walcott responded. "So Bobby, if Carl gets in trouble next door you ain't gonna come help? Ain't that all we're talkin' about? Helpin' each other out?"

Noah jumped in. "It's one thing to help a neighbor out..."

"Good," his debate opponent interrupted. "Glad to hear since I'm *your* neighbor. Trey Nichols." They greeted each other with apparently customary bobs of their heads.

"But Sheriff," Noah continued, "it's another thing entirely to form a government force—with zero legal authority, I might add—to engage in cleansing of the population through mass murder."

"What's *your* plan then?" Trey Nichols asked.

"Okay. How about the Castle Doctrine? Every man's home—his property—is his castle. Right now, the law already says you can defend your home, family, and property."

"That works real nice for *you*," Sheriff Walcott said icily, "since you just posted all them no-trespassing signs." He clearly felt betrayed. "And so if me or my Deputies come on your posted property, you gonna shoot at us?"

"Maybe. Since *you* may one day, God forbid, be the ones who're infected." Noah's audience was listening intently. "But I'm *sure* as hell gonna shoot any militia that's coming to kill my wife and children. And by the way what *does* happen, Sheriff, if and when *you* turn? And your Deputies? And this militia that we've armed and empowered to kick in doors and kill whole families? We've all seen the news. The people who've turned get up out of their sick beds and go back to work doing whatever they were doing before. I assume that includes zombie sheriffs and zombie militiamen. It's pretty easy to imagine *them* taking a vote one day and deciding that it's the *un*infected people who are *their* big threat. That's the road this proposal would start us down."

Sheriff Walcott was an elected official, as was the mayor. They knew how to count noses in a vote, and they glanced at each other before Walcott pivoted. "What about all the public spaces? Roads? The town? The George Washington, Jefferson, and Monongahela National Forests? The Shenandoah National Park? Who polices all those places?"

"Are you sayin'," one man asked, "this militia will be headin' out twenty, thirty, forty *miles* from here? I gotta track my wife's blood sugar every few hours!" There was an avalanche of other loud objections.

"So it's every man for hisself, is it?" Walcott exclaimed.

A hirsute farmer said, "There's this castle thing the new fella said. Nobody goes on anybody's land without permission, or else. We should vote on *that*."

In short order, Noah's Castle Doctrine was approved by the raised hands of at least three-quarters of the people in the firehouse. But after the vote, huddled beneath a row of fire jackets on hooks and helmets on shelves, were the men whose hands had not risen. Included among them were Sheriff Walcott and Noah's neighbor, Trey Nichols.

* * * *

The news on the radio in Noah's SUV ran the full range of modern punditry from pessimistic to apocalyptic, with a huge skew toward the latter. "Well, I guess this is *it!*" proclaimed the host in a broken voice. Previously grounded but now sobbing, she was comforted by her panel of politicians, scientists, entertainers, and clergymen. Noah searched satellite radio. "Breaking news. The BBC has just learned that the Swiss government has granted refuge to the Grand Duke of Luxembourg. To repeat..." Noah tried MSNBC. "The federal government's response to this crisis has been *criminally* inept." He jumped to CNBC. "Trading was suspended when gold hit six thousand dollars an ounce." He had 1,500 ounces in the basement safe and almost ran off the ridge road doing the math. Nine million increasingly worthless dollars' worth of gold. "Whoohoo," he muttered sarcastically. Technically, it was the best investment he'd ever made.

Noah's family was right where he had left them, except that Chloe, sitting on her heels, now read old-fashioned e-mails from a laptop. The servers used by most of her social media apps were slowing or had failed, but she had been thrilled that you could just send an e-mail and get a reply whenever, without having to wait around. "Do you think that's why they call it e-*mail?* Because it's like sending a *letter?*" She was amazed, as if at finding a working telegraph. "Gracie and her fam just made it to Idaho. The one with mountains."

Jake reclined on the floor against displaced sofa cushions, aiming his presumably empty assault rifle at targets on the large flatscreen. "Jake!" He knew the infraction immediately and lowered the high-powered weapon.

Natalie made Noah sit in a chair far away from the rest. "Quarantine. How'd it go?"

Noah briefed them on what had happened at the town meeting.

Chloe interrupted in a whiny voice. "Does the Castle Doctrine mean we're supposed to just...*shoot* people? Whoever wanders onto our *property?*"

Infuriatingly, Natalie said, "She has a point."

"*What* point?" Noah replied.

Chloe's laptop *binged.* "Gracie said *everybody* has guns in Idaho. They'll shoot you if you get too close. Is that what we're supposed to do? Shoot people who come too close? How close? And which people? And without asking an adult first?"

Jake sat up and turned his full attention to whatever his dad was going to say. Noah needed to sound more certain of his reply than he felt. "Okay. Let's start with the fence line around the house. Nobody, *nobody*, comes inside that fence. Even if they're in terrible distress. *Especially* if they're in distress. Anyone who tries—you shoot."

"*At* them?" Chloe asked. "No warning shot?" Noah tilted his head in reproach. "I know, I know. Like the sign said." Her mother looked bewildered. "There was this sign," Chloe explained, "at the gun range that said, 'Due to the rising cost of ammo, I no longer provide a warning shot.' But the instructor said it *really* meant that people who're shooting at each other are already, like, *way* past warning shots."

"Remember that other sign?" Jake asked. "'Trespassers will be shot, survivors will be shot again'?" He was overcome with laughter.

"That's...fuckin'...*horrible!*" Chloe said, kicking her brother.

"Language, Chloe," Noah corrected.

"Language?" Natalie snapped at him. "*Language?*" She turned to her kids. In the same voice as she'd lectured them about stranger danger in preschool, she said, "If anyone tries to come through the fence, or gets inside, you *shoot* them. If you let someone go, they could hurt or infect not just you, but all of us. So we're all depending on each other, no matter how hard it is. You shoot them. Understand? Keep shooting till they quit moving, like Jake's sign said."

The gravity of Natalie's directive settled slowly and in silence. Both Chloe and Jake were taken aback, with Chloe appearing almost sick at what she might actually have to do.

Natalie turned to Noah, who was fighting his own dismay at hearing the words spoken aloud…and from his *wife*. He had worried about Natalie being unable to make the transition to a world filled with unavoidable violence. Now he wondered just how much violence she was prepared to unleash on it. "And I think," Natalie added, "we should all begin regular target practice. Tomorrow morning. Starting with me."

For some reason, this felt to Noah like the formal beginning of their family's personal apocalypse. *Their* trial by ordeal had arrived, or was close.

"What about the property line?" Jake asked. "Where we put up all those signs?"

"What signs?" Chloe asked.

"They say, 'Posted.' It's a warning so we can shoot people legally."

"That's not *fair*. People don't see a sign that says, 'Posted,' and think, 'Hm, somebody will *shoot* me if I step over some totally invisible line.'"

Noah jumped in. "It also says trespassers will be shot, *okay?*" He sighed, rocked back in his chair, and rubbed his face.

Natalie said, "I'm gonna go make coffee."

"It's late," Noah objected, pretty sure country folk got up early every single day, though he still wasn't certain exactly why.

"We need to talk about this. These rules. I'll make coffee. You try to relax a little."

By bedtime at one a.m., after hours of challenges by his wife and children, Noah had hashed out the Miller family rules of engagement. The fence around the main house was to be defended with deadly force—no warning shots. Anyone else on their property was to be ordered to leave and, if the confrontation escalated, engaged with deadly force—one warning shot allowed but not required. Outside their property, they would only use their weapons in self-defense or, if the situation demanded, the defense of others—no warning shots, aim to kill, then get the hell out of there. Natalie's target practice would commence in eight hours. "Have a good night's sleep, kids."

After Noah survived his quarantine, he and Natalie went to bed and made love. Passionate. Energetic. Maybe it was the coffee. Or maybe it was the plan, or the prospect for survival that any plan promised. Noah now felt ready for the fight—for any fight—to protect his family, a fact he couldn't help but think Natalie saw in him, and found every bit as satisfying as the sex.

Chapter 10

"This is weird," Isabel whispered. "I don't like it." They stood outside the cyclone fencing that enclosed the Mass Open-Air Detention facility. What had to be upwards of 20,000 Infecteds stood on the other side, motionless, totally quiet, all staring toward the medical tent where they had been processed—the only way in, or out.

"We've gotta get outta here," Brandon said to Rick, not Isabel. "*Now.* Those detainees in quarantine are way overcrowded. They're totally and completely charged. Hair trigger. One little disturbance, and…"

They were spooky to Isabel. She wandered closer, staring at the statue-like frozen figures. All those people, and no coughs, no whispers, not a scratch of a nose by hands dangling forgotten at their sides. They focused only on the obstacle blocking their path to freedom—the soldiers guarding the processing tent—and nothing else.

Over her shoulder, Mass General across the closed road already looked like a relic in a war zone. Most of its windows were gone. Smoke billowed from the seventh floor where National Guardsmen had used a few dozen hand grenades to "subdue the unrest," as the public information officer had delicately described to the last two remaining members of the press. Someone tossed a bedsheet out of a high window, their now accepted means of biohazard disposal. The sheet fluttered down several stories, snagged on a jagged glass opening, then blew free and fell into the now dangerously contaminated parking lot.

More Infecteds, at gunpoint, filed out of a bus outside the processing tent. "I thought they weren't adding any more?" Rick said. "Did you explain...?"

"*Yes*, I explained!" Brandon snapped. "The density passed thirty per square ten meters hours ago. It's over forty now. I told them it'd be safer to let them roam the streets than to jam them all together."

The Infecteds nearest Isabel, Rick, and Brandon slowly, one-by-one, turned toward them. "Hey, guys," Isabel said. Placid faces now stared their way. In tells, their fists were all clenched and their bodies were like coiled springs. More and more turned their way.

"I think you oughta get back from that fence," advised Sgt. Vasquez. His five men held their weapons pointed at the 20,000 Infecteds separated by the hastily erected and ultimately flimsy barrier.

Brandon said, "Slowly. Slowly."

They backed away. Rick told Vasquez to call the Black Hawk.

Brandon and Isabel continued their unnatural, slow-motion escape despite Isabel's every instinct screaming at her to run. She felt the Infecteds' stares in the prickling of her back. Rick and the soldiers walked backwards, holding their rifles at the ready. No one dared utter a word even after they passed the sandbagged machine gun positions at the hospital entrance. As they entered the lobby, the power went off for an instant, then came back on.

Rick said, "Let's take the stairs."

Easier said than done, at least for Isabel and Brandon. The industrial décor of the fire escapes—bare metal riveted to rough concrete streaked with white paint drippings—seemed never-ending. She was breathing hard, sweating, and adjusting her heavy backpack on her shoulders, her body armor chaffing her hipbones and underarms. Isabel removed her helmet briefly before concluding that carrying it was even harder.

"It's not much further," Rick said as Isabel hopped to readjust her backpack's position and blew sweat from her lips while aiming for a limp strand of stray hair.

Just then, a roar arose. Not the automatic weapons, loud though they too were, but a cacophony of quasi-human sounding voices, which overwhelmed even the percussion of the guns. This wasn't like Rouses Point Bridge. The huge numbers of Infecteds quickly extinguished much of the return gunfire. The next sounds they heard, much closer and louder, were a half dozen doors in the stairwell slamming against walls. People were storming emergency exits. "Let's go!" Rick ordered, not panicked, but not patient either.

When they made it onto the roof, the steady, cool breeze would have felt wonderful were it not for the clamor from the ground below and the total silence from the sky above.

Isabel, Brandon, and Rick descended from the elevated helipad to the railing along the edge of the roof. It was impossible to tell where the detention facility had been in the confusing swirl of violence. Fully-automatic rips of gunfire here and there forestalled the inevitable and added to the hundreds upon hundreds of bodies. The dead and dying lay in the roadway, draped across the flattened cyclone fencing, and scattered amid ambulances, buses, Humvees, and tank-like fighting vehicles, some of which were still trying to drive through the mob to safety. Many of the fallen were crawling wounded over barricades and climbing piles of corpses before being added to those piles by bursts of flame from soldiers' muzzles. "My God!" came Isabel's involuntary cry and shudder.

The mob was winning. A police van ramming its way through got stuck atop a heap of bodies and was quickly toppled onto its side. Its occupants were extracted and dragged into the killing mounds, their screams unheard against the roar.

The sound of gunfire now rose not just from the street, but also from the building, from several stories below, through the door that opened onto the roof. The thunder of approaching helicopter engines relieved Isabel until she saw that it wasn't their Black Hawk. Streaks of fire sparkled off the Charles River and lit the night. A string of six explosions erupted in the heart of the MOAD and buffeted the air on the roof. In the flashes she glimpsed pieces of bodies flying skyward like in some teenage boy's gory video game. Before the boiling orange flames cooled to billowing clouds, the helicopter gunships whirled and began indiscriminately raking the enclosure with automatic fire. Isabel watched hundreds, thousands of shell casings rain into the river with splashes that boiled the surface like a fish feeding frenzy.

The gunship attack masked the approach of their Black Hawk. They climbed the stairs up onto the helipad and knelt to await its landing. The door at the top of the fire escape burst open and men and women in scrubs poured onto the roof.

"Jesus Christ," Vasquez said, tasking his men to turn their weapons on the door, stopping the frantic doctors and nurses with bracing shouts of, "Halt! Halt!"

As soon as the Black Hawk's wheels touched down, Rick led them on a stooped run through the rotors' gale. The engines remained at high throttle, which thankfully muted the pleas of hospital staff, some of whom

Isabel recognized from earlier—the nurse with the big smile drawn on her blue mask, the Indian-American intern who had handed a candy to every child diagnosed with SED until he'd run out, the pretty young nurse who'd hit on Rick. Again hands were clasped in prayer and fists shaken in anger—an awful repeat of the horrific scene on the bridge.

When the last of Vasquez's men scampered aboard, the door slid closed, and the Black Hawk lurched skyward. Isabel crawled across the hard metal deck while dragging her pack, unfolded a seat, and—shaking—buckled its harness as the aircraft pitched wildly from side to side.

In a voice that quaked from the engine vibrating through the bulkhead at her back, she shouted to Rick, "Will there be other helicopters coming for *them?*"

Rick couldn't even muster a reply, and turned away. Isabel dipped her chin to her chest. Only a few loose strands of filthy hair fell to give her face cover. It was all too much. Her eyes sank closed of their own accord. She could stand no more sights. Sounds. Smells. And especially no thoughts or, God forbid, feelings. *If only I were Emma now. None of this would bother me.* She needed to gird herself for survival of the overwhelming trauma and tragedy to come. To climb into Emma's uncaring skin. To shout, *Shut up!* every time a voice in her head recalled how horror-stricken the red-headed nurse had looked before they deserted her on that rooftop to the murderous mob below. *Might as well get used to it,* she thought. Because, for the very first time, Isabel realized that she probably, statistically, realistically wouldn't survive, not uninfected at least. No one would. *No* one!

Rick tried to put his arm around her. Isabel wriggled free. He wasn't her salvation. He was her doom—the chink in her emotional armor—that could destroy her if she let him in. If she let herself love him. Isabel caught Brandon's eye before looking away. She had to keep herself from caring for *anyone* else. She had to emulate her sister.

Chapter 11

Emma was now fairly well equipped. She'd gotten her backpack from the van guy. Her sleeping bag and ground sheet from a family that had only shouted complaints as she ran off with their stuff. A skillet from the kitchen of a farmhouse to go with the eggs she'd stolen from their henhouse. Water bottles from the unguarded flatbed of a pickup truck.

The terrain was growing hillier. She was drawing closer to her destination.

"Hey!" shouted a man a hundred yards away. He held a rifle, but it wasn't pointed at her. He wore hunting gear and a camouflage baseball cap. Off to his side she saw a boy, maybe ten, also carrying a rifle. "You're on our land!"

"Sorry!" Emma replied. The effort of shouting raised the pitch of her voice, making her sound like a vulnerable young girl. That might help.

The man slung his rifle over his shoulder and said something to the boy, who seemed more reluctant and skeptical than the adult. Both approached warily.

You need a better weapon. She had a screwdriver. They had rifles, which was both a threat and an opportunity. The man didn't look menacing, but you never knew for sure. He was, after all, a man. The boy, however, lagged behind and held with both hands the sling of his rifle on his shoulder. He might be the more dangerous of the two. He was, in appearance, a miniature version of the man, minus the height, protruding gut, and scraggly beard. They were probably hunters, but for this outing they had left their orange vests behind. So what, or who, were they hunting?

"Didn't mean to scare you," the man said as he neared. He wore a smile, Emma guessed, to put her at ease or to ingratiate himself for whatever inner purpose he harbored. The boy settled in about twenty feet behind him, watching her and on guard. "Name's Mike. Mike Barnwell."

He held out his hand, but the boy snapped, "Dad!"

"Oh, yeah. I forgot." He withdrew his hand, wiped the imaginary germs onto his jacket, and turned to his son. "Ellis! Git over here!" The boy edged forward until, after repeated urgings, he stood only a step behind the adult. "This scaredy cat is Ellis, my boy."

Emma locked eyes on Ellis, who made no move to acknowledge her. He understood the risk that his father missed. *Children,* Emma reasoned, *are less well socialized to the past and will adapt more quickly to the new world than their parents.* But was that *her* thought, or had it come from that mysterious inner voice? Or was that a distinction without a difference? Increasingly, she was having trouble answering that question.

"Don't worry. We ain't..." Mike didn't finish. *We ain't* what? He removed his baseball cap, and prodded his son, who did the same. "What's *your* name, missy?"

"Emma. Emma Miller."

"Pleasure to meet you, Miss Miller. We don't get much company up here. We was just out lookin' for deer. Didn't mean to scare you."

"I'm not scared."

"Uh, no. I guess you're not. Good. But what...what *are* you doin' out here? I mean, ya *know,* don'cha, that there's been a string of murders, the news said. It probably ain't safe bein' in the woods all by yerself. Bein' a gal and all. A woman, I mean."

He underestimates you, came the voice, and again it was right. "I'm fine," she said. But did he expect more than just pleasantries? Should she elaborate on her sore feet and back, itchy clothes, and possible yeast infection?

But the elder Barnwell didn't seem a particularly adept conversationalist. "Well, *say.* I hate just sendin' a young lady off empty handed. These are tough times. How's about we rustle you up some breakfast?"

"Dad?" said the dangerous boy. Isabel's hand snuck closer to the handle of the screw driver in her back pocket. She would need to get nearer, but when she took a step forward Ellis took a step back. His father gave the boy a lecture on the need to maintain traditions like hospitality, notwithstanding the ongoing total collapse of civilization. "Ma ain't gonna like it," came his son's mumbled reply.

And he was right. The sturdy woman blocked the doorway of their unpainted ramshackle house, really more of a hovel. Smoke rose from its crumbling chimney. Dingy clothes dried on lines. Small, skinned animals hung from the eaves of a tilted, dilapidated outbuilding. Chickens roamed freely all about, heads bobbing with each step. The only thing new about the place was the single black wire that descended into the house through a card-boarded and duct-taped opening in the wall.

Mike returned from a hushed argument with his wife. "That's Hazel," he said with a jab of his thumb toward the surly woman before escorting Emma to a picnic table. "Hope you don't mind eatin' out here." He glanced inexplicably toward the now empty doorway through which Hazel had disappeared. Emma felt a frisson of anxiety. Would the woman reappear holding a shotgun?

Mike leaned his hunting rifle against the table next to where he sat, but rose back to his feet and held out his hand, beckoning Emma to take a seat across from him. The boy perched with his rifle atop a wood pile just outside the leaning, carcass-draped structure.

Emma started when the cabin's screen door slammed behind Hazel, hands full but unarmed. She wore a faded print dress over her shapeless and unattractive figure, and dusty brown boots left untied and loose. Her graying and unwashed hair was pulled back messily into a blue rubber band. A scratched and dented metal plate and a fork bounced on the table in front of Emma. "Hazel!" her husband said for reasons unknown. She scraped a heap of eggs onto the plate with a *splat*. Emma gobbled up the food, which was gone in seconds.

"See?" Mike said. "She didn't even wait for the blessin'. She was starvin'."

"We'll all be starvin' soon enough," Hazel replied, retrieving the empty plate and utensil as Emma wiped her mouth and started her silent clock. Whatever she did with the Barnwells—left them alone, slept with the husband in exchange for provisions, or killed them all—she would have to do it in the next two hours. They would still be ambulatory through first symptoms, and still have ready access to their guns. *Unless...* The voice, however, offered no helpful solutions to the Barnwell problem. Emma could kill Mike then Hazel, or Hazel then Mike, but Ellis killed her in both permutations.

"I feel like I've *seen* you somewheres," Mike said. Emma's anxiety skyrocketed. She began measuring and deepening her breathing. She slowly lowered her hands and pinned them to the wooden planks beneath her thighs.

"Mike!" came Hazel's call from the door. She stared down at an open laptop, whose screen illuminated her creased and splotchy face. "*Mike!*" Emma quivered and shook from a rush of adrenaline. Her anxiety was a weakness, much like Uninfecteds' emotions, and she struggled to overcome it. The sagging new wire that rose from the house looked jury-rigged, running to a tree, not a telephone pole, and on down the hill. But if they had phone service, they had Internet.

Mike headed for their hovel. As an afterthought, he reached back for his rifle. The boy gripped his own rifle with both hands.

Emma let the adrenaline do its thing. She snatched her backpack and ran. *"Dad!"* Emma weaved through trees, rocks, and brush as she flew down the hill expecting at any moment to hear and possibly feel rifle shots at her back. At the bottom of the hill, she leapt over a muddy swale and landed hard, bloodying both hands and knees. Her heart was racing and her muscles were aquiver, but she began climbing in a frenzied assault of the far slope. Sweat poured from every pore. Her lungs burned. She barely contained the primal scream that fought to escape her clenched jaws. By the time she crested the ridge, her fingernails bled from grasping at branches and jagged outcroppings.

She lay behind a tree, breathing hard, watching, and listening. She went from overheated to chilled in damp clothing as it grew darker. No one followed. No one shot at her. They probably were burying her plate and utensils and obsessively washing their hands, and most likely wouldn't fall ill. But they knew who she was.

Double back and cut the wires. If they were going to call the cops, she argued with the voice in her thoughts, they would have done it already. And maybe they'd fear being quarantined if they reported their exposure. Or they could want to keep their location secret. *Or, they could be out hunting me like a deer.*

Chapter 12

THE SHENANDOAH VALLEY, VIRGINIA
Infection Date 46, 2400 GMT (8:00 p.m. Local)

The news on the Millers' TV was unrelentingly bad. Every day brought new towns and cities in which the infection had just broken out. And every day, the cities infected in preceding days yielded some version of the same report. "Authorities in Boston have imposed a twenty-four-hour curfew, although it remains to be seen who will be enforcing it. Police units have barricaded themselves into a handful of precinct stations. The few clinics and firehouses still in contact with the outside world are denying refuge to panicked masses trapped inside the quarantined city. Terrifying reports of roving bands of rampaging Infecteds are too numerous to recount, but CNN is unable to confirm any of the accounts firsthand as all contact with our correspondents on the ground has been lost." The pictures from a high-speed, low-altitude overflight were of a city in flames. Black smoke rose through a gray haze lit by occasional flashes, presumably from guns. Try as he might, Noah couldn't visualize trying to protect his family in the middle of a hell like that.

Just after sunset, the living room of the main house was lit only by the flickering screen of the big TV. His family's faces were masks of intense focus, as if something they might see in the news reports—some small detail or anecdote—might one day save their lives. Natalie even took notes, but Noah had no idea of what. Chloe hugged her knees, which in turn pressed a pillow to her chest in a fragile cocoon from which she watched the horrors wide-eyed. Jake repeatedly flicked the selector switch on the rifle he'd just cleaned from safe to fire and back—*click, click, click.*

"So, Boston is gone," Natalie said, keeping track on her pad. "And so are Paris and Montreal. And just in the last *day*," she consulted her notes, "it's broken out in Toronto, Brussels, Frankfurt, Toulouse, Providence, Kolkata, Buffalo, Calais, Amsterdam, Bangkok…"

The familiar "Breaking News" splash interrupted the broadcast yet again, and Noah braced himself. "This just in. CNN regrets to inform its viewers that the first signs of outbreak have reached our newsroom in Detroit. To repeat, it now appears confirmed that *Pandoravirus* has broken out in Detroit, Michigan."

"It's everywhere," Natalie said, tossing her notepad onto the coffee table. "There's no stopping it. Soon, there won't even be anywhere to run."

"Mo-o-om?" Chloe cried out in fear.

Thirteen-year-old Jake loaded a magazine into his assault rifle. "Not in the house, Jake," Noah admonished. His son ejected the magazine. *Click, click, click.*

"I'm gonna go check the fences," Noah said, rising.

"I'll come too," added a restless Jake, clambering to his feet and again slapping the magazine into his AR. Natalie objected, but Noah assured her it was all right. What he didn't say was that Jake needed some time spent in the darkness, in the woods, with his rifle, getting acclimated. They all did.

Once outside in the brisk night air, both pulled the charging handles of their AR-15s back to chamber rounds with nearly simultaneous *clacks*, but kept their weapons safed. Noah headed past the barn for the fence line. Jake followed too closely, so Noah had him hold back until he could barely make out his son's dark profile. He could, however, hear each crunching step taken by his heavy-footed and ungainly boy.

Noah saw human profiles in every shadow. Kneeling men. Crouching men. Men pressing their backs to tree trunks. Men slithering beneath bushes whose leaves rustled in the intermittent breeze. But he knew that what he really saw were his fears.

The gently sloping ground of the compound was still. They completed their circumnavigation of the unbroken fence having seen and heard no one and nothing. But after Noah's eyes were fully adjusted to the darkness, the main house looked lit up like a Christmas tree in spite of their energy conservation measures. When they returned, Noah locked the door and lowered both sets of storm shutters: inside and outside.

The noise of the electric motors startled Chloe. "Jeez!"

Noah rejoined them in front of the TV as the shades' motors all shut off in rapid succession. The sealed room seemed tomblike. It felt less like they were shutting out the rest of the world than that they were imprisoning themselves, both physically and emotionally. As if it would be possible to wall themselves off from what was happening. Noah couldn't help but wonder how many plans like his had already failed in Asia, and were currently failing in Europe?

"It feels like we're living in a cave," Chloe said. She eyed the shutters covering what had previously been tall and welcoming windows, then wrapped her skinny arms around her knees, which hid the lower half of her face.

The only sound was the low monotone of the TV newswoman. "The White House has resisted calls from members of Congress, now back home in their districts during the temporary recess, for much more forceful attempts to enforce quarantines. Demonstrations in Chicago, St. Louis, Orlando, Dallas, and Phoenix called for shoot-to-kill orders and employment of heavier military firepower to contain the spread of *Pandoravirus* carriers, but Pres. Stoddard has said only that all options remain on the table. As it stands, the only advice given by DHS to citizens who confront an Infected is to flee, phone in a report of the contact, and fight only as a last resort if necessary for self-defense."

"Why did you close the shutters?" Natalie asked. She had been staring at Noah since he'd sat down in the plush armchair: *his* seat in the family's hierarchal seating plan. "Did you see anything?"

The kids listened; rapt. "*No*. It was just...the house was pretty bright. I figured lowering the shutters—just at night—might help with that some."

Chloe said, "That's the truth, right?"

"Of *course*."

"'Cause parents lie to kids all the time when something bad's about to happen. Justin's parents told his little brother and sister that SED was like the chickenpox. Like it somehow makes it better when they find out the truth."

"No, Chloe. I wasn't..."

"Just tell us the truth, okay? I don't mean about the shutters. I mean... whatever's gonna happen. Whatever's coming. 'Cause if we can't trust you to do that, we can't ever relax, ya know? I mean, like, we'll always have to be ready 'cause we'll never know."

Wow, Noah thought. That sounded more mature than almost anything his daughter had ever said. He glanced at Natalie, then said, "Okay Chloe. Jake. You're right. You need to know. I'll...*we'll* always tell you the truth. Promise."

"Okay," Chloe said. Both she and Jake sat up and turned toward Noah as if he'd demanded their attention, which he most certainly had not. "What *is* coming?"

Noah opened his mouth to say, *I don't fucking know!* But he looked at Natalie, who listened to him every bit as intently as the kids, and caught himself. "My best guess," he struggled in saying, "is that the disease is going to spread across the whole country, just like it did in Asia and seems to be doing in Canada and in Europe." That sounded like the beginning of some significant observation, but Noah meant it to be the end of one. His family, however, awaited his plan. The one in which they all survived unscathed.

"Uhm, so the violence seems worst when the infection first sweeps through. If we can ride that out, hopefully things will die down. Isabel told me that a significant percentage, like, I dunno, five, ten, fifteen percent of the Infecteds who turn are highly dysfunctional and won't last too long. After they...die off—get killed—then the other Infecteds maybe won't be so crazy. And they also won't be able to infect you only by breathing after a couple of weeks. If we can keep to ourselves up here long enough, maybe some form of peaceful coexistence might be achieved. Maybe we can join up with surviving Uninfecteds. Or maybe even there'll be peaceful, mixed communities of Infecteds *and* Uninfecteds."

Jake said, "But between now and then...?"

"There will be violence." It was Natalie who had answered. She rose, headed to the hall closet, and returned with her own assault rifle, empty though it was, which she cradled across her yoga pants before turning up the TV news and grabbing her notepad.

Click, click, click.

Chapter 13

Isabel, Rick, and Brandon wore full personal protective equipment as they climbed out of the armored Humvee on the working-class city street. The EMTs emerged from the ambulance in front of them, and soldiers from the two Humvees behind them, including Vasquez and his men, all similarly clad, head-to-toe, in impermeable one-piece suits and hoods, gloves, disposable boots, and face masks and shields. The machine gunner atop the vehicle behind them swiveled his large gun toward the front door of the row house.

Residents of the mostly African-American neighborhood stood in their doorways with cloth covering their noses and mouths, keeping their distance. Someone had called about a possible infection breaking out in the unpainted, narrow, two-story home, at whose front door troops and the medical team gathered.

One of the EMTs pounded loudly on the front door with his fist, then again, then shouted, "New Haven EMS! Open up! Wellness check!"

The soldiers all held their rifles at the ready. When the door cracked open, the muzzles rose to it, then lowered several inches. A child peered out. Her pupils were popped and black.

Everyone backed off the porch without being told. "I'm gonna have to ask you," the EMT said, "to come outside." The girl stared back but did nothing. The paramedic stood with one foot on the porch and the other two steps below. He leaned over, rested his forearm on his raised thigh, and said calmly, "Sweetie, we're not gonna hurt you. But you're gonna have to come out here."

The little girl, maybe six or seven, unchained the door and took a few steps out onto the porch. She was filthy, her nightgown covered in what had to be dried vomit and diarrhea. She jumped when she heard the crinkling sound as the EMT unfolded a clear plastic suit—in a child's size—and then coaxed the girl into it. It had vaguely identifiable arms, legs, torso, and hood. He instructed the girl on how to breathe through what looked something like a snorkel's mouthpiece that vented through filters to the outside air. He then zipped the suit closed, stopping several times to calm the girl by reassuring her that everything would be okay.

But will it? Isabel wondered quietly. Once the Infecteds were all rounded up, the stage was set for a change of policy. Was this the first step in some new Holocaust? Had lowly German soldiers been tricked into roundups of Jews by the fiction that everything would turn out all right?

"Is there anybody else in the house?" the EMT asked, his hand on the girl's plastic-encased shoulder. When she nodded with a rustling sound, he led her off the porch, taking special care to support her as she awkwardly descended the few steps. A sergeant led his three men into the house. Vasquez and his men, there only to escort Isabel and her team, took up positions just inside the front door to support the soldiers clearing the home.

Bam. Bam-bam-bam-bam. The windows lit with each round fired. *Bam-bam-bam. Bam. Bam-bam-bam.* After the brief spasm of gunfire there was silence.

"Clear!" "Clear!" "Clear!" came staggered shouts. The army team streamed back out the door and doubled over, or leaned back against the front wall of the house, or clung to a post by the front steps.

The sergeant yelled out toward the EMTs now gathered at the back of their ambulance, who took turns giving comfort to the little girl in the plastic suit. "We need a body disposal unit!"

The little girl seemed uninterested in the happenings in the house. An EMT shouted back, "How many bodies?"

The army sergeant, who had sunk to the steps and seemed exhausted, exaggerated his shrug so that the gesture would be visible inside his PPE. "Dunno! Twelve? Fourteen? Fifteen?"

A middle-aged woman from down the block shouted, "They took in their cousins from Providence!" She'd uncovered her mouth to speak, but put the scarf back over her face when finished. The soldiers politely urged her to step back off the property, and she complied. "They all get shot?" she asked.

The sergeant took it as an accusation. "No! No, no, no! Most were already dead. Stacked up in the back hall. The ones we shot came flyin' at us with bedposts and tire irons." In a quieter voice to Rick and Vasquez, the sergeant said, "It was a fuckin' horror show in there." He was rattled.

In the distance Isabel heard more gunfire. Another house. More Infecteds carted away in zip-lock baggies. Heads turned to look that way. The sergeant got a call on the radio and ordered his men to mount up. When Rick got off his own radio, Isabel asked, "What's going on?" as they watched the ambulance and Humvee depart.

"Them? Same old, same old. Too many holes in the dike; not enough fingers. But we just got orders to get the hell outta New Haven. Shit must be hitting the fan."

"Where are we headed?" Brandon asked.

Rick looked at Brandon, then Isabel. "New York. *City*," he clarified.

Chapter 14

THE SHENANDOAH VALLEY, VIRGINIA
Infection Date 48, 2300 GMT (7:00 p.m. Local)

The terrain had grown so difficult that Emma was forced to stick to the two-lane state highway. That proved to be a mistake. She heard the car approaching from behind, but resisted the urge to run or to look back at it for fear of appearing apprehensive.

A pickup truck slowed to a stop beside her as its passenger window lowered. It had police lights on its cab, and a sheriff's shield on its door. The driver wore a white cowboy hat, a badge, and a pistol in a holster. "Evenin', ma'am."

Emma didn't risk any reply.

"Sheriff Walcott. I take it from your gear you're just passin' through our fine county." She couldn't tell if it was a question, or a command. "Cat got yer tongue?" Emma knew it was best not to say anything, but that was proving difficult. "What's yer name?"

"Emma," she replied, and to her surprise he didn't demand her last name.

"Well, Miss Emma," Walcott said, "we ain't takin' in anybody new these days. You keep headin' on in this direction a few more hours and you'll be clear outta my jurisdiction. That way we can stay friendly, like now. But you stop in this county—even if you get taken in by one of our more charitable households, bein' as how innocent lookin' you are and all—and we won't be so friendly anymore, you and me. Understand me, young lady?"

"You won't see me again," Emma replied, intending that to be true. She would make it a point to see him first. She would ensure that he remained oblivious to any future plans she might have for him...or for the shotgun in the rack behind him, or the pistol on his hip.

Walcott slapped the side of his truck and said, "Then you have a nice day." He touched the brim of his hat before driving off.

When the taillights receded, Emma took deep breaths. She loosened her grip on the screwdriver she now carried in the cavernous pocket of the camouflaged hunting jacket she had stolen from the clothes line of the Barnwell family. When the lights in their hovel had been extinguished for the night, she had cut their phone line with the sharpened blade of her screwdriver. The jacket, hanging amid the small animal carcasses, was all that she had risked taking. They kept their weapons handy, especially their boy Ellis.

She flexed and then rubbed her hand. Her grip on the screwdriver's handle had been so tight that its imprint creased her palm, and her fingers cramped. Rather than continue her walk down the side of the highway or risk a cross-country hike as darkness deepened, Emma decided to make camp. She was getting close and would spend the next day checking out the town and searching for food and weapons. Noah and his family would be armed.

Chapter 15

The irregularly-shaped and oddly-colored twin American Copper Buildings in Murray Hill were a strange choice of headquarters for the defense of New York City. But the new luxury condo building had several advantages, said the NYPD lieutenant leading Isabel, Rick, Brandon, and their army team to the fitness center. The complex of two buildings was connected by a three-story, elevated skybridge, which Isabel supposed might allow rapid redeployment...or escape. And NYU's medical center was next door, as was the East 34th Street Heliport and the East River Ferry landing on the other side of FDR Drive.

Rick and Isabel exchanged glances. These stout defenders had provided themselves multiple "avenues of egress," Rick had called it, which Isabel remembered because of the importance Rick had accorded the concept. Since most of the buildings' affluent tenants had already fled the city, most of the apartments were empty. Quartering troops, she recalled from a White House NSC briefing, was unconstitutional. *But who cares?*

The entire position was "anchored," their guide said, by the 69th Regiment Armory, home to the New York National Guard's 1st Battalion, 69th Infantry—a 600-person light infantry battalion—of the 27th Infantry Brigade, 42nd Infantry Division. There were lots of numbered units— battalions, brigades, divisions—but China, the Koreas, and Vietnam also had battalions, brigades, and divisions, also numbered, and they had been overrun.

The gymnasium ceiling was high in order to accommodate a climbing wall, creating a cavernous, echoing space. In front was a projection screen displaying a video test pattern washed out by the room's bright lighting. The place was abuzz with the conversations of dozens of soldiers, policemen, firemen, and civilians seated in a semi-circle of chairs facing the screen and the cameras pointing back in their direction. Vasquez and company peeled off when they found other camo-clad soldiers milling about the high stools of a juice bar. Isabel, Rick, and Brandon were escorted to the front row of unstacked metal chairs.

"But if people start throwing themselves into the rivers," said a Coast Guard officer seated behind Isabel, "we'll need those ferries. We gotta get 'em out of the water quickly. Hypothermia sets in fast below sixty degrees."

"Even assuming," the civilian next to him whispered, "we can muster crews, the people they rescue will be Uninfected *and* Infected. We'd expose people in the close quarters."

"Are you proposing that we suspend water rescues?"

"I'm just saying I wouldn't know where to put the people we rescue. And if they jump into the water, it's probably because they just had a close encounter with a fucking Infected."

The test image on the projection screen in front of the climbing wall was replaced by a view Isabel instantly recognized. It was the gold presidential seal on the back of the empty leather swivel chair at the head of the conference table in the Situation Room a hundred feet beneath the White House. The lights in their exercise room were dimmed, causing the picture on the screen to sharpen. Conversations subsided.

A man appeared at the edge of the picture as he slipped into his dark suit jacket and sat. It was President Stoddard. The table around him rapidly filled with generals in camouflage and cabinet secretaries in blue jeans and dress shirts, most out of frame. Everyone in the Situation Room looked not at the camera, but off to the side at the screen on which, Isabel assumed, their view of the New York exercise room was displayed.

"Let's get this started," said Stoddard, whose voice was eerily expansive when boomed through ceiling speakers meant more for bass-heavy spin classes than end-of-the-world videoconferences.

Isabel heard whispering from behind her. "I always knew my last official act on Earth would be to attend a fucking meeting."

"How about an update on your status," Stoddard thundered from his Olympus.

A man introduced himself as the Administrator of Region II, Federal Emergency Management Agency. "There have been no reports of

Pandoravirus yet in the City. The nearest confirmed outbreaks are in Norwalk, Connecticut, and Woodbury, New York. There are fears of infection among first responders in Greenwich, and on Fishers Island, Plum Island, and Long Island after boats fleeing Connecticut and Rhode Island crossed the Sound, but we're still awaiting definitive word."

The president asked the man, "Are you standing by your recommendation against calling for a general evacuation of the City?"

He was clearly uncomfortable in replying. "Evacuate them to *where*, sir? If someone could answer that question, I might change my advice. Otherwise, they're better off staying put, where at least they've got shelter, clean water, electricity, and *some* supplies. I would note, however, sir—as is visible from all the media coverage—that there's a substantial self-evacuation already under way."

Someone somewhere changed the video displayed on their and presumably the National Security Council's screen to show the parked taillights on the Verrazano-Narrows Bridge. It then switched to an identical scene at the entrance to the Holland Tunnel. Then the Lincoln Tunnel. Then stretched out across the Hudson River atop the George Washington and Tappan Zee Bridges. When the picture, taken from a plane or a drone, zoomed in on the last image, both lanes of the bridge had been devoted to west-to-east traffic. A steady line of pedestrians could be seen passing cars, vans, and trucks.

"We estimate," the FEMA man said, "that close to two million residents—about a quarter of the city's population—have managed to evacuate to New Jersey and points west and south. But most won't make it far. Some locals are donating a few gallons of gas per vehicle just to keep 'em heading on outta their communities. And the military is flying gasoline and diesel to the roadsides of I-95, I-80, and I-78, but there's no way they'll be able to keep that much traffic moving. And from what I hear, each of those refueling points is about one thrown rock away from being a riot as people grow increasingly desperate."

"We've also had," came the deep, off-camera voice that Isabel instantly recognized as Marine Gen. Browner, Chairman of the Joint Chiefs of Staff, "over two dozen reported multiple-fatality incidents in New Jersey and New York as locals clash with refugees. Apparently, everyone has learned from the news coverage that refugees are their main threat. They not only carry the contagion, they're living in unsanitary, crowded encampments along the highways where their transportation crapped out on them, and they're fighting each other and locals for supplies. That sparks vigilante counterattacks. Then, of course, come the Infected rampages that follow the *actual* arrival of the virus. We're at most a day or two away from facing that same situation as in New England, but on a much, much larger scale along the I-95 corridor."

"Do you have any plans to deal with that violence?" Stoddard asked in what sounded like an irritated tone.

"We could try to *stop* population migration, rather than facilitate it. Shut down every highway, road, and bridge coming out of the Northeast and upper Midwest."

"But you can't stop it," Stoddard replied. "Your own models tell us that. You shut down every road, they walk through the woods. Killing people only slows it down, and not by very much."

"Doing nothing," Browner shot back, less restrained than Isabel had ever heard, "is not exactly planning for victory. We need time. Pearl River needs time. You heard Dr. Nielsen, sir. Even *days* would help. They've just begun their trials."

"I'm not going to murder thousands, tens of thousands of innocent civilians just to buy Pearl River another few days. You told me your men could hold that Pfizer lab, so *hold* it. It's not like you're facing Nazi panzers. Your men are going to be shooting unorganized, untrained, and largely unarmed *Pandoravirus* victims, many of whom are mentally degraded and physically weakened by the disease."

"But they're not *all* mentally degraded," Browner replied. "And they're unorganized, untrained, and unarmed...for *now*."

Isabel saw heads around the exercise room turn to seatmates. They hadn't contemplated that Infecteds might raise armies against us. But Browner had. He was dying to unleash bombing like in those New York woods, up to and including the use of nukes where targets warranted. And in her heart of hearts, Isabel knew he might be right. This may be the last clear chance to alter the extinction projected by academics' models.

"Your orders," Pres. Stoddard said, "are to hold the Pfizer lab, and the other hardpoints and key blocking positions that I've expressly authorized. Period."

"Sir," Browner said, dropping any pretense of deference other than that first word, "I've got the better part of three brigades, operating at battalion level down to special forces teams, scattered all to hell across what is now Infected territory in New England. Some are establishing perimeters around bastions of uninfected civilians that we're trying to keep resupplied. Others are just barely able to provide for their own force protection and are operating largely independently, although sometimes in conjunction with local authorities, including civilian militias. I cannot, sir, assure you that I know what rules of engagement they're all employing. What restrictions they're imposing on the use of force. Or exactly what they plan to do as every one of their situations deteriorates rapidly."

"What you mean is that they may be engaging in eradication campaigns even as we speak. The very policy I expressly ordered you *not* to employ."

"What I'm saying is that they're fighting for their lives every way they know how. They're fighting violence by Infecteds *and* Uninfecteds. They and the civilians they're protecting are trying to avoid exposure, but when, tragically, their self-isolation fails, they're having to choose from among nothing but terrible options. And they're besieged by pleas for help from fellow countrymen: local authorities, nearby units, civilians for whom our men—*your* men, sir—are their last and only hope. You put men under that kind of threat and stress, sir, and you get breakdowns of order and discipline. Not everywhere, but increasingly, as plans fail and supplies run low."

Everyone in New York was presumably getting their first glimpse into the awful dilemma faced by the dovish president, as posed by the hawks' champion, Browner. But to Isabel, it all sounded like a continuation of the debate that had raged since the beginning. To eradicate, or not to eradicate.

The NSC meeting in the Situation Room returned its attention to New York, which had momentarily been forgotten.

A National Guard general reported on the high level of readiness of his troops. Isabel tried to pay attention. The 27th Infantry Brigade Combat Team, which had been withdrawn from upstate, would mount the principal defense of the city. "The 27th fields two light infantry battalions: 1st Battalion, 69th Infantry, is dug in along 287 west of White Plains to the Hudson River; 2nd Battalion, 108th Infantry, is to the east of White Plains all the way to the Sound at Port Chester and Rye. That's an awfully long line for twelve hundred men to defend—over thirteen miles—even with fire support from 1st Battalion, 258th Field Artillery, which has a mix of 105- and 155-mm towed howitzers. It was the 258th, sir, registering those guns that caused the stir this morning."

"Yeah, can we not practice shooting artillery," the president said, "in the middle of populated areas?"

Off-camera, Isabel heard Browner explain how you needed a few spotter rounds to zero the guns in on pre-planned targets. "You don't want 'em firing for effect inaccurately in the middle of suburbia."

"No, general, I don't want that either." Stoddard had grown far less patient and more frustrated than when Isabel had last seen him just two weeks earlier.

"Since that line north of the City, Sir, will be porous, we're gonna use 2nd Squadron, 101st Cavalry, as a rapid reaction force to close any breaches."

Isabel shot Rick a questioning look. Imperceptible to all except her—and Brandon—Rick shook his head. That line wouldn't hold.

"We're also just now getting 1st Battalion, 182nd Infantry, handed off from the Massachusetts Guard. But they were pretty beat up in the Brockton, Pawtucket, and Middletown scrapes, and they've suffered desertions the farther they've pulled back from their home state, so they're down to about two-thirds strength at four hundred men. They're setting up to defend a secondary line along the northern approaches to Manhattan at the Henry Hudson, Broadway, and University Heights Bridges. They're also tasked with repelling any small boat or raft crossings in between those bridges."

The general described the defense of the Washington and Alexander Hamilton Bridges over the Harlem River by three numbered military police companies: "the 105th, 107th, and 222nd." They always referred to their units by numbers, as if the president or anyone else knew who they were talking about. *Oh, the Fightin' 222nd. Of course!* "Everything from Yankee Stadium on down will be tasked to special weapons teams of the NYPD and backed up by mobile provisional units drawn from the 101st Signal Battalion, 204th Engineer Battalion, and 427th Brigade Support Battalion."

"Dr. Miller?" said the president. Isabel rose, and all eyes turned to the previously anonymous tiny figure in camouflage and webbing. "We miss your company, but we've read your reports. Based on what you've seen, any chance that a more organized defense like the one we've prepared around Manhattan might keep the virus out of the city?"

She glanced down at a glum Rick before making an apologetic face. "In all probability, sir? No."

Her answer drew audible huffs of consternation from the exhausted men in the exercise room, who bolted forward in their seats prepared to rebut the impudent critic. What the hell did *she* know about anything? "Glad to see," the president said, "that we can still count on candor from our lone, plainspoken academic. Would you care to elaborate?"

"Well, sir, I have no doubt they can stop crossings at bridges and tunnels. *If,*" she turned back to the room full of glaring eyes, "your people are willing to kill men, women, and children, day and night, week after week, month after month, with no end in sight. But the spread of the virus is anisotropic. It follows people's migratory routes. And people—Infected *and* Uninfected—seek out population centers where there may be resources like shelter, food, clean water, medicine. Plus, the road-rail network leads them straight into towns and cities. Millions of people are trying to make it down those arteries into or through New York City. Some are going to carry the virus, and some of *them* are going to make it into Manhattan no matter what we do. Swimming across a river. Hiding under a tarp in a resupply shipment. Some act of mercy by defenders or ingenuity by Infecteds. Somehow, some way, they will make it in."

"You *almost*," said the red-faced National Guard general, "sound like you're saying we shouldn't even *try*. Why kill all those *poor* Infecteds when it's not going to work?"

Isabel didn't answer. She turned to look at the president and left the issue hanging. To kill, or not to kill, remained *the* question.

* * * *

The building manager led their entire Pentagon contingent to the fourteenth floor. Rick wanted to keep everyone together. "I could get into real trouble for this," the manager muttered as he unlocked one of the apartments. Vasquez's two men whistled on seeing the luxury accommodations, and raced like children to claim the better bedroom by leaping onto its bed. "You're gonna see to it," the manager said to Rick, "that your people don't trash the places or break or steal anything, right?"

"I'll inspect the apartments before we hand the keys back to you," Rick promised.

Everyone got their own bedroom, and Isabel, as the only female, got an apartment all to herself. It was right next door to Rick. Her view of the river at night was beautiful. It was almost possible to forget what was going on. She stripped out of her filthy uniform, tossed all her dirty clothes into a washing machine, and walked naked across the luxurious hardwood floors to the sumptuous master bath. She stood under the rain shower for what had to be forty-five minutes. When she emerged, she tossed her clothes into the dryer, wrapped herself in a thick towel, and blow dried her hair. She rocked her head back. Her long, thick hair on her bare shoulders made her feel feminine again. The smells were of shampoo, and soap, and makeup, and perfume. Everything was back to normal, for however long that would last.

There was a rapping on the door. Isabel cringed. That wasn't long enough. She tightened the towel and looked through the peephole at a freshly washed Rick. When she opened the door, she saw that he held a bottle of red wine and two glasses.

"Oh, you're not dressed. Should I come back?"

Isabel pulled him inside, kicked the door closed, rose onto tip-toes, wrapped her arms around his neck, and kissed him with an open mouth. Her towel came loose. She let it fall. Rick put the wine down and picked Isabel up. He looked around, saw the sofa in the living room, and headed for it. "No. There," she said, pointing toward the bedroom.

He laid her on the plush sheets as if she might break. She willed her prudish hands not to cover herself as he hovered above her. She tried to pull him lower. "Slow down," Rick said softly, kneeling on the bed beside her, taking off her blouse and looking up and down her naked body. When his T-shirt hit the floor, she again tried to pull his hard chest and flat stomach on top of her. "Wait, wait," he said. "*Slo-o-owly.*"

"*Mmm!*" she groaned in frustration. She followed his eyes down her pale skin. "All these cuts and scrapes and bruises on my arms and legs—I don't normally look like this."

He leaned over her and she closed her eyes, but still she didn't feel the warmth of his skin or press of his weight. "You look perfect," he whispered into her ear before his warm mouth found her neck. She gasped in slow motion. He smelled delicious. His rough hands wrapped almost all the way around her ribcage.

"Am I too skinny?" she asked as her eyes floated open and sunk closed before she flung her head back with a groan upon his further exploration.

"You're exactly what I imagined," he whispered, kissing her neck and down to the bony hollow between her breasts.

"So you've been...you've been picturing me. Without clothes."

"Every five minutes since that flight to Siberia." Her hand reached out and found him. He must've been telling the truth.

His mouth roamed her chest, and she drew her next breath so abruptly he thought he'd hurt her, and he hesitated. "No. Don't stop. Keep doing that." She heard his belt buckle, then he pulled away. "Forget about the boots. Come *on.*"

As his body settled onto hers, their longing found an outlet. He entered her, she convulsed, and he froze again. "I'm not gonna break!" she said, wrapping her arms and legs around him and taking control. Her ecstasy came quickly, and often. It was far, far more amazing than she had ever dreamed it would be. And afterwards, her sleep in his arms was semi-comatose.

Chapter 16

THE SHENANDOAH VALLEY, VIRGINIA
Infection Date 50, 1300 GMT (9:00 a.m. Local)

Emma broke camp early for the final leg of her journey. The signs read, "POSTED: Trespassers Will Be Shot." Vertical silver stripes were painted on trees all along the state highway. She decided to take the overgrown old road up to the main house, not the ridge road, which left nowhere to hide. She was sore, and the long climb up the hill taxed her aching muscles nearly to the limit. They contracted as if shivering on a cold day, but it was warm. She was dry from dehydration when she should have been soaked through from exertion. She had surely lost a dangerous amount of weight. She was tired, not having slept well on the hard ground in the eleven days, mostly on foot and trekking cross-country, since her court-ordered release from the NIH hospital in Bethesda. And she was acutely hungry and thirsty, problems she needed to address before nightfall.

A high-pitched buzzing came from overhead. Emma instinctively took cover. It sounded like a toy lawnmower, crisscrossing the pale blue sky above the treetops. Then it was gone. She rose, hoisted her backpack onto her shoulders, and continued her climb. By the time she saw the tall, newly-erected cyclone fencing around the main house, her vision was blurry. She was on her last reserves of energy.

A high-tech windmill turned atop the hill behind the newly renovated stone house. Emma couldn't see anyone, but they were there. And they were surely armed. It was *she* who had warned them to arm themselves.

She edged around the fence at a distance, losing track of time with each stop. Close to shutting down. She spotted Natalie. Her blond hair shone brightly in the direct sunlight, but it was now cut short. Her sister-in-law went into one of four shipping containers painted in camouflage. Emma opened her eyes and ducked when Chloe burst out of the barn. Her niece, also with shorn blond hair, was in a stoop as she chased a chicken, first one way, then the other, the whole time asking the chicken to stop even though it could not know what she was saying. Or possibly Emma hallucinated that, given how bizarre it would be to talk to poultry. When Chloe caught her prey, she held the wriggling, flapping bird at arm's length, grimacing as she returned to the barn with it.

Where are Noah and Jake? They could be outside the fence patrolling. *We should backtrack and swing wide around the fence.* Emma complied without internal debate, too weak to argue, constantly on the look-out for danger. An hour later, she found the old hunting cabin far up in the hills above the main house. It too had been thoroughly rebuilt, but after a long while of stuporous observation the voice roused her and she concluded that it was unoccupied. A chair strangely sat right in front of the door. She moved it aside and entered.

After a quick inspection of the single room, Emma feasted on the cabin's stocks of breakfast cereal and beef jerky, guzzled water straight out of the sink's faucet, and unfolded one of the cabin's six cots. She put the butcher knife she had found in the kitchen under her pillow and lay down for a rest.

When she woke, it was nearly dusk. It had been a mistake to go to sleep in an unexplored place.

Take another look around before sunset. Emma headed back down toward the main house with the butcher knife in hand. Half way there, she heard distant talking. No, not distant. Hushed. Giggling. Nearby. Emma approached cautiously.

Her niece and nephew sat on a steep embankment twenty yards away. They had military-style rifles. Emma crept to a higher and closer vantage, taking care with each step to avoid brush or pebbles, holding her knife in her teeth when she needed both hands. They sat side-by-side passing a vape pen back and forth. "I can't *believe* you bought that much pot!" Chloe said.

Jacob coughed out a huge plume of vapor. "I cashed in those bonds Mom and Dad gave us. My life savings! Probably worthless now anyway." Emma inched into position above her laughing, inattentive niece and nephew. *Are their rifles loaded?* asked the voice. Probably, she guessed. *A round chambered?* Maybe not. Safeties definitely on, knowing the care Noah would've taken in teaching them. Each impediment to firing would afford an attacker precious seconds. Emma could kick one of the two teens over the cliff on which they perched—preferably Jacob—then yank Chloe's short ponytail backwards to expose her throat. If Chloe was quick, she would shoot Emma. But they weren't expecting an attack, and Chloe would be shocked when she saw that the attacker was her aunt. Plus, they would be buzzed from the pot.

This was her best chance yet to get a firearm, but her heart was pounding and hands vibrating. She was ready to act, but she struggled to control the rush of adrenaline. Losing herself to the frenzy could lead to mistakes. *Like getting killed!* added the voice.

Despite the voice's warning, she coiled herself for the leap with both feet down the hill and right onto the center of Jacob's back, but froze— *Stop!*—when she heard what Jake said next. "I swear to God I think Aunt Emma is up there. I've been looking for her with the drone ever since that college boy got infected, and when I flew over the cabin, the chair that Dad put in front of the door had been moved. Does that freak you out, thinking she might be up there?"

"No. She's family. We are all supposed to stick together. It's our family against everybody else, like Dad said."

Jacob was nodding. Emma hesitated. *If they think that way,* came the voice, *they might prove useful.* They might agree to a contract. Emma needed time to think about what that agreement would say, and how it could be enforced.

Wisps of vapor escaped Chloe's lips with each word. "What do you think they're really like?" She coughed. Emma began edging away, retracing her path of approach. "I mean do you think they're, I dunno, *better* than us, or not as good?"

"Not as good," Jacob said, "of course, 'cause, I mean, they have brain damage. Our same brains, only parts don't work right."

"Or are *different*," Chloe said. Her head jerked around. She stared straight at Emma.

Emma darted away. Chloe shouted, "*Look!*" but no shots rang out.

Instead of returning to the cabin, which they might go check, Emma allowed her adrenaline to propel her on the run down the old road all the way to the state highway. There, she lay totally still behind cover till her breathing recovered and night fell, then climbed the fence without snagging clothes or cutting skin and headed toward the town she had studied from a distance the day before. That's where weapons would be. There was no traffic on the dark road. Emma paused to drink bottled water and eat the dry cereal from her pocket. Up ahead was a mailbox. A driveway traversed the ditch and led through a padlocked gate.

"Nichols," read the name on the mailbox. It held maybe a day's worth of junk mail, meaning mail was still being delivered, and it was checked regularly at this house. Emma climbed the gate and began the march up the mountain alongside the drive.

When she came to the house, it was lit only by a fireplace and candles. But in the darkness, it stood out even at a distance. The windows were all open. Emma saw movement, possibly just the shadow of a branch that occasionally dipped in the wind, but also possibly a sentry. She lay still and saw nothing more until she noticed over time that lights were being extinguished, presumably as people went to bed. She edged closer.

There were no fences, lookouts, or patrols. Voices inside argued. A screen door slammed shut. Emma ducked behind a broad tree. A woman, or a boy, Emma couldn't tell from stolen peeks, went into a dark and sloppily erected shed, which had no doors. A rifle was propped on the outside of what smelled like a latrine. Emma made straight for it and got all the way to the outhouse wall before a teenage boy said, "Who's there?"

Emma raised the rifle high into the air over the top of the irregular boards of the privacy wall and brought it down onto the boy's head.

The rifle butt landed enough of a blow to send him sprawling backwards. He made animal noises as Emma raised the rifle and struck him again. That left him immobile, helpless, but still gurgling and trying to cry out. Sooner or later he might awaken. She took her butcher knife, was careful to avoid the filth of the latrine when kneeling over the boy, about Jacob's age, and put an end to all the noises. Only when it was done did she begin to calm. She searched his pockets and found three spare rifle cartridges.

"Hey!" a man shouted from the house. An adrenaline rush sent Emma running into the black woods with the rifle and ammo. In her weakened state, sapped further by her exhausting agitation, she tired quickly. A prickly feeling crept up her torso. She had tried to use energy she didn't have.

The return trip to the cabin was several times more difficult. Emma was drained and bone-weary. The rifle was a heavy additional burden. It was moonless. She avoided the smooth highway out of fear of discovery, but her footing through the ditch parallel to it was uncertain. Emma had several ankle turns and one trip and fall. The darkness, however, paid off. From the soggy bottom of the ditch, pressed flat into the muck and still as a log, Emma watched a pickup, presumably from the Nichols's house, speed past. Its bed was filled with dark forms, all armed, almost certainly hunting for her.

The second time Emma encountered that truck was when she reached the Miller family's property. In the headlights Emma could see men arguing, and one woman being consoled by another, in front of Noah's locked gate.

Chapter 17

Natalie had consented to serving their family dinner "just this once" in front of the big TV in the living room. The Millers stared at familiar scenes of leafy and green Central Park, made unfamiliar by countless police lights as darkness descended on the metropolis. Noah kept glancing down at his phone, but his last text message—a reply from Isabel as to her whereabouts—still read, "NYC."

Noah had texted back several times. "Iz, get out of there." "It's going to get bad." "What are you doing?" "Are you there?!?!" But none of the texts had gone through. It was as if nature were rolling back human advancement—the Internet era giving way to the TV and telephone—one technological generation at a time on their steady return to the animal kingdom.

"I now have it..." began the local TV reporter into whose feed the national network had patched. "I have just now learned..." He stared into the camera with what could only be trepidation and pressed his earphone to his head. "The rumored outbreak in the Upper West Side has been confirmed as *Pandoravirus*. I repeat, *Pandoravirus* has been confirmed in Manhattan. We've known for about two hours that the NYPD had closed off two blocks: West Eighty-seventh to West Eighty-fifth between Columbus and Amsterdam. Rumors centered on a maid or a nanny of some sort, who grew ill shortly after arriving at work. What I'm being told," the reporter said, cupping his ear, "is that the police got a report from a neighbor that the family for whom she worked all displayed symptoms consistent with acute SED infection. Police are expanding the quarantine to twenty-four blocks, from West Eighty-first at the Museum of Natural History to West Eighty-ninth, and from Central Park West all the way to Broadway."

The reporter stood on the walk along the park side of Central Park West. "If I can ask the camera operator to take a closer shot?" The reporter turned from the lens and pointed across the broad street. "You can see barricades going up." Residents streamed and ultimately sprinted past the orange and white striped sawhorses—one well-coifed couple pushing a tandem jogging stroller—as police blocked the cross street and its sidewalks. A heavy-set middle aged woman ignored shouted police orders and found herself pinned between the last segment of barricade to be swung into place and a piano store's plate glass showroom window, crisscrossed with tape, as if that would help. Then again, who would break into a piano store? A brief but heated argument ensued, which the woman won with a finger shaken in the face of the cop, who shrugged, let her pass, then was besieged by a quickly swelling and clamorous mass trapped behind the barrier, all of whom now brazenly ignored the curfew.

Within seconds, the throng grew on the quarantined side, arriving only moments too late to escape. Everyone wore something over their mouths and noses, from proper masks to absurdly bulky woolen scarves. Cops in masks, goggles, and gloves warned the crowd back with hands raised in air, palms out, as if physically pressing against them, but from a distance. "The people caught on the wrong side of the barricades," the local reporter said, "are growing quite vocal." His microphone picked up angry but indistinct shouting. The camera, however, zoomed in. The scene was shaky and dimly lit, but had the makings of an unmistakable powder keg. Men and women leaned over the sawhorses, straining red-faced in their desperate shouts and threatening demeanor.

"Have they turned?" asked Chloe, who like the others had forgotten her dinner.

"Probably not," Noah replied, "yet. Everybody eat. The food is getting cold."

The news, which was constantly "Breaking," jumped from one outbreak to another, each with scenes eerily similar, no matter the locale. Turkish troops opening fire amid the minarets of Istanbul. Scottish civilians carrying makeshift wooden shields clubbing a human form on an Aberdeen sidewalk. A candlelight vigil outside a quarantined apartment building in Copenhagen. A flyover whose slow-motion video depicted Hamburg fragmented by hastily erected barricades of overturned cars and dumpsters—some manned, some broken, some in flame—all surrounded by toxic, uncollected bodies.

The kids were having an argument in whispers. Annoyed, Noah muted the TV and asked what they were talking about.

"Nothing!" Jake replied.

But Chloe stared back at her brother before turning to her parents. "We think we saw someone yesterday. When we were on patrol."

Noah fought a cringe, silently cursed, and braced himself. "When you were *what?*" Natalie asked. "On *patrol*. You and *Jake?*"

Jake broke quickly under his mother's glare. "Sometimes, Chloe and I go out on patrol without Dad."

There it was. *"What!"* roared Nat. When Noah turned to her, she slapped him squarely on the jaw.

He was stunned and rubbed his face. "Natalie! *Jesus.*"

"You let them go out there *alone?* The two most stupid fucking teenagers who've ever walked the Earth?"

Chloe cried, *"Hey!"* Noah tried to explain.

But Natalie said, *"No!* Not my children! No! You had no right!" Her variations on the same comment filled the next several minutes.

Noah allowed her to vent while checking his teeth with his tongue. Where would he find an uninfected dentist if need be? When Natalie ran out of steam, he said, "Here's the thing. They need to be comfortable out there. You too, Nat. In case we get flushed."

"Flushed? What does that mean? Flushed? Like my life? Flushed down the toilet?"

"I mean, in case we can't hold out here and have to *run!*" Noah was perturbed at having been struck and had barked at her more loudly than intended.

Nat's lower lip quivered, but that could still be anger, so he returned to the main point by saying to the kids, "You saw someone on our *property? Yesterday?* And you didn't *tell* us?"

Jake seemed angry with his sister for reasons that eluded Noah. But Chloe nodded sheepishly. "What the hell do you think a patrol is *for?*" Noah practically shouted.

Natalie wiped quiet tears from her face and demanded details. Apparently, the two idiots were taking a break on a hillside when they glimpsed someone running away. It seemed innocuous enough of an encounter.

"Why didn't you *tell* us?" Natalie asked. The kids looked at each other but said nothing. "Who was this person you saw? Describe them."

"She looked like," Chloe began, again glancing at her brother, "Aunt *Emma?*"

Oh, shit! Natalie quizzed them further. Caucasian female, age twenty, to forty or fifty or whatever, petite, tanned with a bad hairdo and overgrown bangs. The kids had nothing more to add but shrugs and general but unexplained guardedness.

That began close to half an hour of attacks by Natalie and defenses by Noah. He had no idea Emma was coming there. "But you got her released, and she thought of this place just like you did. Or did you tell her to come here?" She's his sister, Noah attempted. What was he supposed to do? "Not get us all infected or killed would be a good start." Emma could be helpful to them, was Noah's final try.

"We'll see," Natalie replied, amazing Noah by then letting it drop. Noah suspected his wife harbored a more evolved and nuanced view of their plight than he yet understood.

On TV, the Vatican had sealed itself off from the rest of Rome, which was aflame. Once-tidy streets in Vienna were glittering with broken windows of looted storefronts. Barcelona was shown from a distance being bombed by the Spanish air force. There were no pictures out of Warsaw, only the YouTube video of a family of four saying good-bye to the world, in English, each listing what had been best about it—"Chocolate. Chopin. Football. Love."

Noah felt more than saw Natalie's eyes on him and turned to her. She sat in an oddly stiff position. Her tray of food in her lap had a full glass of red wine and a daisy Jake had picked on his and Chloe's patrol that afternoon. Her face was frozen in quiet terror.

Noah looked back down at his phone, whose text app still only read "NYC."

Chapter 18

NEW YORK, NEW YORK
Infection Date 51, 2300 GMT (7:00 p.m. Local)

All Rick said to Isabel, in a quiet voice meant only for her, was, "Showtime."

"I think I'm gonna be sick," she replied, startling Rick. "No, I mean, I'm scared. Look." She held her hand out, palm down. It shook visibly. Rick pulled her into his expansive warmth. They were in a conference room, alone for a rare moment. He smelled faintly of dried sweat and the outdoors, but that was okay. She probably did too, although that somehow seemed less okay. She nestled deeper into his arms and under his chin with an unobserved but contented smile.

An hour earlier, after returning with Rick from his obsessive tour of local defensive preparations, they had joined the crowd around a police radio in the offices of the manager of the American Copper Buildings. Once confirmation of the outbreak had been announced and a fruitless expansion of the quarantine zone ordered, Rick had pulled Isabel aside. No need to stay for the bewildered and futile speculation to follow. "We're holding in the north! How the hell did it suddenly show up in Central Park West?"

They had settled into the well-appointed conference room looking east across the verdant St. Vartan Park and waited for their next orders. The outbreak—the one they knew about, anyway—was sixty blocks away. All was still peaceful in Murray Hill as night fell. The streets and sidewalks were oddly empty after a twenty-four-hour curfew had been imposed throughout Manhattan "until further notice."

Isabel abandoned her awkward attempt at cuddling and arched her back, which was sore from the heavy burdens it now routinely bore. Rick described plans for their personal escape. He was such a Marine that he shaved every morning, even "in the field." She ran the back of her hand across his smooth face, which was so unlike the scruffy look more common to their generation, then laid her head on his chest. "Are you listening?" he asked.

"Uh-*huh*," she lied, eyes closed, as his instructions vibrated and his breast rose and fell.

"So if we get separated," he said, "and the Black Hawk doesn't show?"

"We won't get separated."

"Cross the FDR to the Esplanade and get on the East River ferry. Use your White House pass. Don't wait in any lines, and ignore any griping. If they get aggressive, flash your M4. If they get physical, use it. Get on any ferry, they're all going to the same place, which is where?"

"The other side of the *river?*" she answered in a sleepy voice that sounded childlike.

"Hunters Point South, in Long Island City." Then he said something about the Verrazano-Narrows Bridge, some island, and the mainland before she fell asleep.

The conference room door burst open. Isabel was curled up in Rick's lap with her knees pulled into a fetal position. The room was dark save the glare from the hallway and the flickering light of a fire bathing the city outside with an orange warning.

Brandon stood in the doorway looking anywhere but at the two new lovers. "We got a call from the Tank," the Pentagon's pet name for their operations center. "They want us to head up to Central Park."

Rick remained quiet for so long that Brandon looked his way, as did Isabel. Rick's eyes were narrowed and lips pinched. He looked angry. Isabel got off his lap and sat in the adjacent chair. "What is it?"

"You don't have to go. Either of you. You've done enough."

Brandon said, without enthusiasm, "They apparently want us to see if New York's more elaborate containment plans work. They said the Port Chester line was holding."

"The Port *Chester* line," Rick said, his contempt betrayed in his tone, "isn't *urban!* They can't contain outbreaks *inside* the fucking City. They don't even know where they all *are*." Rick's voice was an uncharacteristic mix of scorn and defeatism.

Brandon added, "There was an attack in the Park...outside the quarantined blocks. Near the boathouse. Three couples—one with an infant in a Babybjörn carrier on the dad—were crossing the park toward the quarantine zone on the west side to do some disaster sightseeing, if you can believe that, when they were attacked by a man with a metal garden stake. Five of the six adults were killed. The only one who survived was the dad with the baby, whose wife yelled for him to run. They never found the killer, but the dad told police that the guy was wearing a business suit and that his eyes were pitch black."

"Okay," Isabel said. "So, there are tens of thousands of cops and soldiers out looking for some infected businessman who's breaking curfew. Someone will see him and...and *shoot* him."

"The point is," Rick responded, "if we go up to the Park, it could break out behind us. All around us. Get *us* quarantined. There may be no safe way out from there, unlike there is now, from here. Remember Boston?" Isabel shook herself as if to banish that nightmare. "And what did those mathematicians' models project?"

"The bigger and denser the city," Isabel replied feebly, "the bigger the *boom*."

Isabel knew that, by remaining in Manhattan, of all places, to observe yet another collapse into disease-fueled adrenal atrocities, she was tempting fate in the midst of the worst disaster in human history. This would be worse than the bridge, worse than the woods, worse even than the close call in Boston. The spread of infection in New York City would be the most rapid and explosive of all in North America.

"Dr. Plante," Rick said, "you could escort Isabel across the East River. Get away from here as fast and as far as you can."

"Hey!" Isabel snapped. "I don't need to be *escorted*, okay? Like my fucking petticoats may get soiled."

"We're rolling the dice, Izzy," Brandon said, using his pet name for her from a decade ago. "One of these times..."

Isabel looked at Rick. "Why don't you," she suggested slowly, tentatively, not wanting to offend him, "come *with* us?"

"Not me," he said. "Just you two." She began shaking her head, and continued non-stop through his lecture on risks assumed by soldiers but not civilians, of oaths sworn by the former but not the latter, of training she lacked but that might save him.

Isabel, however, when he ran out of steam, gave him one last shake of her head. "If you stay, I stay." She rested her fingertips on his lips to prevent further quibbles. "Rick, what the hell do you think my chances are on Long Island, or Staten Island, or whatever island, or on the mainland, if I'm out there wandering around through the fucking apocalypse?" With *Brandon*, for God's sake!

"All right, all right," Rick said, rising and beginning the now familiar routine of climbing into his body armor, webbing, and pack. Isabel followed suit, as did Brandon. They met up with Sgt. Vasquez and his five men for the elevator ride down to street level. They wore so much gear, the nine soldiers and scientists had to take separate elevator cars.

As they piled into Humvees, Brandon said to Isabel, "You know I'm not the total coward you think I am."

"I didn't..." Isabel began, but Brandon climbed into a different vehicle.

* * * *

Every storefront and business along the drive to Central Park was closed. Metal shutters or gratings lowered. Windows boarded as if before a storm. There were no cars, taxis, or buses anywhere. Anyone parked on the street had been towed. There were no pedestrians on the sidewalks, but at every apartment building they passed residents crowded stoops and doorways. Some peered left and right down buttoned-up streets and engaged in animated conversations with each other, or arguments with policemen or National Guardsmen, each replete with pointing and animated gesticulations. All had the panicked looks of passengers who'd watched the last lifeboats depart. And all studied the passing three-Humvee convoy as if therein lay some clue critical to their survival. Some secret signal, detected only by them, that now it was time to panic. The machine gunner protruding through the roof of the middle Humvee probably served that purpose for many. Curfew be damned, it was time to flee, or would be soon.

Or maybe not, Isabel thought. Maybe they were stay-put-ers. Dead-enders hunkering down with water, food, and a nine iron by the door. Or deniers, who believed that every catastrophe was overhyped. Or accepters—we're all gonna get sick, so why not fall ill and turn in the comfort of our own home rather than in some government-run concentration camp? Or fatalists—there were, Isabel feared, lots of them—who kept glancing at their gun, or razor blade, or poison, or rope, or plastic bags from the cleaners. The things that they now always kept by their sides, like security blankets. A less awful way out. They had seen what was coming. They weren't going to let that happen to them, or their families.

Isabel jammed her eyes shut. "What is it?" Rick asked.

"My parents told me that imagination was a good thing, but I'm paying the price for it now." Rick cradled the back of her head with his hand. Isabel kissed his warm palm.

At least there was Rick. She tried to smile for him, but it came off every bit as fake as poor Emma's attempts. Where was Emma now? Surely she had made it down to the Old Place unless she had been shot in some ditch and left to die like a rabid dog.

The convoy slowed to pass three successive checkpoints manned first by cops, then a mix of cops and soldiers, then soldiers only. The fourth line, which was pierced by no visible checkpoints—the innermost ring—was being dug into the park's soil and bolstered with sandbags along West Fifty-ninth from the Plaza all the way up to Columbus Circle, where the hansom cabs and their nickering horses used to queue.

They climbed out of their Humvees, left their heavy packs behind, and clambered over concrete barriers only just lowered into place across Fifth Avenue by city workers in hardhats and reflective vests working cranes. Vasquez took the lead—the point, Rick called it—and the two scientists trailed roughly midway through their small formation. The last of his men in their single file spun every few steps and walked backwards almost as much as forwards. It was only when Isabel saw the brief brilliance of a flashlight in Central Park—two soldiers, rifles raised, checking the brush— that she recalled that she too had a rifle slung in its now too-familiar place across her chest.

Pull the charging handle all the way back. Press the carbine firmly to your shoulder. Lower your eye to the sight. Flick the safety to Semi. And squeeze. It was really way too much of a gun for her to handle. She should ask Rick for a pistol instead. It and its ammo also had the benefit of being much lighter.

"Masks on!" Vasquez called out. Isabel, Brandon, and Rick raised their masks and lowered the face shields attached to their helmets by elastic straps. They already wore latex gloves—dark green, not the bright blue of the NIH hospital—issued to them by the army.

They entered an apartment building lobby and joined a man who introduced himself as the Incident Commander. He was a FEMA official, but he wore camouflage combat gear like the troops. The only cops there wore black and had "Emergency Service Unit" patches. "Neighbors next to Apartment 906," the Incident Commander reported, "heard a loud fight and banging sounds, but no gunfire. EMTs placed orders on 906. We've also tagged two suspicious units on the seventh floor and taped their doors too." Troops and SWAT teams finished climbing into full personal protective equipment in the tight, marbled lobby. "Let's see what we can do short of having these guys storm those apartments."

They eschewed the elevators and headed for the stairs. "The doorman reported," the Incident Commander explained as they climbed, "that the couple in 906—an older man and a young blond woman in sunglasses that the media has taken to calling an au pair or nanny—took the elevator to the ninth floor. One of the families in an apartment on the seventh floor that's been quarantined rode up in that car with them. They talked to their neighbors, who also called 9-1-1. We've quarantined them too."

Isabel carried her rifle and other gear, and wore heavy ceramic plates in her body armor. Her legs ached by the third floor. Her lungs caught fire by the sixth. Rick offered to help her with her load, but she declined. She was perspiring and breathing heavily by the time they entered the carpeted hallway on the ninth floor.

Neighbors peered out of doorways up and down the corridor with all manner of fabric covering their faces. One man in ski goggles and ski mask accosted them in muffled tones. "When can we leave?"

"Building's quarantined," the Incident Commander replied. "Nobody's leaving."

Sgt. Vasquez ordered the man to take his goggles off. He raised the amber lenses to his forehead, revealing green irises. Satisfied, Vasquez posted one soldier at the entrance to the stairwell—their escape route—and joined the others outside Apartment 906.

A red sticker was affixed diagonally to the door. Isabel tilted her head to read it. "Do not enter. QUARANTINE NOTICE. No entry, exit, or removal of items without permission of local authorities." Two prickly biohazard symbols formed bookends to the warning. Fine print cited FEMA regulations.

Thick red tape stretched from the doorframe to the door. It wasn't there as a seal. It was there to signal by a tear if the door had been opened. The NYPD SWAT team was arrayed around it. On either side, men with stubby machine pistols pressed their backs to the wall. Across the corridor and at an angle, a man in a black helmet and gas mask knelt with the telescoping stock of a short rifle resting on his shoulder. His goggled eyes were lowered to the weapon's sights, which were aimed at the closed door.

The Incident Commander rapped loudly: a cop's knock. "Federal Emergency Management Agency!" he announced. "Open up!"

On hearing that, timid neighbors leaning into the hallway disappeared behind doors that were bolted and chained with metal rattles. Isabel could hear the scraping sounds of heavy furniture being shoved back into place.

The Incident Commander stepped back. Someone was working the locks from inside 906.

The door opened six inches, tearing the red tape. A lithe blond girl in her late teens or early twenties stared out with black eyes at their menacing weapons.

Isabel said, "Could you, maybe, point your guns somewhere else?"

When the cops and soldiers complied, the infected woman opened the door wider. Her blue jeans, everyone noticed, were covered in dried blood. She blinked in the bright light of the corridor, which poured through her gaping pupils.

The Incident Commander turned to Isabel and waited. *What?* she thought. *What am I supposed to do?* But she stepped forward and drew the infected woman's attention. "What's your name?" Isabel asked, smiling pleasantly—and pointlessly—behind her mask.

"Name? Klara, with a K," the girl replied with a foreign pronunciation. Klara with two *ahs*. She was so light-skinned, Isabel thought, her eyes were probably blue.

"Klara, so, you got sick?" The girl took a look around at the dozen or so armed men, then nodded. "Can I ask where you think you might've caught it?"

"In Boston. Cambridge. At school."

"I hear an accent, but I can't place it."

"It's German. Stuttgart." Like Emma when she had first turned, Klara eschewed the confusing first person pronouns. There was no "I" in there anymore. Her body had survived, but her self had not.

"Klara, why is there blood on your jeans?"

The dark pits of Klara's eyes sank to survey her soiled pants. Her blue irises should reappear in a couple of weeks...if she survives. Then she would pose a new risk to the Uninfected. To men, anyway. She was pretty. When she looked up, she said, "Mr. Jorgensen had to be killed."

"O-o-okay," Isabel replied as looks were exchanged all around her. "Maybe you oughta explain *that?*"

Klara complied innocently. "Mr. Jorgensen and his wife, Marta," she looked over her shoulder back into the apartment, "are friends of...of Klara's parents. Another student had a car and got all the way to Fairfield, in Connecticut, before the sickness started and he drove off. Mr. Jorgensen had a boat that he brought to Manhattan in case he needed to escape in it. But he took it to the Connecticut coast instead. By the time he docked back here, the sickness was very bad."

The damage to her brain wasn't as severe as the worst Isabel had seen at the NIH lab. Like Emma, Klara might soon relearn how to use self-references. Or how to fake their use, Isabel thought, since her "self" had been totally destroyed by *Pandoravirus. Or had it?* Could it be that some small part of her self had survived? Or been regenerated, perhaps, with the promise of a more fulsome recovery over time? They still knew so little.

"And so," Isabel asked, "Mr. Jorgensen got sick too?"

"Yes. And his wife Marta."

"Okay. So how did you end up, you know, killing Mr. Jorgensen?"

"Mr. Jorgensen turned, and then he raped me."

Isabel tried not to let the pause that followed linger. "And then you killed him?"

"There was a big knife in the kitchen. *That* killed him."

Isabel looked around to determine whether the officials wanted anything else. When no one reacted, she said, "And Mrs. Jorgensen? Did you kill her, too?" Klara shook her head. "Can we, maybe, talk to her?"

"No. She doesn't talk." Klara stepped back into the apartment, then returned with a middle-aged woman in a housecoat.

Isabel said, "Mrs. Jorgensen? Marta?" When the woman's head rose and her creepy black eyes focused, Isabel had to force herself not to take a step backward. "Mrs. Jorgensen, I, uhm, understand there was some trouble with your husband."

"It's *Dr.* Jorgensen. MD in Psychiatry. He raped Klara. He'd always wanted to. He had an appetite for younger girls. At some level, he was happy about the pandemic. It allowed him to act out his fantasies. And knowing what I know about them...He needed to be killed."

Klara said, "She is doing much better now. Before, she couldn't talk."

"It was pretending," Dr. Jorgensen said. "To not get killed, too."

Klara nodded. That made perfect sense to her.

Isabel turned to the Incident Commander. Enough with this hallway trial. They had the two infected women don clear plastic coveralls complete with a hood and snorkel-like mouthpiece, zipped them up, and led them down the hall. A few doors slammed closed after getting brief looks at what might be their future: people in plastic bags being marched away by armed men in HazMat gear.

"Let's go down to the seventh floor," the Incident Commander said as Mr. Jorgensen's remains were collected.

In the first apartment two floors below, an adult son of the elderly couple, moaning from a back bedroom, was in the acute phase of illness. As the gurney rolled him out, he writhed, held his head in both hands, and pleaded for painkillers from inside his baggie. His parents both swore they felt fine, but the woman looked peaked, with a narrow band of perspiration along the exposed silver roots at her hairline. They were both escorted out at gunpoint in plastic bags, and a red quarantine sticker was affixed to their door.

The last apartment check down the hall initially appeared uneventful. No one responded to the knocks. The apartment superintendent unlocked the door, but it was barricaded from the inside. The SWAT team and Vasquez's army detail pushed. There was a crash, and the door opened.

A screeching sound preceded the sudden attack by a child, who leapt off the fallen armoire and onto a policeman in the hallway, ripping his helmet and gas mask off as everyone else recoiled.

The NYPD officer tumbled onto his back and flung the berserk girl onto the carpet beside him. A half dozen shots rang out. Isabel cringed but forced herself to look. The wild-haired infected girl, maybe seven or eight years old and in a soiled nightgown, was spurting amazing volumes of blood through the multiple holes in her small torso.

The officer on whom she had pounced stared at his attacker—his face uncovered and eyes wide—before he scrambled away repeating, "I'm okay! I'm okay! I'm okay!" and returned his gas mask to his face. Everyone shied away from him even though it would be at least forty-five minutes before he was contagious. Two hours before he started throwing up. Five or six before he was either dead, or one of them.

"Quarantine," was the sentence handed down gravely by the FEMA official. The cop's fellow officers patted his back and shook his hand as he was led away—in shock, not yet in tears—to join the apartments' detained occupants.

"Hello?" came a woman's voice from inside the infected girl's apartment. Rifles and machine pistols swung toward her.

"Come out with your hands up!" barked a police officer, whose gas-mask covered right eye was lowered to the sights of his ugly black weapon.

A fortyish woman crawled over the toppled armoire then raised both hands above her head. "Coming out! Infected. Infected." True to her word, her pupils were fully popped.

"Anyone else in there?" asked the cop.

"My husband," she replied, "Her father. But he's dead."

The looks exchanged by the cops and soldiers signaled, Isabel understood, silent comments on the infected woman's total lack of concern about her dead family. She had only glanced at her still oozing daughter and not registered any reaction at all.

Although the woman didn't appear much of a threat, cops edged by her to search the apartment as if she were radioactive. Isabel asked the woman what had happened. "Her father barricaded the front door when she got sick. Afraid you might shoot her." The comment was made in a matter-of-fact way. "Then came the illness, and she attacked." The woman held up a forearm wrapped in bandages. "She couldn't move the armoire to get out of the apartment, and she couldn't get into the locked master bedroom. Then you arrived."

And shot your daughter, Isabel thought. She wondered if the day would ever come when Infecteds' complete loss of emotional response didn't shock her.

The cops unfurled a black body bag that was far too large and laid the little girl's body inside it. They also cut out a huge segment of carpeting onto which she had bled and placed it in the bag with her. The Incident Commander halted his men before they zipped it all up. "Do you want some time?" he asked the mother, who stared blankly back at him. "With your daughter?" The FEMA official knelt and tenderly brushed the dead girl's tangled hair from her face, now relaxed and sweet in her blood-splattered repose. "Do you want to say your good-byes?"

"I think she's pretty dead," her mother replied as if baffled by having to state the obvious. She looked at the Incident Commander quizzically, as if *he* were the one with mental issues.

The cops slapped a quarantine sticker on their apartment door. The Incident Commander zipped the little girl up, crossed himself, and said a silent prayer.

Chapter 19

Although they had only been up at the Old Place for two weeks, routines had developed. A rhythm to life. You wake up early, dress, eat while watching horrible news on TV—today, it was non-stop stories about the fall of New York City—and then tend to your chores to help forget what you had just seen.

Natalie lovingly, glowingly admired the miracle of sprouting vegetables and beans in the humid grow labs. Chloe chased chickens and attended to her social media profile on her iPhone, much of which was now chicken-themed. One photo's caption, which a snickering Natalie showed Noah, read, "This rooster I call Justin cuz he's always chasing hens!" Jake went down his daily checklist of mechanical and electrical systems, essentially confirming from a safe distance that they made the same motions and sounds as the day before, and nothing was seized up, grinding, or aflame. Noah checked on the fences, cameras, lights, and other security systems. Their assignments were totally gender-based, but after about a week the complaints about his misogyny and heteronormativity had run their course.

So it was with suspicion that Natalie regarded Noah when he said he was going patrolling. It was a break from their routine. "This early?" she asked. Noah mumbled something about not becoming too predictable. "You'll have your radio, right?" she asked.

"Always."

About half way up to the cabin, he could smell wood burning. At the last of the finger ridges, he lay on his stomach and raised his binoculars. Smoke rose from the cabin's chimney. The chair placed in front of the front door had been moved aside.

Noah slowly made his way down to the rough, one-room structure. About twenty feet away, he called out, "Emma? Emma?" There was no reply at first. He began to fear that maybe it was someone else, and raised his rifle to be ready. "Emma, it's Noah!"

The door cracked open. Emma's now tanned and wind-chapped face appeared. Noah lay his rifle on the ground, removed his backpack, and held it in front of him like an offering to potentially dangerous natives. "I've brought food." She remained motionless and mute. Noah unhooked his pistol belt and dropped his only other weapons—9mm and knife—beside his rifle.

Emma opened the door wide. Noah extracted a mask from his camo jacket's pocket, covered his nose and mouth, and pulled on stretchy Latex gloves. She wasn't supposed to be very contagious, but…His sister wore the exact same jeans, sweater, and boots—all now filthy—that Isabel had brought to the hospital for Emma to don upon her release. She had added an oversized camouflaged parka whose odor, even through his mask, caused Noah to wince. "Whoa! Did you lose a fight with a skunk or something?"

Emma looked down at the garment before shaking her head. "I saw raccoons, possums, deer, squirrels, and birds, but no skunks." She stepped aside and allowed him to enter. Other than her jacket, whose smell she somehow failed to register, the cabin was clean and orderly. Dishes dried beside the sink. A fire crackled in the stone fireplace. Her sheets and blanket were folded atop her pillow on one end of the single cot she'd set up.

Noah unloaded the food from his backpack. "I've been thinking about you ever since you jumped out of that freaking car. I'm glad you're all right." Emma had nothing to say in response. "We stored some emergency rations up here. I guess you found those. But you might like some variety." Emma said nothing, but sniffed and then removed the foul-smelling jacket, which Noah noticed for the first time had brownish splotches along its front and sleeves. Dried blood?

Emma's fists clenched and unclenched. Cords popped through the chaffed and red skin on the backs of her hands. She crossed her arms and pinioned her flattened palms beneath them as if hugging herself.

Noah closed the kitchen cabinet and turned, slowly and non-threateningly, to face his now vaguely terrifying little sister. She was petite, but according to Isabel she would attack with an abandon unleashed by the elimination of all constraints on her behavior. "Watch out for your eyes," had been a cryptic text from Isabel after touring outbreak sites in New England.

Emma walked to the fire, still embracing herself as if she were freezing. Noah followed, but Emma said, "Stay back," over her shoulder.

"Okay." The silence lingered. "You know, at your *habeas* hearing that doctor at the NIH told the judge you weren't really very contagious after two weeks."

"It's not that. It's not safe for you here. I get...nervous."

"But Emmy, it's just me," Noah said limply. He lowered his mask. Isabel had said that would be okay. Wearing gloves was more important. And he wanted her to see his face and be able to confirm from his expression that he harbored no ill will. But then, how could she tell? If she felt no emotions whatsoever, could she understand any of his?

"I don't want to hurt you," Emma said. Noah initially took comfort from the reassurance, though on reflection was unsettled that it needed to be stated and realized it was really a warning. "You'd stop providing food if I hurt you or your family."

"*You're* family too, Emmy."

She sat in a chair, disabling her hands beneath her thighs as if to restrain herself physically. "Maybe...you should go."

Noah took a step toward her, but halted. Her eyes had returned to their natural bright green. But that made her behavior seem more abnormal, not less. Emma had always been lively and animated. Like her twin sister, her eyes frequently betrayed fleeting feelings before her guard rose, suggesting a flourishing inner life.

But now, Emma's face betrayed...nothing. The twins used to play a game with Noah when they were young. They would come out of their room, one-at-a-time, and let him ask a single question to try to identify which twin it was. They took pains to wear their hair the same way and change into the same clothes. They always chose orthodontic bands in contrasting colors, so both curled their lips over their teeth to further the deception in an absurd solution that only a child would devise. To the maximum extent possible, they remained expressionless—like Emma just now—to avoid revealing some idiosyncrasy that might give them away. But if Noah told an R-rated joke and a twin flirted with a smile before its suppression, it was Emma. A blush meant it was Isabel, who would shake herself like a dog emerging from water to facilitate restoration of her lifeless visage. His favorite question was, "You're Isabel, aren't you?" The one whose eyes widened at his amazing guess was Isabel. The one stifling a smug smirk of superiority, that was definitely Emma.

That Emma, Noah thought, *is dead.* The first American victim of *Pandoravirus*. Emma 2.0 now occupied his sister's skin and animated her muscles. She betrayed nothing and stared back with unending patience and abiding indifference.

"Are you," Noah asked, "angry at me for some reason?"

"I don't have feelings like that. Remember? Isabel said I only have reflexive reactions, like agitation, and urges. To eat, sleep, cough, urinate, defecate, and have sex."

Noah could only imagine what *his* face betrayed. But whatever it was, it was lost on Emma even though she tilted her head and studied his changed expression.

"I know it doesn't matter to you, but we all still love you, Emmy."

"I don't love you. I don't really have any idea what I thought love was, or why it seemed so important. Books are filled with words whose definitions, when I look them up, don't make sense anymore. I knew them, once, I'm sure I did, but they're a mystery now. And I suppose that's the issue. I don't have feelings, Isabel said, because there is no *I* inside me anymore."

Noah had no idea how to respond. Again, the conversation faltered. So he said, "Emma, if you see anyone up here, the safest thing to do is to assume they mean you harm. People are spooked. Until things settle down, you should be extra, extra careful. Okay?"

"They'll want to kill me because I'm a *Pandoravirus* carrier."

"And also because people are ignorant and fear anyone who's different."

"Do *you* fear me?" Emma asked, looking straight at him so brazenly he turned away. "Because you should."

"Whatta...whatta you *mean?*"

"Killing, I've discovered, is actually fairly easy. People's trust, and their soft tissues, make them vulnerable."

"Emma...*what?*"

"Don't worry." He relaxed, until Emma added, "I'll kill anyone who comes up here."

"I didn't...I didn't mean, Emma, that..."

"My heart starts pounding. My mouth gets dry. I feel like I have to *do* something." A grimace seized her face. It was sort of *like* an emotion. She clenched her jaws and her captive fists before slowly regaining a calmer, less threatening demeanor.

Noah took a step back in hopes the added space would ease her anxiety. It was also closer to the door, and to his rifle and pistol outside fifteen or so sprinted strides away. "Take it easy," he said both to Emma and to himself.

"It's only me here. And your family. Everyone who loves you. Plus Izzy, who's gonna come here as soon as she can so we'll all be together."

The mention to Emma of her loved ones brought zero reaction. "Maybe I should be with other people like me," she said instead.

"You're with your family, Emma. There's nowhere else you should be."

"Maybe I should be with people who don't have good reason to kill me. Because I understand that reason, and it's a legitimate one. You don't want to get sick and either die or lose the meanings of all those words in the dictionary, and your feelings, emotions, and sense of self, too."

"There aren't any other people here who are…like you."

"There will be. After reestablishing order, I need to resume teaching, publish my research, find a husband, buy a house, get pregnant, and raise a family."

"The Sequence, they call it. You know, the order of life events that historically produced the greatest financial success."

"The Sequence," Emma repeated. "The Sequence." Her eyes darted at what could only be ricocheting thoughts.

"Emma, the world is falling apart. Dreams like those are from a different time."

"They are my plans. But you're probably right. Reestablishing order will take more time than I originally budgeted."

Noah still didn't think she understood. "I'm sure Johns Hopkins is closed. Everything is closed. All the faculty and students have gone home."

"They'll be back."

"Not for a very long time. People aren't gathering in large numbers anywhere."

"They will. People who've turned will. Just not too densely."

"So, you imagine you'll…what? Go back to school and teach *infected* students? Then get married, by a minister, in a church, to someone else who's…who's turned? Get pregnant, go to a hospital, have babies, raise a family? An infected family?"

"You skipped buying a house. We'll need shelter."

"You'll walk into a bank, fill out paperwork, and get a mortgage?"

She shook her head. "We would do it online, my husband and I." Noah was mystified. How did her mind work? "Real estate should be cheap with the population reduced by half. And I need exercise," Emma said, her eyes wandering space as she compiled her mental to-do list. "Being fit will help me survive in an emergency, contribute to my general health, and keep me trim and attractive."

"What?"

"Improved cardiovascular conditioning would allow me to flee dangerous situations and…"

"No. I meant the 'trim and attractive' thing."

"Oh. Jogging and plyometrics will facilitate maintenance of a desirable appearance. Men, including infected men, react at a physiological level when presented with a sexually appealing figure of their preferred gender. In most Western cultures, that means slender, especially for women. That mating preference should be unaffected by any damage caused by *Pandoravirus*."

Noah's myriad questions got jammed when trying to find simultaneous expression. "Wha…? Why…?" He shook his head before remembering. Emma was not Emma anymore. He resolutely abandoned the jumbled queries and tried to compose some kind of rational response. "So, Emmy, in this new future, where you're teaching a bunch of infected kids before going to infected yoga class in a world that's turned, what happens to the rest of us? Do we have any place in that future you see?"

Emma looked at him with an expression devoid of any artifice or fraud. "Yes. If you're like me."

Was she recruiting him? Surely not. "You mean infected? But then, we would never have feelings again? Love, joy, pride, respect?"

"Or fear, or greed, or pain, or a lot of the other words in that book."

Noah followed her gaze to the large dictionary. It was a duplicate purchase, so he had brought it up to stock the cabin's tiny library. It was open to "J." He took a closer look. Emma had highlighted a word, "Jealousy," and written, in the margin, "Like envy? 'Bad.'"

"The words in *this* book?" Noah raised the dictionary from the coffee table.

"No, the other one."

A paperback of *Anna Karenina*, which Noah had bought in anticipation of their long isolation, was now dog-eared. It was Emma's favorite novel, which he had first long ago, and numerous times since, promised her he would read, but hadn't gotten around to it. Its pages were fluffed up and its spine was broken from his sister's repeated re-reading. Words were underlined on almost every page, he saw upon inspection. Love and hate. Anger. Fear. Surprise. Disgust. Trust. Friendship. Shame. Pity. Amusement. Courage. And jealousy, the last of the confusing nouns on the page she had just read.

"Take it," Emma said. "I remember understanding everything in that novel. Now, I don't understand anything. If she loved the Count, why didn't she leave her husband? Why does she *kill* herself? She could have killed her husband." Emma's voice, and her agitation, were on the rise. "None of

it makes sense. But it's useless, anyway. It's all made up. Take the book."
When Noah hesitated, she snapped, "*Take* it!"

She buried her hands in her armpits in a self-imposed straightjacket.

"Okay, okay." Noah retreated toward the door with the paperback classic
in hand. "I'll come back and check on you. Every couple of days. Bring
you some of Natalie's cooking. Okay?"

"Do you have any .308 caliber ammunition?" Emma asked.

"Uhm...no. Ours is all .227, for rifles, or nine-mil for
pistols. Emmy, why...?"

"Never mind. How about paper and a pen?" Noah said *that* he could
supply. The log in the fireplace popped. Emma turned its way, and her
gaze remained fixed on the dancing flames.

Noah closed the door behind him, relieved to be out of there. He strapped
on his pistol belt and slung his rifle over his shoulder. But he'd forgotten
his now empty backpack inside. When he opened the door with a knock
and started to explain the reason for his return, he saw Emma standing
over the fire. In it blazed the now obsolescent dictionary.

Chapter 20

On the computer monitors set up in banks like at NASA's mission control center, Isabel and Rick watched the downfall of New York City. Brandon flitted from workstation to workstation dispensing his expert opinions. How charged was the crowd gathered at Union Square? How close to the tipping point was the mob piling up at Pier Ninety-four? He seemed to Isabel frantic and on the verge of breaking down, as if he alone were responsible for turning back the unstoppable tide.

Several times, his predictions seemed prescient. "Pull them back *right* now! *Right* now! Can't you see? That crowd has to be sixty-plus per ten square meters! They're all facing the barricades! Get them outta…!" But the roar of the crowd, and then of the guns, had overtaken his ineffectual efforts. Commands to retreat shouted over the NYPD and National Guard radio nets came from men and women clustered around monitors displaying scenes that Isabel never wanted to see again. Scenes that always ended the same way: unanswered calls over the radio by forlorn dispatchers and army signalmen while shocking horrors played out on muted video.

After the sixth such dramatic containment failure, each a mass casualty tragedy that left hundreds, thousands of bodies in the parks and streets of Manhattan, Sgt. Vasquez whispered into Rick's ear. "What?" Isabel asked Rick quietly.

"Gather your gear."

Isabel scanned the room. They were trying to manage the hydra-like crisis on two dozen glowing screens, each with its own incident commander and still intact chain of command. But Rick had already played the game out a few moves, and he was ready to go.

"Let me tell Brandon," Isabel said softly.

Brandon, however, was too busy, too engaged to be pulled aside. "Wait!" he snapped at Isabel, then pointed at a map on a glowing iPad as he spoke to a National Guard major. "If we pulled off the blockade here, at Worth Street, that crowd in Columbus Park can unpack some and maybe cool off."

The police captain standing next to the two men, who had been repeating what Brandon said into his cell phone, shook his head. "That won't work. They'll just merge with the already dense crowd in Thomas Paine Park, which puts them right on City Hall's steps. We're trying to hold City Hall."

"Well you're not going to be able to!" Brandon replied. "And you're outta time! Look. Look! You've seen it before, right? How many times? That's a charged crowd! That's what they look like!" The Infecteds were all motionless. They stared silently at the barricades in front of the New York City Marriage Bureau. "That's sixty-five, maybe *seventy* per ten square! One little spark—someone steps on someone else's *toe*—and...! You've seen it before! You *know* what's gonna happen! *Do* something!"

Both the cop and the soldier were on their respective phones and radios, both pleading with superiors. But before either could get an answer, the roar of the crowd and the rattling crescendo of firearms erupted from the tinny computer speakers. Brandon grabbed his head with both hands as the sawhorses were toppled and the first few waves of infected rioters were mowed down. The next waves poured over the flimsy barriers and attacked the cops, who either dropped their riot shields and ran or died in place *en masse*.

Brandon turned to Isabel. He looked deathly pale and, with his hair unkempt, vaguely unstable. "This is pointless! No one is listening to me!"

Isabel whispered that he should get his stuff and meet them in the elevator lobby. There, they joined with Rick and Vasquez's team. Everyone maintained a guilty silence as they abandoned the still striving headquarters. But when the elevator doors closed, Rick said, to Isabel and Brandon, "We can't get the Black Hawk in to pick us up. The airspace is closed."

"What do we do?" Isabel asked. Brandon was in a daze and not listening.

"Catch a boat," Rick replied. She didn't ask how, or where. She simply trusted in Rick's quiet competence, and allowed herself to be carried along on whatever course he set. Head north, or south. Hop aboard a helicopter, or a boat. She had her job analyzing Infecteds' behavior. He had his keeping her alive. Her mind was most at peace these days when it was blank, and she intentionally turned it off until it was needed again.

Outside the American Copper Buildings, the giant city felt like a ghost town. Nothing moved. No one was visible. The noisy tumult of the great city's collapse sounded far away. But on closer inspection, she saw the rounded tops of helmets—some green, some desert tan—just above sandbags. A machine gun protruded through a smashed third-story window. A half dozen soldiers awaited orders at a construction site, whose piles of building materials concealed their turreted armored fighting vehicle.

In the distance, from all points of the compass, came sirens, car alarms, burglar alarms, the buzz of drones, the chop of helicopter rotors, indistinct warnings shouted through feeble bullhorns, and intermittent explosions near and far. Single shots sometimes rose to brief volleys before dying out and other times kept rising into full-on fusillades that were silenced only by some unheard cease fire command, or more likely by a fatal overrun. There were surely temporary victories here and there. But each loss was essentially permanent as the disease spread through one chink in the armor to the next.

The apocalyptic feel was rendered complete when their little detail reached FDR Drive. The wind off the East River just beyond it felt stiffer due to the stillness of their environs. Even though not a single car could be seen in either direction along the normally bustling artery, it still felt oddly dangerous simply to walk across the expressway. But not to fear. Straddling the pavement in the north- and southbound lanes to either side were two main battle tanks whose long guns were slewed broadside to enforce the curfew with fearsome overkill.

Ahead, Isabel could now see, were the crowds. At a distance they seemed largely tranquil. There were vestiges of orderly lines that wrapped through parking lots, along the esplanade, and out onto the ferry pier. But the closer to the boats the civilian mass got, the more chaotic the queues, and the more crushing the press of bodies. In several spots, rival factions in the crowd faced off, shouting at each other and pushing. The lives of the people at the back of the line depended upon order, process, and cooperation. The people at the front, however, were so close to safety that they could almost reach out and seize it.

Rick raised his mask, and the others all followed suit without need for command. Goggles or face shields came down from helmets. Latex gloves that were awkwardly donned days before were now pulled on with practiced ease. They tightened their nine-person formation, all bulked up by the addition of their giant and painfully heavy backpacks, to wade into the sea of humanity, which was bundled against the brisk wind inside thick wool overcoats, brightly colored ski jackets, and puffy down parkas. Most held driver's licenses, passports, and other identity documents in gloved hands and pulled rolling carry-ons. They generally seemed affluent, grim, quietly desperate, and searching for clues in the covered eyes of the troops and scientists who pressed through them toward the river.

"'Scuse me. 'Scuse me. 'Scuse me," Vasquez repeated.

Their progress slowed the closer they got to the water. "Get in fucking line!" some guy shouted. Bodies closed in. People pushed back. Isabel had to scramble for footing as a shove rippled through the crowd. "Go back and fight!", "Cowards!", and a chorus of "Boo!" rained down as they made it from the wooden deck of the covered terminal out onto the pavers on the dock.

There, Isabel stared back mutely into angry faces, one hand on the pistol grip of her rifle even though she would never be able to swing it around in such tight quarters. Rick fended off one crush into her side with a stiff-arm and brandished his pistol several times to silence threats at close range.

When they stopped, Rick squeezed through tiny gaps to talk to the cops guarding a gate under a large sign that read simply, "South." Several times Rick pointed and both men looked at Isabel. "I work for the State of New York," someone shouted. "I have priority!" To which rose a cry of, "*Bu-u-ull*shit! Try and cut line and I'll kick your pompous ass!"

Just beside Isabel, a little blond girl in gray leggings and a hat with two bunny ears sat atop the shoulders of her seemingly mild-mannered father, who craned his neck to monitor their patient progress toward the safety that lay a mere ten feet ahead. The little girl smiled at Isabel. Out of nowhere, Isabel began to cry. A look of concern darkened the girl's small face. At first just a few tears soaked Isabel's mask. But soon, it was a flood. Her jaw quivered. Her lips curled in a fixed grimace. She closed her eyes. There was no place to hide. She felt overwhelmed and lightheaded, but couldn't have fallen even if she fainted given the crush that pressed in on her from all sides.

They began to move again. The little girl whom she left behind waved good-bye with a smile presumably meant to cheer Isabel up.

When the last of their detail squeezed with difficulty through the partially opened metal gate, the thick cop manning it shouted, "That's it! That's it!" and was joined by cops and soldiers on the far side, who put their shoulders into the effort of forcing the gate closed. A man whose face was creased by the gate's bars was panicking, saying he was being crushed and couldn't breathe. A cop used his baton to jab at the people closest to him in an effort to relieve his distress. Isabel relished the relative openness of the gangplank, and felt guilty for the feeling.

The transit officers running the ferry terminal's operations counted out the last nine people in line for the next boat. Isabel expected more curses and complaints as people lost their places to the troops and scientists. But those nine people obviously felt too lucky to be at the head of the line waiting for the next boat to complain about their lot. Examples of a poorer fate pressed against the bowing fences and metal gate and shouted angrily in the direction of everyone on the other side, them included.

"Good-bye, sweetheart," said a man, who hugged a woman holding a young girl in her arms. She was sobbing too hard to reply. The count of nine had split their family of four in half. The father, wearing a calf-length black wool overcoat and scarf, kissed the child held by his wife, who would board the ferry with Isabel's detail. The husband, with his hands on the shoulders of his boy of eight or so, joined the group bumped to the next ferry. The heartbroken woman kept rising onto her tiptoes and craning her neck to peer back at her husband and son.

As a boat approached the dock, it blasted its horn, which seemed to stir up the crowd outside the gate. Everything happened quickly. The ferry was fastened only tenuously to the dock for quick turnaround by a few loops of a single line. Its engines churned the water to pin it in place. The gangplank was lowered. People streamed aboard. The young mother in front of Isabel began calling out, "Alan! Alan!" and failed to keep up with the rapidly receding line. Isabel couldn't help but look, and wished she hadn't. Tears streamed down the woman's face and her daughter's small hand that pressed upon it in curiosity and growing alarm. "Alan!"

Finally at the gangplank, the woman began shaking her head and saying, "I can't! I can't!" She ran back toward the waiting group behind them. Her husband was shouting, "No! Go back! Get on the ferry, Claire!"

Isabel, and everyone in line around her, Brandon most of all, were immersed in the drama. Isabel didn't think that Claire would be able to force herself to part with her husband and son, but she peppered her son's face with kisses, hugged her daughter tight, and rejoined the back of their line, sobbing.

"One forty-seven!" the transit officer called out as Isabel mounted the gangplank. "One forty-eight!" he said, clapping his hand on Rick's shoulder. "One forty-nine and fifty!" he said as Claire carried her clinging daughter aboard. "That's it! Prepare to shove off!"

The pier at the end of the gangplank was filled with rolling luggage that passengers were not allowed to bring with them. Two transit officers were dumping bags into the water with big splashes to make more room. Without warning, a stupendous series of booms echoed through the city and rolled like a crackle across the East River and back. The ferry passengers ducked and gasped. Two jets, flying side-by-side, wheeled in air and climbed from their bombing run with engines shrieking before disappearing into the clouds. Boiling orange flames rose above the skyline and quickly turned black.

The fences holding back the further agitated crowds began to buckle. "I always loved you," Brandon said to Isabel. "I never stopped." Before she knew what was happening, he made his way off the ferryboat and down the gangplank.

"Brandon?" she called out, and found her confusion reflected in Rick's face.

Brandon spoke to the man—Alan—who hugged his son and then pushed the uncertain boy up onto the gangway. The metal gates behind them were groaning as they slowly gave way; the people at the front compressed against it were in obvious peril. The dockworker shoved the boy onto the boat and followed him aboard, as did the two transit workers dumping luggage into the river.

Brandon waved at Isabel as the ferry pulled away. "Brandon!" A quick blast of the horn signaled they were clear of the dock. "Alan!" Isabel heard shouted from nearby but out of sight in the standing-room-only mass. Warning shots were fired into the air from the dock as the fence began to give way. The nine people they had booted off the ferry, Alan and Brandon included, huddled together, recoiling from the encroaching mob.

As the ferry turned, Isabel lost sight of the dock. Over the shoulders of the soldiers who enveloped her, her protective charge, she could see only the tops of skyscrapers and the even taller columns of black smoke merging into gray clouds. Another stunning string of explosions caused another stir among the passengers. Another pair of jets standing on blazing, howling exhaust pipes caused Isabel to duck as they rose over the river in unison and punched holes through the overcast sky. Rick's arm wrapped around her on the slowly rolling deck.

"Can you see?" Isabel asked the much taller Rick, her voice trembling.

"The gate and fence gave way," Rick reported. "I saw Dr. Plante go into the water with everyone else." Isabel lowered her head to his chest and shut down her brain. Closed her heart. Heard nothing. Saw nothing. Felt nothing. Cold air in through her nostrils, warm air out through her mouth, fogging her face shield. Her resolution, made in bed the night before intertwined in Rick's arms and legs, that she would enjoy life for the little while she had left, no longer seemed possible. The naiveté of a silly girl who didn't know, until now, what the end would look like.

"Daddy!" came the little girl's pointless cry. Vasquez ushered her older brother through the crowd to be reunited with his mother. Tears poured down Isabel's cheeks. "Rick," she said, "Brandon…he thought I thought he was a coward. He…He…" Her face was contorted and she shook in silent sobs.

"You're going home," Rick said. Though it was in a whisper, his commitment seemed firm. Her natural resistance to being told what to do made only a fleeting appearance. She nodded, exhausted, and closed her eyes. He was right. This was all way too much. It was time to go home. She was no use to anyone anymore. She had practically murdered Brandon with her own two hands. She wouldn't do that to Rick, too. She wouldn't make him trade his life for hers the way Brandon had for that little boy. *Oh God, when will this all be over?* The tears dried up. Fatigue took their place. Rick removed his gloves and wiped her face above her mask with his rough thumbs.

"Okay," she said, overcoming the last few straggling heaves of her chest and regained control of her breathing. "Okay. I wanna go home." But if Rick was her salvation, then she had to be his. She needed to keep him alive so that she would have something to live for. Some*one* to live for. "What are *you* gonna do?" she asked, now strangely, unnaturally calm. Drained. The ferry bobbed on the slight swell as its engines rumbled through the soles of their boots. The wind whistled by. Claire and her two clinging children sobbed. *Booms* from the city's canyons resounded across the water like thuds from a bass drum. But Isabel's world was tiny. It encompassed Rick, the few inches between their faces, and nothing else.

"I'll find you," he said. "I will come and I will find you." They were only words. Not a plan, but a promise. An oath. She raised their face shields, pulled down their masks, and kissed him. A kiss that was worth the risk. A kiss that prevented any conditions, qualifiers, or caveats escaping his lips. A kiss that sealed the pact and gave her just enough hope to go on living for however long she had left.

Chapter 21

"Dad!" came Jacob's shout.

Noah ran for the door of the humid shipping containers, snatching his rifle from where it was propped against the wall. He saw Jake rapidly descending the hill behind the house. His son was frantically pointing at trucks and SUVs pulling up to the ridge road gate. Noah waved for him to go back. Jake understood, climbed back uphill, and lay behind some rocks with his AR-15 at the ready.

The three vehicles stirred up a dust storm. A dozen men, including Sheriff Walcott and Noah's neighbor, Trey Nichols, climbed out. They all had long guns in hand. Noah gripped his assault rifle tightly.

He had chambered a round before leaving the house that morning. His right thumb felt for the selector switch. He had practiced in the dark. *Click.* Fire. *Click.* Safe. *Click.* Fire. *Click.* Safe. Noah stepped onto the front porch forty meters from the gate. *"Sheriff?"*

"Mr. Miller!" Walcott said with a touch of the brim of his cowboy hat. "We're checkin' the area. Can we take a look around your property?"

"You've been on my property since you passed that locked gate and those Posted signs down on the highway!"

The eyes of the militiamen flitted back and forth between Noah and "the tower." They hadn't seen Jacob with his rifle on the hill, but the tower looked like an obvious threat. The front door opened. Natalie appeared holding the shotgun, which she had apparently found beside the umbrella stand.

From the barn, Chloe said, "Dad?"

"Back in the barn!" he snapped. The militiamen argued inaudibly. A window in the barn opened. The muzzle of Chloe's rifle appeared in it.

"We can get a warrant!" Walcott threatened. "Judge Parker is down the hill. But we was hopin' you'd consent."

"Tell the judge he can come on up. I'd like a hearing. You tell him that. A *hearing*."

"We're searchin' everybody's places," Walcott said, "'cause we had a murder three nights ago at the Nicholses'. Trey's fourteen-year-old nephew was stabbed to death. Trey said he's seen a suspicious woman on your property down by the highway."

"What does a suspicious woman look like, Sheriff Walcott?" The militiamen were paying close attention. They were civilians, not soldiers; more of a jury than a posse. And with three armed members of the Miller family having shown themselves, they seemed open to persuasion. "What was this suspicious woman doing?"

"Jogging," Walcott replied.

Several militiamen laughed. *It was Emma!* Noah knew.

One militiaman waved. "Hey, Mr. Miller. I'm Angus Bishop from down at the Quickie-Mart. My wife Margie said to tell you *hey*."

Noah waved back. This militia wasn't solid in backing Walcott. Noah addressed Trey Nichols, but played to his neighbor's comrades. "I'm real sorry, Trey, for your loss. That's truly awful. And I don't mean, folks, to be inhospitable. Ordinarily, I'd invite you all in. But if I open those gates, somebody could bring the virus in with 'em. That's a death sentence for my whole family." There were looks exchanged and a nod or two of agreement.

Sheriff Walcott spoke into the radio handset clipped to his khaki uniform blouse. "The judge is on his way up. I guess we'll just wait *here*, instead of spendin' our time searchin' the valley for Infecteds."

Noah joined Natalie in the house. "I don't want them coming in here!" she said.

"I'm doing every fucking thing I *can*."

"Don't you curse at me, Noah Miller!"

Chloe slipped in sideways through the open front door, and Jacob entered through the back. Natalie's fierce gaze barely left Noah. "Are you not gonna do anything to stop those people from coming in here, raping us, stealing our supplies, and infecting us all?"

"*Jesus*, Nat. None of that's gonna happen. That militia out there are our *neighbors*."

Jacob, being young, was also stupid. "Will they check the cabin, you think?"

Noah tried not to deflate on the spot. Maybe Natalie had missed it. "What *about* the cabin?" she asked instantly. Natalie turned her quizzical gaze onto Noah.

He took a deep breath. "Emma's living up there."

Natalie looked at him as if the words were puzzling; as if he'd made no sense at all. *"Emma?* Your...your *sister* Emma? Your *infected* sister, Emma? At our secret hideout, where we're supposed to run off to...to avoid all getting *sick?"*

"She's nowhere near as contagious as before. Now, it's only like...like AIDS, or Ebola." Natalie could only stare at him. He'd perhaps chosen the wrong diseases for comparison. "I didn't *invite* her to move in up there. She just showed *up*. And again, technically, this place is one-third hers. Legally."

"Noah, don't take this the wrong way, but Emma is a fucking *zombie*."

"That's not fair! You shouldn't use that word."

"Uh, hello?" Jake said to his parents from the door. "Can you not *hear* that?"

In the silence that followed, Noah heard a distant engine sound. "The judge?" he asked. Sure enough, he saw through the window the arrival of a dust-covered black Lincoln.

"No," Chloe said, peering out the door at the sky. "That's not it."

"Judge Parker has your warrant!" Walcott shouted, waving paper in the air. "Now if you'd put down your weapons and open this gate, we won't waste any more time!"

Noah stepped outside. "Judge, that warrant is unconstitutional! They have no probable cause!"

"There!" Chloe said from the porch beside him, shielding her eyes. Jacob, too, searched the sky. "Dad," Chloe said, "do militias have helicopters?"

A helicopter! Shit. "Look," Noah said to Walcott, "let's talk this thing over calmly."

Natalie hustled the kids inside and joined Noah on the porch, still holding the shotgun. The Sheriff began issuing orders. Only a couple of his men, however, did what they were told and fanned out to either side of the gate. The rest argued among themselves. Some also began gazing at the sky. Walcott said, "There's ten of us, Mr. Miller! And four of you! Yeah, I see your boy up there!"

A giant green helicopter descended out of the clouds overhead. Noah's heart sank. It had a huge Gatling-type gun in its door. Behind it stood a man in a large green helmet with a black visor. If Walcott had full-on military shit, it was game over.

It didn't orbit overhead, however, but settled into the small, level clearing—Jake's "droneport," where Chloe had dragged a lawn chair to work on her tan. When its tires set down, soldiers leapt out. Helmeted men ran off to either side out of sight.

Other soldiers approached the house as the engines wound down. One was tall; the other looked smaller than the rest, and waved.

"Izzy?" Noah called out. *"Iz!"*

When they met, she threw herself into her big brother's bear hug. Isabel's escorts focused their attention on the gate. Hand signals sent serious men off to the left and right of Walcott's now outgunned and outmaneuvered search party.

"Is there trouble here?" asked the tall soldier who'd given the troops orders.

"They wanna search our house!" Natalie said from behind Noah.

"And you don't want 'em to?" Natalie shook her head. The soldier headed straight for the gate.

Natalie watched him depart while giving her sister-in-law a distracted, perfunctory hug. Isabel was filthy. Every square inch of her was overlaid with layers of dusty flak jacket and grimy pouches that appeared full of rifle magazines. "So, who's *that?*" Natalie asked.

"Rick Townsend." Isabel's face lit with a smile she seemed incapable of suppressing. "He's a Marine," she explained with faux nonchalance. "A captain."

"Hmm. Are you...?"

"Uh *huh.*"

Isabel got another hug, this one genuine, from her sister-in-law. "Way to go *Isabel!*"

"They may be talking about that warrant," Noah said. "I'd better..." He took one step.

Natalie grabbed his arm. "Nope."

Noah was instantly frustrated. "Do you think, Isabel, you might explain what the hell is going on here? You flying in on a helicopter gunship and all?"

"Technically, it's a medium utility helicopter. A UH-60 Black Hawk."

"Not the point!"

The militiamen loaded up to leave. Trey Nichols shouted, "This ain't over!" before he was dragged into Walcott's truck. They departed in another dust storm.

The tall Marine—Townsend, by his nametag—returned.

"What just happened there?" Noah asked.

"They showed me their warrant. I told them to leave or we'd kill them all. They left." Townsend was called back to the helicopter by the door gunner.

"*Yum,*" Natalie actually said—*out loud.*

Noah couldn't recall ever seeing his sister look happier. Chloe arrived. Isabel quickly related how she'd met the Marine on the trip to Siberia to pick up Emma after her infection. "He's in charge of my '*personal security.*'" Natalie and her clone-of-a-daughter suppressed their amusement at the vaguely ribald job description. Isabel, Noah knew, so unlike Emma, had had only two boyfriends in her entire life to date. This was clearly a big deal to her.

Townsend called Isabel over. "Uh-oh," Natalie said, her spidey sense picking up on some cues Noah missed entirely.

"Is he dumping her?" Chloe asked.

What?

"Looks like it."

"How the hell can you tell that?" Noah asked in even greater frustration.

Townsend had to pull Isabel's arms from around his neck. As she tried to kiss him, his hand signals reeled in the troops deployed about the property. The engines wound up from a whine to a roar. Isabel held Townsend's face, speaking words audible only to him.

The Marine climbed aboard as a stooped Isabel shielded her face from the flying grit. The giant aircraft rose skyward and thundered away, thrashing the treetops with its ferocious rotor wash.

A crate-like box lay on the ground beside an enormous backpack, which Isabel impressively hoisted onto her shoulders, but with effort. When she returned, slumping under her load and staring at the ground, her tears had turned to mud from the dust and ran in streaks down her face like mascara. "He'll be back," Isabel said, presumably to herself. "He always comes back. Rick said Marines never leave anyone behind." Natalie and Chloe wrapped their arms around Isabel as if she might topple over at any moment. "He'll be *back*. He *will.*"

Natalie offered Isabel a long, hot bath, tea, then a meal with the last of the semi-fresh food.

"Rick left *that,*" Isabel said to Noah, glancing back over her shoulder at the crate in the landing zone.

"What is it?"

"Dunno. He said it was a house-warming gift. He's from very, you know, considerate, Midwestern people. Dairy farmers, from Wisconsin."

"And I bet that's pretty much all you know about him, right?"

"We're getting there! *Christ.* Just try being happy for me, Noah."

The three women in his life all glared at him as they left. "Jake, buddy, we need to spend more quality time together, you and me." Jake followed his father to the crate. On it were stenciled incomprehensible strings of numbers, and the words, "30 Grenade, Hand, Frag Delay, M67, Bursting Charge."

"Wo-o-*ow!*" Jake half-said, half-cackled. For him, this was like the Christmas morning when he'd gotten a hoverboard. For Noah, it felt more like that Christmas night spent in the emergency room. They each took one end of the crate by its rope loop and lugged the heavy box down to the basement. Noah held up a clawed crowbar, triumphantly finding a manly tool for a manly job. The grenades inside were smooth and round, not knobby and pineapple shaped.

Jake searched the Internet on his phone. "Okay, it says that, for right-handed people, you hold the grenade and the *spoon*—the safety lever thing—with your right hand, pull the *safety clip*—the pin—out with your left, throw the grenade like a football," he pantomimed the motion complete with a *whoosh*, "then take cover. You should be able to throw it thirty to thirty-five meters. That sounds kinda far. Maybe we could practice with rocks or something that are about the same weight. It says the grenade blows up in four to five seconds, and to make sure you don't hit a tree limb or something, or throw it up a steep hill so it comes rolling back. If you're standing near where it goes off, it's guaranteed to kill you inside of five meters, and wound you within fifteen meters. *But*—and this is in big black letters—it says the fragments *could* fly as far as two-hundred and *fifty* meters out, but they generally go up, like an upside-down cone, so you should get down low."

Noah let Jacob hold one grenade to judge its weight before sending him out to find rocks for throwing practice. At the top of the stairs, Jake collided with Chloe, who was head-down typing on her phone. "Justin thought the army helicopter story was *really* cool."

"We've got grenades!" Jake informed her.

"Sweet!" Chloe said. "Lemme see. Justin's family only has *baseball* bats." Noah knew what she really wanted to do was take a selfie with their new arsenal to send to her boyfriend. They thundered downstairs past their father.

"No playing with the hand grenades!"

In the kitchen, Natalie was making tea. Isabel said, "So, she's here? Emma?"

"Oh. Yeah. She hitchhiked down from Bethesda. She's been here about three days."

Natalie, wearing an oven mitt, removed the whistling kettle from the stove. "That Nichols boy was murdered three nights ago." Isabel and Noah waited, but Natalie didn't complete the thought. From the hush that followed, however, they all harbored the same suspicion.

"How...*is* she?" Isabel asked. "I mean, any difference?" Noah shook his head. "And that Sheriff was up here looking...for *her?*"

"Apparently Emma went jogging and got spotted." On seeing Isabel's surprise, Noah said, "She wants to keep her figure so she can find a man of her choosing."

Isabel snorted. "*That*, kinda, makes some sense, I guess. Her *plans* again? Hubby, kids, picket fence, station wagon?"

"She might be lonely. She told me to tell her when *Pandoravirus* hits the valley."

Natalie said, "So she can get first pick of the infected widowers, I suppose."

Chloe arrived with arms full of clothes from the laundry room. Isabel picked out a pair of blue jeans. "Oh, this top is cute," Natalie said. Chloe added accessory suggestions.

"How about this one," a winded Jake said upon arrival, placing a rock on the breakfast table with a thud.

Noah tossed it in air a few times. "Feels about right. So, Jake, it's about time. To go. You know. Do that thing?"

"What thing?" his idiot son asked.

Noah sighed. "Um, sweetie? Natalie? You're gonna hear a loud *bang*. But don't worry. That's us. Let's go, Jake."

Natalie peppered Noah and Jacob with repeated questions all the way to the SUV.

"They're gonna go throw *hand* grenades!" Chloe let slip.

"*Chloe!*" Jake snapped. "You *narc!*"

"You are *not* going to start playing with *hand* grenades, Noah Miller!"

"No," Noah said. "We're not. We're going to detonate four blocks of C4—seven and a half pounds of plastic explosives—and permanently sever the ridgeline road so we won't get any more visitors like today."

He was prepared for an outburst. So when she said nothing he grew defensive. "I paid a guy at the highway department a hundred K, and he and some other guy, ex-military or something, got the explosives from God knows where, pre-wired everything, and showed me what to do. The C4 is in a bore hole underneath the road. I don't have to go anywhere near it. We'll be back in an hour, max."

Chloe listened, mouth agape. "You mean we've been driving a huge SUV over a *bomb?*"

"*Noah!* She's right. But, now that it's done, be careful," was all Natalie said.

"*What?*" Chloe burst out. "*Mo-o-m!*" Noah hustled Jake into the SUV. "It's not fair! Just because he's a *boy*, it's *Jake* who gets to blow shit up?"

"Language, Chloe."

Jake fastened his seatbelt wearing a look of absolute wonder. "I thought we *were* just gonna blow up a grenade. She's actually letting us *do* this?" Noah ignored him and drove down the hill in silence, trying to make sure he hadn't forgotten any of the steps they'd walked him through. "It's rained, you know," Jake added, "since they put the dynamite in that hole." Noah frowned but declined to respond. "What if it got wet and doesn't blow? Do we, like, pull it out and see what's wrong? What if a wire is loose, and we tug on it?"

"It's gonna *work*." Noah had no other answer to the fairly legitimate concern.

They turned the SUV around in a tiny level area about a hundred meters from the detonator—three hundred from the charge. They climbed out with their rifles and found the blasting unit where Noah had hidden it under now dried-out, brown brush.

Father and son lay on their stomachs on the side of the ridge road behind the black plastic box. Noah handed the loose end of a bright orange wire to Jacob. The cable ran just outside the raised lip delineating the road's cliff-side edge and off into the distance around the bend ahead. Noah extracted the remote blaster from its waterproof enclosure. When he pressed "Power," the display lit and beeped. He smiled to his son at their success thus far.

"This goes in here," Noah said, inserting the plastic connector into the remote blasting unit, which beeped again. The display cycled through a series of checks. "Line continuity—OK. Rounds wired—1. Delay—0 ms. No errors." A green light lit above a button labeled, "Fire." The word, "Armed," flashed on the small LCD screen. But Noah didn't exult in that final milestone. His anxiety prevented premature celebration.

Jacob stared at him. "Ready?" Noah asked with a dry mouth. Jake covered his ears.

Noah couldn't figure out how to plug his own ears while also setting off the charge. He probably should've brought earplugs, or put the blasting unit on a timer, but instead just counted down. "Three, two, one."

He pressed and held the "Fire" button. When nothing happened, his heart sank.

Boooooom!

Both jumped reflexively at the stupendous detonation. Noah was jarred. His nerves embrittled. Church bells rang in his ears. The explosion had instantaneously pounded his body and rattled his chest. He coughed as jangled echoes reverberated through the hills.

Jacob was saying something and starting to rise. Noah restrained him until the last debris fell onto the road ahead. Smoke fouled the breeze with

144 Eric L. Harry

a noxious smell. Jacob shook Noah's arm. "Dad!" he mouthed through the cotton of Noah's throbbing eardrums. "It *worked*."

"Let's go check it out!"

"You're yelling, Dad."

They carried their rifles into the clearing haze. Around the curve, a thirty-foot section of road had completely disappeared. Unstable dirt tumbled into the gap. The ridge walls were now nearly vertical. No one could traverse it or the dominating hill above it.

"Wow!" Jacob said while taking photos on his cell phone.

On the short drive back, Noah kept trying to pop his ears like on an airplane.

Natalie, Chloe, and a freshly showered and changed Isabel met them at the SUV.

Natalie said something about "loud" and "spilled my tea."

"*What?*" Noah shouted. Jacob explained something through the loud ringing tones, then showed them pictures. "It's, like, *wrecked!*"

Noah couldn't tell what Natalie said about their accomplishment, but she didn't seem appropriately impressed. She raised her voice and mumbled something.

"*What?*" Noah replied.

"*Emma!* Let's go see her! Now! Before it gets dark!"

Chapter 22

THE SHENANDOAH VALLEY, VIRGINIA
Infection Date 53, 1730 GMT (1:30 p.m. Local)

THE SHENANDOAH VALLEY, VIRGINIA
Infection Date 53, 1730 GMT (1:30 p.m. Local)

Emma drank another cup of coffee at the cabin's small dinette. The caffeine stimulated her. Objectives, plans to accomplish them, necessities required for success, the identification and sequencing of subtasks and prerequisites in a hand-drawn Gantt chart—details poured forth. She sat at the table trying to keep track of it all. When she heard her brother call to her from outside, she looked at her phone. Over an hour had passed since she had heard the loud *bang*. She had been sitting in the same place and position since she had breakfast that morning. Her muscles felt stiff when she rose.

Outside, Noah stood at a distance with Natalie, Jake, Chloe, and Isabel.

"Hi!" Isabel said. A green mask, not the usual blue from the hospital, dangled beneath her chin, but she didn't raise it before coming over to give Emma a hug, no longer worried by Emma's significantly lower level of contagiousness. Emma patted her twin sister's back until Isabel pulled away. *"Surprise."*

It wasn't actually much of a surprise. When Emma heard the helicopter, she'd assumed it was Isabel.

"We brought you some more supplies!" Noah shouted. "And some pens and paper!"

Both would help. "My hearing was unaffected by SED, Noah. No need to yell." Her brother and his kids each carried sacks. Everyone but Isabel had rifles. Emma jammed her fingernails into her palms and took deep breaths, slowly, slowly, until the worst of the trembling passed.

Noah told the kids to follow him inside with the supplies, but Natalie said to stay outside. Natalie's look at Noah led him to agree instantly with his wife. She controlled Noah quite effectively. *Sex is a powerful tool,* the inner voice suggested helpfully. Noah and the kids nodded at Emma awkwardly as each laid their bags beside the front door. Natalie directed everyone to the shade of a steep hillside—outside, not inside the cabin.

Natalie sat on old stump. Noah, fittingly, sank to the ground at her feet. The two kids settled cross-legged onto grassy patches. Jake tossed pebbles down the hill. Chloe stared piercingly at Emma. Isabel and Emma sat on a flat rock outcropping roughly in the center of the semi-circle formed by their family.

Isabel held Emma's hand, gloved fingers interlaced, just as she had on the Air Force transport from Siberia to Washington after Emma had been infected. Isabel patted and rubbed Emma's jeaned thigh. "I was so *worried* about you after you ran off."

Emma said, "In retrospect, it was a dangerous trip down here."

"Did you run into any trouble?" Noah asked.

"There was a truck driver. He wanted sex in exchange for the ride, but he was disgustingly ugly."

"Did he…?" Natalie began before glancing down at her kids.

"Did he what?"

No one uttered a word until Isabel, haltingly, said, "I think she's asking, you know, whether he, you know…?"

"Raped you," Chloe explained.

"Oh. No."

Natalie put a hand to her chest and exhaled loudly. "*I'm* sorry, Emma. I was just afraid, you know…"

"That he raped me? No. I killed him." They all froze. Emma looked from face to face. Natalie's mouth hung open. Chloe's brow was knit. Jake now stared back at her too. What were they thinking? Why did they react like this? What did the looks and silence mean? "With a screwdriver," she added, hoping for some more enlightening feedback. Natalie shot her husband a look. He avoided it. "Up through the chin." Emma demonstrated with a thrust of her empty right hand. Isabel slowly, by degrees, let go of Emma's left hand.

It was Noah who next spoke. "Anything…*else* you wanna tell us?"

Emma had no idea what he meant. "There was this family driving to Atlanta. A mother and her three kids."

After a long silence, Noah said, "Did you...?" Once again, an inchoate question.

"Did you kill them too?" Chloe supplied.

"*Oh.* Thank you. No. I did not." Noah, like Natalie before him, heaved a sigh, which he slowly let out as he looked up at the sky. Emma quickly checked. There was nothing above them but a sheet of stratocumulus clouds.

"Do you think it's possible," Natalie asked, "that you might have infected them?"

Emma shook her head. "Probably not. They kept their windows open. One of the children had problems with flatulence."

Jake and Chloe laughed, but Noah and Natalie caught each other's eyes before returning Isabel's gaze. They were communicating—something—without words. Emma began to grow anxious again. She dug her fingernails into her palms and tried to deepen her shallow breathing.

"Did you meet anyone else on the way here?" Isabel asked.

Emma nodded. From the pause in the questioning, she surmised that they wanted details. "A tall, gangly man with a van and yellow teeth. He wanted sex too, so I also killed him. Then a college student. A cute freshman boy. We had sex, and he *did* get sick, but survived, I think."

"Did he go to George Mason?" Chloe asked. When Emma nodded, Chloe burst out, "*That's* the guy we saw on *TV!* Under *arrest!* You're practically *famous* now."

"And I also met a family living in the woods." That, apparently, was less exciting news. "They fed me, but then they recognized me from the DHS video."

"You didn't...?" Noah began.

Emma wished these people would finish their sentences. She turned to Chloe. "Did you kill them too?" she translated.

"Nope." Natalie sank from her stump to the ground next to Noah, her cheeks puffing out as she exhaled. She hugged her knees to her chest and Noah put his arm around her. Since no other questions immediately followed, Emma added, "The family in the woods had better weapons than the screwdriver, so I ran away."

Natalie looked at everyone in turn until she finally said, "Emma, how many people *have* you killed?"

"On the trip down here? Just the two: the guy with the truck, and the guy with the van."

"So," Chloe said, "those two creepy guys tried to have sex with you, and you didn't want to, so you killed them? But you had sex with the college boy? Uhm...*why?*" Now Chloe, too, had stopped making sense. Emma had already covered that ground.

"Because I didn't want to have sex with the first two, but I did with the third, who as I said was cute."

Chloe pursed her lips and nodded slowly. "Makes...*sense*, I guess." *There,* commented the voice. She *understands.*

"Emma?" It was Noah. "You qualified your answer, that you'd only killed two people, 'On the trip down here.' Does that mean...have you killed anyone else?"

"Yes. But those two were the only people I killed on the trip here."

Again, there was a long silence.

"I think he means who else did you kill?" Chloe interpreted again.

Before Emma could answer, Isabel slipped off the rock that the two sisters had shared and seated herself on another nearby ledge.

"I killed a boy at your neighbors' house. The Nicholses'."

Chloe gasped. Everyone stared at Emma so intensely that she felt a trickle of blood cross her palm. Jake casually lifted the rifle that he had leaned against the rocks and placed it across his lap. "Did he try to rape you, too?" Chloe asked.

Emma shook her head and pinned her bloody hands under her thighs. "He was only a boy. He had a rifle. I needed a better weapon, but all I found in the cabin was the butcher knife, which was good enough for the boy."

Noah startled Emma by rising, throwing his arms in the air, and slapping his thighs in a confusing jumble of vaguely aggressive gesticulations. "You *killed* that Nichols boy? Emma, he was four*teen!* A *child!*"

Emma nodded. "Yes, a boy. It would've been a lot more dangerous to try to kill a grown man with only a butcher knife. Maybe, with enough surprise, but..."

"Emma!" Isabel shouted.

Emma rose to her feet to pace like Noah, but Chloe, Jake, even Natalie reached for their rifles, and she froze—the only safe response to feeling the sudden torrent of anxiety. Her breathing became panting. Her heart pounded. Her ears popped. Her muscles quivered. They thought she might kill them too, but that was ridiculous. There were too many of them. They were armed. Her rifle was hidden behind the folded cots. She only had four cartridges. But she concluded she should focus instead on her last point. "That boy wasn't family," she said.

"But Emma, for God's sake," Noah shouted, "he was...!" *Again.* Noah was a successful lawyer, and one would imagine normally reasonably articulate. Natalie reached out and grabbed his forearm. Noah met his wife's eyes and fell silent. *What are they saying with those looks?* Emma's pulse throbbed audibly in her ears. She dug her nails deep.

"Your hands are bleeding," Isabel said softly, slowly approaching Emma. "You should trim your nails." Her sister's manner was calming. Emma began first to breathe, then to relax. *Cutting fingernails is a good idea,* said the voice.

Time passed before Noah said, "Emma, if you see anyone—anyone other than *family*—you need to...you need to run, okay? There are people out there who think you're...dangerous."

"I *am* dangerous," Emma explained, hoping that would clear things up. But they all stared back again as if at something unexpected she'd said. "To them," she added.

"But not to us?" It was Natalie. "You won't hurt *us?*"

"No."

"You promise?"

The voice in Emma's head remained silent. Emma said, "A contract?" They all looked back and forth between each other.

"Yes, a contract," Isabel replied. "And we agree not to hurt you, and to share our food. Deal?"

Emma said, "A contract. Yes. I agree to that."

* * * *

Isabel brimmed with thoughts about—and fears for—her sister. But the banter of her niece and nephew on the walk back down the hill distracted her.

"Can you *believe* it?" Jake said to Chloe. Both exploded in nervous laughter. "She was like, 'He wanted to hook up, so I killed his ass. *What*-ever.'"

"I *know!*" Chloe exclaimed. "She's so freaking badass. A player, *and* a killer!"

"Stop it!" Natalie snapped. Her two children shot sheepish looks toward Isabel and Noah. Chloe mouthed an exaggerated, "Sorry!" Isabel absolved the teenager by flashing her a smile.

Natalie asked Isabel, "Do you think we can trust her?"

Isabel, the world's leading authority on the behavior of *Pandoravirus* victims, decided not fritter that status away by betraying uncertainty. "She kept saying, in the lab, that she wanted to talk to you, Noah, about contracts. From reading her notebooks, it seemed like she was considering, I don't know, founding a society based on social contracts. She seemed *especially* focused on how to make sure one side doesn't do its part first, then be forced to rely on the other side to live up to some future end of its bargain."

"That's actually a pretty common…"

"How does *any* of this," Natalie interrupted, "have *anything* to do with whether or not Emma will kill us all? *Jesus!*"

"Well, I guess," Noah said falteringly, "we keep supplying her with food, and…."

"And as long as we do, she doesn't kill us?" Chloe asked.

"No one's killing anyone!" Noah snapped.

"That's hardly true," countered Chloe. "Aunt Emma killed, what, three people that we know of? It sounds to me like everybody is killing everybody."

"Every*one*," Noah corrected. "Everyone is killing everyone."

"And every*one*," Chloe continued, "is *infecting* everyone, like Aunt Emma and that college boy."

"I thought you claimed she wasn't contagious," Noah said to Isabel.

"I said she wasn't shedding the virus *prodigiously*, like by *breathing*. I didn't say someone could safely have presumably unprotected *sex* with her."

"Come on, Isabel," Noah said. "Just admit you don't know what you're talking about."

Isabel halted. The others turned her way. "Excuse me kids, Natalie, but *fuck* you, Noah!" She turned and headed back up the hill toward the cabin.

"Where are you going?" Noah called out.

"To continue my research!" she replied over her shoulder.

Noah first objected, then told her to be careful and to get back inside the fence by five p.m. "It gets dark earlier in the mountains!"

As Noah's family continued downhill, Chloe asked if she and Jake could visit Emma too. "Absolutely not," Isabel heard their mother reply before they disappeared.

Back at the cabin, Isabel saw that Emma had taken the bags of supplies inside. She stopped herself from going straight to the front door, and like Noah had done called out to her sister from some distance away. Emma appeared, saw it was Isabel, and stood aside.

When her eyes adjusted to the gloom of the cabin, Isabel noticed that notes already covered several loose pages spread across the dinette. "Back at it, huh?" Emma tilted her head in confusion. "Your notes? More epidemiological research on *Pandoravirus*?"

"Oh. No. I finished that."

Isabel edged closer to the table, but didn't feel comfortable turning her back on her sister. She pivoted awkwardly, exuding a pleasant demeanor as if to allay any suspicion over her odd maneuver. But she saw no alarm in

Emma's blank face. Isabel slid a page with a few notes off another covered top to bottom with words, figures, and diagrams. "So what's this, then?"

Before Emma could reply, Isabel saw that she had hand-drawn, in the midst of her text, a series of lines with numbers corresponding to the local state highways and more distant Interstate, all connected to the names of towns and cities, though not to scale.

"It's my plan for surviving the arrival of SED."

"Okay. And when, do you expect, that will happen?"

"It already has happened."

"You mean *you*. No, I meant, when do you think it will break out, you know, in the rest of the population?"

"As a rough guess? Tomorrow, most likely."

"Tomorrow!" Isabel snorted, though it wasn't funny. "But, Em, they're still fighting in New York City. It hasn't even made it to Philadelphia, much less the D.C.-area."

"Yes, it has," came her sister's innocent-sounding reply. "We just don't know about it yet."

Isabel found the prediction so disconcerting that she had to hold onto the kitchen countertop. "So, it's what? Everywhere?"

"No. But it's everywhere between here and New England. It's in the refugee camps. The private homes of people who took relatives in. Charitable shelters at churches and community centers. Long-haul drivers, aircraft and train crews, and emergency and security personnel and troops."

"And tomorrow it'll be here."

"And a few days after that," Emma explained as if it were a mathematical certainty, "the authorities will know about it, word will leak out, and the killing will begin."

And that's that. Isabel had thought they had more time. She'd thought her only worry for the next couple of weeks would be whatever godawful hell it was to which they sent Rick. Turned out the godawful hell had followed her there.

Emma's musings on paper had a section entitled, "Militia." Under it were notes about organization: keep units small, look for veterans to train and lead, equip with light arms and large vehicles, feed well. "Looks like you're clairvoyant." Emma clearly had no idea what she meant. "The sheriff showed up today at the gate to the main house with a militia. They were looking for you—or, rather, for the murderer of that boy. They said they'd seen some woman jogging in the hills."

"I'm trying to stay in shape."

"Emmy, you can't *kill* people."

"Not the bigger, stronger, or better armed and prepared people." Emma's face remained uncreased by any cares, concerns, or guilt.

How could Isabel explain ten thousand years of human moral development to her brain damaged sister? Why would an Infected even care about morals with zero empathy and no self to be held to account to any standards of conduct? "This sheriff's militia," Isabel said, "is out there looking for you right now."

Emma strangely exhibited absolutely no sign of anxiety even though, this time, it was warranted. "The loud explosion today," Emma asked, "was that Noah blowing up the ridge road?" *Maybe she's calm,* Isabel thought as she confirmed her sister's speculation, *because she's already worked out how she'd kill me.* She resolved never again to return to the cabin unarmed. Rick would admonish her for such an error. Emma said, "Sheriff Walcott probably doesn't know the old way up here. It's overgrown."

"You know that sheriff?"

"I met him," Emma replied. "He seemed reasonable. Professional."

"But the neighbor—Nichols—won't be reasonable. And some of his good-ole-boy militia buddies might side with him. That militia is a huge threat to you."

"That's not the militia I'm writing about. Although..." she began, then leaned onto her elbows and resumed taking notes. Isabel followed along, mumbling, "Consider...reforming...Walcott's...militia...after..."

Emma put down the pen and stood erect. Isabel met her uncomplicated and direct gaze. "You're talking about forming a militia of the *infected?*"

"It would be helpful, now that you mention it, simply to recall the previously uninfected militiamen to their posts. There's pre-existing organization, equipment, maybe even a modicum of training."

"I didn't mean that!" Isabel said for no particular reason.

"I just thought," Emma said uncertainly, "that I would credit you with a good idea."

"No! Don't 'credit me' with that." Isabel was exasperated. "Emma, that's an *army.*"

"A militia."

"Men in big trucks with guns!" Emma searched Isabel's face, presumably in an effort to understand her sister, who after all did have the great idea of founding an army of Infecteds. "What is this militia of yours going to do, exactly?"

"Help me survive. And you, too, possibly."

Isabel filled her lungs and exhaled noisily, which increased Emma's scrutiny of her. "Jesus, Emmy. What's gonna happen? To us? To the world?"

The gears clearly turned in her sister's damaged head before she extended her thumb to keep count of her points. "The virus is going to overrun the Earth." Her index finger was next. "If we plan carefully, we may survive." Her middle finger joined the first two. "The world, as it existed before the outbreak, will be replaced by a new world that's dramatically changed by massive depopulation, the wars, and the altered nature of Infecteds, who will quickly predominate demographically."

She was finished. So was Isabel. Again, she reached out to steady herself on the countertop. "I...I'd better...I'm heading back down now."

"Okay," Emma said. She sounded almost cheerful, except "cheer" was one of those emotions that Infecteds had lost, along with everything else that made them human.

When Isabel's hand found the knob at the front door, she heard from behind, "That Nichols boy that I killed..."

"Yes?" Isabel replied without turning.

"Maybe I shouldn't have killed him." Isabel turned to face her sister. Was Emma's remark evidence of self-doubt? Was it possible that the ever amazing brain had sufficient plasticity to work around the damage it had suffered and reconstruct an identity—a self—from the wreckage? A self against which standards of behavior—morals, ethics—could be measured and guilt applied to enforce societal norms? "Killing the boy seems to have caused trouble."

"Yes, it did."

"And..." Emma fell silent.

"Yes?" Isabel prodded. Emma's eyes were darting about empty space. *She's thinking,* Isabel realized. *Something is happening in there.* "And *what*, Emma?"

"And could you bring some artificial sweetener on your next trip? The coffee doesn't taste good just black." That was it. Isabel felt deflated.

"Okay. Sure. Sweetener. The zero-calorie kind, for your...*figure*." She felt relieved to be outside and to not see the muzzle of a stolen gun aimed at her back. But it took Isabel getting over the first ridge for her to envision a world in which everyone was like Emma, or worse. She stopped, squatted, wrapped her arms around her knees, and rocked herself back and forth. But the only thing that calmed her was to close her eyes and repeat, silently, her mantra. *Rick, Rick, Rick.*

Chapter 23

Isabel's niece beamed with pride as Natalie put the eggs from Chloe's hens on the table for the family.

A phone rang with a previously unheard tone. It wasn't any of the cell phones, all checked in unison, of anyone in the kitchen or breakfast room. "What's *that?*" Chloe asked.

"The land line!" Noah replied. His chair scraped the floor as he hurried to answer.

"The what?"

Isabel and Noah's curious family crowded around Noah, who pressed the speaker button on the handset's base.

"...has activated your county's disaster response plan. A credible report of an outbreak in your county of *Pandoravirus horribilis* has been received. You should remain indoors, if possible, and should limit contact with persons not known to you to be uninfected until further notice. You should exercise extreme caution in public, avoid all large crowds, and report any suspicious persons to your local medical or law enforcement authorities. If you see something, say something. To repeat, the Virginia Department of Emergency Management has activated your county's disaster response plan." The reverse 9-1-1 call reiterated the previous warnings. Noah hung up.

"Emma was right," Isabel said, feeling both begrudging respect for her sister's prediction and fatalistic resignation at the foretold arrival of the pandemic.

Everyone turned to Noah. "Okay. Starting now, we all carry a radio and a rifle with us everywhere, and all the time. We'll patrol different parts of the property, in pairs, every four hours during the daytime, and once at night before we button the place up. Jake, the drones will go up in between foot patrols and check the areas not covered. I'll make out a schedule. If anyone sees *anything—kids*—they let everyone know. Immediately."

"Do you think it's Emma?" Natalie asked. "Who triggered that call?"

Noah shook his head. "I'm guessing it's someone else. Walcott didn't seem too convinced by Trey Nichols's accusation that the murderer was an Infected. But I'll go check on Emma to make sure she hasn't done, you know, anything else."

"I'll come with you," Isabel said. Why, she didn't know. She needed to abandon this hopeless goal of reconnecting with her brain-damaged sister, which if truth be told was really a continuation of a lifelong, failed effort. They were identical twin sisters. It wasn't supposed to be this way.

* * * *

When Noah met Isabel on the front porch after distributing the patrol schedule he'd printed out, she said, "Look at us!" She left her helmet, body armor, hydration system, huge backpack, and smaller rucksack behind, but wore her army camouflage, webbing studded with bulging pouches, and combat boots, and carried her assault rifle. Rick would be proud.

"Look at *you*," Noah commented. She grew self-conscious, checking herself in the hallway mirror for something that appeared comically out-of-place. Noah, too, wore camo, but hers looked government-issue, his bought from a sporting goods store. "What's in all those pouches?" he asked.

She tucked her chin to her chest to look down, which warped her voice. "These four are ammunition. I don't know, exactly, about all the rest. I think this one's first aid. This one I've never looked in. That one has a compass. This is where I keep my toiletries."

Her brother took a look at her rifle, tilting his head, his attention lingering around the trigger. "It's full auto." He sounded impressed, or possibly concerned.

Isabel looked at the switch, which had three positions: Safe, Semi, and Auto. "Yeah. You're only supposed to use Safe and Semi." *Because*

Rick said. Noah perhaps felt somewhat inadequate, in a Freudian sense. "*Your* rifle is a lot longer than mine," Isabel said in an attempt to make him feel better.

"Yeah. And semi-automatic only. Yours is, like, *totally* illegal. Barrel's too short, and full auto. Jeeze."

Isabel fished a small purse from the cargo pocket on her right thigh. In it was her California driver's license, UCSB faculty ID and health insurance card, VISA and American Express cards, and the card that she was looking for, which she handed to Noah.

"Retired Federal Agent?"

"Former FBI agent, please, to be precise. Remember, I was a snitch? But I can now legally carry guns for the next fifteen years."

They headed out through the small gate on the uphill side of the compound, which Noah tapped lightly before opening. Isabel quickly lost the main house's WiFi, which put a halt to her obsessive checking for text messages. She had awoken that morning, looked at her phone, and cursed that it hadn't chirped to notify her of the middle-of-the-night message. Rick couldn't say where he was, probably some military secret, but he'd texted that he wasn't "too far." That must have meant he was still at the Pentagon, where he'd headed the day before.

He'd told her, during their escape from Long Island, that there were four sites in Washington that would be defended to the last: central D.C. encompassing the White House, Capitol Hill, and the Supreme Court; the cluster of the NIH and Walter Reed hospitals in Bethesda; Joint Base Andrews; and the Pentagon across the Potomac in Arlington.

"So," Noah said when she put her phone away, "this Marine guy…"

"Rick Townsend."

"Are you and he…?"

"Sleeping with each other? Uhm, *duh*."

"I was gonna say serious, but okay. What about that ex-boyfriend of yours, Brandon what's-his-name, from the University of Illinois?"

"Indiana," she corrected. "And he's dead."

Saying it out loud stabbed Isabel in the chest. She recounted to Noah Brandon's self-sacrifice at the Manhattan ferry dock and was surprised to end the story in tears.

Noah stopped and embraced her. "You know, if all Townsend saw was him jumping into the water…"

"Being pushed," Isabel amended. "Fully clothed, wearing all the same heavy gear I've got on, plus a backpack and body armor. Just ahead of a panicked crowd that shoved a few hundred more people in on top of him in a fifty-degree river. In a city that's right now lost all control after outbreaks at the DHS headquarters, City Hall, NYPD headquarters, everywhere, and has descended into something like the late stages of a medieval siege."

They were silent for a while as they continued on uphill. Then Noah said, "So, you love him? The Marine?"

"I don't know. I mean, I guess I do. I think about him all the time. I want to be with him and hate every second we're apart. I worry about him, scared to death about where they might send him. And…and I worry he won't, you know, come back. For me." Her lower lip quivered, and she bit it.

Isabel looked up at her big brother. Surely he'd picked up on her deepest fears and would reassure her that she was smart, and witty, and pretty, and of course Rick loved her and would move heaven and earth to return to the only person that mattered in his life. But naturally, Noah totally missed the pleading look on her face and said, "Something tells me Marines are gonna be pretty busy the next little while. I wouldn't hold my breath."

"*Je*sus!" she snapped, confusing Noah completely.

Isabel walked the rest of the way to the cabin in wounded silence. As before, Noah called Emma's name repeatedly some distance from the front door. There was no answer. They knocked. Nothing. Noah opened the door.

They stepped into the dark, single room. Before Isabel's eyes could adjust, Noah exclaimed, "Shit!"

Sitting still on the sofa and on a chair were the African-American embassy guard Dwayne, whose breathing was fast and shallow, and the young blond ambassador's daughter, Samantha, who had infected Dwayne during their evacuation from China and who now pinned both hands beneath her legs. In a miniature imitation of Emma, the young girl said softly, to Dwayne, "In through the nose; out through the mouth." In the kitchen, holding a broom in a white-knuckled death grip, stood a wide-eyed Dorothy, the infected tourist and housewife, also Emma's NIH roommate.

"Ho-o-oly, shit," said Noah. "They're all here. *Fuck* me."

"*Noah,*" Isabel admonished, nodding at the twelve-year-old girl. She then said, as cheerily as possible, "Hi," giving the silent Infecteds a cursory waggle of her fingers.

"Hi," replied Sam in her high-pitched voice as she returned the wave. Dwayne just stared at their weapons. Dorothy didn't know what to say, but she had always been more addled than the others.

"Hello." Noah and Isabel both jumped at the greeting from behind them. "Christ!" Noah exclaimed. "Emma! You scared the hell outta me!" Their sister was flushed and breathing hard, and her T-shirt was soaked through. "Where have you been?"

"Jogging. We talked about that."

"Right. Nothing else? No...*trouble?*"

"Jogging?"

Noah turned to the three other Infecteds gathered in the cabin. "How about any of you? Did you, by any chance, run into any trouble on the way down here from Maryland?"

Sam said, "No." Her voice was so childlike it seemed to put Noah at ease. But Isabel knew better. That cute little girl had used her thumbnails to gouge out the eyes of her Navy SEAL rescuer in Beijing.

Noah's ease proved to be short-lived. Isabel nudged him. His gaze followed hers to the coffee table. On it lay neatly arranged personal effects. Wallets. Cell phones. A mace canister. A revolver with five bullets and one empty casing standing upright beside it. A pink, bedazzled plastic bag that looked like it contained a young girl's makeup kit. All resources presumably collected on their trek south and cataloged on the paper Noah had brought the day before, which lay on the table next to a pen.

"Did you bring sweetener?" asked Emma as she poured herself a glass of water. Isabel put the blue box with its individual packets on the counter. At Emma's urging, Dorothy resumed sweeping.

Emma rejoined her siblings by the front door and said to Noah, "From now on, we're going to need rations for four. And in return we'll help you in the defense of the property and share any deer that we kill. That would be an amendment of our contract. Do you agree?"

"Uhm, it'll be tighter..." Noah glanced at Isabel, who stared back wide-eyed—*can you believe this*—and attracted Emma's close attention, but ultimate confusion. "But instead of the venison," Noah said, "I'd like you to agree to give us four days' notice if you ever intend to terminate this contract."

Emma's eyes darted all about. She opened her mouth—not as if to speak to them, but to someone else...who wasn't there. Eventually, she focused on Noah. "One day."

"Two days' notice."

"Agreed," Emma replied. "And it's reciprocal."

Emma turned and looked at each of her roommates, but no words or gestures were exchanged. "And as for the defense of the property, tell Jake he doesn't have to patrol the cabin all the time. We'll take care of everything here."

"Emmy, I don't know what you think, but I didn't tell him to spy on you."

"The drone was here for five minutes during my outdoor shower yesterday. Explain to him that drones are louder than he thinks. Also, I washed and aired out that camouflage jacket. Would you mind smelling it to make sure it's okay?"

She handed the jacket to Noah, who seemed dumbfounded and frozen. "Emma, I'm very, very sorry. This is so embarrassing."

"What is?" When Noah couldn't manage a timely reply, Emma said, "Does the jacket still smell?"

"Did you lose your sense of smell?" he asked.

"No," Isabel answered, raising the jacket to her nose. "They can smell, they just aren't offended by smells. It's clean, Emma. No problem."

"Thank you," she replied. "Did you come up here for any other reason?"

Noah seemed dazed. "Uhm, yeah, I guess." Isabel tried to remain motionless and to forego the newfound comfort of resting her finger on her rifle's trigger and thumb on the selector switch. "We got a reverse 9-1-1 call this morning saying that the virus is now in this county. There's been an outbreak."

"That was them." Dwayne and Samantha agreed. "Someone stole Samantha's water bottle in the Red Cross soup line and must've ingested pathogens from it."

"The Salvation Army," the normally taciturn Dorothy corrected. Everyone turned her way. "The ones with the kettle and bell. They're the Salvation Army."

Isabel's eye was drawn toward the corner of the room to an ice chest, a canvas tent, and miscellaneous camping supplies. "After they ate, they went off and found a camper with those things in them, then headed back by the soup line and the sheriff had already quarantined it."

"The sheriff?" Noah asked.

"Yes. Sheriff Walcott."

"You *know* him?"

"Yeah," Isabel said. "She's already met him."

"He seems competent," Emma opined.

Noah shook his head and took a deep breath. "Emmy, can we talk to you outside?" When the twins followed Noah out, he said, "You can't kill people for their stuff. That's…That's…" He didn't complete the thought, perhaps realizing all the reasons why Emma couldn't kill people no longer applied…to her, anyway. It's immoral? Illegal? Cruel? Why would that persuade an Infected?

"If you start killing the uninfected," Isabel tried, "then they'll start killing you."

"They're already killing Infecteds, if that's who you mean by *you*."

* * * *

"What the hell am I gonna tell Natalie?" Noah asked on the trip back down the hill.

"The truth?" came Isabel's naïve reply. *She's obviously never been married*, Noah thought but didn't say.

But then again, what else *could* Noah tell his wife? His every alternative to the truth seemed worse. "Okay. But how can I spin it as a positive?"

"Oh, I dunno. Try, 'Nat, there are some homicidal Infecteds at the cabin, but we have that deal that they won't slaughter us without first giving two days' notice'?"

"You see, that's what's wrong with the truth."

"Do you think we actually *can* trust them?" Isabel asked.

That pissed Noah off. "Aren't you the world's leading fucking expert on Infected behavior? Why are you asking *me?*"

"Because I'm *worried* about it, Noah. Jesus. I mean, who the hell could know whether they'll honor their side of any deal? And it probably varies based on which Infecteds you're talking about, and what the circumstances are in a situation that's going through radical changes every couple of hours."

As they neared the small gate in the fence, Isabel's phone buzzed. They were back in WiFi range. She read her only message with growing concern. "Shit. The helicopter is on the way back here to pick me up." Noah detected a hint of a smile on her face.

"Is that this *Rick's* helicopter?"

"*Maybe*. Yeah." She grinned. "I'm on the E-4B list." Noah had no idea what she was talking about. "The president's plane? I'm supposed to get on it at Andrews."

"The president is evacuating Washington? When?"

"Like they told me that, Noah!"

"Why the hell are *you* supposed to be on his plane?"

"Because I'm the world's leading fucking zombie expert, remember?"

"Just tell them no."

"I can't," Isabel said. Noah guessed it had something to do with her Marine. She packed and said her good-byes. When the same helicopter as the day before picked Isabel up, Noah waved one last time, but his little sister didn't notice. She was too busy kissing Townsend.

"I guess he *didn't* dump her," Natalie said to Noah, perplexed.

"I've got, uhm, something to tell you," Noah said to his wife. "Remember when I told you that Emma had a bunch of roommates at the NIH hospital?"

Chapter 24

Rick and Isabel were nearly alone in the large Black Hawk helicopter. The only crewman in the rear sat beside his door gun and avoided the couple who, despite the many empty seats lining the thrumming bulkheads, pressed close to each other.

Rick seemed distant. "What's the *matter?*" Isabel asked repeatedly.

After dodging, he eventually said, "There was this church bus full of kids. We...didn't get there in time. I don't wanna talk about it." His mood darkened further.

She wanted him to share everything with her. But their intimacy had come to an abrupt halt. Rick now stared at the cabin's deck instead of at her.

The gunner slid his door open and roiling wind blasted their cabin. He swung his multi-barreled gun out and pointed it down. They were descending. Rick seemed relieved by the interruption and went from handhold to handhold to stand near the opening, lowering his goggles against the gale. Isabel joined him there, squinting.

The helicopter settled lower and lower as they tracked the Potomac River headed north. The familiar monuments of the District of Columbia were directly ahead, and Arlington, Virginia, on their left was dominated by the Pentagon. Ugly concrete barriers interspersed with hulking green tank-like vehicles surrounded the huge complex. The bridges were blocked, and the nearby streets were empty.

The helicopter began a big, sweeping turn to the right. Ever lower, Isabel could now see the still quiet residential neighborhoods of suburban Maryland. All seemed calm other than the fires that rose here and there in the distance closer to Washington. But as they passed an oval track that at first Isabel thought was a football stadium but on closer inspection appeared to be some sort of motor raceway, she and Rick both saw the fencing, the troop tents ringed by sandbags, and the giant green reception tents emblazoned with red crosses on white circles. Although the infield was empty, it would soon be filled with detained Infecteds. Elevated man lifts topped by umbrellas, presumably impromptu machine gun towers, encircled the Mass Open-Air Detention facility just like in Boston despite their report of its total failure there. Her eyes met Rick's, and in them she saw reflected the same thought. These plans, too, would fail. Isabel's concern deepened on sensing Rick's internal disquiet. He appeared to be at risk of losing hope. Brandon had given up too.

The helicopter landed on the airbase tarmac amid dozens of others. They were directed to a breezy tent with open sides. A nurse in full combat gear stood behind a small table beside an air policeman holding an assault rifle at the ready. Both wore masks and gloves. The nurse did temperature and pupil checks on Isabel. The air policeman asked Isabel questions. "You like football, ma'am?" Isabel nodded while trying to hold her eyes open as the nurse shone a pen light into them, but she flinched at how bright the beam was. "What's your favorite team?"

"The Giants. I grew up in Connecticut. We were Giants fans."

"What do you like about football?"

They were checking her emotional responses. She needed to show that she had them. "I loved the thrill when we scored and the crowd went crazy. When you're at the game, it vibrates through you like you're sitting on a speaker at a concert. It was," she was going to say infectious, "scintillating, blood-tingling, electrifying." She couldn't think of any other emotive synonyms.

The air policeman gave the nurse a thumbs-up. Isabel marveled at how easily their test could be passed. The thermometer held to Isabel's forehead beeped. "She's good," the female medic said.

The air policeman relaxed slightly, but he never lowered his weapon. He was committed to living and taking no chances.

Rick said, "This is where I say good-bye...again."

"Now? You can't, at least, come inside with me?"

He shook his head. "I've gotta get back across the river. But they've tasked me to the staff of the Joint Chiefs, so I'll probably stay in the area...

at least until it's time to come meet up with you again. You're the one who's headed off God knows where."

They hugged and kissed, but Rick was more reserved than in days past. She thought about saying, "I love you," but settled on, "Be careful. I'm depending on you, you know?"

"You'll be fine." He tried to smile. "You'll literally be in the safest place on Earth."

"I mean, stupid, that I'm depending on you to take care of yourself and come back to me. I need you to. Do you understand?" He nodded, but that seemed too noncommittal. "No. That's not good enough. You *have* to find me. It's very, very important. If you understand that, then *say* it."

"I'll make it to you. I'll find you."

How? she thought but couldn't bring herself to ask. It would've been unfair to Rick.

She looked back as Rick strode toward the helicopter and the air policeman drove her across the base in an open-air golf cart. She focused on controlling those pesky emotions of hers. She had to keep herself from crying so much, especially on military bases. Her escort parked beside sandbags manned by heavily armed troops, saluted, and reported to an officer.

Another PPE-clad medic checked her vitals again. Temperature normal. "They should fuckin' kill 'em all," an armed airman said, sitting on the mound of sandbags. "As soon as it breaks out. Wipe everybody the fuck out." Pupillary response normal. "Ever seen fuel-air ordnance? Big canister filled with gas that gets sprayed out over a wide area and lit. *Boom!*" Knee reflexes normal. "The blast wave's the trick. Breaks every bone in your body like you jumped outta the World Trade Center." Blood pressure and heart rate in the elevated range.

"She's good," the medic pronounced. "And shut the fuck up," she said to the bloodthirsty airman.

Isabel was escorted by a female air policeman to a lounge. A TV mounted high on the wall was tuned to CNN, but the volume was low. Scattered about sprawled on sofas and in recliners were crewmen in their flight suits, most asleep. Isabel settled close enough to the TV to watch, if not hear. It amazed her to see a video like those she'd viewed weeks earlier in the underground White House Situation Room. A crowd of Infecteds in some midsized American city, not far-off Asia, confronted troops. It would've been classified Top Secret just a short while ago. She could anticipate what was going to happen as she watched the still, quiet crowd. A hulking black vehicle with the emblem of some police department sprayed water from behind barricades onto the stoic front ranks of Infecteds, whom Brandon would have called charged.

She had tried not to think about Brandon, but now she winced. It had been too much for her to digest when they'd made it across the East River to the Hunter's Point South ferry landing. Their helicopter crew had been searching for fuel, so their remaining entourage had hiked south on Long Island. Her huge pack had wrecked her back, and every previously insignificant pressure point in her combat boots had become a blister. Rick talked their way across the Pulaski Bridge with the aid of Isabel's White House pass. "Did you see him…after he went into the water?" she had asked. But when Rick had shaken his head, Isabel let it drop. Brandon was gone.

Rick had gotten in touch with an Annapolis classmate stationed at the Brooklyn Navy Yard. The lieutenant had driven to meet them in a gray pickup truck wearing gray-themed camouflage. Vasquez and his five green-clad troops had filled the bed in the back, and Rick and Isabel had crowded into the cab. The Navy guy had a million questions for Rick. Can you catch it from bodily fluids? When do they go from rational to crowd-crazed? Had he ever seen them use weapons? Had he heard about the survivors of the New York National Guard unit that had turned and were now fighting against us?

On the nearly muted TV, the camera displaying the crowd shook once as if a blow had fallen on the cameraman. But it wasn't a physical blow, except to the extent of the concussive effects of so many guns firing all at once, which was only a slight hiss at the set's lowered volume. Masses of Infecteds fell in waves. This time, the line held, with only a few infected attackers topping the barricades and being shot point-blank by PPE-clad troops. Piles of the dead and dying soon formed a second barrier that attackers found difficult to surmount, climbing bodies that still writhed, brushing aside hands that still grasped, slipping on blood and viscera, only to be shredded by steady fire from a few feet in front and added to the height of the obstacle.

"Dr. Miller?" Isabel jumped. The female Air Force officer at her side apologized, glancing at the carnage on the screen above a graphic— "Recorded earlier today in King of Prussia, Pennsylvania"—before saying, "I guess we won that one."

"Yay for us," Isabel replied. The woman erased her polite expression. Isabel left her rifle and pack in the lounge and was led down a short hall for her E-4B orientation. "So, E-4B is…what? The name of the plane?"

"Yes, ma'am. It's the name of the equipment model, a heavily modified 747-200. Call sign *Nightwatch*." At the end of a long hall, she opened a door into a hangar large enough to engulf the huge jumbo jet. The scale of the everything was so out of proportion that Isabel's head swam. "You're now on twenty-four-hour ground alert. You're not to leave the hangar. You sleep in your gear and listen for the call—*Nightwatch*—over the PA. You'll have six minutes to board, but you oughta be there in two. Go to the aft stairs." She pointed at narrow steps that had been lowered from the rear of the plane. "Show this badge." The woman handed her an ID with Isabel's hideous White House security pass photo. "Never take it off." Isabel slipped its strap around her neck before showing it to the air policeman guarding the wider steps up to the front of the plane.

The 747's interior was more Spartan than Isabel had imagined. The only luxury was in the smallish presidential quarters, of which she got only a passing glimpse. The cockpit looked old-fashioned, with dials, gauges, and knobs instead of glass touchscreens. "Analog," her escort explained, "not digital. Not networked. Unhackable." Three large cabins, filled with workstations, took up the rest of the plane. In the very back, Isabel would "hot bunk," sharing a bed on a rotating basis with other crewmen, or she could sleep in her assigned seat, whose upholstery was a shockingly bright blue. It stood out against the décor in the rest of the plane, which was in the style of late-Twentieth-Century-beige-computer-case. "But since that seat's also where you'll spend all your waking hours, you might wanna stretch out for variety's sake. We'll exit down the aft steps. Any questions?"

That was it? "Uhm, yeah," Isabel replied. *Any idea what the fuck I'm doing here?* What she actually said was, "When do we take off?"

"Fifteen minutes after the National Command Authority says go, ma'am, and about sixty seconds after he and his family are aboard."

Isabel took a last look around in disbelief. The woman escorted her back to the giant hangar's lounge, introduced her to a newly arrived aircrew, and said, "Make yourself comfortable. I hear different things about how it's going in D.C., but you may be here a while."

Isabel dumped her M4 and pack, draped in body armor with her helmet hooked onto it, beside an empty plush recliner in front of the TV. The three airmen she had met, spread out to either side, wore one-piece flight uniforms and cast tired but curious glances at G.I. Jane. Isabel inquired politely what they all did in the Air Force. The dark-haired man with graying temples, sitting on her left directly in front of the TV, said, "I'm a pilot, she's my co-pilot." The blond female officer to her right was about Isabel's age. "And he's our loadmaster." A younger man—a sergeant with a bunch of stripes—leaned forward and gave her a wave. He then grumbled, "But since we just maxed out our flight duty hours, we'll probably get handed shovels and ordered to dig."

The co-pilot filled her mouth with yoghurt and mumbled, "Somebody's gotta fly that bird outta here 'fore Andrews is overrun."

"Why? Pretty soon we're gonna have way too many planes and way too little fuel."

"Yeah, but not yet. Plus, I saw a *lo-o-otta* flight plans being filed for Texas." She thumped her chest with her fist several times before burping.

"Gross," the loadmaster said.

"Gross *ma'am*," the co-pilot corrected.

"Gross ma'am," came his perfunctory revision.

"Fuck-off," the co-pilot responded with a single, two-syllable word before stuffing an entire white donut into her mouth and licking her fingers.

"Ma'am?"

The co-pilot turned to the sergeant and spat puffs of confectionary powder. "Fuck the fuck *off*, Chapman!"

"You on *Nightwatch*?" the pilot asked Isabel. "Better chow down, 'cause it's rationed MREs, 24/7, unless you're the NCA and family."

Isabel grabbed some fruit and a coffee and returned to her place. The others all reclined in the comfortable, padded chairs, so Isabel did the same. The news anchor was on a split screen alongside shaky aerial photos that pixilated every few seconds. The caption said they were from suburban Buffalo. Streets and lawns were dotted with bodies that now represented hazardous waste sites. Large Army trucks filled with soldiers in gas masks held rifles pointed outward. A line of police cars all had lights flashing. Police in helmets and gas masks held large clear riot shields. The picture switched to recorded video of a brutal, primitive orgy of gouging, stomping annihilations. Too late, a warning about graphic violence appeared.

"You gonna eat that?" the co-pilot asked Isabel about the half-empty plate she'd rested on the broad arm of her chair with its disposable plastic fork, half a dozen cantaloupe slices, and semi-picked over grapes on a stem. Isabel shook her head. The woman instantly seized the sagging paper plate and shoveled the fruit into her mouth.

"Ma'am?" the loadmaster said to the co-pilot.

"Yeah. Gross. Copy that. Could you...?" She looked at the pilot, but motioned toward the TV.

The senior officer used the remote to raise the volume. "Scenes like this," came the anchorwoman's funereal tone, "are being repeated all across the northern tier of States and are, well, one has to admit frighteningly reminiscent of the last footage we saw out of China, South Korea, and

Vietnam before they went dark, and have seen in Europe and Japan in the last few weeks."

Barricades, smoke, burning buildings, the lingering fog of tear gas, rioters, looters, bouncing rocks, spinning tear gas canisters. Wounded crumpled against a building. People steering wide berths around them. *They're not wounded,* Isabel realized. *They're sick.*

The expressions on the faces of the flight crew around her had darkened, but none more than the co-pilot's. The blond woman stared at the screen looking pallid and waxen. Winces made brief appearances on her otherwise guarded face. The abandoned plate of half-eaten food now seemed of no interest.

The pilot, watching scenes from Buffalo, said to Isabel, "We just got back from up that way. Took a C-17 with supplies to Syracuse." He glanced at his crewmen, who stared back from beneath knit brows. "It got...bad. Some of the Guardsmen wanted to get the hell outta there. I can't say that I blame 'em."

"The stacks of the dead," said the co-pilot on the other side of Isabel, looking as if she might grow ill right then and there, "were piled, like, one story high? Two? Practically the whole length of Runway 2-8. Nine thousand feet. They were bulldozing bodies into long trenches, and when we opened up the ramp, *man*, the fuckin' *stench*...."

"And the fuckin' Guardsmen," came from the loadmaster. "They stormed aboard, before we could even unload our first pallet. Screamin', 'Take off! Take off! Right now!' I had to explain that we were too heavy. We had to offload our cargo. I swear to God I thought they were gonna shoot me right then. They were arguing with each other. Fuckin' terrified, is what they were. Then, I thought they were gonna shoot their colonel, who came marchin' up the ramp with his hand on the butt of his pistol. Did you see that? Like, what? Quickdraw fuckin' McGraw there with his Berretta was gonna take on two dozen desperate motherfuckers with M4s? Tryin' to get home to their families?"

"I gotta take a crap," the distressed and bloodless co-pilot said. Gone was her bravado, and her color.

"How'd you get outta there?" Isabel asked.

The pilot said, "The colonel convinced the lieutenant, the lieutenant convinced the sergeants, and the men followed the sergeants." He seemed deeply disturbed. One of the signs of the apocalypse, Isabel imagined. U.S. troops...mutinying.

"Probably all dead by now," the younger airman said. "Or infected."

"To recap," they heard on TV, "there are reported outbreaks in all regions of Vermont and New Hampshire. In Maine west of I-95 from Bangor to Houlton. In Massachusetts north and east of a line running from Springfield to Pittsfield. In Connecticut east and south of I-84 from Hartford to Danbury. In New York north of the Buffalo-Rochester-Syracuse-Utica-Albany line, and down the Hudson River Valley from Albany all the way into New York City. There are pockets of outbreaks in Newark, Princeton, and Trenton, New Jersey, in eastern Pennsylvania principally clustered around Philadelphia, and overnight in Baltimore, Maryland, the greater D.C. metropolitan area, and further south in Virginia as far as Lynchburg. In addition, reports have just come in of vigilante fighting in a displaced persons camp along I-91 north of Greenfield in western Massachusetts, with estimates of, and this is what I'm being told, thousands of casualties."

"We oughta just nuke the whole lot of 'em," the sergeant said.

"You're a fuckin' idiot," shot back the surly co-pilot, returning from the bathroom and heading for the food. Isabel joined her there. The Air Force officer's eyes turned toward Isabel before swishing orange juice about her mouth, spitting it out, and rinsing it down the drain. Isabel got another coffee. The co-pilot poured herself a soda water.

"Are you pregnant?" Isabel asked softly. By looking not at Isabel, but back over her shoulder toward her crewmates, the woman confirmed Isabel's suspicion.

"We gotta stop 'em somewhere!" the loadmaster persisted, ever more loudly.

"What's your plan?" Isabel asked.

The co-pilot drew close to Isabel's ear. "My *plan?*" She almost spat the "p" in her whisper. "My fuckin' *plan* is to not get *clawed* to death by a rampaging mob of fuckin' zombies. Not to get shot through and through by some chicken-shit Guardsmen tryin' to quit the jobs they swore they'd do! Not to get *breathed* on by some infected motherfucker who lied her way past the Mickey Mouse *medical* checks at this *base*."

"Okay," Isabel said. "Thanks for sharing." She returned to her seat. The co-pilot took her place to Isabel's right, but pointedly avoided looking her way.

The TV anchor continued her inventory of approaching dread. "I-90 has been shut down east and south of Buffalo." Full-screen video showed cars at a stand-still filling all four lanes and both shoulders of a highway, with chaos in the median, for as far as the camera could see. Angry drivers shouted at each other across safe, isolated distances.

"Reports of panic, looting, and unprecedented disorder are pouring into CNN. Some as-yet unsubstantiated reports are that there have been military attacks on back roads used by refugees seeking to avoid checkpoints."

"They're true," said a gray-haired African-American man standing behind their plush seats. Isabel's new friends all leapt to attention. Isabel, also in uniform, stole looks at them and aped their posture and bearing. They relaxed, but only slightly, when the older man said, "At ease." He had a gold fabric star sewn onto the shoulders of his dull green flight suit, and he watched the news for a moment, sort of in spite of their presence, lost in thought. He then marched off with his cup of coffee without another word. Everyone settled back into their seats.

"So-o-o, who was that?" Isabel asked.

"Incoming *Nightwatch* commander," the pilot replied. "General Grier. This must be the real deal."

The anchor on CNN said, "Hospitals in West Bloomfield, Troy, and Sterling Heights north of Detroit have been abandoned by authorities. But before cell service was cut, callers reported that those hospitals remained open with wards overflowing with the sick and manned by a skeleton staff. Hospitals all across Michigan are desperately begging for supplies…Just a moment. We're getting breaking news."

"Maybe it's *good* news," the co-pilot mumbled sarcastically.

"Could you repeat that?" A "Breaking News" graphic splashed onto the screen with the biohazard symbol CNN had adopted for the apocalypse. "This just in. CNN can report that Beaumont Hospital in Troy, Michigan… that Beaumont Hospital has been bombed by U.S. military aircraft earlier seen circling overhead. Dozens of bombs—large bombs—were dropped directly onto the hospital over a short span of a minute or two."

"Jesus," the loadmaster said.

"Yes!" replied some reporter on the scene as the picture switched to a Google Earth map that zoomed in on the hospital. "It's impossible to find words to describe what we witnessed! We had *just* retreated to the Health and Wellness Center across South Boulevard from Beaumont Hospital after vigilantes attacked infected patients there, when all of a sudden there was a series of *giant* explosions that blew out all our windows and filled the building with smoke. We thought *we* were being bombed. The smoke is clearing and I can now see that the hospital across the street has almost completely collapsed, and there are fires raging throughout the complex."

The anchorwoman struggled to make herself heard. "Were there…were there *people* in the hospital?"

"Yes! Yes! It was *full* of sick patients. And there were medical staff on duty, including, we were told by a nurse who'd fled the building, physicians who'd gotten sick yesterday, turned, and gone back to work treating the Infected."

"Wait," the anchorwoman interrupted, "are you saying that, among the medical staff who remained on duty, some were doctors who had turned?"

"Yes. Yes. The nurse said, and I'm just quoting her, that it didn't even feel like *her* hospital any more. That two nurses had also turned and now cared for infected patients, but had sparked panic among the dwindling number of Uninfecteds."

The reporter suddenly began shouting over a roar of gunfire. "Heavy fighting has broken out! I'm taking cover." Confusing sounds came from her jostled microphone.

The anchorwoman kept repeating, "Who is fighting whom?"

"...all along South Boulevard are being riddled with bullets! They're flying into our room! I'm moving again. Crawling."

"Who is attacking you?" the anchorwoman asked for the fourth or fifth time.

"Yes! Yes! We're under attack! By the Infecteds! They have guns! There's a small team of soldiers here—Green Berets—who are fighting back! They're who called in the airstrike. I can see...I see what looks like *policemen*. Eight or nine. A lot of policemen. The people shooting at us are police officers. Many are wearing bullet-proof police vests over hospital gowns. They must have turned and are now attacking this command post." Away from the phone, she shouted, "There! There-there-*there!*" Then back into her phone, she whispered, "Tell somebody we're in...in the reception area..." the signal dropped, "...the cancer center...need help. We're moving deeper inside...as soon as possible!"

After that, there was silence as the anchorwoman futilely repeated, "Can you hear me? Can you hear me? Can you hear me?"

Chapter 25

Justin Kovic, on the other end of the line, whispered to Chloe, "My dad tried to join, but the Neighborhood Watch guy, this real asshole who used to yell at us to get off his lawn, told him he couldn't go on patrol without a gun, and nobody would loan him theirs. My mom won't let any of us go out after dark 'cause she's afraid we could get shot."

Chloe sat in her favorite place in the whole compound. It was on the far side of the barn, with a tool shed to her right and two tall black water filtration thingies to her left. She had even dragged over one of the plastic stackable chairs, which her lame mother must've bought for parties or something. The WiFi signal was weak but still passable. A chicken, head bobbing, pecked at the dirt ever closer to Chloe, the source of all sustenance. She kicked at the bird. "That's not *food*, Kim." She'd named her chickens after the Kardashians. The skinniest and cutest chicken was Khloé, with a K. "That's dirt, Kim. It's *bad* for you."

"Are you talking to your chickens again?" Justin asked, a smile evident in his voice.

"Yeah. Kim's on an all-dirt diet before bikini season. They're really pretty dumb. So, Justin, what I don't get is why you'd *wanna* go out after dark? I mean, you could run into one of them. An Infected."

"The army has 'em under control. But Chloe, you wouldn't believe the kickass parties I've been to these last three nights. There are all these abandoned houses. And you remember Lardass—Billie Faign, that senior last year—who got kicked outta McLean?"

"Yeah, hm, let's see. Do...I...remember...him? Of *course!* Justin! The whole cheer team went to the principal and showed him that *creep* video. It was the most embarrassing moment of my entire life. Poor Mr. *Sims* had to call the school nurse in 'cause he felt weird watching it with us, but not half as weird as *I* felt."

"Well *you* have nothing to complain about. I mean, you looked really *good.*"

Chloe lowered the phone and appealed to the jury of hens who wandered about her, instantly understood her look of disbelief, and supported her side one hundred percent.

When Chloe raised the phone to vent her righteous indignation, it turned out Justin had moved on. "Anyway, he's at Langley High this year, or was. And I think they call him Billie there, not Lardass, but whatever. Same guy. Anyway, he organizes these, like, flash raves. He cases a house, makes sure it's empty, sneaks in, covers all the windows so you can't see inside, rigs up a DJ station with these, like, wireless headphones that everybody wears so you can't hear a sound outside. I mean, it's freaky, but kinda cool. When you walk up, it's all dark and quiet, but when you get inside everybody's raving. All you gotta do to get in is either be a chick, or a guy with liquor, pot, or a hot girl. You'd be my freakin' season pass, babe." He laughed at his combination joke-compliment.

Chloe was leaning forward, coiled, mouth agape. "You're hanging out with that fucking perv *Lardass?* After what *he* did? To me, *and* to Janie? *Your* girlfriend, at the time, as I recall?" Justin remained silent, unprepared for this turn in the conversation. Chloe scoffed, intentionally and noisily, straight into the phone's mic.

"We're not *hanging out?* He's throwing these great parties, and I'm blowing off steam before, you know...Plus, *everybody* goes to his raves."

"Who?" Justin acted as if he didn't understand her. "Who goes? You said everybody had left town. You said Janie and her family had finally bugged out."

"She *did*, but..." He acted frustrated.

Chloe was boiling. Two steps ahead, she would watch Justin plummet into the pit he somehow failed to see before him. She took special care to lower her voice, and slow her roll. "But...*what?* Let me guess. Did Janie go to the party, too?"

"Just the first one. They left the next day. I wasn't supposed to tell anybody, but you're my *bae.* They went to their lake house in Ohio. The one where I learned to water ski that summer." *Water ski!* Every picture

Janie had posted was of her wearing a slutty thong and hugging her prize of a boyfriend.

Chloe had to command her teeth to end their clench in order to force words past them. "So...you two...*went* together?" He could now sense the danger in general terms despite her seemingly calm demeanor. If he'd had any wits, he would've noticed that she was *too* calm. But not paying attention to his girlfriend was a specialty of Justin's.

"I didn't have any pot or booze, so she was my way in."

Chloe emitted what sounded like a laugh, but wasn't. "She was your *hot girl*? Janie? My *former* friend," that *bitch*, "and your, I guess, now *former* ex-? What'd she wear? Was it that backless, sparkly, side-boob show-and-tell thing she wore to Trey's end-of-the-world party?" Justin claimed he didn't remember, which could've been true. "I guess a Lardass rave is a guaranteed lay, huh Justin? Like, like, senior prom?" She had resolved to do it no later than *junior* prom, but that deal with herself was now off. "And it's a party in somebody's house, their *home*, that you've broke *into*. The house of some poor family—mom, and dad, and little kids," she was spending too much time on the point she cared least about, "who ran away from the city like *anybody* with half a *brain* would." She tried to rein it back in. "A party thrown by a guy who took videos of our whole cheer team—of *me*, and of *Janie*—in the shower at school after practice?"

"You could mainly just see your back and your butt," Justin said, apparently imagining that to be some kind of defense.

"You told me you hadn't *seen* it!"

"I *hadn't*, I swear it, when I said that. But, Chloe, I mean, it's all over the Internet." Before she could speak, he said, "And it was mostly, like, you know, Janie, mostly. I mean, not because of it being her versus, you know, you or the others. It was just you could see more of her. With you, it was just a little boob. *And-and* I don't mean your *boobs* are little, I meant..."

"*Are you fucking out of your* mind!" Chloe squealed.

"Everything okay?" her mom called out from the direction of the house.

"I'm *fine!*" Chloe snapped, not even bothering to sound fine since all her mother wanted to know was that she wasn't being eaten alive or held hostage. Chloe ignored whatever ignorant thing Justin was in the middle of saying. "What's *wrong* with you?" she snarled. "You've *changed*. Breaking into houses to get fucked up. Hanging out with," she didn't say Janie, though that was what angered her most, "with convicted *perverts*."

"They didn't convict him of anything. They just expelled him."

After a few deep breaths, Chloe said, "So," wondering if now was the time to devise some loyalty test that she could administer, "are you done? The defense rests?"

"De*fense?* Look, my dad isn't some rich *lawyer*, okay? He's just a working guy."

"He's a *tax* accountant," Chloe shot back. *And also a perv*, she thought, for letching on Chloe's mom every time she was around.

"Look, *whatta* you want me to say? *Huh?* I'll say whatever you want me to, Chloe."

That did it. Fuck, *On a scale of one-to-ten, how much did you love Janie, and how much do you love me?* This was no longer eighth grade. The whole world was being turned upside down. Time to grow up and be mature. "All right. You're free. We can break up." She grimaced. The tears began, first a drop, then two, then a flood.

He was shouting professions of love that she heard in tone, if not specific word, as she wiped her face with the back of the hand that held the phone. As his protestations petered out, she said, "I didn't hear any of that. I wasn't listening." It was clear, as she heard her own voice, that her nose was heavily congested.

"You're *crying?*" Justin said. Finally, he got it. How much he had hurt her. "That's typical! Instead of *listening* to me, to my explanation of everything, you just start crying and it's *game over.* Now I've gotta apologize, *sorry*, there, for just having a little fun before my life ends or whatever, at six*teen*, when some mob of fucking zombies...."

Chloe hung up on him, finished drying her face, and rose. They might technically still be boyfriend and girlfriend even after she released him because he hadn't officially exercised his option to end it. But she was moving on. She slung her rifle over her shoulder and said, "Oh *shut* up," when Kourtney, who was boy crazy, clucked at Chloe for possibly ending the last chance Chloe had at having a boyfriend.

Chloe emulated her charges by wandering about the compound, dwelling on her thoughts to the point that she managed to bore herself. At least, maybe, the *P.* would wipe out the Internet and all traces of Lardass's video. Her walkabout ended with a sigh at the kitchen counter where her mother opened more cans of the same food she had already grown sick of. With her rifle still slung over her shoulder, Chloe slumped on the cool granite top with an even deeper sigh that sounded like the air going out of a tire.

"So, what's up?" her mom asked with one of her annoying, all-knowing smiles.

"Nothing," came out muffled from behind Chloe's crossed arms. "Everything. I dunno." She sat up, but wouldn't return her mom's gaze. "That local hick boy living down the hill, he's around my age, right? They, like, live behind that gas station on the highway?"

"Margus Bishop," her grinning mom replied.

"*Mar*-gus?" Chloe slid off her stool. "Never mind."

"Why? Because of his name? It's traditional, you know, European."

"I've never heard it before. And it sounds stupid. He's probably some knuckle-dragging Neanderthal dunce."

"Well that sounds pretty prejudiced. Just because he didn't grow up rich like you."

"We weren't rich."

"Yes, we were. We are, I guess, still. For a little while longer. And you are spoiled rotten. Who the hell says a kid like Margus would want *you?* Don't imagine that just being pretty is gonna get you as far as it used to. Pretty is a luxury. Good to have if you can afford it. But don't expect to be taken care of by some guy just because of your looks. You need to contribute something more than that to surviving. Learn some skills. *Provide*, for yourself and for others. Make yourself useful, not just *hot*."

"*That's* funny," Chloe said, "coming from you."

"What the hell does *that* mean?"

"Never mind."

"No. No! You finish that thought, young lady. You think I was just your dad's arm candy? Some gold-digging cheerleader he met while he was in law school?" Chloe's dad walked in, heard her Mom, pivoted, and reversed course. "*No*, Noah. Come back in here." He approached reluctantly, clearly anxious to bolt at the first opportunity. "Your daughter, here, thinks she can make it through the apocalypse the way she's made it through life this far, which is to look real cute and get her stupid parents or, now, some stupid guy to give her everything she wants."

"Nuh-*uhhhh!* I didn't say *any* of that. I just asked about that redneck boy down the hill!"

"Margus?" her dad contributed. "What about Margus?"

"He's your daughter's meal ticket, apparently."

"Nuh-uh! *Jesus*, Mo-o-om!"

"You know, Chloe," she replied, "*Neanderthals* might just be the way to go these days. Not too witty around the campfire, but they can probably defend the cave and bring home the protein."

"*Stop* it," her dad said. It wasn't loud, but it surprised both Chloe and, apparently, her Mom, who went back to work preparing dinner, only with more vigor than before.

Chloe and her dad exchanged looks of warning, and neither moved a muscle or said anything.

"I think you need to go down to town and mend fences," her mom told her dad, although Chloe hadn't seen any broken fences when they drove through. "Isabel's boyfriend threatened to kill the sheriff and his men, then you blow up the ridge road, and they already suspect us of harboring an Infected but don't realize that we've got a whole prison block full of them up the hill who're doing God knows what at night…"

"We can't assume, Natalie…"

"You've heard that gunfire. Every night for the last two nights there's been shooting. And I'm not even mentioning the gunshots we hear during the daytime. I'm willing to assume they're just hunters. But at night? Nobody hunts at night."

"I think, maybe, they do, for things like boar, and…"

"Noah, do boar shoot back? Does it take twenty or thirty shots by different guns in some big boar shootout?"

Chloe drew the ire of both parents when she snorted. "What? It was *funny.*"

"So you want me to go down there?" her dad asked. "Where that shooting is? Where the virus is? Then come back here and possibly infect the whole family? Why? What could possibly be worth that risk?"

Chloe's eyes followed the ball back across the net to her Mom, who paused her furious cooking to face her dad. "Find out what's going on. Not on TV in Buffalo or Philadelphia, but where it matters most. Down in that valley. Where the people are. If they think we're protecting your sister, and that she murdered that boy at the Nicholses…"

"Which she did," Chloe said, the weight of her chin on her palm mushing the words.

"Thank you for that," her mom replied before turning back to her dad. "They could hike up here, with their guns, and there could be trouble. You're a very persuasive lawyer. You could go down there and convince them to leave us alone."

Her dad seemed reluctant. But when he didn't refuse, her mom rewarded him with a kiss, then a second, then allowed him a hug. When his hand brushed over her yoga pants bottom, Chloe said, "Ughhh!" and got out of there. *Yeah, Mom,* she thought in bitter triumph. *You send Dad off maybe to get killed with one feel of your ass, and* I'm *the one who gets her way with her looks!*

Chapter 26

JOINT BASE ANDREWS
Infection Date 56, 0510 GMT (1:10 a.m. Local)

"Attention on base. Attention on base," the loudspeaker in the crew lounge blared. "*Nightwatch* crew, report to stations. I say again. *Nightwatch*, to your stations."

Isabel bolted upright in her reclining chair. She had six minutes. She blinked until she could read her glowing cell phone. It was one-ten a.m. Her pals, the crew of the C-17, were nowhere to be seen. A few other people wearing flight suits were curled up here and there, but none of them stirred. Isabel ran to the bathroom, rinsed her mouth with the conveniently supplied wash, and pinned her hair up so that it looked slightly less of a mess.

"You need to board the E-4B, ma'am!" said an agitated young airman as she entered the bathroom behind Isabel, wearing a sidearm and full camouflage.

"Yep. I just need to…"

"You need to go *now*, ma'am."

Isabel followed the woman back into the lounge, aggravated her when she stopped for her backpack and rifle, and jogged heavily with her load down the hallway toward the hangar. Several times they had to make way for airmen racing past at even higher speeds. "Is the president here?" Isabel asked.

"I don't know, ma'am." She replied in similar fashion to questions about whether they were taking off now, what was happening, and whether containment in D.C. had failed. She was led directly to the aft stairs of the giant aircraft, which was now sitting outside the hangar on the dark tarmac with engines running.

There was a short line at the bottom of the stairs filled with a mixed lot of civilians in suits towing black carry-ons, and soldiers and airmen in camouflage and flight suits lugging backpacks or duffels. Air policemen wearing blue berets and blue ascots tucked into their camo blouses and holding rifles stood all around the jet interspersed with Secret Service agents wearing suits and carrying small, ugly, black machine pistols out in the open.

In line up ahead, the Director of the CIA, Phillip Struthers, acknowledged Isabel over his shoulder, then showed his ID to the Secret Service agent just like everyone else. The agent handed the ID to an Air Force officer, who checked the Director's name off a list. Isabel scrambled to find the ID she had been given. Was it in her wallet? Purse? The outer pockets of her pack? Her fatigues pockets?

"Ma'am?" the Secret Service agent at the front of the line had to shout over the engines.

"Just a…" Isabel remembered and pulled the ID, on its strap, out of her blouse.

"Miller," the agent said to the Air Force officer, "Isabel." The stern-looking military man looked back and forth from her ID to her face, then checked her name off the list.

Isabel ascended the long staircase. At the top waited several airmen wearing sidearms. One pointed Isabel to her pre-assigned seat. She put her backpack, rucksack, and body armor in a storage closet, and rifle and helmet in the overhead bin, then streamed forward amid the line of boarding passengers in hopes of finding some purpose for her being there. Near the front, she stopped beside an open door into a small conference room. "Dr. Miller?" the CIA Director said on seeing her. FBI Director Pearson greeted her with a silent bob of his head.

"We've got to stop meeting like this," Isabel said, sounding ditsy when she really was on edge. She was the only one even to crack a smile. "What's up?" she asked, expecting to be invited in.

"Apparently my blood pressure," the CIA Director replied. Both men glanced out the lone, small window. The headlights of a motorcade lit the tarmac. "Behold…POTUS," Struthers mumbled. That sounded odd to Isabel, who caught a glimpse of the First Lady, with one hand on the shoulder of each of her two children, directing them at a fast clip toward the stairs. Isabel was expecting some announcement over the PA system, but within seconds the aircraft was moving. She grabbed the doorway as the sound of the engines rose steadily through a high-speed turn to full power. The giant aircraft picked up momentum down the runway until its nose rotated skyward.

Director Pearson said to Isabel, in a voice raised over the noise, "There are reports out of France that the gendarmerie is going house-to-house, rousting out Uninfecteds, and forcing them to go sit in crowded halls with recently turned townsfolk."

His CIA counterpart said, "Like one of those old chickenpox parties before they developed a vaccine." He shook his head.

Both directors half rose to their feet. Isabel turned to see the president. "No, keep your seats." He edged into the room, forcing Isabel inside first. Pres. Stoddard shut the door and squeezed into a seat beside the CIA Director. "Did you hear about Kansas City?" When no one replied, Pres. Stoddard said, "There's been an outbreak there. Nobody knows where it came from."

The silence was doleful and oppressive.

The president said, "MIT now projects that the virus will be in all forty-nine continental states within two weeks. *Two.* Hawaii may hold out a bit longer, or not. They say we'll hit eighty percent infected in about three months. Among the twenty percent who're left—sixty million or so people—should be large swaths of the mid- and southwest, our military bases, and random pockets of population behind Infected lines here and there probably not exceeding a few tens of thousands in any one location."

"What about…?" the CIA Director asked cryptically.

"I don't wanna hear the words 'impulsive eradication' again. Do you have any idea what ordering troops to kill Infecteds would do to their morale? As it is, there were 137 summary court-martials and twenty-nine executions by firing squad as of my last update. We had over a dozen fragging incidents—officers killed by their own troops. We need a Plan B."

"There *is* no Plan B," CIA Director Struthers said, barely masking his anger.

"What about a vaccine?" Isabel asked.

The president frowned. "Pearl River is keeping fingers crossed about their human trials. And there's some progress down in Atlanta in mitigating the virulence of *Pandoravirus* with antivirals. The subjects don't get *as* sick. Their survival rates are better—over sixty percent. But they still turn, every last subject."

"Prisoner," Pearson corrected. "They're testing it on prisoners condemned to death or life without parole."

"It's all being done by court order," Struthers said to Isabel. She tried harder to suppress the revulsion that must be shown on her face.

"Soon," Pearson added, "we'll be testing vaccines on jaywalkers and litter bugs."

"What is it that you don't get?" the CIA Director suddenly snarled in a raised voice. Struthers directed his ire at his fellow agency head. But Isabel couldn't help but think the president was its target. "This is *it!* Our backs are against the wall. We've got to fight while we've still got an army and a navy and an air force to fight *with*. You heard the projections. In three months, our forces will be greatly reduced, and our enemy will be far stronger than we are."

"Maybe they're not our enemy," Isabel said.

"Oh!" the CIA man replied. "*There* it is. 'Why can't we all just get along?' *Kumbaya* and all that bullshit."

"Maybe we could try to look at it from *their* perspective," Isabel said.

"I thought *you* were the one," Struthers accused, "who said that they don't *have* a perspective. That they're empty husks who used to be human."

They all waited for Isabel's reply. "They may not have a consciousness. Okay," she amended, seeing her accuser's scoff, "they *aren't* conscious. That part of their brain—of their human experience—is gone. Forever. But my sister was tortured by..."

"Oh, *please!*" interrupted the CIA Director.

"They shocked her with electrodes!" Isabel protested. "Burned her. Intentionally inflicted pain."

"Which you said yourself she couldn't feel," Struthers responded. "And which those experiments, by the way, proved. Just like others done in more suspect corners of the globe like Russia without all the assurances that the tests would be conducted safely."

"But her ill treatment *did* have an effect," Isabel rebutted. "She may not have any sense of self or emotional reaction to pain, but she knows who it was that locked her up and harmed her. And she remembers from her upbringing in the pre-plague world that good, honest, trustworthy people don't torture, even in the name of science. She knows why there were always guns pointed at her, ready to shoot her dead if she made any untoward move. She ran away at the first opportunity. She so distrusted *us*—the Uninfecteds—that she jumped out of her brother and sister's car after they sprang her and ran off into the freaking woods. She thought that she had to do that to survive based on how we were treating her."

"So if we start a war with them," the president said, "and they fight back, how long do you think *we'll* survive? Wouldn't we be better off avoiding war with them for as long as possible to give our scientists more time to find a vaccine?"

Director Struthers frowned. "I guess I'd rather go out on my feet than on my knees."

"But what if there's another way?" Isabel asked. "I bet the models didn't assume that a negotiated peace was possible. A separation—a partition—of the Infected and the Uninfected. If the mathematicians added *that* to their calculations, I bet the models might show an equilibrium develop between the two populations. Maybe even ultimately a recovery of the uninfected population."

"Sure," replied the CIA Director derisively. "You can make models show anything you want. The key is to vet the assumptions you use for their reasonableness. Do you think it's reasonable to assume that we'll agree to peacefully segregate the world into a 'Theirs' and an 'Ours'? Which are *their* farm fields? Their oilfields? Their factories? Their mines? Their tanks and planes? And also, keep in mind that infection is a one-way street. We can turn into *them*, but they can't turn back into *us*."

With that, the president rose. Although these arguments were fresh to Isabel, they obviously weren't to Stoddard. He exited without a word into a flurry of demands for his immediate attention.

Isabel headed back to her cabin, passing cabinet secretaries who didn't know her from Adam and military officers whose faces were knit deep in concentration at glowing screens. When she sank into her seat, she looked out the window. In the dim moonlight she could see, off the starboard wingtip, two small fighter jets whose lights were extinguished.

She didn't feel like sleeping. She had nothing to do and no reason, really, even to be there. A female crew member walked past. "Excuse me," Isabel asked, "do you happen to know where and when we'll be landing?"

"Where, no ma'am. But we'll land sometime in the next week."

"Week?"

"Yes, ma'am. We'll refuel midair a couple of times a day. We're provisioned with consumables for over a week in flight. It's just the fluids and lubricants that limit our flying time." She smiled cheerily and headed off.

A week, Isabel thought, staring down at her phone in airplane mode and then out at the two little military jets. Their pilots were doing their small part in the grand saga but seemed to be rendered insignificant by the vastness of what was happening…just like Isabel.

Chapter 27

After breakfast, Noah stuffed ammunition, meal rations, and an extra canteen into his backpack for his trip down to town. "The Internet is out," Chloe said, entering the kitchen staring at her phone rather than getting after her chores in the barn. "First the cell connection, now this."

Noah looked at his own phone. "I've got WiFi."

"Yeah, but no Internet."

He tried a random Google search, but instead of results he got an error message. He reset the router. Nothing. Chloe stared at him with a look of deep concern. "You don't think," she said in terrible trepidation, "like, the whole *Internet* went down. That couldn't happen, could it?" Noah checked the land line. The phone was dead.

"I'll follow the cable downhill and make sure some branch didn't take the wires out or something."

"What'll you do if it did?"

"I don't know. Fix it, maybe?"

"Yeah, right," his daughter scoffed.

"Be careful," Natalie said, kissing him good-bye. "And wear your mask thing when you get around people."

"Here!" Chloe said. "Take my phone. It's useless without the Internet, but maybe I'll get my texts and messages if you get cell coverage down in the valley. Don't turn it off, and *don't* look at anything!"

Noah slid the phone into his backpack and headed off. "See ya, squirt!" he shouted across the compound to Jake, who waved as he knelt over the drone he prepared to launch. Noah found the first telephone pole, and began following the black line to the pole's nearest neighbor. Conveniently, the line mostly followed the old way down the hill.

Everything looked fine until the last pole before the highway. A single black cable drooped to the ground and disappeared into the brush. Noah found its frayed end. He couldn't tell for sure, but from a few slices in the insulation he guessed that it had been cut by vandals.

He decided to ask in town if anyone could repair the line professionally. Luckily, the break was right beside the highway and easily accessed.

The hike along the smooth roadway went much faster. He felt uncomfortable as he passed the Nicholses' mailbox. When he reached Bishop's Mini Mart, Margie came out and waved. Angus followed right behind her. Their store was actually open, though all the nozzles on the empty gas pumps were covered in yellow plastic bags. Noah felt compelled to head over to greet the friendly couple.

"Hullo, Mr. Miller!" called out Angus. Noah halted the prescribed ten steps away. "Hey, listen. I feel like I need to apologize for comin' on your property uninvited. I can see how you mighta felt like we were, I dunno, threatenin' you or somethin'. With the sheriff and the judge there, it all seemed official. But some of us—*most* of us, actually—didn't sign on to harass our neighbors like that."

"No hard feelings, Angus," Noah said as the bell on the store's entrance jingled and their eighteen-year-old son Margus emerged. He didn't look particularly friendly, wearing a glum expression, but he wasn't armed that Noah could tell, nor were his parents. "So... 'Margus' is, like, Lithuanian, or something like that?"

The boy looked at his parents, who glanced at each other before Angus replied, "If you say so. We thought we'd made it up. Half Margie; half Angus."

Noah nodded agreeably. "Oh. Cool. So, Margus, you're in the military, right? Are you on leave or something?"

No reply came, but the son exchanged looks with his parents. *He's AWOL,* Noah thought, deciding to drop the touchy topic right there.

"You headed down to town?" Margie asked. She prodded Angus with her elbow.

"Lemme give you a lift," he said. Before Noah could decline, the man disappeared into the store.

In the silence, Margie asked, "Did you get that recorded phone call? About the virus breaking out in the valley? I ain't seen any of 'em, have you?"

"Nope."

"Got 'em," Angus said on returning, jingling his keys in air and heading for his ancient pick-up truck.

"Have a nice day," Noah said to Margie and Margus.

Noah donned his mask before opening the incredibly loud, creaky door and settling onto the massively perforated and duct-taped seat cushion. The engine sputtered to life, emitting a pre-climate-conscious cloud of exhaust smoke. Angus was looking at Noah's mask.

"Oh, this? It's, you know, just a precaution."

"I ain't complainin'," Angus replied as he pulled out. "It protects me as much as you, right?" They passed wary refugees camped along the rural state highway. "Say, Mr. Miller, we were all kinda scratchin' our heads tryin' to figure out what that army helicopter was doin' up at your place."

Noah tried to decide how to play it, and opted for ominous mystery. "I'm not really at liberty to say, Angus."

He got a knowing nod in reply. "That's what we all figured. I tol' 'em 'bout all yer fencin' and yer radio tower, and that big explosion ever'body heard. I'm glad our gov'ment ain't just rollin' over and playin' dead."

Noah gave the man a thoughtful expression that could have been agreement.

When they passed the city limits sign, Angus said, "So, where can I drop ya off?"

"I guess at the sheriff's office."

"Has Trey Nichols been givin' you trouble?"

Noah shook his head, but was now alert and stared back at Angus. "Why?"

"Oh, he's just been actin' all…I dunno. I guess it was the shock, ya know, him findin' his brother's kid all cut up like that. His brother is in the Reserves and got called up. Trey was responsible for his niece and nephew and he, you know, took it hard. He's usually fairly even-keeled. I've never seen him like this. Been drinkin' some, too. It's probably a good thing that you check in with the Sheriff. I told Trey that there's no way of tellin' who might have done what was done. There's all kinds of outsiders roamin' around these parts nowadays. And obviously they had that outbreak down to Rawley Springs."

"But not up here?"

"Not that we've heard. But Walcott gets calls about suspicious sorts all the time, and it coulda been any one of them, I was tellin' Trey."

"So, is Trey somebody I oughta be worried about?"

It was far from comforting when Angus took his time replying. "Gotta worry about everybody these days, I guess. Best you talk to Walcott. I told him everything I know."

"Which is what?"

Angus shot a look over. "Trey was really wound up last night when he came by the store. He'd been drinkin' a lot, from the smell of him. He was just blowin' off steam, I figure. But I called Walcott and told him he was talkin' some stuff, ya know?"

"No, I don't. What stuff?"

There was a long delay. The brakes squealed as the rattling, faded blue truck pulled to a stop in front of the sheriff's office. "He was tryin' to, I guess, recruit me to join his little posse. Tryin' to get us to go with him back up to your place to 'get justice,' he was sayin'. Walcott wasn't surprised. Trey had been hittin' up the other members of the militia, but Walcott assured me they'd all said no and that he'd calm Trey down."

Noah thanked him for the ride and entered the sheriff's building with newfound urgency. Walcott's office was crowded with a couple of deputies and several civilians, but when Walcott saw Noah he came straight out. "Mr. Miller? Everything okay up there?"

"Well, no, actually. I've been hearing that Trey Nichols is...I dunno, riled up?"

Walcott took a deep breath and caught his secretary's eye. She resumed her typing. "Has he done anything?"

"No. But...is he somebody I should be worrying about?"

Walcott led Noah outside and away from prying ears, which now included the deputies and civilians in his office. Down the street, the large brick army reserve building was a hive of activity. A man in combat dress stood at the door holding an assault rifle at the ready. But his hair was longish, not regulation length.

The sheriff turned to Noah. "Look, I've known Trey Nichols since Sunday School." The words seemed to pain him as he spoke. "But I, honestly, Mr. Miller, cain't answer your question. Everything's changin' so fast. Up is down, and wrong is right." He tilted his cowboy hat back. "I talked to him—tried to talk some *sense* into him—but he's just convinced you're harboring some Infecteds up at your place, and they's the ones who kilt Trey's nephew. Said he saw one of 'em runnin' off back toward the highway in the direction of your place the night it happened. Then he said he saw that girl out joggin'. Said it was the same person, although he hadn't mentioned her bein' a girl in his first report."

"So you're saying, Sheriff, that he's got it in for me and my family?"

"I didn't say that." But he ended his denial there.

"I'd better get back," Noah said. Walcott gave him a lift in his police pickup. "What's going on in the National Guard armory?"

"Well sir, they's tryin' to figure out what to do with the weapons in there. Since you successfully kilt my idea for a citizens' militia, we're just guardin' the armory for the time bein'. Waitin' on orders. But if those orders never come, we gotta make the call on our own."

"And the virus has reached the valley?"

"We quarantined a Salvation Army soup line where it broke out. And Rawley Springs PD pulled a car over with New Hampshire plates, and they scattered. Kilt one, winged another, but two got away. The one they wounded had black eyes. They're lookin' for the others, but…these woods 'round here are thick."

"What'd they do with the one they wounded?"

Walcott looked at him in silence before he said, "She expired. From her wounds."

Noah didn't ask for more. Walcott pulled up beside the locked gate to the now severed ridge road. "You didn't drive?"

"That ridge road you took up to my place—it's now out."

"That didn't have anything to do with that big *boom* I got reports on, I s'pose?"

"Good luck, Sheriff."

"You too, Mr. Miller." Noah hesitated, searching the man's face for any deeper meaning. He waved as the sheriff drove off. The more he thought about Walcott's send off, the more anxious he grew.

But everything seemed normal on his climb up the hill, and the physical effort took the edge off his nerves. It was nothing. Paranoia of the times.

About half way up, Noah practically jumped out of his skin when a slim blond girl stepped out from behind a thick tree. Samantha's blue eyes had returned to normal, but her total lack of expression was off-putting. "*Oh!* Jesus! You scared the *crap* outta me."

"I'm sorry," she said in her reedy girlish voice, thin arms dangling at her sides. "Emma told me to wait for you."

Noah's guard rose. "Why? Is there any trouble?" He pulled his radio out of his backpack. "Shit!" It was turned off.

Samantha waited for Noah to look up at her. "No," she replied, and Noah relaxed. "But your son is probably dead."

Chapter 28

"Jake!" Emma's brother Noah shouted from atop a rocky crag. *"Ja-a-ake!"*

"He's dead," Dwayne said quietly. Emma agreed.

"Here's more!" Emma's niece Chloe called out.

They all joined her. Dwayne smelled one of the numerous singed shell casings that lay scattered among the rocks. Noah took it from him and said, "It's 5.56." Noah's head darted all about. His eyes were wide, and his breathing was shallow.

"Noah," Emma said. "In through the nose. Out through the mouth."

"What?" He got on his hands and knees and frantically searched the ground, presumably looking for a blood trail. He was acting erratically. His emotions were getting the better of him.

Even Chloe was disturbed. "Dad? What are you *doing?*"

"I see a body." Dwayne pointed into the gully beneath where they stood. A blue-jean clad leg was draped over a rock. Jake had been wearing jeans.

Noah scampered down the hill. There was little need to hurry. The body was deathly still. They all followed, but before they were half way to Noah, he announced, "It's not him! It's not...!" He squatted and covered his face with both hands. The dead person was a middle-aged woman with a drying blood stain in her chest. Noah kept his distance, reclining against a rock, trying to breathe.

"Dad?"

Noah's radio crackled. "Anything?" came Natalie's scratchy voice.

"No. More bullets, and a dead body. Shot. Jake was…He's fighting."

Again Dwayne caught Emma's eye. They had been up at the cabin when they heard sporadic gunfire coming from downhill, and had immediately headed for the main house. Natalie and Chloe both came running out to the fence with rifles. "It must be Jake!" Noah's wife had said. "He's out there somewhere."

Standing at the fence, everyone had turned toward the sudden but distant sound of more gunfire. Samantha had arrived from the cabin, and they had sent her to meet Noah. Before Emma and Dwayne found the first of the spent rounds, they had heard more shooting and kept up their pursuit. But they hadn't heard anything at all for almost an hour.

"Do you know anybody named Nichols?" Dwayne asked as he looked at the driver's license he'd removed from the dead woman's wallet.

"Fuck!" Noah said. "They're our neighbors." He looked at Emma. "The ones whose young nephew was butchered." That made sense to her. They must be seeking revenge, another emotion for which this woman, and probably Jake, had ended up dying unnecessarily. Noah glared at Emma with his teeth bared and jaw set.

The radio crackled. "He's here," Natalie said. "Jake. He's back ho… home." Her last word was broken and choked.

Noah clawed at the hill as he climbed, with Chloe right behind.

"What should we do with this body?" Emma called out to their backs.

"Don't care!" Noah shouted before disappearing over the ridge.

They retrieved the woman's shotgun and a half dozen shells from her jacket's pocket, and left her body there for the wildlife.

* * * *

Jake hyperactively regaled his family and Samantha with his exploits. "Then all the sudden this tree beside me went *smack* right *before* I heard the gun. It was like…*backwards*. The gunshot echoed so long I didn't realize they were still shooting at me. When I did, I hauled ass all the way down to the highway. They followed me, and I shot back. I don't think I hit anybody, but I fought *back*, Dad, just like they taught us."

"You killed one," Noah said. "A woman."

"A woman?" Jake repeated, his pubescent voice breaking. "I *did?*"

"It's okay, Jake," his father said.

"You did good." Natalie kissed the boy, who no longer seemed excited to tell his story. She pulled Jake's head all the way down to her shoulder, closed her eyes, and cradled his face.

Jake broke free of her embrace. "They shot at me *first*," he said even though no one was blaming him. "I didn't have a choice," he pleaded to no one. "I…They were trying to *kill* me." Emma tried to figure out what his problem was. No one was questioning the propriety of his actions. Could it be that voice in Uninfecteds' heads, accusing him? His conscience? *Is that what feeling guilty is?*

"Something's gotta be done about the Nichols," Natalie said, turning to Emma. "They're gonna come back. Now there are *two* of them dead. You started this, Emma. You need to fix this."

Emma nodded, and headed for the gate. Dwayne and Samantha followed her.

"Wait!" Noah called out as they departed. "What are you gonna do?"

But when they stopped and turned, Natalie was whispering to Noah, holding his forearm and shaking her head. "Let them go. Let them *go*," she repeated. Noah seemed shocked, but his wife's logic was sound and decision-making level-headed.

"Natalie…*really?*" She nodded slowly. Noah's mouth hung open, but he had nothing more to say and stared back at his wife as they departed.

Emma and Dwayne developed their plan on the hike back to the cabin. When it was settled and they fell silent, Samantha asked, "How old is Jake?"

"A year older than you," Emma replied.

"He's good at fighting. And tall. And he's cute, right?"

Chapter 29

ABOARD E-4B
Infection Date 57, 1400 GMT (10:00 a.m. Local)

Two days in the air. Two *days!* Isabel twisted and turned in her assigned seat, which she had initially thought was comfortable but now revealed previously concealed lumps and hard spots. But the worst thing was doing nothing. Knowing nothing.

What was Rick doing? At least she had Pentagon anecdotes to read on her iPad app. That one portal through the *Nightwatch* firewall was open.

One entry caught her eye. "From: Townsend (Cpt. USMC)." Her eyes popped open and she sat up. His report was dated a month earlier from Vladivostok. She had run into Rick at the White House upon his return from that mission. He'd seemed shaken.

"Four nuclashes," the Pentagon abstract read, "over 60 sec., range 8-60 km. Substantial blast and heat effects from nearest airburst at 3,000-5,000 ft. Observed 1st and 2nd degree burns of exposed Russian troops, and 3rd degree burns on Chinese Infecteds along Tumen River (est. 2 million total) closer to ground zero, who immediately overran Russian blocking positions (100% KIA/WIA/MIA). Began emergency egress with WHO field team (Lange, Groenewalt), but were overtaken by Infecteds. Russian army helicopter secured LZ with 2 x miniguns. Cpt. Townsend expended all 700 rounds of 5.56 mm before reaching LZ with Lange/Groenewalt, and fired 9 mm from wheel strut at three naked, burned Infecteds clinging to undercarriage and to Townsend (in full MOPP gear). Second helo overcome by Infecteds with 100% KIA (incl. 3 x USA SF; 1 x USN SEAL). Lesson learned: river ice singed by Russian artillery barrage absorbed radiant energy from detonations and melted, preventing passage across Tumen River into NK by Chinese Infecteds."

She searched for "Townsend," and found numerous abstracts of his reports from Asia. The longest one was from China. "Est. 1.2-1.5 million uninfected refugees. No food, water, shelter, sewer, medical, security. Dysentery and disorder rampant. Several false rumors of SED outbreaks triggered multi-fatality violence. Refugees self-segregated into groups of 2-20 members guarding perimeters 10-50 sq. meters in area. Muddy space between perimeters was heavily rutted by foot traffic, which froze razor-sharp overnight and was obvious vector through camp for pathogen. Every morning, bodies were piled in informally dedicated collection sites. Repelled major, coordinated attack and two lesser efforts by refugees and renegade PLA soldiers to seize WHO field team's supplies. Est. 150-175 enemy and 2 friendly KIA."

That sounded horrible, but it got worse. "*Pandoravirus* arrived on Day 3. Successive waves of panic washed through camp from all directions. Encroachment on defended perimeters by recoiling masses resulted in generalized close-in combat. Continuous, low-level, but lethal engagement of refugees and PLA by WHO field team security during fighting withdrawal through disorganized and confused battlespace. Est. 275-350 enemy KIA; 7 friendly KIA/MIA. Lesson learned: supply cough drops to prevent violence from false positives."

Cough drops? Isabel thought. But on further reflection, she realized a deeper truth: no list of proposals could stop the spread of the virus. It was nature, flicking aside its self-proclaimed dominant species as if in some parting taunt to almighty *Homo sapiens*.

She found no further abstracts of Rick's reports. The last entry in the Asian archives, Isabel read, was, "Only remaining contact is with Infecteds. No uninfected commo lines survive." It had taken only a month for a complete collapse of China, North and South Korea, Vietnam, and the southern two main islands of Japan.

She looked out the window at the sunny day above the clouds somewhere over something. Even their location was a secret, and she couldn't see the ground or the water beneath them as clues to her whereabouts. Isabel rose to do some more strolling, and quickly ran into the air force crewmen who were power-walking up and down the aisles with hand and ankle weights to work up a sweat. Maybe she could do calisthenics tomorrow before her scheduled five-minute shower.

She left the rest area at the very back of the 747 with its combination of blue seats and a precious few curtained bunk beds, always full, and headed forward into the cramped and hot little cabin that seemed to have something to do with communications judging from the labels atop the consoles, though she wasn't sure what. "Tech 1" and "Tech 2" were mysterious titles given a man and a woman staring at glowing screens and wearing large over-ear and well-padded headphones like from the heyday of high-fidelity stereo.

"May I help you?" the female Tech 2 asked.

"Oh, I…" *I'm bored out of my mind.* Isabel quickly scanned the woman's console. "What does 'GEP' stand for?" she read from a label.

"Ground Entry Point," the woman replied pleasantly enough, but unhelpfully.

"Oh. Okay. Thanks."

The operations area, where most of the work seemed to take place, was much roomier and felt almost spacious. A few dozen airmen sat in clusters of four facing each other across desks filled with yet more consoles. They all appeared exhausted and she wondered if they ever took breaks. She could smell the dried sweat. "They're evacuating the subs from New London," she overheard and slowed. "Sending them all down to Kings Bay in Georgia. I guess that's lights out Connecticut. Not much of New England left."

When the two buzz-cut airmen looked up at her, Isabel walked away pumping her arms in ridiculous, exaggerated fashion like a housewife on a morning jaunt.

The titles at workspaces grew ever more impressive the farther forward she walked. Rather than vague names like Tech 1 and Tech 2, these labels were more descriptive: controllers, launch system operators, planners, and weather officers. The airmen at those stations were almost all officers, some senior as suggested by the graying hair and the star on the epaulettes of a man whose workstation was labeled "Chief of Battle Staff." The other general on board, Grier, must have been in the cockpit.

The next cabin forward, which she called the theater, but that presumably wasn't its name, was like business class to her economy. There were rows of plush chairs, half filled by crewmen she presumed were off-duty because some were napping. All faced a conference table and wall-mounted flat-screen behind it on which were displayed an indecipherable series of circles, lines projecting from or to them, and numbers denoting range, or speed, or something else.

Beyond that, the door was guarded by men in dark suits: Secret Service, she guessed. From glimpses through the door, once left open, she'd seen a small conference room and table with its own screen. The map on that screen had looked similar to those displayed in the Situation Room under the White House. Red shading of various intensities covered most of New England, and to her surprise also bathed new areas of outbreak along all the northern tier of states around the Great Lakes. On her second pass by the open door she'd made out Buffalo, Cleveland, Chicago, Minneapolis, and Detroit in medium-intensity magenta. On her third, she noticed a pale pink descending into Virginia that almost certainly included the Old Place, and isolated pockets of deep crimson in Philadelphia and St. Louis, and around Washington, D.C. The last—the nation's capital—was ringed in dark red but lily white and uninfected at its center, where she had last seen Rick. On her fourth pass, and on every trip forward since, the conference room door had been closed.

When she returned to her rest area, a small semi-circle of airmen were kneeling, and a chaplain was placing wafers in their hands. *This must be Sunday,* she thought. It appeared to be a Catholic communion service, and she was Presbyterian, but the chaplain held a wafer out to her in invitation, and she knelt without thinking. She wasn't religious, but the first tears began when she ate the sacrament. By the time the cup of wine appeared, she was sobbing but trying hard not to. The male and female airmen to either side of her patted her on the back and stroked her dirty hair. They had no idea who the petite woman in stinky army camouflage was or why she was there, but they shared that moment with her. Her fears and anguish were theirs too. Isabel's feeling of despair transcended religion, politics, race, gender, and nationality. For the time being, they all belonged to the same dwindling identity group: the Uninfected.

Chapter 30

Emma called out to her niece, who sat beside the barn door with her rifle. "Chloe, could you let me in?" The girl darted from tree to tree as she came over to unlock the gate. "Where are your parents?"

"In the house," Chloe replied, taking cover behind a thick trunk. She waved her arm, and Jake returned the gesture from the tower.

"I don't think you need to be quite so careful," Emma told her. "We took care of the Nichols problem."

"You did?" She still remained in a crouch beside the standing Emma. "Well, Dad's gotten to be a total asshole since they came up here and shot at Jake. He's acting like we're in the army or something. Always shouting orders. He gets really pissed if we don't, you know, play soldier." Emma had nothing to say in response and headed for the house. "Hey," Chloe called out, "if you're gonna see Dad, could you please, please, *please* ask him for my phone back? He took it down to town the other day, and he yells at me every time I ask him for it. 'Get your head in the *ga-a-ame*, Chloe! Pay attention! Head on a swivel! You'd just get distracted by your iPhone!'"

"I'll ask him."

"Oh, and did you hear? The local TV stations both went off the air. They, like, played the national anthem, showed pictures of wheat fields and flags, then just turned off."

Emma found Natalie in the kitchen cooking. "Is Noah here?"

"He was up in the tower all night. I told him he could just watch the security cameras on his iPad, but…So I made him get some shut-eye. He hasn't gotten more than a couple hours sleep at a time since the attack. Is it…*done?*"

"Yes. They're all dead." Natalie appeared on the verge of asking another question, but hesitated a moment, then handed Emma a tray with a plate of bacon and eggs and a mug of coffee. "He needs to eat. Tell him that's the last of the bacon, so enjoy."

Emma carried the tray to the master bedroom, knocked on the door with the toe of her boot, and managed to turn the knob without dropping or spilling anything. Her eyes took time to adjust to the darkness. There was a rumpled form on the King-sized bed. "Noah?"

"*What?*" came Noah's startled response as he bolted upright.

"I've brought you breakfast." Emma put the tray on the bed. "The last of the bacon."

"What about the Nicholses?"

"You don't have to worry about them anymore, but there's plenty more trouble coming." Noah asked only about the earlier threat. "They're all dead. We burned their house down and shot them as they came out. But you do need to worry about the violence when the contagion passes through. I've got plans."

"What kinda plans?"

"Plans for the future. For survival. I need your help. You're a lawyer, you majored in political science, and you took economics courses too, right?"

"Emma, I'm too busy for this." But he wasn't doing anything.

"While you're eating breakfast, maybe I could ask you a few questions?" He took a bite, which she interpreted to be an invitation to continue. "Question one. What should be done with Infecteds, in an Infected society, who are unable or unwilling to work?"

It was dark. Emma couldn't see Noah's face, but she wasn't good at reading expressions anyway. "What the hell kind of question is that?"

"It's mainly legal, but also economic. Post-infection society is going to be impoverished and food-insecure. Ensuring that its members are all economically productive will be vital in staving off starvation and disease. *Other* diseases, not *Pandoravirus*. Infected societies won't be rich enough to support a class of the idle, except possibly for children, who are needed long term."

"So what's the question?" Noah asked amid a huge yawn.

"What should be done with people who can't or won't work? If we compensate workers with food to incentivize them, then the non-working will resort to violence to feed themselves."

"Why do you even *care* about this shit?"

"I'm trying to organize society to help ensure order and survival."

In the darkness, she could tell Noah rubbed his face from the sounds and the rocking bed. "Okay. What are you thinking the rules might be in Emma's brave new world?"

"Imprisonment is costly. Banish people and they will come back. Execution works, but seems imprecise."

"Execution? For not *working*? Emma, that's freakin'...*crazy*. And how do you define not working? One day's absence? A week of slothfulness? A bad quarter?"

They talked for the next few hours, interrupted by Noah's potty break and shower, and his opening of the shades and arranging of two chairs. Democracy seemed like an unnecessary luxury despite Noah's repeated attempts to sell Emma on it. Private ownership of property made sense, but beyond the essentials required for survival the topic lost her interest. Capitalism and the accumulation of wealth felt as archaic as feudalism. Some centralized form of capital and resource allocation made more sense, especially for a society perpetually at war with well-armed uninfected survivors.

Noah shouted a request for his wife to bring more coffee. When Natalie arrived, Emma found the coffee she brought stimulated even more questions.

"So," Noah said, "you're proposing a command economy. Like the old Soviet five-year plans, production quotas, things like that."

Natalie asked, "Will this new society of yours admit Uninfecteds?"

That was actually one of Emma's questions. But she had refrained from asking Noah about it for fear that the answer would be an obvious, "No," and the implications he might draw from that answer. Emma instead replied with a list of complications. "Even after a couple of weeks, when Infecteds cease shedding the virus through respiration, Uninfecteds will fear close contact...like this. Being infected will remain a stigma."

Noah seemed to agree. "Uninfecteds will want to segregate themselves."

And kill us, came the voice in Emma's head. She carefully avoided a furtive look up in search of the comment's origin.

"How big will this new society you're planning be?" Natalie asked.

"However many Infecteds there are."

"I mean hundreds? Thousands?"

"More like a hundred to a hundred and fifty million."

Noah chuckled even though she hadn't told a joke. "You think this society of yours is just going to...*spread?* The Infecteds will all sign up and whistle while they work?"

"I don't know about whistling, but if they're provided with food, medicine, shelter, clothing, security, and sex, then yes. They'll join."

"Sex?" Natalie said. It sounded like a question.

"Society will have to meet their needs. And it will also, as I mentioned, long-term have to perpetuate itself with future generations of workers."

"How are you gonna regulate *sex?*" asked Emma's sister-in-law.

"I was thinking that it should be used, along with the other things I listed, to incentivize work. If an Infected was incapable of working productively, or refused to, those necessities would be withdrawn until, at some point, execution was appropriate. And as to who decides whom to execute, that would devolve bureaucratically to the administrators of the rules and regulations that prescribe rewards and punishments."

"Meaning you'd have state-sanctioned brothels and death chambers?" Noah asked.

Although Emma was the one who came prepared with questions, she was finding this give-and-take to be useful. *State-sanctioned brothels*, she noted mentally. Uninfecteds were far more creative and imaginative than her cabinmates, with the possible exception of Samantha. "And permits and permissions," Emma said, "for recreational sex, or for intercourse leading to reproduction, which would necessarily imply a general prohibition of sex absent those permits."

"How can you stop people," Natalie asked, sort of giggling despite the seriousness of the topic, "who wanna have *sex?*"

"Punishment. Death, in the case of rape or repeated disregard for the rules."

Emma looked at her phone, which she now used only for its clock. Dwayne would be returning soon from his reconnaissance of the town. She should meet him back at the cabin. "Oh, Chloe asked for her phone back."

Noah fished in his camo backpack and handed the iPhone to Emma.

At the door, Natalie reached out for Emma's arm. "You never said whether we'd be invited to live in your new society."

Say yes, came the voice. *Lie!* "Yes," Emma said. "But you'll have to agree to abide by the contract...and the punishments."

"Meaning death for breaking the rules?" Noah asked.

"Yep." Emma departed the silent bedroom. Just as she thought, they wouldn't agree. Would any Uninfecteds agree to that deal? Infecteds would...in droves.

"You were in there a long time," Chloe said as she sat incorrectly in a chair, dangling her legs over an arm. She muted the TV news. They still received many of the national satellite signals. There was video of a small crowd of people outside a tall fence pleading with the thin line of soldiers guarding it. Kneeling. Wailing. Gesticulating. Clearly Uninfecteds, who shouted across the line of troops and tossed bundles of food or containers of water into the enclosure to Infecteds. Former loved ones, probably. Small, vicious fights broke out where the supplies landed.

"Did you get my phone?" Chloe asked.

Emma handed it to her. Chloe hesitated, then used her paper napkin from the lunch she'd eaten in front of the TV to take the phone from Emma. *Unnecessary, but smart,* came the voice. *She's careful. We could use Uninfecteds like her.* Chloe pressed a few buttons and wiped her fingertips on her jeans.

"Hey, Chlo, it's Justin," the recording played from the phone's speaker. Chloe instantly smiled ear-to-ear. "Texts aren't going through, so I thought I'd call. Where you been at?" *Where have you* been*!* noted the voice. "You're not answering. Call when you get this." The boy, "Justin," then related to Chloe the story of two classmates whose families were evacuating to different parts of the country. The boy had asked the girl to marry him. The girl had responded by breaking up with the boy. "Can you believe that shit?" Justin said before concluding, after a long pause, with, "I love you."

It was unclear whether Chloe was happy or found Justin's story or profession of love to be humorous, but she was grinning broadly. "It's gotten really creepy," Justin reported in the next voicemail. "Nobody goes out at night." No *one.* "And if you run into anybody," any*one*, "during the daytime, everybody," every*one*, "keeps their distance." As Justin relayed an anecdote to which he inexplicably ascribed immense significance— coming upon an overturned, burning SUV, whose occupants fired on anyone attempting to rescue them—Emma considered whether remedial grammar and diction courses should be a priority. "I kept waiting for them to scream when the flames, like, exploded, but those last shots must've been, you know, suicides 'cause they didn't. Scream. It really shook me up, babe. I mean, why would somebody *do* that?" But while uniform rules of communication were beneficial, they didn't rise to the level of importance of food production and societal security.

The map shown on the muted TV displayed outbreaks of *Pandoravirus* all across the northern tier of states, meaning Canada just beyond was succumbing rapidly. But isolated pockets farther south in the U.S. were misleading. They were only the known, reddish-tinted outbreaks. But the intervening, all-clear, unshaded areas around them were, in truth, being infected home-by-home, town-by-town, hour-by-hour, Emma knew, in an inexorable biological process.

Justin's third voicemail seemed to depress Chloe's mood. "It's like, I dunno." He wasn't articulate, even for a high school boy. "This rumbling that you feel and can almost hear. It rattled my mom's decorative plate right off the shelf even though there wasn't really any sound. It's like what I bet an earthquake must be. And this red glow in the sky at night. They're bombing all around D.C. My dad says Infecteds are trying to find a way to bypass the defenses around the city. Last night, the bombing was closer. You could hear *boom-boom-boom-boom*." Chloe leaned forward, listening intently to the phone cradled in a napkin. *She's too smart for him,* came the voice.

His next message pled for Chloe to respond, and she groaned. "Our parents said nobody goes outside any more. A bomb broke all our front windows even though it landed a block away. It was a mess. We've pushed our heavy furniture up against the doors, but the windows are wide open. My dad was gonna go take some of the plywood the neighbors put up before leaving, which is what *we* shoulda done, but my mom said that was stealing. Stealing! Who the fuck *cares?* Ya know? *Really?* I don't know what's gonna happen. The last few nights we heard people shooting, and it's gotten closer and louder. Then, today, the shooting kept going after sun-up. *There!* Can you hear that? There. Hear it?" Chloe's brow was creased and mouth drooped open. She looked up at Emma. On the muted TV were images from Fort Worth, Texas, where tanks were being unloaded from rail cars.

Justin's next message, probably his last, was recorded in whispers. "Chloe! They're inside our house! They're coming up the stairs!" His voice was quivering. Moisture welled in Chloe's wide eyes, and she covered her mouth with her free hand. In the background, the sound of tramping feet, children crying, and adults praying could be heard. "This is it! They're coming to the closet door. This is…!" There was a crashing sound. A woman begged for the lives of her children. A man grunted and then screeched in pain like a wounded animal. Their feeble attempts to confront their attackers were obviously ineffectual. The phone was dropped, shouts, of "No!" and "Please!" were ended with piercing shrieks and wails that went on and on. Agony after agony ensued, grew weaker, and was followed by relative calm. Pants from exertion or rage could be heard. Superfluous blows rained hollow thuds on by now surely lifeless bodies. Then, a woman's voice. "Somebody's in the kitchen getting at the food!"

Off the footfalls went. After the brief rustling as the mob departed and a few seconds of shouting and crashing sounds from a distance, a deep and permanent silence descended on the recording.

Chloe was ashen, shaking…and staring wide-eyed at Emma.

"So," Emma said, "you got your *messages*." But from Chloe's reaction, that wasn't the right thing to say. What about, *You're gonna need a new boyfriend 'cause that one's dead? Don't say that!* advised the voice. "See ya later," she tried in an upbeat tone.

Chloe started sobbing. "*Mo-o-om!*" Emma began to calm after getting out of there and heading up to review Dwayne's plan for seizing control of the town.

Chapter 31

ABOARD E-4B
Infection Date 59, 1700 GMT (1:00 p.m. Local)

Isabel knew something was happening when the ever present, level whine of the engines fell an octave and her ears popped. Air policemen began donning full combat gear and, upon completion, pounded their comrades' body armor like football players in shoulder pads. A Secret Service agent in a dark suit appeared at Isabel's seat. "Please come with me." She wasted no time with futile questions and followed him up to the small, crowded, standing-room only conference room in the front, which was usually off-limits.

First Lady Angela Stoddard stood in the doorway on the far side, which presumably led to the presidential quarters, hugging little Ginnie and Bill Junior tight. The First Son kept stealing looks at Isabel, and Ginnie waved vigorously—her face lighting up as if on sighting an old friend. Isabel had attended a private dinner and question and answer session about SED with the First Family at the White House residence.

The normally polite greeting from the president was missing as the harried man listened to Marine Gen. Browner, Chairman of the Joint Chiefs of Staff, whose image was displayed on the room's screen. "This is a game-changer, sir, if it's true. Real hope. Maybe our last chance." She'd never heard him lay it on that thick. "But we've got to take full advantage of it. We've got to think strategically."

"Like ordering all our forces back to Texas and the Rockies?" Bill Stoddard said.

"You gave us discretion on redeployments, sir. And our forces weren't exactly proving useful in their previous positions."

"But now, General, you want to take the gloves off, I'm guessing."

Vice Pres. Anderson appeared on a split screen with Browner. He was at the head of his own conference table in some windowless bunker. "Bill, we're down to the lick log here. Skip is proposing marshalling our forces inside a defensible perimeter around self-sustaining resources and pharma plants that can crank out what we all hope is a working vaccine. Given where the virus came across the border, that's the corridor from Houston up through Denver. We can set up a reverse quarantine there. Now, that's going to require some draconian policies. Expulsion of Infecteds, lethal force at the border, etc., but…"

"There's that word again," Stoddard interrupted. "*Border.* Right down the *middle* of our country. We're going to be massacring fellow citizens, Infecteds *and* Uninfecteds, who're fleeing for their lives. And what about all those desperate calls for help you say, Gen. Browner, that we're getting in the rest of the country? You heard the DHS estimates. Thirty percent of the population in rural Vermont, where it first broke out, are *still* uninfected. What do we tell them? Certainly not, 'Get yourselves to Texas,' as impossible as it would be to cross, what did you call it, 'Injun Country.'"

"Sir," Browner continued in an exasperated tone that must have represented his hundredth attempt at persuasion on the point, "this is about playing the hand we're dealt." Around the E-4B's conference table, the directors of the CIA and FBI and the Attorney General stared at the president, as did the vice president and secretary of defense from their bunkers. "It's not something any of us would've chosen as the plan for our future. Hell, none of us could possibly even have *imagined* these circumstances even two months ago. But it's reality, and we all have to deal with it."

The president covered his face with his hands. Browner's gaze scanned the room as if pleading not to the president, but to his National Security Council. No, not pleading. Polling. Counting. Possibly canvassing.

"No," Pres. Stoddard replied. "We're not abandoning the rest of the country for some last stand in the Midwest." He asked the Secret Service agent behind Isabel to close the door. "Dr. Miller, your colleague Dr. Nielsen at the Pfizer lab in Pearl River, New York, has reported successfully completing human trials on a vaccine that will inoculate Uninfecteds against *Pandoravirus.*"

Isabel almost burst out laughing. "That's…*wonderful!*"

But the other faces around the room remained grim. "Yeah, well, let's hope so. We've had our hopes raised before. And Nielsen was pretty cagey on the call. We're putting down in upstate New York. We can't safely get you any closer to Pearl River because one of our guard units, which is equipped with state-of-the-art surface-to-air missiles, has turned and is taking pot shots at aircraft flying over the Hudson River Valley. I need you to go meet with Nielsen, see what she's come up with, and call back with your dead-eyed-serious appraisal of the vaccine's efficacy. I'll redirect every resource this government can bring to bear on producing mass quantities of her vaccine, but I need to know if it works. Understand?"

"Yes," Isabel said, then added, "Sir."

They descended through the clouds to the dreary day beneath them. Browner said, "You're putting down at Stewart International Airport and its co-located Air National Guard Base. They've had a rough go of it and are barely able to defend the strip. I've called in your personal security team, but I've got to inform you that this mission entails substantial risk."

"It's okay," Isabel said a bit too quickly. "I mean, I'm good with it, general."

* * * *

The aisles filled as soon as the E-4B touched down. An aide motioned to Isabel, who retrieved her backpacks, body armor, helmet, and rifle. He gave Isabel a bulky satellite phone with the president's number stored in it and a bag with charging cables just in case. At the top of the stairs, the commander-in-chief and his family wished her luck.

The lines on the president's face were worn deep. His hair, even his skin, seemed grayer. "You know Nielsen from Bethesda. I'm hoping you can tell whether this is the breakthrough we've been praying for, or she's just angling for more support like everyone else."

"I'll do my best, Mr. President."

"We'll be here, on the ground waiting for another aircraft or until we get a green light on a sketchy engine. Call me when you know something, and be careful."

Isabel deplaned in a line of staffers, mostly military, who milled about on the tarmac stretching stiff backs, lifting faces to the cloudy sky, and drawing deep breaths of air that was fresh, but also hinted at an encroaching foulness from nearby. Airmen wearing oven mitts at the top of a ladder shone a flashlight into an engine cowling on the 747.

"Dr. Miller?" Rick called out from the crowd at the bottom of the stairs. She broke into a toothy, broad grin before restoring something approximating adult behavior. He wore full combat gear like the men in the Humvee behind him. A soldier in goggles protruded through the roof behind a machine gun. "You ready for this?" Rick seemed chilly, distant, and on edge. It should have been a warning.

Rick removed Isabel's body armor and draped a new vest over her shoulders. "This seems heavier than the old one," she said as several vehicles pulled up in front of and behind their Humvee.

"Extra plates," was Rick's only, dispirited explanation. *Something's wrong with him,* she realized. She studied his face for clues. Rick studiously ignored her.

Isabel's nerves frayed as Rick checked her equipment in silence and their convoy formed. There were two tracked armored hulks: one low-slung with a bulldozer blade; the other like a boxy tank with a long, slender gun in a small turret. Then a vehicle with a V-shaped bottom like a boat high above knobby tires. A fourth, also wheeled, had antenna masts and a satellite dish atop a boxy cabin. The fifth was a regular, canvas-topped truck filled with soldiers. The sixth was a green tanker truck. Bringing up the rear was a second Humvee on which was mounted a short and stubby, wide-barreled gun with a giant ammo box.

"Where's Sgt. Vasquez?" Isabel asked. Rick gave her a single shake of his head. "Oh." She said a short prayer for him. "And his men?" Another no. "All five of them?" She added another prayer. She was growing more religious as the world neared its end.

A soldier returned Isabel's rifle after a quick confirmation that it was operable, loaded, and clean. "Are we expecting trouble?" she asked.

Rick snorted. "It's forty-seven miles down I-87. *Toward* the City. So... *yeah.*" He sounded like a different person, though it had only been five days since they'd parted. That was, however, an eternity during times like these.

Two small jets roared down the runway side-by-side. As the screech of their engines receded, their exhausts' black smudges dropped low over the treetops instead of climbing, as if weighed down by their full loads of underwing bombs. A dozen helicopters were parked nearby, but the only ones being readied for flight were small, wasp-like aircraft that bristled with rockets and missiles.

After a radio check, they drove off, slowed by the lumbering tracked vehicles. The smell of diesel was noxious. Through the grimy, presumably bullet-proof windows she watched them pass two rings of trenches and sandbagged machine gun nests. "Stewart Air National Guard Base," read the sign at the gate. Burned out cars and trucks lined the road. There was the source of the stench that wafted across the airstrip.

Forty-seven miles, she thought. *Oughta be there in an hour or two.*

Her ETA was proven wrong as soon as they reached the ramp onto I-87. The tracked bulldozer—an "M9 Armored Combat Earthmover," Rick explained tersely following her attempt to start a conversation—plowed cars and trucks out of their way with grinding noise and sparks.

They then proceeded down the interstate highway in slow motion, stopping to clear more obstacles every few miles. Rick stared out the window and talked over his radio, but never acknowledged Isabel's presence despite her near constant focus on him.

"Where are all the people?" she asked. "From all these cars and buses?"

Rick just shrugged. He was starting to both frighten her, and piss her off.

At their fourth stop, one of their machine guns opened fire, followed by a much louder, slower rattle from what Rick called, "The Bradley," in answer to her question. Its armored rear door lowered to the pavement. Out poured six soldiers, who spread out among the abandoned cars and were joined by a half dozen more from the truck. All fired at unseen targets. When the machine gun atop their own Humvee opened fire, Isabel plugged her ears. Rick exited the vehicle, took cover behind a dusty Lexus, and began firing his rifle. Isabel joined Rick, who tackled her to the pavement. "Ow!"

Glass exploded on an abandoned yellow cab nearby. Someone was shooting back.

Isabel raised her helmeted head above the hood. A hundred people streamed toward them across a field. Cows galloped to and fro, but the humans all ran straight at them. Some carried pistols or rifles whose muzzles flashed. Attackers fell with every passing second.

Rick pulled her back down. "Goddammit! These men are risking their fucking lives for you!" She asked who was attacking. "Who the fuck do you think? *Them!*" Rick fired over the hood. The whole time, the armored bulldozer plowed the path ahead.

"Why?" Isabel shouted. "That isn't a densely packed crowd! And they aren't agitated individual Infecteds, they're a group! Why are they doing this?"

Rick said, in between aimed shots, "They're a third category!" *Bam.* "You think this highway is blocked by accident?" *Bam.* "They want our food, water, weapons!" *Bam.* "Most of these cars are already shot up!" *Bam.* "They've been at this a while!" *Bam.*

A third category of Infecteds' violence, Isabel thought. Organized and armed resistance.

The troops suddenly sprinted back to their vehicles at some unheard radio command. One fell, shot in the hip, and was hoisted—grimacing—into a sitting position atop his rifle, which was held on either end by laboring buddies. He was deposited into the arms of a waiting female medic inside the Bradley's troop compartment.

Isabel and Rick made a stooped dash back to their Humvee. Its mounted weapon kept up its fire even as they drove off. Star-shaped pockmarks appeared in the side windows in time with loud *thumps.*

Rick resumed his watch out his window. The drive continued much the same as before. They stopped to engage largely ineffectual ambushers every half hour or so, always winning with overwhelming firepower. Always leaving fields strewn with the dead. Unlike, presumably, the civilian cars that had strayed into these ambushes before them. Rick declined Isabel's every attempt to engage him in conversation until, randomly, she asked, "Have things been, you know, tough? Since Andrews?"

He looked at her with disbelief, or contempt. She didn't have time to amend the evidently stupid question. "So I led a patrol into Silver Spring," he said. "The police chief had sent two patrol cars into a neighborhood, and neither came back. We went in quietly, at night, dismounted. Edged our way through back yards. Got spotted by a man taking out the trash in his bathrobe. They're picking up garbage now like…like normal."

"He was infected?"

Rick wasn't listening. "Sometimes they run away. Sometimes they charge. You lay your sights on 'em and let God decide. This guy ran at us in his slippers. I dropped him. My mixed bag of reservists, Guardsmen, Marines, and Vasquez's two remaining men then shot the guy's wife, three kids, and two other men, whoever the hell they were, who poured out of his house like some jail break. In seconds, every door on that street swung open. Some were Uninfecteds calling for help. Some of *them* got dragged to the ground by their neighbors. It was a fucking 360-degree shitstorm."

Rick chose just then to put on his wraparound sunglasses. To hide behind them as he gathered himself. "Every other house lit us up. There were rounds flyin' *every*where. I started that patrol with eleven men. When the sixth got hit, we couldn't carry the wounded anymore. They fuckin' cursed at us. I almost shot one when he raised his rifle, but he did the job *for* me and shot himself. I can still see the faces of those wounded men, clear as day under a streetlamp. Eyes wide. Sweat pouring out on a freezing cold night. Knowing this was the end of the road. Remember when I told you that Marines never leave men behind? Well, I left them behind. Just left 'em there. They cursed us till we were outta earshot, then we heard shooting. Wild, crazy fire, then, *bam-bam-bam-bam-bam*. Five shots. Maybe they were executed. Maybe they shot themselves. That's where I last saw Vasquez and his two men."

All she could come up with was, "Rick, I'm *so* sorry."

"And I can't get in touch with my parents in Wisconsin," he said. He faced away from her. The faint reflection of his face in the window was indecipherable.

"Oh, *God*, Rick. I had no..."

"I don't wanna talk about it."

"I'm sorry. I should've asked about them."

"I don't wanna *talk* about it! I've got a job to do. People are counting on me. *Still*." He resumed his watch out the side window and radio checks with the other vehicles. Several times, Isabel raised an unseen hand to his shoulder and almost touched him. Each time she decided it might make things worse.

After four hours and seven firefights, they exited the Interstate at Pearl River. Uncollected bodies in a shopping center parking lot lay strewn around barricades of cars, furniture, and shopping carts at the site of someone's unsuccessful last stand. On the next block over, looters— Infected or Uninfected, who could tell—loaded minivans and warily watched the convoy pass.

When they eventually slowed, a curious, sickly sweet smell entered through the open gunner's hatch. Bodies lay in piles or singly, splayed or in fetal positions, some intact, some just limbs and a head around brown, contaminated stains. The convoy wound its way slowly through a slalom course of immobilized concrete mixers and dump trucks parked in a road pitted with craters large and small. Their Humvee bounced over bodies it couldn't avoid. The tracked Bradley in front simply flattened them. Some of the dead Infecteds had guns. Others lay next to sharpened wooden fence posts, clutched iron bars, or held a chunk of concrete in an outstretched hand.

Infecteds' bodies were stacked by the dozens near the sandbags at the gate. "Pfizer Pearl River Life Sciences Campus," read its bullet-riddled sign. Men, women, and children had attacked the two tanks on either side of the road. And there had to be a hundred helmeted heads protruding from trenches running off in both directions in front of parallel, chain-link fences topped by barbed wire.

As soon as they entered, the gates closed behind them, but no one approached when they got out. Troops in gas masks and gloves encircled them, keeping their distance, weapons in hand.

"Which one of you is Isabel Miller?" came a shout from behind a mask. Isabel raised her hand like a schoolgirl. "Come forward. Only you!" She walked toward the voice. The ring of troops parted. She followed instructions and stood atop a blue tarp. "Please remove your equipment and clothing, ma'am." Isabel looked around. There had to be a hundred men on the lawn. "Sorry," the soldier said, sounding drained, not apologetic. "Protocol."

Isabel lay her rifle, webbing and body armor on the ground, unlaced her boots, and pulled her blouse off and trousers down. Her bare skin erupted in goosebumps. "Everything off, ma'am." She looked back at her convoy. Rick was checking on the wounded man. She unclasped her bra and stepped out of her panties. She had never felt more naked.

Men in PPE hosed and brushed her down. The icy disinfectant stung. She fought the brushes twice, when they were too rough. Finally, freezing water from a garden hose rinsed her off. Soldiers' gazes were averted when they handed her a towel and blanket. She was led, shivering, to a guardhouse. A female nurse and armed soldier in full PPE joined her in the small but, thankfully, heated shack.

The nurse did temperature and pupil checks, then said, "Dr. Isabel Miller?" Isabel nodded. Her stringy, cold hair tickled her face. "I'm going to ask you a few questions." She seemed tired; the questions rote. "Can you describe this picture?" She held up a glossy, 8.5 by 11 photo of a flattened human in a puddle of viscera with a sickeningly misshapen head.

Isabel winced and turned away. "*Jesus!*" The nurse asked her to describe the photo. Isabel took a sidelong peek, cringing. "It's a body. A dead body. Someone, I don't know, who jumped off a building, or got run over or something."

"And this?" The woman flashed a second photo from her stack.

Isabel guardedly glanced at it. A little girl sat in the lap of a middle-aged woman. An elderly female stood behind them. All wore loving looks. "It's a grandmom, mom, and daughter, I'm guessing." Isabel knew what they were testing for, so she elaborated. "They're happy. Three generations of women gathered for a birthday, or family reunion, or holiday."

"And this?" A deer floated in a swimming pool. Isabel overplayed her revulsion. "Aw, a little baby deer fell into a pool and drowned. Probably lapping at the water and got startled, then couldn't climb its way out. Poor thing."

"And this?"

"A proud veteran of an old war, crying at a funeral, or maybe the national anthem."

"And this?"

"Oh, for Christ's sake, an autopsy photo? Seriously?"

The door opened. Dr. Nielsen entered, wearing no PPE. "It's okay," she said. The nurse and soldier departed. "Isabel!" They hugged like old friends. "We've done it! A vaccine! Let's get you dressed and I'll show you."

Isabel climbed into hospital scrubs that Nielsen had brought while they washed her camouflage army uniform and undergarments for her. The former head of the Bethesda NIH hospital asked Isabel if it was bad out there. "Yes," was all Isabel said. "So how effective is the vaccine?"

There was enough of a pause in the reply that Isabel sensed a problem. "It's one hundred percent effective. Total immunity is achieved in less than four hours; partial in less."

"Any side effects?"

Nielsen's eyes darted away. "Almost everyone gets a lump and itching at the injection site, and suffers from some fatigue. Two out of three get painful inflammation. One-third headaches, joint pain. One in eight fever and diarrhea."

"No allergic reactions?"

"Not in our test group of less than a thousand." Dr. Nielsen wasn't making eye contact. "I can't overstate how hard my team worked on getting to this breakthrough, and how amazed we all are at our success. A vaccine, in *weeks*, Isabel, not months, not years."

"But...?"

"The Roche and Novartis labs in Switzerland tried deactivation of the virus but got overrun before anything came of it. AstraZeneca in Sweden has tried working with the toxoids—inactivated toxins released on infection—but have gotten nowhere so far. Sanofi tried conjugates— attaching antigens to carrier proteins—but now that the disease is out of control in France they're in the process of moving their work up to Bayer in Germany. We elected to go with attenuation of the virus."

"So, you inject live *Pandoravirus* into people?"

"Attenuated *Pandoravirus*," Nielsen corrected. "Like the vaccines for measles, mumps, rubella, chickenpox, oral polio, rotavirus, yellow fever, and some flu shots. Plus the typhoid and typhus vaccines in the bacteriological arena. Attenuated vaccines engage all phases of the immune response and provide more durable immunity, requiring less frequent boosters. They're also cheap, and immunity comes in hours, not a week."

Isabel was now dressed in scrubs. "Bottom line? What's the downside?"

Nielsen took a deep breath. "Six percent of the subjects contract *Pandoravirus*."

Isabel sank into the chair opposite the woman. "Six *percent?*"

"Plus or minus a fraction. But it *works!* For the rest."

"And of the six percent, half die and half turn?"

"In rough numbers, but pretty consistently. Yes."

"Can that be reduced? Attenuated further?"

Nielsen shook her head. "This bug is slippery. High mutation rate. The six percent get sick not because of insufficient attenuation, but because of post-exposure viral mutation."

"Is there any way to know who should get the vaccine, and who shouldn't?"

"Immunocompromised patients shouldn't take it," Nielsen replied. "They couldn't fight off even the attenuated virus. And we haven't tested children, the elderly, or pregnant women. But we can achieve communal immunity at a ninety percent vaccination rate. There's no way, however, to predict who'll get sick from the vaccine. The mutations seem statistical."

"Meaning random? So people have to decide whether to take the vaccine, or try to avoid infection 'in the wild,' as you people refer to the real world out there?"

Nielsen looked exhausted. "Assuming we give them that choice."

"Have *you* taken it?" Isabel asked. Nielsen furtively glanced at Isabel, then shook her head. "Has anyone on your *team* taken the vaccine?"

"I've only got a *thousand* people at this lab! I can't lose sixty of them to the virus."

"But you'll provide your vaccine to *billions* of people? A chance to play Russian roulette with their families?"

Isabel expected Nielsen to bristle. Instead, she slumped, betraying an even deeper level of exhaustion than was first evident. "The mutagenesis team is trying to identify genes that facilitate reversion to virulence. Genetic modification of the attenuated virus may improve the odds. But that'll take time, and there's no guarantee. This vaccine, however, is still a miracle! It could stop the spread of the virus. *Save* billions."

They exited the guardhouse into the pale afternoon. Isabel was instantly freezing. Her hair was wet and her scrubs and slippers were thin. She crossed her arms over her chest as they walked toward the building complex. Rick sat in the open doorway of their Humvee, oblivious to her passing, cleaning his rifle, as always.

Nielsen led her to the one out-of-place building on the placid green campus. Where previously there had been trees and an expansive lawn, now were freshly cut stumps beside a metal monstrosity. No one had bothered to blend the new facility into the red-brick theme of the older buildings. The only indication of the new facility's purpose was an already fading poster board mounted beside the door. "Testing."

The building was heated, but Isabel strangely felt no warmer as a shiver rippled up her torso. "We're going in," Dr. Nielsen said to a soldier at a security desk. He requested no ID and used a magnetic card to unlock a sturdy steel door. Two armed soldiers accompanied them down a long, T-shaped corridor that disappeared in opposite directions at the far end. The floors were concrete. The lighting was industrial. Every other door had a small square window crisscrossed with reinforcing wire, a slot for trays, and a big hole for physical keys. It looked like a prison, not a lab.

Most of the small windows they passed were lit, but Isabel saw nothing inside. Nielsen led her through one of the unlocked ordinary doors in between. A bleary-eyed woman in a lab coat raised her head from a nap at a desk in front of a large observation window like at the NIH hospital in Bethesda. Nielsen introduced Isabel as being, "from the White House."

Isabel's attention was drawn to the room next door. A man in a hospital gown that barely covered him lay on a bed with one leg crossed over a raised knee, thumbing through a magazine. A woman in scrubs sat in the lone chair—motionless, expressionless, eyes black. The man licked a finger and turned a page.

"This is Subject One Zero Nine," Nielsen said. She took a clipboard from its holder and read, snorting in amusement. "Again?" she asked the nurse. "One-Oh-Nine is something of a star. Age twenty-seven. Good health. Recreational drug and alcohol use. Non-smoker. No major disease or surgical history. He got the vaccine," she flipped back to page one, "eleven days ago. Fever of 101, nasal congestion, gastric distress, and a headache, which led to an anxiety attack. But all that passed in a day."

The guy had short hair, but was unshaven. His left arm was heavily tattooed.

The girl had thick, dark hair, which when brushed might have been her best feature. It now hung around her face as she sat impassively, hands on her thighs, doing nothing.

"We introduced her four days after One-Oh-Nine's inoculation," Nielsen said, "and less than four hours after she had turned."

"She was *highly* contagious," said the nurse—beaming member of the victorious team.

"And One-Oh-Nine didn't catch it," explained Nielsen simply. "He's immune."

That announcement of their triumph seemed highly anticlimactic.

"So presumably," Isabel said, "you've had repeated success at achieving immunity. Why is he your *star* test subject?"

Nielsen and the nurse smiled each other's way. "At first, of course, when we introduced her into his room, he reacted like every subject does. Fled to a far corner, shouted obscenities, covered his mouth and nose, threatened her to keep her away. But a day passed. Nothing. Two days. Zip. She was shedding the virus like crazy. We tested her. They were in a closed room. Sealed in tight quarters. No PPE. And...he's fine."

"And that makes him your star?"

"Hm?" Nielsen said, looking up from the chart. "Oh. She no longer sheds much virus now through respiration, but it still contaminates her biofluids. Intracellular, extracellular, interstitial. Bile, feces, gastric acid, lymph, mucus, tears, saliva—all contagious. Vaginal secretions and female ejaculate too."

Slowly, it dawned on Isabel what she was suggesting. "They had sex?"

"Unprotected. Eight times as of...10:09 to 10:12 this morning." She put the clipboard back in its rack.

This was all too much. "Wait a minute, they're having sex. And you're... watching, and recording?" *Like with my sister in Bethesda!*

"This is science, Dr. Miller," Nielsen replied icily, "not some peep show. I'm fed up with complaints about the ethics of our testing! We're trying to save the human fucking race!" She reined herself in. She was biting the hand she wanted to feed her.

Isabel, however, wanted the truth, so she pressed the buttons Nielsen revealed. "Let's talk about ethics. How did these people come to be part of your testing program?"

Her host was visibly angry. Nielsen pressed her lips closed as if to prevent the wrong words escaping. The nurse seemed frightened of her fearsome boss, who said, with forced calm, "One-Zero-Nine is a National Guardsman caught stealing opioids from a medical locker. He was sentenced to the vaccine trials by a three-judge military tribunal."

"Sentenced to be a guinea pig? In a potentially fatal medical experiment? I thought they only tested on prisoners sentenced to death or life imprisonment."

Nielsen said, "Military punishment is harsher."

"And the girl?"

A look of pain creased the nurse's face as her gaze darted toward the hospital room.

"She was a lab tech here," Nielsen said. Isabel asked if they had intentionally infected her. "Good God, no!" Nielsen replied, happy for the opportunity to be offended. She turned to the young nurse. "You knew her. Want to explain?"

"She talked a soldier into letting her slip out. She's a single mom, and *her* mom called to tell her that her daughter, in town, was sick. They caught her trying to sneak back in to steal antivirals."

"So, she tries to help her daughter, gets sick, and ends up being that asshole's sex slave."

Nielsen glared at her, but wouldn't take the bait.

"She wants to do it," the young nurse said. "She has orgasms almost every time; sometimes multiple. There's been no violence, no coercion. They sleep in the same bed, and he's been sweet to her."

Over the observation room speakers, Subject 109 said to his infected companion, "You wanna look at this?" He held the magazine out to her. She shook her head. He tossed the magazine at the trash can and missed. He sighed, acting bored, and rose to urinate in the stainless steel toilet. "You gettin' this?" he asked toward the observation room window, which was clearly opaque on his side. "Subject pissed at...what time is it? Morning? Afternoon?"

"Afternoon," the infected lab tech replied.

The observation room door opened. A soldier delivered to Isabel her now clean and disinfected clothes, still warm from the dryer. Her sanitized rifle and other gear had been returned to the convoy except for the proffered satellite phone, which Isabel accepted. After Isabel dressed, the nurse lent her a hairbrush, and Isabel removed tangles from the mess on her head. "What happened to the soldier who let the lab tech sneak out?" she asked. Nielsen and the nurse exchanged a glance. "You know what he did, so he obviously got caught."

"One-Thirty-Four," Nielsen said. "He didn't make it. Got sick, never pulled out." Isabel's heart wasn't in further harangues, so she let the tragedy pass. "We've tested 894 subjects, almost all inmates from Attica, with over a thousand more volunteering for the trials. Fifty-three contracted SED. That's 5.93, or roughly six percent. Twenty-five died—forty-seven percent. Twenty-eight turned."

The Guardsman wandered his prison cell/hospital room, putting the splayed magazine into the trash, inspecting a pimple in the mirror, ending up at the desk, where he began to massage the infected lab tech's shoulders. She straightened her back. He whispered into her ear. She tilted her head. He kissed her neck. His tattooed forearm pressed on her breasts.

Unbidden, she rose, trailing her hand, and towed him to the bed.

The nurse got out the clipboard.

"Okay, I've seen enough," said Isabel. She and Nielsen spent the next few hours touring the limited manufacturing facilities of the lab and meeting a dozen scientists, physicians, and medical engineers. Isabel then went outside onto the lawn, alone, and auto-dialed the only number stored on the phone—"POTUS."

"And?" was the president's greeting.

"It works." A chorus of cheers from his end surprised her. "There are negatives. Six percent contract *Pandoravirus*, with the usual results."

"Six *percent?*" came the president's reply. His questions about improving the odds led to the same dead ends as Isabel's queries of Nielsen had.

She heard the deep voice of Gen. Browner, who must have joined the president while his plane was grounded. "We'll have to make inoculations mandatory, sir. To get high enough vaccination rates for herd immunity."

"I'm not about to condemn," Pres. Stoddard said, "six percent of the healthy population of this country to *Pandoravirus* infection."

"What about the ninety-four percent you'll save, sir?"

"Give it up, General. This is America, not North Korea. We've got time for a public information campaign as we ramp up production."

"Public information...!" Browner choked off his reply. "Sir, you heard those reports. New York City, eighty-five percent infected. Chicago, seventy. Detroit, Cleveland, Philadelphia, all over fifty. Like we said when you turned down our request for special measures, we're losing this war!"

"Let's call your special measures what they are, General. Genocide. Which is what, General, I'm hearing that your men are already doing!"

There was silence. The rupture, long in coming, appeared complete.

The president tried to walk it back through a change in tone. "*I'll* take the vaccine myself. Go on national TV, report our success, and roll up my sleeve. Dr. Miller, please bring back with you as many doses as they can spare. We'll inoculate everyone on the plane who *volunteers*. Because, General, that's the American way."

After a pause, Browner said, "Sir, you've got a 112 people on the flight manifest. That's about three or four, if everyone volunteers, who're gonna turn."

They discussed creating isolation space, which satisfied the president.

It took the lab hours to prepare a large enough batch of the vaccine. Isabel napped fitfully, alone, in the Humvee while Rick went from vehicle to vehicle, talking to soldiers.

Just after midnight, Nielsen delivered an ice chest filled with two hundred doses of vaccine and said good-bye. "You'll be getting all the support you need," Isabel informed the ecstatic scientist. "And I imagine your testing is fully documented? If I were you, I'd destroy all that in case there are investigations and trials...by whichever side wins."

Chapter 32

THE SHENANDOAH VALLEY
Infection Date 59, 2000 GMT (4:00 p.m. Local)

"Whatta we do?" Chloe asked her dad.

Her father counted heads along the highway. "I see thirteen people between the camper on the left and those two cars—the SUV and the coupe—on the right."

"Okay. They're over the fence. They're on our *property*. Your rules, and those signs you nailed up, say we start *shooting*, right?"

"No they don't."

"Something like that. And isn't that why you made me bring *six* magazines, plus the one that's in my rifle. That's, like, almost 200 *rounds*, Dad. They're freakin' *heavy*."

"We fired twice as much in a day at the Big Jimmy's tactical course."

"Okay. So, do we start *shooting?* I can take left. You take right. I'll have a lot fewer rounds to lug back home, *uphill* I'll remind you. And leaving all their bodies down there would be a better warning to trespassers than a few signs that say *Postal* or whatever."

"Are you *high?*"

"What?"

"Chloe, let me see your eyes."

"What? Why?"

"Seriously! You go out on patrol carrying a rifle! *Stoned?*"

"Shhhhh. They could hear you," Chloe whispered.

Her dad skidded over to her. She turned away. "You're in *huge* fucking trouble, Chloe. Eject that magazine and the round you chambered *right* now."

"Dad, I'm not *that* high. I can handle an A*R*. It's not like I'm carrying *grenades* like *somebody* we know. I just did a little microdose right before my shower. It was supposed to be *Jake's* patrol."

"Eject that magazine and that round. I'm not fucking *kidding*, Chloe."

"Are you sure that's really smart, Dad? On a patrol? Two hundred meters from thirteen potential *hostiles?*"

"*Hostiles?*"

"They could have patrols out *too*, ya know, Dad? And while we're here arguing about this *nothing* burger, they could be..."

"It's *not* nothing. I want your stash before Jake gets into it."

Chloe guffawed. "Me giving weed to Jake? *That's* funny. The point is we're on this patrol, we haven't even *talked* about the potential hostiles issue, and you've completely lost situational awareness. And I'd never get *stoned*, okay. I'm *responsible*. And you're *not* getting my *'sta-a-ash.'* No way. I have *rights*. If I carry a rifle, I get rights. To vote, and stuff like that, and to the pursuit of happiness. So..."

"This isn't over," her dad said.

They left the trespassers unmolested and headed back home in silence. The hill seemed twice as steep as she'd remembered it on the way down. To top it off, her dad stopped them, made her get down on the ground, waved and waggled his hand and pointed to his eyes—"*What?*" she'd pantomimed—like she could possibly know what he meant by all his monkey motion. And all of it was only paranoia. She'd mentioned patrols by potential hostiles completely theoretically. Of *course* nobody else went on patrols. Normal people didn't have guys like her dad. *Jesus.*

He eased up after no major loss of life and joined Chloe for the last of their climb. "Where'd you get that potential hostiles thing? Did I miss it in class or the reading?"

"I made it up." He looked down at her. "I'm *creative*." Her dad smiled. Situation handled. "We really could've taken 'em, ya know. Those settlers down there."

"Now they're *settlers?* I think potential hostiles is better. It includes Infecteds, *and* Uninfecteds who're starving, or driven to depravity by trauma, or just ordinary felons."

"PH is shorter," Chloe remarked. "But the P stands for *potential*, Dad. They could just be settlers looking to raise some crops, you know, and support, like, the local arts and crafts. But we coulda taken 'em. I could have hit all mine on the left, and then come and helped you out on the right. My aim is *real* steady when I microdose."

"Wait!" He grabbed her arm. "Chloe, you've gone shooting *before* while high?"

"You train like you fight. That's what the big instructor said."

"High?"

"Like I said, it was *Jake's* patrol. I'd *finished* my chores." She gritted her teeth. "*Microdose*, Dad. I put an entire magazine, twenty-seven rounds, inside the five ring while microdosing. It looked like a *cannon* ball had shot straight through the target. That's when the instructor gave me that thingie, remember, that *pin?* Expert effing marksman. 'Marks*woman*,' he called me, remember? My hands were, like, totally calm. My heart steady. Breathing slow."

She waited to see which way this thing was gonna go. More lectures and criticism, joined in by her mom, God forbid? Or full-on police raid of her panty drawer, where the vape pens Jake had given her were hidden?

"Uhm, Chloe, could *I* maybe, you know, have a little? Pot, I mean? Just a little."

"What?" Oh, the irony. Un-fucking-believable! After her reflexive roller coaster of an eye roll, she said, "You know what *hypocrisy* is, don't you? And yes, okay, you can have *one* vape pen, but only if you prove you understand the microdosing concept. I'd like to see a good definition on the hallway floor outside my room by eight o'clock tonight, double-spaced, 200 words, handwritten is fine."

Her dad laughed. "You woulda been a good lawyer." He meant it as a compliment.

"So, what am I gonna be *now?*" she asked, hoping the pot conversation was over before her mom got to join it.

"Maybe, I dunno, travel the country doing sharpshooting exhibitions at rodeos, hoe-downs, barn raisings." He hugged her. *"Ew!"* She pried herself free from her sweaty father.

Chapter 33

THE SHENANDOAH VALLEY
Infection Date 60, 1000 GMT (6:00 a.m. Local)

Emma, Dwayne, and Samantha arrived at the first encampment along the state highway leading down to town, which Samantha had numbered "1" on her map. It was occupied by Infecteds of varying capabilities from indolent and inactive, to industrious and energetic. The latter would work; the former could be disposed of. They took photos on Emma's iPhone for future use in organizing. Camps 2, 3, and 4 were also full of Infecteds, but 5 was Uninfected: blasting loud music on an RV's stereo system, with boisterous children playing noisily atop an immobilized SUV. Camp 6 was evidently mixed, with Uninfecteds wearing masks and Infecteds chained to a tree. Camp 7 was impossible to categorize from the observable actions of their grimy, barely subsisting occupants. The scientist in Emma noted the convergence of Infected and Uninfected behavior at the very edge of subsistence living. All were wary of the three armed passers-by, but none challenged or confronted them.

Before reaching town, they climbed the hill above the highway and lay on their bellies behind a rock. Samantha sketched the town's layout and took note of Dwayne and Emma's comments. "I estimate about two hundred refugees in that enclosure," Dwayne said.

"More," Emma corrected. Sam added a plus sign after the 200 she had written on her map next to the fenced back lot of an auto-body shop that looked more like a junkyard. Emma noted for Sam the only guard they saw: a shaggy man in jeans and a camouflage blouse with a hunting rifle propped on his hip and a sleepy dog at his feet. "See those young men over there?" Emma pointed at four boys and men seated behind the hulk of an old truck, hidden from view amid piles of rusting metal. "They're sharpening tools."

"Weapons," suggested Dwayne.

Sam asked, "Are they Infected, or Uninfected?"

"Uninfected." Emma pointed. A boy of ten or so chased a girl somewhat younger through the junkyard playing a game of tag. Samantha put a big "U" in the center of the fenced-off pen she had drawn. "Look," Emma said. "They're gonna feed them." A line of gray-haired ladies carried trays toward the fence from one of the four nearby churches. A sheriff's deputy with a shotgun escorted them, and the refugees in the camp quickly crowded the fence nearest them. Even the males making weapons and the two playing children raced to join them. The lone guard with the hunting rifle knew enough to be concerned, and retreated several steps as the commotion grew.

"They're starving," Emma said. The Uninfecteds jostled for position, with shoves and elbows thrown, and snarls revealing a more primitive underlying substrate. *They're dangerous,* said the voice.

"Why are they wasting food on them?" Samantha asked.

Emma ventured, "Maybe the promise of a little food keeps them under control."

Dwayne was shaking his head. "Right now, they're in a fairly secure enclosure. But before too long they'll work their way through that fence."

The fence bowed outward with the pressure of the refugees. The women with the food stopped short. In what appeared to be the routine, they placed the trays on the ground and began tossing sandwiches, wrapped in paper, over the fence. Each descending packet became the center of a fight. Bigger men generally fared better in the scramble for food, but some groups appeared organized with men blocking their competition and women seizing the sandwiches. The noise of it all, including the useless barks of the guard's dog, rose to a crescendo as the last of the food rained down into the melee. The women, looking behind them in concern bordering on fear, departed with their empty trays. The deputy shouted unheard commands as men and women wrestled over the last unclaimed bundles.

"That man doesn't look very interested in doing his job," Dwayne said. The civilian guard with the hunting rifle had backed all the way across the street from the fence. His slumping dog looked ancient and decrepit.

"Could he stop them if they broke out?" Emma asked.

Dwayne shook his head. "Not with a bolt action rifle against 200 starving people."

"Then why are they staying penned up in there?"

"They're doing what they're told. They're getting at least *some* food. They're staying free of the virus. It would take five or six men with magazine-fed semi-automatic rifles—or one with a belt-fed machine gun from that armory—to cut them down to a manageable number." Samantha neatly wrote "5-6 rifles or 1 MG" underneath dashed lines of bullets ripping through the roughly square enclosure drawn on her map.

They saw no evidence of a larger armed militia. A second deputy sat in a folding lawn chair at the door to the large brick Army National Guard building, to which Samantha paid particular attention in her drawing. "Could you hit him at this range?" Dwayne began to raise his rifle to his shoulder. Emma rested her hand on his arm. "I mean, hypothetically."

"From here? Three hundred yards? Sure." Samantha drew a dashed line from their vantage point to the stick figure she'd placed by the armory door, wrote "300 yards," and drew a smiley face.

Emma had Sam note every door and window into the armory, fire station, and sheriff's offices, and the doors into the church's kitchen to which the ladies had returned.

"This town isn't big enough," Emma commented as Sam completed her map.

"You said you didn't want a big city," Dwayne noted. "Too attractive a target."

Emma said, "Sam?" The girl was so absorbed in her map that she jumped in surprise. "What was that list of mid-sized Virginia towns that we came up with at the NIH hospital? Between 75,000 and 150,000 pre-outbreak populations?"

Samantha had recreated most of her notes from their combined recollections in a spiral notebook like those she had presumably used in middle school. Only this one lacked the flowery doodles and hearts and stars, and bore instead, on its bright blue cover, only the word, "Notes."

"Uhm, Lynchburg."

"That's a possibility," Emma said. "But it's close to D.C."

The next three—Suffolk, Portsmouth, and Hampton—were nixed on Dwayne's advice. They were all adjacent to Norfolk, still a flourishing and heavily defended U.S. naval base. "Plus," he said, "anywhere near the coast and we'd be exposed to naval artillery and the possibility of an amphibious assault."

"And the last town is Roanoke," Samantha interjected in her high-pitched yet still confident voice. She looked expectantly at Emma. Roanoke was nowhere near the coast. Could she be thinking on her own, not simply reciting the requested list? Could she possibly be hearing voices too, prodding her with advice? Voices that were, somewhere deep in her mind, doing their own analysis of the data?

"That's reasonably close to here," Emma noted.

Dwayne added, "And in the Blue Ridge Mountains. Remember when I was telling you about raising semi-regular forces without all the complex and heavier systems."

Emma looked his way. "Forces that could break down," she said, "under pressure into semi-*ir*regular units, like guerrillas. In the mountains?" Samantha began drawing large apes on the map next to Roanoke. Emma said, "So, Roanoke it is. But we'll need numbers. First, this town. Then on to Rawley Springs."

Chapter 34

UPSTATE NEW YORK
Infection Date 60, 1100 GMT (7:00 a.m. Local)

The gunner atop Isabel's Humvee had opened fire repeatedly after they left Pearl River, but they hadn't exited their vehicles to fight even once. Nevertheless, the trip back—in the dark early morning hours—was several times scarier than the daytime trip down to Pearl River had been.

Once, the ghostly figure of a woman, almost certainly infected, had stood staring straight through Isabel's side window from under ten feet away as they edged their way slowly through the narrow channel of stalled cars cleared the day before. The woman had fallen backwards like a bowling pin when their machine gunner had cursed and fired as fast as he could swivel his weapon around. But in her spooky final moments on Earth, she had never taken her eyes off Isabel.

They returned the way they had come, driving north up the southbound lane. At their plodding pace, it would take hours more to make it back to the president's plane.

A flurry of radio traffic changed that calculus. They pulled off the Interstate and into the parking lot of a long-ago looted Walmart. "What's going on?" Isabel asked Rick.

"Changing rides," was all he said, opening his door even before the Humvee stopped. Their convoy was arranged in a tight circle in the huge, empty parking lot, its vehicles backing into place so that their headlights illuminated their surroundings. Old shopping bags and free newspapers swirled in the breeze amid overturned carts and volume discount packaging.

Isabel opened her door, but Rick leaned back inside. "Stay there!"

She ignored him and exited inside the circle of vehicles, which reminded her of a wagon train bedding down for the night. The wind was cold. There was thunder in the distance. Men growled orders, moved between vehicles, and unfurled belts of brass ammo to feed the machine guns placed in the gaps between the fenders. "Alvarez," a sergeant barked, "you got from Garden Supplies on the left to that burned out flatbed. Mazelli, that flatbed is the leftmost edge of your field of fire. You got all the way over to that last lamppost in front of the barbeque grills. You see which one I'm talkin' about?"

"Yes, sergeant!"

"If they take cover behind the flatbed, you both keep 'em pinned and we'll lob forty mike-mikes down on 'em. Got it?"

"Yes, sergeant!" both men replied.

The thunder on the horizon seemed odd. It came in waves, not randomly. Isabel found the gap between the tall MRAP, Rick had called it, and the Humvee with the stubby, automatic grenade launcher and watched the lightning that was associated with the rumbling. They were explosions, not weather. She counted the time between the strings of flashes and the sounds of *boom-boom-boom-boom*. Seven seconds. Seven miles.

"I told you to stay in the fucking Humvee!" Rick snarled at her.

She was more disturbed than offended by him cursing at her, but held it together. "What's going on?"

Rick's eyes followed hers to the flashes that lit the treetops. "They found and fixed that renegade National Guard unit. So, Stewart thinks it's safe enough now to fly helos, and you're getting picked up. They're in a hurry to get you back."

"To get that ice chest back, more likely."

"I take it this wasn't a beer run?" he ventured. She simply shook her head. She'd already decided it was best if no one knew what was in the cooler. Someone might go a little nuts if they heard she was carrying a working *Pandoravirus* vaccine. It may be the single most valuable substance on earth.

"Movement!" someone called out from the opposite side of the circle.

"Hold your fire!" came another shout.

Rick hustled to the source of the warning. Isabel followed. "Five people," said the sergeant, alternating between night vision goggles mounted atop his helmet and hand-held optical binoculars. "Looks like a family. Mom, dad, three kids."

Despite that report, the soldier next to Isabel took aim; nervous, jumpy, ready.

A lieutenant showed up with a bullhorn and handed it to Rick. "You there!" his voice boomed. "Halt! United States military! You are approaching a restricted zone! We will use deadly force if you come any closer!"

There was a shout in reply from the distance. "What did he say?" the lieutenant asked Rick.

"Fuck if I know." Rick pointed the horn toward the family and raised the handheld mike connected to it by a long, curly cord. "I say again. *Halt!* This is a restricted military zone! Do not approach this convoy! We *will* use deadly force! This is your final warning!"

There was another shouted reply. The only word Isabel made out was "food."

One of the soldiers said, "They're starving."

"Yeah?" the army officer replied to his man. "And I haven't been paid in a month. We all got problems."

"Yeah but…They got little kids."

"Helo is ten out," Rick said to his fellow officer, lowering a radio handset. Isabel thought ten minutes was no time at all. But the two officers exchanged a glance that suggested otherwise.

The family was now clearly pleading. "They're just hungry," the soldier again piped up.

"You don't think Infecteds get hungry?" his commanding officer answered.

"Please!" came the now audible shouts of the approaching family. "They're everywhere! The woods are full of 'em! We risked coming out because we're starving! We've got kids! Just take *them!* Please!"

"That don't sound like Infecteds, sir!" the rebellious soldier implored.

This time, it was another soldier who responded, not their officer. "If we let them inside this perimeter, we could all get sick."

But the first guy wouldn't give up. "We're out in open air. That's not as dangerous as indoors, right?"

"Shut the fuck up!" the lieutenant snapped. "We've got a mission, and we're gonna complete it." He glanced at Isabel—their mission—and she felt guilty.

The rifle of the hesitant soldier was no longer raised to his shoulder. He muttered, "The mission, the mission," and avoided looking directly at Isabel. "When we get this woman back, what then, sir? What are our orders? 'Cause it seems like we're just about at the end of the road. What if there's nobody out there to give us our next mission?"

A string of explosions miles away drew their attention. "They're still out there," his lieutenant replied.

"Fuckin' *Air* Force. That's hardly fightin'. Droppin' bombs on some poor bastards who may or may not be sick? Then drinkin' beer back on some airbase?"

"Shut the fuck up!" came the increasingly menacing curse from his commander.

A woman from the family in the distance screamed. Her high pitch caused everyone to rivet their gaze on that gloomy patch of parking lot. "They're coming!" the head of the starving family shouted. "They're coming! Let us in!"

A searchlight swung their way. The family was running straight toward their guns.

"Shit!" Rick said. He raised his rifle to his shoulder.

"You're not gonna *shoot* them!" Isabel said.

Rick shouted, *"Ha-a-a-alt!"* at the top of his lungs. His command jarred Isabel. She could see them now. Five people. A mom, a dad, two boys, and a girl. They were sprinting toward the convoy.

"Your call," Rick said to the army officer, a lieutenant.

"Fuck you. *Sir! Your* fucking call!"

"Rick!" Isabel said.

It was the wrong thing to do. He took one side-long glance at her, set his face in a grimace, and literally growled out a loud, "Ahhh!" His muzzle flamed. The family dove to the ground. Rick surely would've hit someone if he'd aimed at them, but no one appeared wounded. Soldiers' helmets swiveled left and right. Hushed arguments broke out.

The family rose and resumed their run toward them, this time in a stoop. Rick looked at Isabel, then raised his rifle again and fired a single shot. The man fell instantly. A girl screamed. *"Daddy!"* The family gathered around him.

Isabel burst into tears. She tried to stop and walked away from and out of sight of Rick. But she doubled over, instead sobbing even harder. She heard more calls of, "Movement!" and "Contract!" Through her blurry vision she saw figures emerge from the tree line. "Oh, God!" she said just before the entire unit opened fire.

Dozens of running figures came straight at the family and at their armored wagon train beyond. These weren't pathetic pleading figures. They were shooting back.

The family lay flat underneath sheets of fire that had to be passing just over their heads in both directions. Spent cartridges spat from Rick's rifle.

Bullets zipped through the air. "Get your fucking weapon!" Rick shouted when he saw Isabel.

Through eyesight still obscured by tears, she stumbled back toward their Humvee. Muzzle flashes sparkled in her liquid vision. She ducked low on hearing a *bzzzt* fly past her head. At the Humvee, she grabbed her rifle and ran back to the fight.

She knelt on the hard pavement behind the huge tire of the MRAP and raised her M4. The scene was alive with sprinting figures. She aimed at the Infecteds closest to the prone family, unsafed the rifle, and pulled the trigger but missed. She reached up and wiped her eyes clear, then her runny nose, and focused. A woman in jeans and a high school letter jacket with something that looked like a hatchet in her hand didn't weave or duck, she just ran. Isabel kept her in her sights while slowly increased pressure on the trigger till the recoil surprised her. The woman's legs seemed to outrun her torso as she fell backwards, half rolled onto her side, then lay still.

Isabel fired again, and again. It took her several shots to fell her next kill—an old man, who dropped to his knees, tried to rise, then crumpled forward in a heap like a Muslim in prayer. Just as the number of targets began to dwindle, the steady *thump-thump-thump* of the Bradley's small cannon opened fire from the opposite side of the circle.

Soldiers ran to the sound of that gun. Isabel followed. Sure enough, there was a second mob of people approaching the opposite side of their circle from the tree line as if in a coordinated, two-pronged attack. One hurled a burning, spinning object toward them, but it fell well short. The parking lot, however, erupted in a blaze where it landed. They were making Molotov fucking cocktails! Several more rained down, ever nearer, lighting up the killing fields with their barbarous glow.

She fired at a man in a police uniform who was shooting a pistol at them. Strangely, she felt no fear despite the bullets clanging off their vehicles. She was sprayed with debris from a shattered taillight. She could practically feel shots *whiz* close by. She heard the shouts of "Medic!" from the opposite side of the convoy's circle.

When the policeman she'd wounded rose to his knees, she killed him. Fired straight into his torso as Rick had taught. Then a skinny man, dragging one leg behind him, moving slowly, an easy shot. Then what looked like a teenage boy, who would run a few steps, kneel, and fire his shotgun. On his third kneel, as he was loading another two rounds into the open, double-barreled gun, her bullet struck him squarely in his face. The shotgun flew from his hands. A woman picked it up. Isabel wounded her. She rose again, wobbly, and was riddled with fire from someone else.

Above the *pops* of the guns and *thumps* of the Bradley came a new sound. Deep. Throbbing. Growing louder.

The chop of the helicopter's rotor was quickly punctuated by a howl from the sky. That was the word that came to her—a mechanical, banshee-like howl. The helicopter swept in low over the parking lot, its green fuselage lit by a blaze four feet in length. Clearly visible at that low altitude was a man in an oversized helmet standing behind a spinning, multi-barrel gun that fired at a prodigious rate. A second after it passed over them, spent cartridges rained across their vehicles' formation. Dozens of shell casings clinked off rooftops and bounced off pavement like hail. The helicopter orbited, raining fire down on the attackers. The rifles, machine guns, and cannon of the convoy slowly fell silent. The shrieks of the helicopter's door gun grew less constant, ending in short rips that must have been brief pulls of its trigger.

The aircraft flared out and touched down gently amid a tornado of debris.

"Isabel!" Rick shouted. He jabbed his finger at the helicopter, which kept its rotors turning, ready to take off. "Get on board!"

She ran back to her Humvee. He joined her there. She got her backpack. He got his gear and her ice chest. They and three nervous soldiers with rifles raised to their shoulders jogged the short distance to the Black Hawk. Rick hoisted the chest into the open doorway. The door gunner pulled Isabel aboard.

"Come on!" she shouted to Rick, holding out her hand.

"I'm staying!"

"No! You have to come too!" He shook his head. She shouted, "The mission, remember?" She pointed at the ice chest. He hesitated, looking at the circled wagon train, which was profiled by a half dozen gasoline fires. "What if we don't make it back to the airbase?"

Reluctantly, Rick tossed his heavy pack into the cabin and climbed aboard. The second his boots left the pavement the helicopter was airborne. The gunner had to hang onto Rick to keep him from falling out. Isabel crawled away from the man's fearsome six-barreled weapon, which again began to shriek, and leaned her back against the bulkhead. Rick did the same, but on the opposite side of the cabin. He never once made eye contact with her on the twenty-minute, twisting and turning, low-altitude flight. The helicopter gyrated so wildly that Isabel craned her neck to see what the hell the pilot was doing. He and his copilot sat behind their sticks, pointing, shouting warnings to each other constantly, and pulling sickening Gs to avoid whatever threats they had spotted or imagined.

Amazingly, they didn't hit a radio tower or power line, and slowed to settle onto the brightly lit tarmac next to a 747 with "United States of America" written on its side.

They bounced once, then settled. The pilots killed the engines, and the door gunner raised his weapon so that it pointed harmlessly skyward. He sank onto his butt, wiping sweat off his face and flexing his cramping gloved hands.

Isabel and Rick climbed down wearing their heavy packs. Isabel held her rifle. Rick's was slung over his shoulder to allow him to carry the ice chest for their short walk to the E-4B. It was bathed in blinding lights and surrounded by air policemen with rifles raised and at the ready.

A small delegation left a cluster of Humvees at the base of the forward staircase leading up to the president's plane. From outside the glare from the spotlights, Isabel couldn't make out who the dark profiles were that were headed to meet them, but some wore camouflage and others business suits. They intercepted Rick and Isabel half way to the staircase.

"Dr. Miller," came the booming voice of Gen. Browner. Rick stiffened, but couldn't salute because of the ice chest he carried. "Capt. Townsend. Glad to find you both well."

The two civilians who accompanied Browner were the Directors of the CIA and FBI. No one smiled even though they surely knew what she'd brought.

"This is for the president," Isabel said, indicating Rick's cargo.

"Two hundred doses?" Gen. Browner asked. "Good, good. Wonders of modern science. We'll take them from here." Browner reached for the ice chest himself.

Isabel rested her hand atop the white plastic lid. "The president asked me to bring them back to *him*."

"We'll take care of it."

It seemed strange to Isabel. The high-level welcoming committee. The fact that Gen. Browner asked for the ice chest himself, rather than having some flunky carry it.

Isabel hesitated. "Can I have one dose?"

"You'll get yours on *Nightwatch*."

"I mean one *more* dose."

Browner's gaze flitted to Rick and back to Isabel. He opened the latch and lifted the lid. From the rising fog inside, he extracted a syringe from a form-fitting foam pocket and handed it to her. Rick gave Browner the ice chest and saluted. CIA Director Struthers maintained a poker face, but FBI Director Pearson appeared troubled. The three men returned to a waiting black SUV.

"That was strange," Isabel said. Rick nodded. Seconds later, an officer in full camo emerged from the SUV and carried the ice chest up the stairs to *Nightwatch*, whose engines were powering up. The two Directors followed the man onto the plane seconds later, and the black SUV drove away with Browner inside.

Isabel handed Rick the syringe. "There's a six percent chance this will give you *Pandoravirus*. But if it doesn't, you'll be immune in a few hours."

"Are you gonna take it?"

Isabel looked at the giant 747. "I imagine everyone on the plane will. So, yeah."

Without further hesitation, Rick dropped his pack and body armor, rolled up his sleeve, and injected the thimbleful of precious amber serum into his biceps. "I guess I'll go find someplace secluded while I wait." He climbed back into his gear.

The air policemen withdrew from their wider perimeter at all corners of the jet toward the stairs deployed in the back. "I've gotta go," Isabel said, staring at the concrete beneath her. "Hey, are we okay? I mean, you'll still come and find me? Like you promised?" She held her breath and couldn't look his way.

"I hear they're evacuating the Pentagon to Pennsylvania. My guess is I'll be headed down that way. But yeah. I'll find you, Isabel. I'll try. Somehow. Someday." Isabel rose onto tiptoes and kissed Rick's lips, scratching herself on his stubble. Rick, always clean shaven, hadn't shaved in days. But he crushed her to his chest for a second, deeper kiss. In that instant, the Earth resumed its orbit and the ground beneath her firmed. The world felt right again, in spite of everything else. And then he left to await his fate.

Chapter 35

"He's on!" Natalie called out to Noah, who joined her and Chloe at the TV. He could hear the buzz of Jake's drone landing outside. Natalie pointed at the flat screen.

A picture of the presidential seal switched to Bill Stoddard, seated in front of a blue wall. The lighting was poor and the room cramped. They were obviously on the airborne command post, not in a studio. And Stoddard wore a dark blue, short-sleeved, collared golf shirt that said, "USAF" over a logo.

"My fellow Americans, I come to you today to announce wonderful news. Our scientists, who've been working tirelessly since the outbreak of this terrible disease, have made a stunning breakthrough. They have developed a vaccine that will prevent infection from *Pandoravirus*." Natalie sank into a chair, closed her eyes, and mouthed a prayer. "We are, right now, employing every available resource this country can muster to initiate large-scale production of the serum, which we hope to begin distributing to regional health authorities within a few weeks."

"This is great!" Chloe said, turning to her parents with a hopeful look. "Right?"

"What's great?" Jake said as he descended the spiral staircase from the tower.

"Shhh!" both Natalie and Noah responded.

"This godsend will allow our nation, indeed our entire world, to turn the corner and begin to bring an end to this horrible nightmare, which had previously seemed unstoppable. We are sharing the vaccine, of course, with every nation on earth as all of humanity attempts to halt the scourge of *Pandoravirus*. What I ask of each of you, my fellow citizens, is to stay calm, stay safe, and hold on because help is on the way. Victory over this dread disease is in sight."

"But if it's gonna take weeks, or *months* maybe, to make the stuff," Chloe said, less enthusiastically than before, "can we hold out till then?" Noah realized she was asking him. He couldn't bring himself to answer. He had promised her he wouldn't lie.

With Jake back from the tower and his drone patrol, the house was undefended.

"There *are* side effects," Pres. Stoddard said, "that our scientists are striving to reduce. I will not deceive you by telling you that this vaccination is without risk. A small percentage of the people who take the vaccine will get sick with *Pandoravirus*."

"That's not good," Chloe said.

"But that should not dissuade you from inoculation just as it will not dissuade me or my family. In fact, when given the choice, fully informed of the risk, every single crewmember and government official on board this aircraft elected to take the vaccine, which I will now do."

"Isabel is supposed to be on that plane," Natalie noted.

A woman in a white lab coat over camouflaged fatigues appeared on TV with an alcohol wipe and a syringe. As the president raised his sleeve to his shoulder, Chloe covered her mouth with both hands, cringing melodramatically as the needle went in.

"There," said the president. "I should achieve full immunity from *Pandoravirus* within hours."

Chloe looked up at her mother and father to confirm whether this was something she should be excited about. Noah acted as if he didn't notice his daughter's searching gaze. It was far too early for them to celebrate.

"The initial allotments of the vaccine will go to medical workers and first responders. The second round will go to our troops, law enforcement personnel, and key officials. We hope to have every citizen of this country inoculated by the end of the year."

Natalie said, "Can they make 300 million doses in a *year*?"

"We won't need that many," Noah replied. "Every day that goes by, we need fewer."

Stoddard ended with praise of everyone for everything they're doing, uplifting statements about the triumph of human ingenuity and the can-do American spirit, and exhortations to keep calm and carry on. The scene cut to a network studio. The talking heads began what would surely be hours of speculation about the treatment based on no more information than they had all just heard. Noah muted the television.

"We should listen to what they're saying about…" Natalie began.

"Shhh!" Noah replied. There was a steady uproar of clucking in the barn.

"Hey, my chickens," Chloe said, rising and heading for the front door.

Noah grabbed her arm and motioned toward her rifle. "Jake, get back up to the tower but stay *low*." Noah retrieved his rifle and was the first to make it to the door. He chambered a round, took the safety off, and headed across the yard for the barn from which chickens were busily scattering. Everything happened quickly. Natalie called his name. Chloe shouted, *"Lookout!"*

A figure appeared beside the barn raising a weapon. Noah dropped to the ground just ahead of a *boom* that jarred him even more than blowing the ridge road.

Crack.

The man dropped his shotgun and fell. Noah hadn't even had time to raise his rifle. He looked back at the porch. Chloe's smoking AR rested atop the wooden railing.

"Sorry!" she called out in horror toward the man she'd shot, who lay deathly still. Natalie knelt beside Chloe and held her as their daughter began to sob.

The chickens were settling down, bobbing their heads and pecking at the dirt around the fallen intruder. Noah's heart threatened to burst out of his chest with each thud as he lay on his stomach gripping his rifle so hard his hands quickly grew sore. He could see no other motion through the barn's windows and doorways. The man hadn't moved. "Anyone see anything?" Noah called out.

Natalie said, "No!"

Jake shouted, "Clear!"

Noah ensured his rifle's safety was off and approached the barn with his AR-15 at his shoulder and eye to his sight, ready to fire with a single twitch of his finger, as taught.

"Noah! Sweetheart! Be careful!"

He peered into the darkness of the barn. His eyes hadn't yet adjusted. *Wait!* he cautioned to restrain himself. *Slowly. Carefully.* The chickens seemed unconcerned, approaching him as if he bore seed for their morning feeding. He cleared the room as he'd been instructed in the tactical course. Left. Right. Proceed to cover. Left. Right. Behind. The nooks and crannies were danger zones. He remained ready to fire at any hint of movement. But the barn was empty save the chickens. He saw where the fencing outside had been cut and bent inwards, but there was no one in the woods beyond the breach.

Noah exited the barn on the side facing the house. Chloe and Natalie were lying flat on the porch behind their rifles.

"Clear!" Noah called out.

"Clear!" Chloe replied, as taught, in her high pitch.

"Clear!" Jake shouted from the tower.

"I don't see anything," Natalie said. "I mean...*clear!*"

Noah rounded the corner of the barn at which the would-be chicken thief lay.

"Noah, your mask!" Natalie reminded him.

He jogged back to the house to gear up. "Is he dead?" Chloe asked.

"I dunno. Probably. Stay right there and shoot anyone you see. Or shoot that guy again if he moves a muscle." He donned a mask and blue latex gloves from the boxes in the foyer, but his hands shook so much the gloves' fingers were never pulled on fully. When he returned to the porch, he asked in a voice that he heard tremble, "Anything?" as he knelt and surveyed the scene.

Chloe looked ill, but both she and her mother shook their heads in reply.

Noah again crossed the yard. The fallen intruder lay face down. He had sparse gray hair and smelled as if he hadn't showered in weeks. His dark jacket had a single hole in the middle of his back. Blood spread black around it. Noah kicked the shotgun away, then used the toe of his boot to roll the man over.

The intruder stared straight up at the sky through pupils that were totally black. Dirt stuck to the sweat on his forehead. A small hole in his chest corresponded to the larger one in his back. As taught by the instructors, Noah held his rifle one-handed, pointing down at the man, finger pulling firmly against the trigger, as he thumped the man's eyeball with a gloved index finger. The infected man didn't react at all. No involuntary flinch of a living person who was "playing possum."

"He's dead!" Noah announced.

Natalie and Chloe arrived a few moments later but kept their distance. His daughter looked mortified, staring out from her mother's embrace at the man she'd killed. Noah wanted to help relieve her anguish. "Good shot, Chloe. Thank you for..."

Chloe vomited. In between spasms, she repeated, "I'm sorry. I'm sorry. I'm sorry."

Jake arrived. "It's okay, Chloe. You feel bad for a little while but then it goes away."

Noah realized in that moment that both of their teenage children, whose lives their parents had committed to protecting, had now killed people, but neither he nor Natalie had fired a single shot in their defense. What sense did this new world make?

"Chloe, sweetie," Natalie said, "you did the right thing. Like Dad said, good shot. *I* couldn't have made it. And if you hadn't done it, Dad would've been hurt, or even killed."

"He was just hungry," Chloe said. She was doubled over, hands braced on her knees, and spitting the foul taste from her mouth as Natalie rubbed her back.

"He was infected," Noah replied. "And stealing the food that we need to survive."

"Everything okay?" Emma shouted from the side gate that led up the hill to the cabin. She, Dwayne, Samantha, and Dorothy all stood outside the fence carrying long guns.

"Yes!" Natalie replied.

"Did we miss one of the Nicholses?"

"No. Some guy was trying to steal our chickens, we think."

"Okay then. Here's our notice," Emma said, waving a single sheet of paper in air, rolling it up, and inserting it into the fencing. "Bye."

Noah sent Jake back up to the tower as Natalie guided Chloe inside. He went and retrieved the single page Emma had left behind. "We hereby terminate our contract." Signed "Emma Miller, PhD." Emma and friends were long gone. Noah felt overwhelmed. His circuits overloaded.

He got a shovel from the barn and began digging a grave near the septic tanks, where there was soil, not rock. It felt good to sweat from hard labor instead of anxiety. It calmed him. When the hole was a few feet deep, he dragged the body into it. He shoveled the topsoil from where the thief had fallen, dark with blood, into a trash bag, which he buried unceremoniously with the *Pandoravirus*-tainted remains and his blue gloves. Noah made a cross from two pieces of wood and wrote on it the man's name he got from his wallet, Chet Perkins of Bridgeport, Connecticut, and the dates of his birth and death...today. Noah then used wire to repair the hole in the fence.

Over the radio, Natalie asked if they should turn the electric fence on during the daytime. Noah replied, "I don't know if we're producing enough power. But we can try it and see if the battery holds up."

When the fence was fixed and he'd thrown the long red handle to electrify the fence, he took a long, calming shower, holding onto the walls as he allowed himself to admit just how close he'd come to dying, and how great the risk to his family remained. He then joined Natalie, whose tanned arms were wrapped tightly around Chloe as she repeatedly kissed their daughter's short blond hair. The TV was tuned to a grainy, off-air channel.

"The Rawley Springs station is back on," Natalie said quietly as if not to disturb her daughter's fragile calm. Her eyes directed Noah's gaze to the screen.

The anchorwoman from the station in the valley sat woodenly in front of the camera reading the news. "Brazilian authorities believe the outbreak in Rio de Janeiro, which marks the first known arrival of *Pandoravirus* in Latin America, traces back to a charter flight evacuating wealthy Portuguese refugees from Lisbon."

Noah felt Natalie looking his way, and turned to meet her gaze. "Do you see it?"

"See what?" he asked.

Natalie nodded at the TV again.

Noah leaned forward. The picture quality wasn't great. "The weather today is expected to be fair, with a high of 64 degrees and no precipitation in the forecast. There are no local sports scheduled. The local school district remains closed until further notice. Traffic on the main highways continues to be heavy out of northern Virginia…"

Noah gasped. The anchorwoman's eyes were jet black. She was infected.

Chapter 36

ABOARD E4-B
Infection Date 61, 1545 GMT (11:45 a.m. Local)

Isabel sat in her blue seat, mask and goggles on, airsick bag at her side, staring at the numbers—"1436/62"—written in black marker on the back of her left hand. The first number was clearly the time of her injection with the vaccine—1436 Greenwich Mean Time, about an hour and ten minutes ago—when her entire cabin had been vaccinated in their seats or bunks. The second number was either her order in the 112 injections being given to the people on board, or the number written on the vaccine's syringe, or something like that.

She passed the time by occasionally catching the wide, goggled eyes of off-duty crewmen seated around her, who themselves warily monitored neighbors for any signs of illness. Statistically, seven of them should catch *Pandoravirus* from the injection.

No movement through the aircraft was allowed. Air policemen armed with pistols stood at the opposite ends of their cabin and, Isabel presumed, each of the other cabins on the 747. They periodically took slow strolls down the two aisles searching for any signs of medical distress. A cough. A sneeze. A gag. A hiccup. Squirming. Sweating. Moaning.

A nurse in camouflage arrived to take everyone's temperature. The frequency of the checks was increasing as the two-hour mark approached. This check and the next one, two spins of the wheel, should inform Isabel and the others of their destinies.

The nurse didn't smile when she got to Isabel. Nor did the armed air policeman accompanying her. Any bedside manner they might once have exhibited had yielded to tension writ firmly onto their faces. "How do you feel?" the nurse asked from behind her mask and goggles.

"Great!" Isabel said. Her voice quivered.

The nurse pressed the contact thermometer to her forehead. Isabel couldn't help but close her eyes. *Please, God, I'll be good!* There was a *beep.* The nurse made a notation on her iPad and moved on. Isabel resumed breathing. The airman followed the nurse to the next row. "How do you feel?" she asked the airman in the seat behind Isabel.

Another *beep.* Another all-clear.

But shortly afterwards, Isabel sensed a break in routine and turned to look down the aisle. A man, around her age—an officer—had approached the nurse and her escort. He was speaking to her in quiet tones. Sweat trickled down his brow. The thermometer went to his head and *beeped.* The nurse read the instrument, and raised it again to his forehead. *Beep.* Her brow furrowed.

The officer willingly climbed into a full-body coverall and calmly said his good-byes as he walked forward with one of the cabin's two posted guards following him. Isabel didn't know the man, but she got a nod as he passed, which she returned.

Jesus. He was so calm. *Could I be that brave?* His life was over, or irrevocably changed, but he seemed serene. She was shaking and covered herself in her blanket. That got her noticed. "You doing okay?" the nurse asked as she came back up the aisle.

"Yeah. Sure." She held her breath again as the thermometer *beeped.* The nurse and her airman moved forward to the middle cabin.

Minutes passed like months. An officer arrived and called an airman to duty. "That's two," said the man across the aisle from Isabel. It took a moment for her to understand. Someone else, up front, had fallen ill. The man from their cabin was his or her replacement.

"What are they doing with them?" she asked the man. "With the people who…?"

"They outfitted the aft lower lobe as an isolation ward. It'll be tight for a half-dozen people."

Isabel imagined the scene as, one-by-one, sick people filled the small compartment. Were there tears? Prayers? Vomit? Was there gallows humor, or a camaraderie among the condemned? She shivered and took a deep, ragged breath. Her seatmate paid greater attention to her after that. She didn't feel sick, exactly, she didn't think. Hers were symptoms more of terror. She felt cold, but not feverish...probably.

She needed to go to the bathroom. But was that diarrhea? She shivered, but her temperature was normal or else they'd have escorted her down to that nightmarish dungeon. Her stomach made a gurgling noise. She glanced at the airman across the aisle, who returned her gaze suspiciously. Had he heard the noise?

She checked her phone. Only twenty minutes had passed since they'd led the sick man off. Time was stuck in super slo-mo. Another airman was called to duty presumably to replace a crewman who'd fallen ill. *Three.* Isabel's nerves began to settle. She felt no worse than before inoculation, which meant cramped, sore, and stir-crazy. But that beat the hell out of the alternative. She resisted the urge to rub and scratch the sore and itchy injection site.

She couldn't think about Rick. He was ninety-four percent okay. She instead pictured Emma, Noah, and his family tending their gardens in their idyllic and safe mountain hideout. *Tick. Tock. Tick. Tock.*

The nurse arrived at the front no longer wearing her mask and goggles. "This cabin is all clear." There was an explosion of cheering. Caught by surprise, Isabel didn't join in but grinned in quiet celebration. Not only did they not die or turn from the dread disease, they were now all going to be immune! "Please stay in your seats until you're notified that you can resume normal rotations."

The nurse turned to leave, but stopped when someone called out, "How many?" The woman knew what he meant. "Eight, sir." That was one more than the 6.6 infections, rounded to seven, that Isabel had calculated based on the average Nielsen had reported.

Her cheer at surviving the inoculation was tempered by two thoughts. There were eight people, somewhere down in the bowels of the jumbo jet, who were facing death or life-altering brain damage. And there was Rick, somewhere amid the horror down on the ground, who may or may not have been one of the lucky ninety-four percent.

Chapter 37

When Emma, Dwayne, Samantha, and Dorothy reached the state highway at the bottom of the Miller property, they looked uphill toward the eruption of gunfire. Dwayne said, "That's coming from the main house. We only gave them notice yesterday. We're still under contract."

The shooting soon turned desultory and disorganized. Probably just a few more starving stragglers. "They can handle it," Emma said. Dwayne seemed unconvinced and inclined to return. Was that because he wanted to help defend the providers of their food, or because he, too, heard a voice in his head? A voice that was telling him to keep his promise? Emma said, "We can get food in town." When Dwayne kept glancing back at the sound of fighting, Emma concluded it must be the latter. What remained of the Marine in him was troubled by his broken oath.

They stopped at a distance when they came to the first of the roadside camps—number 1 on Samantha's map. A half dozen infected refugees slowly gathered on the road's shoulder. One held a shotgun. None of the others possessed any visible firearms. Emma did all the talking. "We've come to organize a community," she called out from thirty or so yards away. "Offer a chance to join."

Looks were exchanged, but no words until an older woman said, "What's in it for the ones who sign on?"

"Food, shelter, clothing, security." Emma decided not to mention sex, the prohibition of which was as much a stick as its provision was a carrot. "But there's a contract to be entered into."

"What kind of contract?"

Emma gave her the outline of the unwritten compact she was slowly developing. "Agree to abide by the rules—no violence unless it's authorized, everyone works in return for benefits, no forming into crowds, and other things that we'll inform you of, with any breaches being punishable by penalties up to and including death."

"What if people don't join?" asked a man.

"Then they won't be part of the community, and they'll have to leave."

They outnumbered Emma and her small party, but they didn't outgun them. The few adults and more mature children exchanged views out of Emma's earshot, then all agreed. Dwayne picked out the adults and older teenagers save one woman who would stay behind with the younger children, and off they went to Infected encampment number 2. There, the promise of necessities, especially food—"Work first, then eat," Emma explained—quickly sealed the deal, and their numbers grew yet again.

They passed the gate up to the Old Place's severed and therefore now dangerous ridge road. When they came to the Nicholses' mailbox, Emma stopped. *You should have run off with the boy's rifle without killing him*, said the voice. "What is it?" Dwayne asked.

"Nothing," Emma lied.

By the time they reached Bishop's Quickie-Mart and Gas, there were almost thirty fighting-age Infecteds in her group, about half with some sort of weaponry.

The adult proprietors emerged from the store; the woman carrying a rifle and her husband a shotgun. Their blackened pupils confirmed their status. But from around the back of the house, a teenage boy appeared holding his own rifle. His pupils looked normal. Dwayne turned to Emma. "No," she said, "but keep an eye on him."

She addressed the couple, who she assumed were the boy's parents. "I'm here to offer the chance to join a community."

"Why would somebody do that?" the woman asked.

Emma went through her persuasive litany of benefits. "But it requires agreement to a contract." So far, all the Infecteds they had met had gladly exchanged their freedoms for the promise of necessities. "Following the rules, which I'll publish, or being put to death if they're broken."

The uninfected boy called out from the side of the store. "Mom! Dad!"

But his parents were uninterested in his objections. Both fell into formation with their weapons for the hike down toward town. Dwayne caught up with Emma at the head of the silent army. "That boy ran up the highway toward your family's house. Should I let him go?" She shrugged. Dwayne allowed it to drop.

When they reached the first camp of Uninfecteds—number 5—spread out around an RV, with clothes on lines, a deer carcass lying on a bloody tarp, venison cooking on an open fire, and the men, women, and older children all armed, Emma halted her much more numerous procession of Infecteds. "We mean you no harm. We're just passing by."

The Uninfecteds took up threatening positions behind cover. Emma directed her growing band of Infecteds to pass along the opposite shoulder of the highway. Dwayne and a subset of the armed men and women he'd been organizing during the march stood arrayed against the wary Uninfecteds, but their passage proceeded uneventfully.

"Thank you!" Emma called out when they were clear. The bypassed Uninfecteds appeared dumbfounded as they stared at the receding crowd.

Camp 6 had been mixed when they had reconnoitered the highway, but now they were all infected. A woman couldn't join without abandoning her young daughter and son, but she volunteered nonetheless. "No. You stay and take care of them. What about those two chained to the tree up there?" Emma asked, shielding her eyes from the sun to peer at what looked to be the woman's husband and mother or mother-in-law.

"Them? They haven't eaten in days and are too weak. They should die soon. The food was running low, so…" Emma understood. They had to ration. She led the procession off toward town.

The only other cause for conversation was a long-distance appraisal of the final campsite they approached—number 7—along the highway just before they reached the city limits. "I don't see anybody," Dwayne said. "But there's a pot hanging over that campfire."

The people in number 7 had hurriedly abandoned the food they were cooking. The situation did seem threatening. Emma could feel her anxiety rise. A quick look back at the others in her group revealed signs of similar agitation. "Take care of it," she told Dwayne.

Samantha, carrying one of the Nicholses' hunting rifles, which looked far too large for her small frame, came up to Emma. Dwayne led a group of armed Infecteds off the road to the uphill side of the highway. Three or four minutes later, the woods exploded in shooting. Emma turned back around to those remaining on the pavement and instructed them to breathe deeply in through the nose and out through the mouth. Samantha turned and demonstrated, and ended up leading the breathing exercises. Their agitation remained under control. The rapid firing from the woods was replaced by single killshots.

Dwayne and the others returned. "Uninfecteds. I think we got 'em all. We only lost one." Emma led them past the abandoned campsite on the final leg of their journey into town. About a hundred yards past the camp, however, a shot rang out and a woman from their group fell to her knees clutching her throat. Blood gushed through her fingers, and she gasped and coughed additional, copious quantities from her mouth. Dwayne led his war party off without being told what to do. No more shots were heard until there was a cascade of firing. The wounded woman was turning purple from lack of oxygen and had sunk to sit on her heels.

Emma raised her rifle to put the woman out of her misery, but hesitated. Not because that one bullet was precious. In town, they had an armory full of ammo to plunder. Emma hesitated because she didn't know why putting someone out of her misery made any sense. The woman wasn't *in* misery. She was just dying slowly. Emma also was baffled at why she hesitated pulling the trigger. It shouldn't matter—shoot, or don't shoot—but for some reason, it did. She felt...troubled.

The woman crumpled to the ground dead. Emma shook the strange thought from her head, but something of it lingered. Samantha was staring at her—studying her—looking perplexed.

At the woman's side lay a revolver. "If anyone knows how to use a pistol," Emma called out to the group, "there's one available."

A man stepped forward, took the pistol, and searched the woman's body for ammunition but didn't find any. He then counted the bullets in the gun's cylinder.

Dwayne returned with his soldiers. "We'd missed one. A kid. He's dead."

The rest of their march into town was uneventful. But they halted at the top of the last rise. There were bodies lying uncollected everywhere. "Where is Dorothy?" Emma asked, searching their group.

"She went to get a pregnancy test from the drug store," Dwayne replied.

"I wanted to ask her this question too. All of these others," she looked back at her patient army of black-eyed Infecteds, "have just turned, so it's too soon. But I'll ask you two. Have either of you recently started hearing... voices? Not out loud, but in your heads?"

"Yes."

"Yes."

Samantha added, "I thought there was something wrong with me."

Dwayne said, "I asked Dorothy about those out-of-nowhere thoughts, but she had no idea what I was talking about. Sometimes, the voice makes me a little sick."

"Like when you wanted to go back up to the main house and help out my family?"

"Yes. Exactly. The voice kept saying I had cheated them. How did you know?"

"Just a guess. Let's not say anything about this to anyone. Agreed?"

Samantha and Dwayne both nodded.

"Okay, Sam, you make note on your map of where we left bodies for clean-up, and where we find them in town." The girl immediately undertook the task.

Emma stopped when they neared the fire station, and Dwayne held up his hand as if the people behind him knew what his commands meant. But they all stopped on seeing the dozens of dead splayed wildly in the street, draped over a bicycle rack, and spilling out of open car doors. "What a mess," Samantha said, trying to make note of it all with stick figures, arms and legs all akimbo, on her hand-drawn map.

A man emerged from the fire station and donned a cowboy hat. He carried a shotgun, and wore a badge on his chest. "Stay here," Emma told Dwayne. The other Infecteds they'd gathered along the way stood still, quiet, staring straight ahead. "But spread them out. They're packed too close and starting to freeze up. Be ready, however, to crowd them back together again if there's trouble and we need them ready to fight."

Emma walked down to meet the man in the hat, whom she recognized as Sheriff Walcott despite his dark sunglasses. "Sheriff?"

"You? You said you were passing on through."

"I was lying."

"You're infected?" Walcott asked. Emma confirmed that she was. "And they're all infected too?" She turned to see Dwayne physically separating the group by dragging some across the street and barking orders to the others. Samantha's head was tilted almost horizontal as she tried to count the tangle of bodies lying behind a burned-out truck.

"Yes. What happened here?"

The sheriff surveyed the corpses, which had not begun to smell. "Somebody tossed tainted food into the enclosure where we'd penned up the refugees. They all got sick."

"That was us," Emma confided.

"Thought you'd hurry things along?"

"Looks like it worked." Tendrils of smoke rose from the dozen or so buildings and homes that had burned to the ground. "Are there any Uninfecteds left in town?"

"A few. They're hiding. Whatta y'all want?"

"Can I see your eyes?" Emma asked. Walcott removed his sunglasses and winced at the bright light. Despite his squinting, she could see that his pupils were fully blown. He wore a khaki blouse with its sheriff's star, but blue jeans. He must have changed after soiling his uniform trousers. "We're here to form a new community."

"The uninfected citizens aren't going to like that too much."

"We'll deal with them." She explained her idea for the contract that would bind them all together.

Walcott raised issues with which he was most familiar. "So who decides on punishments? Judge Parker's dead."

"I do," Emma replied simply.

Walcott drew a deep breath, surveyed the bodies strewn all about, and said, "This town *could* use some tidying up."

"You work with Samantha on mapping the occupied houses. Then come with me and we'll visit everyone who's left: Infected and Uninfected."

"There could be trouble," Walcott said.

"We'll bring Dwayne and his people with us."

Chapter 38

RAVEN ROCK MOUNTAIN, PENNSYLVANIA
Infection Date 63, 1245 GMT (8:45 a.m. Local)

The 747 made what felt to Isabel like an emergency descent. The jumbo jet corkscrewed through the darkness in a tight spiral. Her seat fell away beneath her like a ride at an amusement park. They broke through the clouds just above a runway visible only in the flicker of burning barrels that ran down both sides of it. It was impossible to tell where they were, but she'd given up asking anything. Out of her window, however, the dim shapes of wooded mountains rose.

After a fierce reverse thrust and desperate braking that threw Isabel forward against her seatbelt, the plane came to a stop right at the end of the runway. "Dr. Miller!" called an air policeman who had replaced his blue beret and ascot with a combat helmet.

Isabel retrieved her gear and was ushered to the forward door. She exited into the fresh pre-dawn air as the first two of the three waiting helicopters rose noisily into the air. Marine One—the president's aircraft—and an identical green helicopter extinguished all lights upon taking flight. At the bottom of the stairs, a Secret Service agent in a dark suit led her to the third helicopter, which was much smaller and purely military, with a machine gun mounted under one stubby wing and a green cylinder full of what looked like rockets under the other. They stowed her backpack and rifle in a compartment, and she strapped into one of the bucket seats behind the pilots, whose faces were covered by night vision goggles. The agent, looking out-of-place in his civilian attire, settled in beside her. "Let me guess. You can't tell me where we're going."

"No ma'am," he replied before donning large, over-ear headphones. She did the same, but there was nothing but silence over the intercom. No tour guide narration like, "Out of the left side, you'll see the mighty Mauna Loa volcano." At least the headphones dulled the noise as the rotors spun up.

They leapt into the air with surprising agility, pivoted in a hover, and shot off with nose dipping toward the dimly visible earth below, all of which messed with Isabel's head and stomach. When the co-pilot punched a few buttons, a large, bright screen on the console between the two crewmen switched from touchscreen buttons to a moving map. Isabel followed its changing display. The agent didn't seem to care that she snooped. Amid the squiggly contour lines on the map displaying the terrain that slid by in darkness beneath the helicopter was a dot that read, "Hagerstown, MD." A few minutes later they passed, "Gettysburg, PA."

They slowed and began to descend. In the gray light of dawn, the only distinguishing feature of the mountainous, wooded terrain had been the communications towers on a rocky hilltop, painted a fading white and red, and a small, peeling, cinder block building. It could have been some obscure weather or communications relay station but for the double fences that surrounded the facilities, the helmeted heads swinging bright flashlights into the underbrush, and the dogs on leashes rearing up onto hind legs. Their helicopter set down on the "H" of a helipad next to a waiting gray Humvee.

The Secret Service agent whisked Isabel into the vehicle. Dark mountains loomed all around. The twisting drive through the thick forest was short. They passed an outer checkpoint manned by combat troops behind sandbags, and an inner gate with a guard shack that appeared to be the facility's original, permanent security. The road ended at a heavily reinforced concrete tunnel leading straight into the mountainside. Above the arch of the tunnel's entrance was written, "Raven Rock Mountain Complex."

Isabel had never heard of it.

Inside the large blast door were exposed rock walls and the unnatural smell of steel like the musty gust that preceded arrival of trains at a Manhattan subway station. All here was industrial and utilitarian. No effort had been wasted on ambiance.

The regularly spaced lights on the ceiling of the tunnel went on and on and on. Isabel's ears popped. There was a growing chill in the cave-like air through the machine gunner's open, sun-roof perch. They slowed as they entered a large, hollowed cavern, then pulled to a stop. The agent handed

Isabel off to a woman in a civilian suit. "Thank God," she said to Isabel's Secret Service escort. "They didn't waste any time. It's already under way." Isabel asked what was under way, again feeling under-dressed in her smelly camouflage army uniform amid the business attire of everyone around. The woman introduced herself as "Special Assistant to the First Lady," which Isabel found odd. "I apologize for the rush, but I'm taking you straight in. They're waiting."

"*Who* is waiting?" Isabel asked even as she followed the woman toward a metal building erected in the center of the huge, subterranean grotto.

"The Supreme Court. Their hearing is in session."

"*What?*"

The door opened to reveal a crowded improvised courtroom. All eyes turned her way as Isabel rested her pack and rifle along the wall just inside the door. People tapped seatmates' shoulders and pointed at her. Whispered comments rose. At the front sat nine black-robed justices. Lesser cabinet officials and Congressmen lined the walls in the standing-room-only assemblage.

A lawyer at a podium was saying something about "Section One, Article Two," until he saw Isabel. "Ah! Our witness has arrived. Professor Miller? Please take the stand."

Isabel was in a state of semi-shock as she proceeded to the indicated chair atop a slightly raised platform. She recognized the black-robed man at the center of the even more elevated panel from their one legal briefing in the Situation Room. "Chief Justice," the placard before his seat read. "Dr. Isabel Miller?" She nodded, but the Chief Justice admonished her to reply out loud. "Yes," she said as she turned to face the room.

A video monitor displayed a live image of Pres. Stoddard staring impassively at the camera. His pupils were totally blown and black.

*Oh-my-*God*!*

In that moment, it all became clear. The president had gotten sick from the vaccine. He was one of the eight—one more than the seven who, statistically, ought to have contracted it. The Chief Justice explained to her that this was a competency hearing. The First Lady, seated at the counsel's table, held Isabel's eye, looking tense but hard. An opposing set of lawyers with no obvious client among them sat at a table across the room's central aisle.

"Dr. Miller!" the Chief Justice snapped. Isabel turned his way with a start. "These proceedings are of the utmost consequence both to our nation, and to our constitutional system of government. May I please have your full and undivided attention?"

"Yes...sir," Isabel replied in a chastened tone.

"This is an unusual hearing for this Court," the Chief Justice continued, "in that we're acting as a trier of fact, not as an appellate body. Therefore, we are the taker of original witness testimony and need to swear you in."

A man in a suit approached the witness stand. "Please rise," he said, then in a lower voice asked, "Christian?" Isabel nodded. He held a Bible out to her, and she placed her left hand on it. A Torah and a Quran lay on a table beside her seat. She raised her right hand.

The Chief Justice said, "Dr. Miller, do you solemnly swear to tell the truth, the whole truth, and nothing but the truth, so help you God?"

"I do."

"Take your seat. Given the need for an expeditious ruling, and following prior if begrudging consent by both counsels, I'm going to undertake to determine this witness's qualifications to serve as an expert." The Chief Justice asked Isabel her occupation, what papers she had published, and what research she had done on the effects of *Pandoravirus*.

He then briefly glanced left and right at the four robed justices to either side before turning to each counsel and announcing, after less than a minute, "This Court accepts this witness's testimony as expert on the subject of the effects on the human brain of infection by *Pandoravirus*. Is counsel willing to so stipulate?"

The client-less lawyer opposite the First Lady's table rose and said, seemingly reluctantly, "In view of the Court's stated desire for haste in this matter, and despite the numerous substantive objections we have raised in this..."

"Might I remind you," the Chief Justice interrupted, "there is no appeal from this Court, so there's no reason to preserve your objections for the record." The lawyer quickly stipulated that Isabel was an expert. "Good!" the Chief Justice replied before turning to the man's adversary. "You may proceed."

Despite the judge's prior admonishment, Isabel's eyes kept straying to the monitor on which was displayed the image of a stoic Pres. Stoddard, who seemed to be following the proceedings without any real interest. *What are the odds that* he *would be one of the people to catch it?* Isabel couldn't help but think.

The First Lady's lawyer approached Isabel. "Dr. Miller, this hearing will determine whether or not, under Section One, Article Two, of the Constitution of the United States of America, the duly elected president, William Lloyd Stoddard, remains competent to continue in office. Do you understand the question at issue?"

Isabel glanced at the court reporter, cleared her dry throat, and said, "Yes, I do."

Among the few dignitaries who had found seats together were Gen. Browner and Directors Pearson and Struthers of the FBI and CIA.

"I am counsel to the president," the lawyer continued, "who is the Petitioner in this proceeding. At that table is counsel to the vice president, who is the Respondent." Isabel didn't know what any of that meant. "You have had the opportunity, have you not, to study survivors of *Pandoravirus* infection?"

"Yes." That seemed too short. "That's correct."

"In fact, the patient you studied most in depth was your identical twin sister, Dr. Emma Miller, former professor of epidemiology at Johns Hopkins University, who was the first American victim of *Pandoravirus horribilis* after contracting SED in Siberia during her work on the WHO's Surge Team Two."

"Objection," the opposing counsel said, rising to his feet. "Leading."

But the Chief Justice was already directing the man to return to his seat with a patting motion. "Let's keep the evidentiary and procedural objections to a minimum. This panel is not a jury, but a Court fully capable of assessing the probative value of a witness's testimony. And I would also remind counsel to the president that opposing counsel has just stipulated to this witness's expertise, so there's no need to continue laying foundation."

"Yes, Mr. Chief Justice," the lawyer questioning Isabel replied with a courtly bob of his head. *Where did they all find suits?* The lawyer turned back to Isabel. "Following your scientific observation, you gave testimony as an expert witness before the District Court for the District of Maryland in your sister's successful *habeas corpus* hearing, did you not?" Isabel confirmed that was correct. "And in that hearing, did you express an opinion on the question of whether or not your sister was a *person* for purposes of that Court determining whether *habeas* rights lie pursuant to the Constitution?"

Before Isabel could answer, the opposing counsel jumped up. "I'm sorry, Mr. Chief Justice, but I have to object. The matter at issue before the Maryland Court is inapposite to the issue before this Court. Furthermore, this counsel was not present at that hearing to cross-examine the witness. *And* the ruling was by a *District* Court, which of course has no precedential value in the United States Supreme Court."

"You will have your opportunity to cross," the Chief Justice replied. "And it's for this Court to determine what precedent is persuasive. Objection overruled. Proceed."

Everyone waited. For Isabel. "Oh, ummm, yes. I testified to that effect. And the judge released her, Emma I mean, from quarantine."

"And one of the linchpins of the District Court's ruling..." the lawyer began.

"I'm sorry," his opponent apologized to the Court, reluctantly rising again, "but I *have* to object. This witness is in *no* way competent to analyze what grounds underlay an unpublished opinion of a District Court's *habeas* ruling."

"I'm going to admonish you one last time," the Chief Justice responded. "Overruled! Counsel, get on with it."

But instead of repeating his question, the lawyer questioning Isabel said, "Dr. Miller, you have doubtless noted from the monitor in this courtroom that the president has survived infection with *Pandoravirus horribilis*, have you not?" Isabel replied that yes, she had noticed that. "In your expert opinion, despite having *turned*, is Pres. William Stoddard still a human being?"

Isabel hesitated at the novel way in which the question was phrased. "Well...*yes*. Of *course*. He hasn't transformed *genetically* into some different...*species*."

"And you assert that to be a scientific fact despite some commentators having taken to calling the Infecteds who turn members of the species *Homo* in*sapiens?*"

"That's just a pejorative term that someone"—*Like me!*—"made up to describe people suffering deficits due to their brain damage. In order to be a separate *species*, people would need a different genetic code, as expressed in the DNA contained in almost every cell in their bodies. Therefore, genetically, *Pandoravirus* victims of *course* remain members of the species *Homo sapiens*."

"Thank you, Dr. Miller." The lawyer surveyed the nine justices before returning to his questioning. "Now you mentioned deficits. Please define that term for the Court."

"A deficit is an impairment."

"A handicap? Like FDR in his wheelchair?"

"Well, yes, except in the case of *Pandoravirus* the impairment is cognitive."

The lawyer didn't appear to appreciate her clarification. "A yes or a no will do. *So*, Dr. Miller, when patients suffer mental impairment, don't they often experience compensatory improvements in *other* aspects of cognitive function?" Isabel said that yes, that happens. "And do *Pandoravirus* victims experience such compensatory enhancements to *their* brain function?"

"There's anecdotal evidence suggesting that *Pandoravirus* victims who have turned—who have suffered substantial damage to the right hemispheres of their brains—compensate for their loss of abstract thinking by developing additional capacities for logical thinking in their relatively less damaged left hemispheres."

"They become more logical, less emotional, like Dr. Spock on Star Trek?"

"Um, I think that's *Mr.* Spock." A nervous titter rose from the courtroom. "And something like that happens, sometimes, sort of, I suppose. In other cases, however..."

"Thank you," the lawyer interrupted, cutting off her attempted foray into the profound dysfunction suffered by substantial percentages of the more severely damaged survivors. Pres. Stoddard didn't seem as damaged as them. "And do they have a soul?"

"Pardon me?"

The lawyer rephrased. "While you were at the NIH hospital in Bethesda, you opined that *Pandoravirus* victims had lost their *self*—the 'ghost in the machine,' you called it."

His opponent could take it no longer. "Perhaps, Mr. Chief Justice, we should just put opposing counsel on the stand and have *him* give you the testimony he wants."

This time, the Chief Justice said, to Isabel's questioner, "Please do remember that Dr. Miller is the witness, not you. Objection, which you were going to make, sustained."

The chastised lawyer to the president asked Isabel, "Do you believe that *Pandoravirus* destroys the thing we call a *self?*"

"Yes, I do. But there's so much we don't know about how the amazing plasticity of the brain—its resiliency, malleability, adaptability— might one day develop workarounds that restore some circumscribed sense of self that..."

"Thank you." The lawyer wasn't interested. Isabel was speculating about a neuroscientific development that could possibly have far-reaching, even decisive consequences for mankind. But the lawyer to the president only heard the two words "one day." He was concerned only with right now. "And this thing—the self—in what part of the brain does it reside?"

She opened her mouth to speak. But before she could get her somewhat complex answer out, the lawyer 'man-splained' it for her.

"As I understand it, there's the brain, and the mind. The brain is obvious. It's that gray mass that sits in our crania between our ears. But the location of the mind is in doubt, is it not?"

"As I was about to say, it's an age-old question, the mind-brain duality. Some people think that the mind is like software that runs on hardware—the brain."

"So, the *mind,* or the *self,* is the ghost in the machine?" Isabel confirmed his understanding, sort of, with a nod modified by a shrug. "And what proof do we have that that the mind actually exists?"

"There is no proof, really. It's just a common, shared perception. But there is another school of thought that consciousness is merely an artifact. Something that doesn't actually exist, but is conjured up to explain our everyday experience."

"And so consciousness—a self, a mind—is just a construct manufactured by our brains out of thin air?"

"That's *a* theory," Isabel replied.

"Do *you* subscribe to that theory?"

"I'm not sure." The lawyer abruptly walked away from the witness stand and said, in a booming voice, "*Now,* Dr. Miller, switching subjects..."

"Hold on there, counsel," interrupted one of the previously silent Associate Justices, a frail looking elderly lady whose name Isabel couldn't recall. "Dr. Miller, you said you're not sure. You're not sure about *what*, exactly?"

"I *used* to believe, ma'am, like most modern neuroscientists, in conscious inessentialism. That all activities undertaken in the cognitive domain can be explained by the natural functioning of the physical brain without resorting to the more convoluted explanation that there's some separate thinking entity inside each of us, looking out at the world, watching the 'theater of the mind.'"

"But you don't believe that anymore?"

Isabel looked at the president, who stared blankly back at the camera, and at the First Lady, who leaned forward on both elbows and was boring holes into Isabel with her stare.

"No, I don't think I do," Isabel answered.

"So, ergo, you now think," the same associate justice asked, "that there is something *to* the concept of a self, or a soul, or a *ghost* in the machine?"

Without meaning too, Isabel sighed. "This is just my opinion..."

"That's why we certify experts," the associate justice interrupted. "To give us their presumably more informed opinions. So what is *your* opinion, Dr. Miller?"

Isabel paused to compose her thoughts, which had the unintended consequence of heightening the significance of her reply. "The whole point of conscious inessentialism is that, if you can imagine a person, called a philosopher's zombie, who has no consciousness whatsoever but still behaves in exactly the same way as you and I, then consciousness would *not* have evolved, because natural selection operates only on traits that affect behavior."

The associate justice looked at her brethren before saying, "I'm sorry, but if there was an answer in there—an opinion about whether or not consciousness is real—I didn't hear it."

Isabel looked apologetically at the First Lady. "The behavior of *Pandoravirus* victims is markedly different from the behavior of the Uninfected. So that thought exercise I described, where you assumed *identical* behavior—by one person *with* a self, and another *without* one—is irrelevant. Whether you call the change in Infecteds *deficits* resulting from physiological alterations to the structure of the brain, or alternatively the death of the self, doesn't matter. Infecteds and Uninfecteds are *not* the same. Their behavior *is* different."

"No more questions," the president's lawyer said icily and abruptly.

"Does counsel to the Respondent have any questions?"

"Oh, yes I do, Mr. Chief Justice," said the energized lawyer to Vice Pres. Anderson, rising and buttoning his jacket. "I most certainly do. Thank you."

The president's lawyer began a whispered and heated exchange with the First Lady. Pres. Stoddard on his monitor scratched his nose. The vice president's counsel stepped up to Isabel. "And thank you, Dr. Miller, for appearing here. I know of your prior service during this crisis, and I applaud the sense of duty that brought you before this Court today. And I also understand how close you have been to the First Family, and how difficult this hearing must be for you."

The lawyer wasn't speaking to her. He was reminding the nine justices that Isabel had been called as his opposition's expert, despite her testimony helping his case. "As I understand it, you believe that when someone survives infection with *Pandoravirus*, the brain damage that he or she suffers results in substantial behavioral changes."

"Objection!" said counsel to the president. "He's leading the witness."

"He's *cross*-examining her," the Chief Justice replied in apparent extreme annoyance. "She's *your* witness."

"Do you remember the question?" the patient vice president's lawyer asked.

"Yes. And the answer is yes. Their behavior changes substantially."

"Thank you. Now," the lawyer said, beginning to pace the room, "as you are aware, the issue before this Court is whether or not the current president is competent to continue in his office. The vice president and a majority of the president's cabinet..."

"Objection!" said the president's counsel, bolting to his feet.

The Chief Justice instantly sustained the objection. "I will not warn you again, Mr. Solicitor-General. You are not to introduce, before this or any other witness, the opinion of others regarding the competence or lack thereof of the president."

The lawyer gave the Court an exaggerated, deferential nod. But Isabel now knew that the vice president and the Cabinet had voted the president out, and that the president—the *Petitioner* who had requested this hearing—was fighting that decision. Or the First Lady was, on his behalf.

"Dr. Miller," the solicitor-general resumed, "you are familiar, generally speaking, with the complexity of the job of President of the United States of America? With the myriad decisions, large and small, that constitute a day-in-the-life of this nation's commander-in-chief?"

Isabel said, "Yes. Sure. Generally speaking."

"And during an emergency such as this one—an existential crisis that has gripped every citizen of our nation, and indeed of the entire world, in a life-and-death struggle with an apocalyptic plague—would you not expect that the decisions this country relies upon its president to make are not only *more* complex, *more* novel, and *more* difficult, but also far, *far* more momentous in their importance?"

The president's counsel held out his arms in supplication and began to rise. "Overruled!" the Chief Justice said before the man could even speak.

Everyone waited. Isabel said, "I'm sure it's an extremely demanding job, yes."

"And your testimony today has been that the person on whom we currently rely to make decisions that affect the fate of our nation, of our entire *species*, is suffering from mental deficits that cause his behavior to deviate substantially from the norm?" Isabel gave him a sheepish yes. "And by altered behavior, do you mean that some of the decisions that the man elected to this office might have made *before* infection can now be expected to be decided differently today, *after* his infection, as a direct result of his brain damage?"

The First Lady's gaze was riveted on Isabel. But she couldn't lie. "I'm afraid so."

The lawyer was nodding, encouraging her. It felt like betrayal even though her answers were the God's-honest-truth and the president didn't seem to care in the least that she was stabbing him in the back. "And whether that's due to the death of Pres. Stoddard's *self*, or just the cumulative effect of his post-infection mental handicaps, the president is not the same man who was elected to his office, would you agree?"

Isabel licked her dry lips and swallowed. "Uhm, I guess I would, yes. Agree."

"No more questions," the satisfied lawyer said, thanking her as she was dismissed by the Chief Justice. She cast one last glance at the First Lady and was met with complete indifference. Isabel was dead to Angela Stoddard now. Just another in what must have been a series of betrayals that had led to this hearing. From the president's lack of any reaction at all on the television monitor, she was also dead to him, but in a different and much more profound way.

Gen. Browner dipped his head in acknowledgement as Isabel passed. The Directors of the CIA and FBI both avoided eye contact. "Counsel to the Respondent," the vice president's lawyer said, "would like to call, as *our* expert witness, Dr. Henry Rosenbaum."

The door opened just as Isabel reached it, and Hank Rosenbaum entered. Hank had lied to her to trick her into participating in an NIH twins study with her infected sister. All her ill feelings toward the man came flooding back. They exchanged the briefest of nods on passing. Rosenbaum would surely demolish any shred of a case left to the president...to the extent Isabel hadn't already. The Supreme Court would probably end up declaring Infecteds to be non-human, and it would be open season on all of them, Emma included.

The Secret Service agent who had brought Isabel there waited for her outside the metal building. Isabel only then remembered that she was in a cave. Somehow, the venue seemed appropriate. It was probably in caves that mankind's morality and ethics had first emerged. It was fitting that they would also be discarded in a cave.

Browner called out to her as she was putting her pack and rifle back into the Humvee. He asked for privacy, and the soldiers and Secret Service agent gave them space. "Thank you for your honesty in there. I know your feelings for your sister, and for the First Family. That must have been difficult."

"So, we're going to start impulsive eradication?"

Gen. Browner didn't hedge. "The vice president agreed with that policy. But the vaccine changes things."

"Are you going to kill the president?"

"Good God, no. We'll find a place for him to live out his days. That may seem inconsistent with...what *is* coming, but now that we have a vaccine we don't need to eradicate *all* Infecteds. We no longer have to fear extinction. We just need to defeat them militarily. Not genocide; war. I take it, however, that you still don't even agree with that?"

"Honestly, I don't know what I believe anymore. I just want all this to be over."

Browner wore a sympathetic expression. "The times do test one's faith. In God. In mankind. In institutions and principles."

But Isabel's concern was more practical. "If you start exterminating them, their logical response will be to start exterminating us."

"They're already doing that. We'll just be going all-in on our side."

"And do you think we'll win if we do?"

The Marine regarded her for a moment before replying, "I can't say that I do. The deck is stacked against us. It's going to take a lot longer than Stoddard suggested in his speech to manufacture mass quantities of the vaccine. And the Infecteds seem to be organizing more rapidly than we expected. But we have to try. We can't just give up on art, literature, scientific achievement. They won't have any of those things. They've got no spark, no creativity. They may keep farms and factories going, but they won't write *War and Peace*, or compose Beethoven's Ninth, or paint the ceiling of the Sistine Chapel."

"No," Isabel said with a loud sigh, "they won't. That's all inessential."

An officer summoned Browner. "Duty calls," the Marine general said to Isabel. "You've been a true patriot. We're falling back to what surveys suggest may be a defensible corridor from the Port of Houston and its petrochemical and refinery complex, up to the Denver/Boulder area. We could use your continued assistance." Browner waited, then took her silence as a no. "Well, if there's ever anything I can do for you, please let me know."

Isabel considered asking him how it was that the anti-war president was so conveniently one of the eight people who got sick from the inoculations on the plane…but she didn't. What would've been the point?

It was time to think about survival of *her* self. "I do have one favor I'd like to ask."

Chapter 39

"I think I hit one behind that big dead tree," Chloe whispered to her father, pointing. Noah radioed his intentions to Natalie and Jake, who covered them from the tower.

Their plan for daily target practice had been overtaken by hourly attacks. Natalie was learning how to shoot on the job. "We don't see anything moving," she replied in a low crackle.

When they got to the thick trunk of the fallen tree, they found a smallish rifle and a crimson pool that still glinted in the sunlight. Like an Indian tracker, Noah searched for and found droplets and drag marks leading downhill. He moved from cover to cover as he followed the blood trail. Chloe took up each position he abandoned, her AR-15 at the ready and her face frozen in a cringe that Noah, by now, recognized as meaning ready-to-kill. These nearly continuous attacks on their compound were taking a huge toll on everyone. It was a relentless grind of sleeplessness and stress punctuated by sudden onslaughts of fear and trauma. Everyone waited for their luck to run out. No one was more sick in anticipation of that happening than Noah.

He saw soiled tennis shoes protruding from the brush—unnatural in pose and unmoving. He raised his mask with a gloved hand and, with his rifle to his shoulder, crept closer. It was a middle-aged woman. Her hands clutched loosely at the sucking wound on her chest, which made a gurgling rattle. He couldn't tell if she was infected, but there was blood everywhere. She wasn't long for this world.

Noah backed off a few yards, raised the radio, and whispered, "See anything? Over."

"Nope," Natalie replied. "It's all still. I don't think I hit anyone. And you've gotten all of Jake's. Looks like that's the last." After a moment, she said, "Oh. Sorry. Over."

"What's that?" Chloe said from behind Noah on hearing the sounds emanating from the dying woman's last labored breaths.

"I gotta take one shot," Noah radioed while looking at his daughter. "To finish it."

He waited, but didn't know for what. "Okay," was all Natalie said. It was less than the full moral absolution for which he longed. Noah caught Chloe's eye and raised his rifle in a pantomime of what he was about to do. His daughter shrugged before turning away. She seemed drained, or distant, or closed off from what was happening. Whichever, it came off as uncaring, like an Infected. Like her Aunt Emma.

Noah aimed at the nearly lifeless form, first at the underside of the woman's chin. But what a mess that would leave. He shifted positions to the side so he had a shot straight at her heart. He was surprised how hard it was to pull the trigger. Harder than when they were shooting back. Enough time to think about it. He fired a single shot into the mortally wounded attacker, who jerked once before falling still.

He grabbed the woman's tennis shoe and dragged her across the sloping forest floor back toward Chloe. "Where'd I hit her?" his bored sounding daughter asked in an incongruously high-pitched, girlish voice. He too had endured the violence of the past few days, but Chloe's callousness still disconcerted Noah. He surveyed the carcass, whose arms were raised directly over her head from his dragging as if in surrender to death.

"Chest. It was fatal, but it was taking too long."

Another shrug from his daughter. Another casual dismissal of a life lost. Chloe had donned gloves and mask to retrieve the woman's small-bore, bolt-action rifle. "She stood up," Chloe said. "I don't know why. Maybe it was that ant pile behind the rotting tree. But she just stood straight up right in my cross-hairs." Noah could think of nothing to say. It was just chatter—small talk—he decided. "Was she infected?"

"It doesn't matter," he replied.

"Just curious." With the toe of her boot Chloe lifted the woman's eyelid. "Infected." She began rummaging through the dead woman's pockets and extracting a handful of .22 long shells and a folding pocket knife.

"Make sure you wash that stuff, and your boots, before going back inside."

Noah dragged their latest victim to the new pit. They'd used the little Bobcat to dig a third trench for the dead a short distance from the other two and the lone individual grave of their first kill. Noah slid the body down onto the growing pile of corpses of all ages and genders and in all manner of clothing at the bottom of the long and narrow mass grave, then removed his blue Latex gloves and tossed them in after her. Flies were beginning to gather. He wondered if *they* might spread the disease.

"That makes twenty-three," Chloe said dully. "Fourteen Infecteds, and nine Uninfecteds, not counting the Nicholses and those camps down on the highway where Emma and Dwayne got their weapons."

"Let's leave this hole open a little while longer," Noah said.

"It's starting to smell."

Noah gazed up at the sun through the canopy of trees. "Yeah, but it's in the shade, and it's still early."

The walk back up to the side gate was circuitous. The cyclone fencing was still intact—no one had made it inside since the first day—but it was growing frayed by bullets fired through it in both directions. Both the barn and the house were randomly pocked with an alarming number of pits and holes like a World War II urban battle photo. Two chickens—Kourtney and Khloé—had died in the crossfire. Chloe and Noah kept their distance from the growing number of contaminated black patches in the dirt where Infecteds had fallen.

It was just a matter of time, Noah reasoned—time, and statistics—before one of the bullets meant for a member of their family struck home. Noah had imagined it dozens of times as he had tried to grab an hour or two of sleep. Each time, some small detail had jolted him awake. The fleeting image of his frantic, inexpert, and ultimately failed first aid attempt. Calls not returned on the radio. Another search, like the one for Jake, only with a different outcome and a different family member each time. Natalie. Chloe. Jake.

He hadn't slept in four days.

Each of them had suffered close calls that had troubled them more and more in the quiet hours that followed the fights. Noah and Natalie were emotionally exposed to each and every near miss—of them, *and* of their children. The cumulative toll taken on their nerves was starting to tell. There was no more laughter. Their conversations were brief. Gone was the warmth and love shown just days earlier. Chloe hadn't even cried at the loss of her beloved chickens.

Noah's daughter said, "How long can we keep doing this? I mean, eventually we're not gonna hear 'em until it's too late and a whole bunch of 'em are inside the fence." She was right. He had known it for a day or so now. The attacks on their compound would continue until one finally succeeded. "Whatta we do, Dad?"

With his back to his daughter, Noah allowed himself a wince. If only she hadn't said, "Dad." That word encompassed both her trust and faith in him, and his duty to protect her. Everything depended on him and the decisions he made. On no sleep. Hands now constantly trembling, spoiling his aim. How much longer could he keep his family safe there? He silently cursed himself for ever thinking that he *could* just by renovating a house and stocking it with things. *Millions in worthless gold in the basement.*

"Dad?"

Noah's original Plan B had been to evacuate to the cabin, which apparently had been abandoned by Emma and company. But after the attacks they'd barely managed to repel on the relatively well protected main house, the cabin seemed like a death trap. His new Plan C—or was it B now?—was to abandon both houses and live in the hills around their property. Noah, together with either Jake or Chloe, in alternating patrol schedules, had begun stashing bags of food, water, supplies, and ammo in various caches scattered at a distance. Once they abandoned the compound, the house would surely be picked clean. Those cached supplies would buy them a few weeks, maybe a little more with replenishment of water snuck from the main house's or cabin's wells.

"On the news," he finally replied to his daughter without looking her way, "they're talking about some last stand in Texas. Defending big pharma plants there that're manufacturing the vaccine. I'm thinking maybe...we could head that way."

"To *Texas?*" Noah shrugged as they entered the side gate and locked it behind them. "Will they even let us in if we make it there? I mean, they might think we're Infecteds."

"They'll have some procedure," Noah made up. "A test or something." Chloe's concern, while valid, lay at the end of a thousand other life-threatening obstacles between Virginia and Texas, which in the aggregate made staying and defending the house or hiding in the hills look more attractive by comparison. They hosed off their boots, and Chloe washed the .22 rifle, bullets, and pocket knife with soap and water in the buckets kept for that purpose beside the front porch. Both then scrubbed hands that were raw from previous scouring.

At the front door, which had at least a dozen bullet holes in it, Natalie had left lunches for them made of stale, rock-hard bread and peanut butter. Noah and Chloe ravenously consumed the food in joyless silence and washed it down with cool well water. They were almost out of bread, whose increasingly mold-covered edges Natalie excised like a surgeon, reducing the slices' sizes to miniature versions of sandwiches.

Natalie or Jake fired a single shot from a rifle in the tower above them. "I see four!" Jake called out before firing several more shots. Natalie added, "It looks like two men, a woman, and a boy or girl! Down the hill just past where we burn the trash!"

Noah stuffed the rest of his sandwich into his mouth, wiped the crumbs from his lips with the back of his hand, and took cover behind the column opposite where Chloe lay with her rifle. His shouting was made difficult by the peanut butter. "Are they running...or...are they staying?"

"They went to ground!" Jake replied. *Pop. Pop.* His wife and son kept up steady fire meant to keep them heads-down. "I counted two long guns!" *Pop.*

Chloe was already donning a fresh pair of gloves, which Noah did as well. "We'll swing around the back," he said, "past the grow labs, and out the side gate again."

"We should climb up the rocks to the left of the path up to Emma's cabin," Chloe suggested. "That'll give us a clearer shot."

That was just what Noah had been thinking. He explained their plan over the radio to Natalie and Jake, and led his teenage daughter on the flanking maneuver. Ten minutes later, Noah dragged the first of the dead family of Uninfecteds toward the pit. "Twenty-*seven*, Dad," Chloe said as she kept watch with her rifle.

Texas was looking—and probably smelling—a fair bit better.

* * * *

As night fell, Natalie brought dinner—the first of their twenty-five-year shelf-life freeze-dried packages—up to Noah in the tower, keeping her head below the level of the walls. "Pasta alfredo!" she announced with her smiling, newly adopted forced optimism. Noah turned off the battery-powered thermal imager. He'd wait to use it until it was fully dark. "The first of 192 pasta alfredos to come, so I hope you like it." Noah took a bite and tried not to grimace. The boiled dinner tasted bland with overtones of plastic. "I noticed that some of the buckets of bulk food were gone. Is that what you've been hiding out there on your hikes?"

"Patrols," Noah corrected. "And yeah."

"That's the new backup plan? If things get worse here? Live off the land?"

"Nat, we need to talk. I don't know how much longer we can stay in this house." She was sitting on her heels and blinking. "I mean, if people keep coming—and I don't know why they'd stop, especially after the food in town runs out—then we're constantly going to be attacked, and sooner or later..." He couldn't bring himself to speak his worst fear aloud.

"So that's it?" she asked, her eyes flitting about the bare concrete of the tower, which was pocked with bullet holes. "All these preparations—the grow labs, the supplies—and we're just gonna abandon everything? Sleep in tents? Live like homeless people?"

"Everyone seems to know where we are, and that we've got a lot of supplies. We're too big of a target. One of these times our luck is gonna run out. I mean, what's Chloe's count? Twenty-seven we've killed? How many rounds did they fire back our way that missed? Two hundred? Four hundred? Have you seen the front of the house? The hurricane shutters look like Swiss cheese. The windows between the inner and outer shutters are all shattered, and some of those bullets went clear through into the living room and kitchen. The breakfast room TV got smashed. It just takes one bullet."

"I know how many fucking bullets it takes, Noah!" Natalie replied. "What about the cabin? Emma and her crew are all down in town now. We could air the cabin out for a day or two and scrub it down."

"Nat, as soon as they pick over the main house, they'll come find us up there. And that cabin is completely undefendable." He shook his head. "Nothing is working."

"What about going into town? Joining Emma?"

"We can't agree to Emma's *contract,* whatever the hell that's gonna be. She's serious, you know, about killing undesirable people and rule breakers. That would include us if we stepped out of line. Forget sentimental family ties. I'd rather take my chances in the woods. Or on the road, like the rest of America."

"Noah! You've seen on the news how *bad* it is out there. And it's worst on the refugees! The army is trying to stop them. The towns treat them like invading barbarians. People assume you're infected, just like you do them. They prey on each other for food and water. *And* they've got to contend with the *real* Infecteds. Without any electrified fence, stone walls, or towers. It's *horrible.*"

"Pick your poison." The expression seemed agonizingly apt. "I sure would like not being such a juicy target. Or at least being a more mobile one."

Natalie absorbed the comment before sighing. "I see you brought a sleeping bag and a pillow up here. Are you spending the night in the tower again?"

"Yeah." He expected her to lecture him about how tired he looked; how important sleep was; how not to overtax himself. But she didn't. He finished his dinner—410 calories that were supposed to be sufficient but left him feeling almost as empty as before—then flicked on the huge thermal imager and raised it into one of the crenels in the low wall. The imager was meant to sit atop a rifle like an enormous telephoto lens. Through the eyepiece he quickly confirmed that the woods were dark. Nothing glowed hot. Anything 98.6 degrees would shine brightly against the duller, cooler black-and-white background.

"So what do we do?" Noah's wife asked. This time, his eyes found hers boring into him, waiting for the next plan that would save them from the brutal end they had witnessed—and *caused*—twenty-seven times now.

"We head to Texas."

"*What?*"

"It's where the government is reforming after D.C. fell. You saw the news. They're moving all their troops down there to defend the pharmaceutical factories and refineries. Everywhere around *here*—it's gonna be all-out war."

"And we're gonna drive straight thorough the middle of that war zone, Noah. They're going to be blasting the holy *crap* out of anybody who tries to flee down there, *and*, oh by the way, everywhere between here and there that turns. And where do you think you're gonna find gasoline for that guzzler you parked down by the highway?"

"We can't take the SUV." She screwed up her face in confusion. "We'll have to hike it." Her jaw dropped in utter disbelief. "It'll be safer ultimately. In a car, you'll drive right into an ambush and never see it coming. On foot, you'll have a sense of what's around you. 'Situational awareness,' the shooting instructors called it."

"Noah, that's…*Walking?* To *Texas*? Through towns and cities that are all—every one of them—in the middle of their very own Armageddon? Assuming that's even *possible*—that we *can* actually hike that far, and nobody will shoot us or bomb us or strafe us or whatever—how can we *possibly* carry enough food and water for what will take *months*, I presume?"

"About fifty-two days, taking a more or less straight line and making eight hours a day."

"So…*months*, like I said. Do you realize how heavy those buckets of food are down in the basement? It took all my strength just to bring one upstairs today."

"Four ounces per packet, three packets per day, figure sixty days, that's forty-five pounds per person."

"On a thousand-mile *trek*, Noah!"

"It's 1,260 miles. But the load will get lighter and lighter as we consume stuff."

"Water is even *heavier* than food. We can't carry that much, plus all the other stuff we'd have to bring—sleeping bags, flashlights, first aid kits… and *guns*, I'm sure, and lots and lots of ammunition."

Noah said, "I figure we'll take about half that much food, plus some water, and we'll forage the rest along the way."

"You mean steal it. Take it from some poor people who aren't armed as well as we will be. Right?"

"Nat, bullets and purification tablets are lighter than food and water."

"Jesus Christ. That's what it's come to? This is who we are now? We're no different than those twenty-seven starving people we've killed."

"You're wrong there," Noah replied. "We *are* different." Natalie cocked her head. "We're better armed." He took another check through the thermal imager.

A half dozen glowing figures approached in the darkness. "Go get Chloe and Jake. We've got more coming."

Chapter 40

Isabel and Rick wore their goggles in the breezy open doorway of the Black Hawk as it slowly circled the Old Place. "My God!" Isabel gasped seeing the bodies strewn all about. "Oh-my-God-oh-my-*God!*" Rick's arm wrapped around her as she began to shake while searching the dead for her brother and his family.

The door gunner was on high alert behind his multi-barrel weapon as they settled into the tight clearing, which looked too small for the large aircraft. The tree limbs flailed this way and that only feet beyond the spinning rotors. Dust shot up just before the tires connected solidly with the ground.

There was no Vasquez or Army detail anymore, just Isabel, Rick, and the three-man crew, who remained in the cockpit or behind the door gun as their two passengers climbed out into the dying gale.

Rick took the lead, rifle raised. This time, Isabel held her finger on her trigger, and her thumb on her selector switch. She felt sick, needing to vomit but unable to. Somewhere in that dark house, she felt sure, they would find her brother, sister-in-law, niece, and nephew—dead. Slaughtered. Raped. Tortured. Butchered. She was petrified to discover her worst fears come true, and tried several times to pray for it not to be before abandoning the dangerous distraction and focusing on killing whoever did this.

Bodies rotted in the sun. Their weapons still lay beside them. No one had even bothered to collect the guns, valuable as they and their ammunition were. The entire place looked abandoned but not yet looted.

The front of the house was peppered with hundreds of holes and gouges. How could anyone have survived that hail of bullets? "Stay here," Rick said at the open front door before disappearing inside with his rifle raised to his cheek. There were dead people all across the grounds. Two by the barn. Three by a hole cut through the cyclone fencing. At least half a dozen more in the woods beyond. They all lay where it appeared they had fallen.

And there were shell casings glinting in the sunlight all about, many of which must have rained down from the tower above the porch. Every square foot of the front wall of the house was pitted and chipped. The storm shutters had been shot straight through. It was impossible to imagine that Noah's family had prevailed in that all-out war.

Rick reappeared and handed two sheets of paper to Isabel. One was a handwritten note from Noah. "They're alive!" Isabel blurted out, elated despite the carnage all around. She read the message from her brother aloud. "'Isabel, we are under constant attack by Infecteds and Uninfecteds both, and have decided that we can't defend the house any longer. Natalie, Chloe, Jake, Margus (the kid from the Quickie Mart), and I are headed to Texas on foot. I attached a map showing our intended route in case you find this.'" Isabel took a quick glance at the second page. A red line ran down the Appalachians to Knoxville, Tennessee, then cut west to Memphis and on to Hot Springs, Arkansas, then southwest to the Dallas/Fort Worth area. "'I hope you catch up with us along the way (we'll check in with authorities or aid services, where possible), or join us in Texas. If not, I love you and wish you the best of luck and a happy, long, and healthy life. With all our love…'" Her relatives had each signed the note. Under the names of Noah, Natalie, and Jake, her niece had added, "'Chloe (and Margus)'".

"After all this, they bugged out," Isabel said in a tone of wonder.

Rick surveyed the compound and its killing fields full of the uncollected dead. "This would've been safe before. But it's not fortified. It could never have been defended militarily. For that you need troops and shovels."

"At least they're alive." Noah had written a postscript, which Isabel read out loud. "'Emma is organizing her Infected society in town. She seems to be taking over everything.'"

"I wanna go down to town to see my sister," Isabel said.

Rick sighed. "Of *course* you do." He was being surprisingly sarcastic. He looked at the Black Hawk. "If we come flying in, it'll probably spark trouble. Plus, they've only got enough fuel for a direct return to the nearest refueling point."

"So, we walk down to town."

Rick conspicuously disapproved of that idea, but he refrained from saying so. He insisted that they carry their enormously heavy and bulky backpacks, which normally remained on the helicopter, perhaps to discourage Isabel, which it didn't. She sat beside the door gun with her boots dangling in air and the heavy pack resting on the cabin floor. When she dropped to the ground with a grunt as the full weight bore down on her shoulders, her legs almost buckled. Almost. The weight required her to hunch forward at an awkward angle and seemed to prevent her from taking deep enough breaths.

They exited through the open side gate where two more bodies lay. Infected or Uninfected, it didn't really matter, as they were now both vaccinated and immune. They passed six more bodies on the hike down to the state highway, which they inspected, but none of them were Noah and his family. All of them were riddled with bloody holes, some in their heads. "Kill shots," Rick called them to Isabel's horror. "Probably put the wounded out of their misery. And these wounds are all from 5.56 mm," Rick commented, kneeling beside a corpse. "You can tell 'cause the entry wound is tiny, but the exit wound is huge from the meta-unstable round tumbling, and sometimes like this one it's deflected at a sharp angle from internal ricochets off bones. Come look."

"No thank you."

He stood up with ease despite his pack, the rows of bulbous 40mm grenades that he wore outside his body armor, and their launcher mounted beneath his carbine barrel. He had the unfair advantage of a foot in height and a hundred pounds in body weight. "I also counted three grenade craters between here and the house. Looks like your brother and his family have turned stone cold killer. Good for them; bad for everybody else."

Isabel couldn't believe what he said was true, despite the evidence. Noah, maybe. But the kids killing people? *Natalie?* That seemed unimaginable. Those thoughts, however, were soon crowded out by the pain that began to burn in her legs and lungs. When they dropped their backpacks at the bottom of the hill, her head was swimming and she had to rest for a few minutes, wiping the unbecoming sweat from her face. Rick then tossed their packs onto the other side of the barbed wire fence, and they leapt over the rickety barrier to join them. Isabel had to climb into her pack's broad straps while still seated. Rick pulled her to her feet. At least walking generally downhill along the smooth highway proved easier.

After passing the gate to the ridge road, which now bore a sign that looked vaguely like Emma's handwriting—"Road Out. Be Careful"—they passed a couple of abandoned camps and an empty Quickie Mart. The next half dozen encampments were also deserted. When they reached the sign marking the city limits, Rick made them depart the easy pavement and climb half way up a hill before continuing their march across the sloping, uneven terrain. The off-road path proved ten times more difficult for Isabel than the highway, and they had to stop twice more for her to regain her wind.

Rick found a boulder on a wooded hill. They lay behind it to observe the town. He surveyed things first, then handed his binoculars to Isabel and continued his reconnaissance through the sight atop his rifle. Work crews were sweeping up the streets. A wrecker was dragging a burned-out hulk of a truck, tires gone and rims spraying sparks, up onto its bed to be hauled away. Bodies were being piled into a pickup truck. No one wore masks, though most wore gloves.

"They're all infected?" Isabel said.

"Yep," came Rick's reply as he squinted through the sight. "That's my guess."

"So how should we do this?"

"I say we sling our weapons over our shoulders and walk down there like we own the place. If we don't mask up and keep all our reactions in check, they might mistake us for Infecteds. But if things turn bad, Isabel, we gotta be ready to kill every last one of them, your sister included. So, are you absolutely sure you're up for this?"

"No. But it sounds like the right plan."

They did just as Rick suggested. The first workers they passed ceased sweeping and stared at them with hollow black eyes, but made no move suggesting alarm. Rick and Isabel both wore camouflage battle dress and carried military-issue weapons and gear, and their eyes had normal color in them. But they acted as if they belonged, and they took no precautions against infection. They didn't acknowledge anyone, smile, or in any other way act human. It was far more likely that they'd be regarded as soldiers who had turned some weeks ago than Uninfecteds who'd been among the very few to have received the vaccine.

Dwayne, the Marine embassy guard from Isabel's hospital room, met them carrying an assault rifle. He of course recognized Isabel instantly. They slowed, but made no move to unshoulder their weapons. Dwayne stiffened, slung his rifle over his shoulder, and saluted Rick, who returned the greeting crisply.

"What's the situation here," Rick inquired officiously, as if this were a normal encounter with a fellow Marine.

"The fighting has died down, sir. Took a few incoming pot shots last night, but nothing today. The Uninfecteds are mostly staying behind closed doors, and we're leaving them alone for now. There are some out-of-control Infecteds causing trouble down by the junction with the east-west county road," he said, turning to point farther down the valley, "so I'd steer clear of there until we've put them down."

"Is my sister here?" Isabel asked.

"Yes, ma'am. She's in the sheriff's office. I'll take you to her."

They followed the lance corporal. Isabel made a face at Rick at how weird this all was, but he shook his head and she forced her expression back to the bland persona of the new world order. Inside the building, they were led to a crowded office with a plaque that read, "Sheriff Walcott." She heard Emma issuing orders. "Have that hot tub guy from Hoboken organize showers outside the workers' barracks. But no one gets food until *after* they work no matter how hungry they are. Except the young children. Let's go ahead and keep them alive for now." Emma sat behind Walcott's big desk and fell silent as Isabel and Rick entered. All heads turned their way.

Rick nodded at a man in a cowboy hat seated on a sofa and said, "Sheriff."

The black-eyed man returned his greeting in kind. "Captain."

"Hi, Emmy."

"Hello, Isabel. You just missed Noah and his family, and a neighbor boy. They headed south for Texas."

"I know."

Emma turned to Rick. "I recognize you. You were on the plane that brought me back from Siberia." When the conversation stalled, Emma said, "Is there anything more?"

That was it. Emma was busy and wanted to get back to work. A tear sprang loose. Isabel caught it on her cheek, but not before everyone noticed.

"You're not infected?" Emma asked, tilting her head as she studied her now more interesting sister. "And not *afraid* of infection." All around were black-eyed, recently turned Infecteds, who were spewing the highly contagious virus with each and every breath. The office was thick with their pathogenic miasma.

"We've been vaccinated. We're immune now."

Isabel and Rick waited for a reaction from the gathering of Infecteds. Dorothy hugged a huge bag of baby diapers. Little Samantha huddled with Sheriff Walcott and continued writing a "U," an "I," or a "?" on a map of every property in the county based on Walcott's whispered knowledge of that household's condition.

"We could use your help," Isabel said, "in setting up our new community. Being immune would allow you to liaise effectively between Infecteds and Uninfecteds."

"If you want Uninfecteds, why didn't you convince Noah and his family to stay?"

"It's not that we *want* Uninfecteds. It's that we have them. But if they keep shooting at us, we'll have to do something about them. You could convince them to quit fighting, sign onto the contract, and become productive, contributing members of society."

"So you're implementing your plan then, Emma?"

"Yes. We're going to organize, restore order, then expand. We need scale to provide for the basic needs of our community—food, water, clothing, power, self-defense—and territory for what Dwayne calls defense in depth."

Rick gave his fellow Marine an approving nod.

"So this is your new world based on social contracts? Are you just gonna settle right into the Oval Office now that Washington has fallen and the president has turned?"

Emma shook her head. "Too big of a target. Plus, the White House burned down. So, will you join us and help?"

Isabel took a look around the office. All except Emma and her NIH hospital roommates had black, inhuman eyes. The fists of several were balled tight and straining. Emma seemed to be keeping an eye on them, too, but hadn't yet needed to intervene.

"No, I think we'll go...and find our own kind." Emma accepted her answer, then after a moment seemed to find it curious that Isabel and Rick were still there. "So we may not see each other again," Isabel said.

"You're probably right. If you're heading to Texas like Noah, there's a pretty high chance none of you will make it."

"I love you, Emmy." Isabel's voice cracked. "Even if you can't love me back. I guess...this is good-bye."

"Bye."

After an awkward hush, Rick led Isabel out by the elbow. It didn't seem like enough of a farewell. A hug and a kiss, at a minimum, now that Isabel was immune. But what more could she expect of her sister, or any Infected?

In the corridor, a high-pitched voice called out from behind, "Tell Jake I said hi." They turned to see little Samantha, long blond hair and bangs all perfectly in place, leaning into the hall from the doorway.

"What?" Isabel asked the girl.

"Tell Jake that Samantha said hi." She disappeared back into Emma's office.

Isabel looked over at Rick, whose eyebrows were arched. "What the fuck *next?*" she said. Outside in the sunlight amid the street sweepers, she took a deep breath. The air mainly smelled of smoke, but was joined by the faintly sweet stench of decomposition.

As they retraced their steps back up the highway toward the Old Place, Isabel said, "I was thinking about, maybe, a slight detour?"

"Okay. You're the boss. I've never gotten a direct order from a four-star before, but Gen. Browner was pretty explicit. I'm to provide for your personal security until you've come to your senses and decided to resume your work for the government."

"And that's exactly what I plan to do."

Rick caught and held her eye. "In Texas? So, we're gonna *hump* it?"

"Pardon me?"

"Walk? To Texas? Across country that'll almost certainly be turned by the time we pass through? Or tur*ning*, so the needle will be pegged to max on the fucked-up meter?"

"Yep. We Miller girls are into our plans, and that's mine. But you don't have to come if you don't want to. I hereby fully release you from your orders and oaths. I think I can handle myself now...and know my way around this rifle. Trigger. Selector switch. Magazine. Sight. Hole where the bullets come out. I don't really know what's in this little compartment in the bottom here." She raised the base of the rifle's stock.

"That's called the butt plate. There's a cleaning kit inside there."

"Oh. *Cute.*" The corners of Rick's mouth turned up, and his eyes confirmed it was a smile. He reached under her helmet and brushed clear of her eye a loose strand of hair. "You seem to be in a better mood," she said, "than on the drive down to Pearl River. You even shaved." She ran the backs of two fingers along his sharp jaw line and grinned.

"I spoke to my parents yesterday." Isabel stopped, hugged him, and told him how happy she was for him. "They've moved to my uncle's farm. He has his own well. There was a rumor that the Infecteds were contaminating the city water supply, although that sounds unlikely."

"I've still got that satellite phone they gave me on the president's plane. You could call them if you want to."

Rick shook his head. "No. They were real happy when I told them I had gotten outta D.C. I could only imagine what they'd say if I told them I was walking to Texas."

"You could lie."

"To my parents? *No.*"

"Really? Okay." Isabel realized how little she knew about who Rick was.

They marched on in awkward silence until Rick said, "Finding your brother, you know, is gonna be like looking for a needle in a haystack. And no matter how bad-ass they are, or *we* are, Emma was right. It's still a pretty low probability that everybody makes it."

"Does that mean you're coming?"

They stopped. "It *would* be a good chance for us to get to know each other better," Rick said. "Favorite color, favorite food, things that annoy us."

"Oh, I've got lots of those. We may not have enough time to cover them all."

Rick radioed the helicopter and told the pilot he could head back without them. Isabel threw her arms around him as best she could and kissed him on the lips.

"Come on," Rick said. "Time's a wastin'."

"First tell me something about yourself that I don't know."

"Okay. Let's see. *Oh.* I majored in English at the Academy."

"No. Really? *English?*"

"Somebody had to."

"Some*one*. Really? Not engineering or something? I don't believe you. Prove it. Recite some poem or something...*other* than *The Charge of the Light Brigade.*"

"Okay. But I do know that one by heart. Let's see." He couldn't resist looking at the black wristwatch he wore. "*Oh.* I know. How about, 'The woods are lovely, dark and deep, But I have promises to keep, And miles to go before I sleep. And miles to go before I sleep.'"

Chapter 41

THE SHENANDOAH VALLEY
Infection Date 64, 2130 GMT (5:30 p.m. Local)

Emma climbed up onto the park bench in front of the gathered townsfolk. Some were newcomers; others were long-time residents. All, it seemed to her, were infected.

"The postings on this bulletin board," she indicated the cork board that Dwayne and Samantha had placed on a stand under the awnings of a barber shop, "are the rules for this community." At the top was a bold-faced banner that read, "Infection Date 64."

"If you agree to abide by them," Emma continued, "you may stay and all your needs will be met. If you don't, you've got one hour to leave. Every time the rules change, you'll be given another opportunity to quit. But if you remain, you are bound by the rules until your next chance to leave. Failure to follow any of the rules will result in punishment ranging from withholding of food, water, shelter, clothing, and sex, to execution. You've got five minutes to study the board."

Emma climbed down off the bench and started the stopwatch on her phone.

There seemed to be some fuss around the bulletin board. Emma couldn't tell if it was disagreement with her rules, or merely ordinary jostling for position.

But Dwayne and Samantha joined her, and the former said, "What do we do if they don't agree to the rules, and don't agree to leave?"

"Have your people kill them all," Emma said. At the urging of the voice, Emma had begun to prize Dwayne and Samantha's lives almost as highly as her own. Dorothy, despite carrying Dwayne's child, she could take or leave. "But be careful," Emma said to Dwayne, who didn't seem to know what to make of that instruction. Samantha, however, nodded in concurrence with it. "What's your plan for clearing the road junction?"

"We're going tonight. I've got twenty guns I can count on, including Samantha."

"Leave Samantha here. Sam, you and I can come up with tomorrow's work schedule. It needs to be posted before sun-up tomorrow. Where's Dorothy?"

Samantha pointed. "I told her to set up a daycare center for the children. She's putting mattresses and blankets on the floor of the Methodist Church's basketball court."

"Good idea," Emma noted. *Samantha is a natural planner,* observed Emma's inner voice. Emma's phone's timer chirped. She climbed back onto the bench. "All right! Everyone back in their places! Time's up!"

The crowd finished their last reading of the several printed pages mounted to the bulletin board and wandered back into the square in front of Emma's bench. "Anyone who doesn't commit to following all of those rules—every last one of them—you may leave now." She set her phone's timer to one hour, raised it for the townsfolk to see, and started its countdown.

No one left the square, but one man said, "Who decides on the punishments?"

"*I* do," Emma replied.

There was a brief delay until another man asked, "Who the hell are you?"

Emma could feel that the voice in her head wanted to make some point. Emma waited. *Say it,* was all the voice commanded. *Say it!*

"*I*...am Emma Miller!"

Pandora: Resistance

Don't miss the next exciting novel in the Pandora series by Eric L. Harry
Coming soon from Rebel Base, an imprint of Kensington Publishing Corp.

Keep reading to enjoy a sample excerpt…

Chapter 1

NEW ROANOKE, VIRGINIA
Infection Date 122, 1415 GMT (10:15 am Local)

"Who was the first person you killed?" asked the interviewer in her monotone.

"Do you mean last night? Or ever?"

The infected bureaucrat on the far side of the bright yellow line, uncaring and yet persistent, said, "Last night." The count began on a thumb and ended on a pinkie. "The man coming through the door." The typing resumed. "The woman and boy outside. The old man on the stairs. And the girl and old woman in the parking lot. Five."

The expressionless scrivener was both doll-like and grotesque. Brown, helmet-shaped hair, loose clothes draping a scrawny, non-descript figure, no make-up of course, maybe thirty-five, maybe fifty-five. The Infected chic of shabby automata. Spartan shells, like the interview room all drab colors…save the bright, impossible-to-miss line down its middle. On either side of the optic yellow border, dark hardwoods were worn tan by countless trudges. But the neon boundary between was untrod. Our side. Their side. An involuntary reach up found no mask—a defining post-apocalyptic twitch.

"Did you kill anyone before the outbreak?" the infected woman asked.

"Of course not."

"What were you before the outbreak?"

"Why?"

The interviewer turned worn, yellowing laminated pages in the ring binder on her desk across the room. "Is it difficult to talk about 'before-the-outbreak'?"

"Is that what it says? What to do when they don't talk? 'If they say this, ask that'?" The interviewer stared back, repeatedly blinking. *A tell? Getting jumpy? Welcome to the club.* The door and ground-floor windows in what signs said had been a title company were wide open. *That'll help her nerves.* But talking was what she really needed to calm down. Doing her job. Typing mindlessly. "Life was easy." The clacking resumed. "So, *yeah*, it's hard on me. All the *emotions*. You know?"

The interviewer nodded. *No, you don't know shit. You have no idea what that means.* She typed every word, then looked not at her binder, but at a form on a clipboard filled with notes in neat handwriting in multiple colors. *So, her boss knows I'm here.* "It says you have insights into the *Pandoravirus* epidemic. The Outbreak, the Killing, the Schism." *They've* named *everything.* A first draft of their history of the world.

"*What* says that I have insights? What is that on your clipboard?"

"The intake form. Please describe what's happened since the Outbreak."

"I thought this was a trial or whatever. About the five Infecteds last night."

"It's an inquiry," the infected woman replied.

"Into what though?"

Silence. *You know* when *to lie, just not* how. "You can start at Infection Date Zero."

"What? From the beginning, to now? All three months?"

"No? Okay." She turned plastic pages. "How about begin with the Killing?"

"And when was that? It seems like to me the killing began at the very beginning."

"Why don't you describe what happened around the time Vice Pres. Anderson took over?"

"We just call him *President* Anderson." The barb was lost on the woman.

It would get dark early. The fresh smell of rain was in the air. It would make for a choice between a damp, miserable night in the woods, or breaking into an empty house that every once in a while turned out wasn't abandoned. It wouldn't matter whether its occupants were cold-blooded Infecteds or a desperate, bypassed Uninfecteds—you were in for a fight. *Better to get this over with.* "People told stories, you know. Maybe some were made up."

"Lies?" asked the interviewer.

"Very good. *'Embellished,'* more likely. Learn that word and you'll be ready for your SATs." The infected woman opened her mouth, presumably to correct the record about any impending college boards. "I *know*. You're not taking the SATs. It was a joke."

Apparently, there was a page for jokes. Her finger traced the line as she read. "Please just say what happened." Page 11, Option 24 or whatever, in the binder.

"Well, in the beginning everything was normal." She typed. "No guns, Exclusion Zone, yellow lines. Happy people living happy lives. Then, out of fucking *nowhere*, in three months everything got totally fucking fucked never to be unfucked again. The End."

She typed it all, then said, "So, you decided to start at Infection Date Zero?"

The woman wanted the apocalypse in chronological order, please. Was she judging? And, if so, whom and what? The events of last night? Or all Uninfecteds on their record since the Outbreak? The woman's finger found the question she was looking for. "On what Infection Date will you begin your recounting of events?"

"That's your new calendar? Infection Dates? 'Cause January, February, and March are outdated now?" The interviewer stared back. "Never mind. What's today's date in Infection-land?"

"It's Infection Date 122 today. On what date will your history begin?"

"Oh, I guess I'd say…" The math was pretty simple. Sixty-one days ago. Half the way back to the beginning. "Infection Date 61. *Okay?*"

The woman nodded, fingers poised, ready to type. What she didn't know, however, was that she was the one being judged. It was her life, and the lives of her fellow Infecteds, that were being decided.

Meet the Author

Eric L. Harry launched his Pandora series of science fiction thrillers with *Pandora: Outbreak* and now continues it with *Pandora: Contagion*. He is currently working on the third book in the series, *Pandora: Resistance*. Raised in a small town in Mississippi, he graduated from the Marine Military Academy in Texas and studied Russian and Economics at Vanderbilt University, where he also earned a J.D. and M.B.A. In addition, he studied in Moscow and Leningrad in the USSR, and at the University of Virginia Law School. He began his legal career in private practice in Houston, negotiated complex multinational mergers and acquisitions around the world, and rose to be general counsel of a Fortune 500 company. He left to raise a private equity fund and co-found a successful oil company. His previous thrillers include *Arc Light, Society of the Mind, Protect and Defend* and *Invasion*. His books have been published in eight countries. He and his wife have three children and divide their time between Houston and San Diego.

Contact him on Facebook or visit him online at www.EricLHarry.com.

Pandora: Outbreak

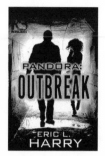

BEGINNING OF THE END

They call it Pandoravirus. It attacks the brain. Anyone infected may explode in uncontrollable rage. Blind to pain, empty of emotion, the infected hunt and are hunted. They attack without warning and without mercy. Their numbers spread unchecked. There is no known cure.

Emma Miller studies diseases for a living—until she catches the virus. Now she's the one being studied by the U.S. government and by her twin sister, neuroscientist Isabel Miller. Rival factions debate whether to treat the infected like rabid animals to be put down, or victims deserving compassion. As Isabel fights for her sister's life, the infected are massing for an epic battle of survival. And it looks like Emma is leading the way . . .

Made in the USA
Middletown, DE
08 March 2020

86031832R00168